PUNISHING EMBRACE

Kenna's eyes opened wide and her lips closed in a mutinous line as Rhys's mouth met her own. She recoiled from his harsh, punishing embrace and tried to push at his chest with her palms.

He caught her wrists in his hands. Then he gave her a little jerk and moved Kenna so her back was flush to the ice-flowered window panes.

Her head swayed weakly to one side as if too heavy to be supported by the slender column of her throat. She did not know what was happening to her. How could she desire someone she feared and despised?

Yet Kenna could not deny the peculiar drugged sensation she felt, nor could she ignore the uneven beat of her own heart and the warm, oddly liquid feeling that seemed to radiate within her.

"Rhys?" She choked on his name as his lips were evoking pleasant sensations on the cord in her neck. Kenna wanted to make him stop; he was confusing her with his experienced kisses. "Please. No more. Don't . . ." Her voi⬚ ⬚f his mouth to hers.

She was helpless ⬚ ⬚

Zebra Historical Romances—
Dare to Dream!

MOONLIT MAGIC (1941, $3.95)
by Sylvie F. Sommerfield
How dare that slick railroad negotiator bathe in Jenna's river and sneak around her property! But soon her seething fury became burning desire. As he stroked her skin, she was forever captured by *Moonlit Magic*.

SAVAGE KISS (1669, $3.95)
by Sylvie F. Sommerfield
Rayne Freeman thought he was dreaming. But one moment in Falling Water's arms and he knew he would never betray the ecstasy of their *Savage Kiss*.

REBEL HEART (1802, $3.95)
by Lauren Wilde
From the moment she stepped into the ballroom, Desiree felt her eyes drawn to one man: a womanizing rogue named Captain Jason Montgomery. And when Jason gathered her into his strong embrace, a feeling of fire burned through her veins.

SURRENDER TO DESIRE (1503, $3.75)
by Catherine Creel
When Marianna learned she was to marry a stranger once she reached the Alaskan frontier, her fury knew no bounds. But she found herself falling under the spell of passion's sweet fire, destined to welcome defeat and *Surrender to Desire*.

PASSION'S BRIDE (1417, $3.75)
Jo Goodman
"Don't make me love you," Alexis whispered. But Tanner was a man used to having his own way. The Captain would keep her prisoner rather than risk losing her to her quest for revenge.

Available wherever paperbacks are sold, or order direct from the Publisher. Send cover price plus 50¢ per copy for mailing and handling to Zebra Books, Dept. 2063, 475 Park Avenue South, New York, N.Y. 10016. Residents of New York, New Jersey and Pennsylvania must include sales tax. DO NOT SEND CASH.

Velvet Night

Jo Goodman

ZEBRA BOOKS
KENSINGTON PUBLISHING CORP.

ZEBRA BOOKS

are published by

Kensington Publishing Corp.
475 Park Avenue South
New York, NY 10016

First printing: May 1987

Printed in the United States of America

For Yvonne and Twin Weirdness!

Prologue

Kenna Dunne edged closer to the banister, keeping her body in the shadows on the landing. Between the smooth oaken posts smelling faintly of beeswax, one eye was opened wide and scanning the flurry of activity in the lighted hallway below. Kenna fought back a giggle as Henderson assisted the most recent guest with her pelisse. The manservant swept back the young woman's cloak and his superior height gave him an unrestricted view of the ivory bosom swelling above a tightly laced bodice. At the rear of the woman's unsuspecting shoulder Henderson's white brows wiggled in appreciation. "Poor Henderson!" Kenna whispered conspiratorially, nudging her stepsister. "I shouldn't be surprised if the Lord smote his eyes by evening's end. If Mrs. H. doesn't smite him first. That's the fourth shepherdess nearly popping from her bodice."

"I only counted three," Yvonne answered softly. She turned her head so Kenna could hear, a worried line between her brows. "I think we should leave the staircase. Someone is bound to see us." Yvonne started

7

to rise but she was pushed back in her place by Kenna's firm hand on her shoulder.

"Not yet! I want to see everything. There never has been such a party at Dunnelly before. Did you include Lady Dimmy as a shepherdess?"

"No."

"Then that accounts for it."

"But she looked like a housekeeper," Yvonne protested.

Kenna muffled her laugh with the back of her hand, never taking her eyes from the guests. "Yes, I know she did. But she meant to be a shepherdess so we must count her as one. At least I think that's what she meant to be. It is rather hard imagining anyone would come to a masque costumed as a housekeeper. Though it's difficult to say why anyone would come as a shepherdess, for that matter."

Yvonne's smile was wistful. "I think it's romantic."

"Pooh! There's nothing romantic about tending sheep. Smelly work if ever there was. But I don't suppose they gave that a thought." Kenna's wide mouth curled in derision as the newest shepherdess was escorted into the ballroom. "What do you think would happen if we were to release a dozen ewes?"

"We would never leave the schoolroom in this lifetime, Kenna Dunne," Yvonne said firmly. "You may not mind it, for Mama says she will have to take you in hand if you are not to become a bluestocking, but I should wither and die if I have to refine upon the geography of India yet again."

That dramatic pronouncement brought Kenna's attention fully on her stepsister. Immersed as Kenna was in her studies, it hadn't occurred to her that Yvonne found them painfully dull. To Kenna's young and curious mind the notion was inconceivable. Her head fell thoughtfully to one side and she drew a strand of hair through her lips, worrying it as she often did when struck by a particularly fascinating anomaly.

At thirteen Kenna was not often given to introspection, but she believed she was aware of the admirable qualities she possessed as well as those in which she was found wanting. Without conceit she listed the former attributes in her mind: intelligent, curious, daring, loving, honest, fair, and possessed of an independent spirit. Opposite that list she concluded she was sadly lacking wisdom to compliment her intelligence, common sense to temper curiosity and daring, and tact to sooth the sting of her earnestly honest tongue. She knew she was spoiled by her father and older brother. But one thing she had never thought she lacked was regard for others. Now she added selfish to her list.

Overjoyed as she was to have Yvonne in the family after a lifetime of being raised in the near exclusive company of males, Kenna had assumed she and Yvonne would share confidences and adventures. Now Kenna reflected that she had not really listened to her sister's secrets and all their adventures had been at Kenna's urgings. Kenna could find no other explanation for the fact that not above a week ago she and Yvonne had been locked in the tower room for nearly eighteen hours while everyone at Dunnelly Manor had been searching for them in the lake. Looking back, Kenna remembered Yvonne's softly voiced reluctance to go into the tower room but with characteristic impetuousness Kenna had dismissed her fears and pressed on. That was why this evening, instead of joining the masked celebration their parents were hosting—the first since their marriage three months ago—Kenna and Yvonne were confined to their bedchambers.

Supposed to be confined, Kenna reminded herself, for her father had been loath to lock them in and had accepted their word of honor they would remain unseen and unheard. Yet here they were, once again at Kenna's insistence, hidden on the shadowed stairs and acting for all the world like Peeping Toms in their own home. For herself she did not mind terribly much but with her new-found insight she knew Yvonne was deeply disappointed. Yvonne wanted to be entering the ballroom now, mixing with the pirates and queens, the devils and clowns, and, of course, the four shepherdesses.

Kenna reflected that Yvonne would have made an excellent angel. Her white-blond hair, braided for bed and coiled on her small head, formed a natural halo. Her expression, aided by a pair of clear blue eyes and dark, fanning lashes, was most frequently winsome, perhaps even a little other-worldly. She was a madonna, petite and soft-spoken, with beautifully molded features, delicate and serene.

Kenna felt compelled to make another list. She had no illusions about her own looks. In contrast to Yvonne's ethereal nature, which was best suited to pastel gowns and silver slippers, Kenna was firmly of this earth. Taller than every woman she knew and able to look most men of her acquaintance in the eye, Kenna thought of herself as unflatteringly tree-like. Thin and gangly, still possessing the awkwardness of youth, she viewed her limbs as slashing branches most often slapping out of control, guided willy-nilly by an uneven temperament. Her mouth seemed too wide for her narrow face; the lower lip certainly too full to copy the serenity of Yvonne's smiles. Unconsciously Kenna ran the tip of her index finger along the narrow bridge of her nose. There was nothing to recommend this appendage as retroussé. If she slept face down in her pillow for the next seventy years, with the tip of her nose arranged just so, she doubted it would ever achieve the charming effect that was often remarked about her sister's countenance.

Kenna spit out the strand of hair she was pensively

chewing and examined the wet tip with a measure of disgust. Even damp her hair was still the color of a flame, a blend of orange and red so striking that it was likely to elicit comments as to its combustability. Thick and unruly, it frequently required the attention of a comb, which Kenna was reluctant to use. She was more likely to cut out her tangles with a dull pair of sewing scissors which accounted for her oddly cropped style.

Her brows and lashes were dark, which she supposed served her well enough. Had they been the same color as her hair she would have been blinking fire and how was she to feign engaging expressions when her face was a veritable beacon? And her eyes? In Kenna's present frame of mind they did not bear scrutiny. At this moment she felt it was a kindness to say they were the same deep shade of brown as mud.

It was not Kenna's way to refine upon what could not be changed and envy served no purpose that she could understand. She was glad enough that Yvonne was a diamond of the first water because any young woman who abhorred the schoolroom needed something to recommend her.

Coming out of her reverie, Kenna realized she had missed the entrance of several new arrivals. Yvonne's dreamy sigh warned her they had been of particular interest and Kenna suddenly had an idea. If it was in her power—and Kenna had yet to experience a situation that was not—Yvonne was going to attend the masque.

Kenna tapped Yvonne's shoulder. "Let's go back to my room. I have a marvelous idea." Kenna knew Yvonne had good reason to be wary but she thought her stepsister rather faint-hearted to show it so plainly. Yvonne might have all manner of beauty but she lacked spirit. Kenna thought it a very good thing that she had Yvonne's full measure now. It was not too late to correct this regrettable character flaw.

11

Kenna overcame Yvonne's resistance by taking her by the wrist and pulling her up the stairs. Bent on her mission, which she now likened to saving a damsel in distress, and feeling very fine about her intended good works, Kenna raced along the darkly paneled hallway with Yvonne firmly in tow. Oblivious to the fading music in the background and the faint laughter of her father's guests, Kenna also failed to notice the approaching footsteps from the south wing which marked an end to her secrecy.

It was difficult to say who was more surprised when Kenna took the corner at full tilt, her slippers sliding on the polished floor, and barrelled heavily into the unyielding arms of a highwayman. The highwayman rocked back on his heels and there was a distinct and unflattering whoosh as air left his lungs from the force of the collision. Kenna's heart firmly lodged in the region of her throat and she lost her grip on Yvonne's wrist as she sought purchase and balance on the rogue's broad shoulders. She knew herself to be every bit of graceless as her feet trod hard upon the highwayman's boots and her dressing gown tangled about his legs. They tottered briefly and might have managed to remain standing had Kenna not heard the familiar sound of her brother's laughter coming from beyond the highwayman's shoulder. She brought her head up sharply to reprimand Nicholas for finding his amusement at her expense and squarely connected her forehead with her unwitting assailant's chin. A muffled curse followed and though Kenna vowed she had never heard it before, she somewhat fuzzily thought it appropriate to this occasion. Behind her, Yvonne's squeal of fright turned to wailed distress and Kenna knew she and the highwayman were going to take a tumble. Seeing nothing for it but to make the best of an awkward encounter, Kenna closed her eyes in the hope that not seeing the floor rise to meet her would make for a softer landing.

A moment later there was the expected thud but none of the bone-jarring pain Kenna anticipated accompanying it. Her eyes were still squeezed tightly shut and her face was comically distorted while she waited for her body to signal monumental injury. It took her several moments to realize she was lying fully on top of the highwayman and he had chivalrously taken the brunt of the fall. Cautiously she opened one eye and stared into the face of her much abused gallant.

It was altogether a rather handsome face that met her wary gaze. The highwayman's mask had slipped in the fray and rested awkwardly about his neck, but the absurdity of his present posture did nothing to detract from his roguish attraction. His black felt tricorne had been dislodged in the fall and a lock of hair, nearly as dark as his disguise, fell neatly across his smooth forehead. The firm thrust of his jaw was softened by the merest suggestion of a dimple and Kenna wondered why her head didn't feel the better for making contact with it. His eyes were closed and Kenna could detect no movement behind them or from the ebony lashes that fanned them. His mouth was parted slightly and she could make out the white even line of his teeth resting on his lower lip. She was glad she hadn't disgraced herself by knocking any of them out, though she reflected darkly that a loose cuspid may be just the thing to keep him from skulking around corners in the future. Kenna would have waited patiently for the highwayman to come to his senses if he had shown the least desire to do so, but he seemed so completely at his ease that Kenna was inspired to hurry matters along.

"Oh, Nicky, I think I've done murder!" she cried out, feigning alarm at the stillness of the body beneath her. "Never say this blackguard was a dear friend of yours for I'd hate to be the cause of a most untimely but permanent separation!" As Kenna expected, it was not her brother

13

who answered.

The highwayman's eyes opened like a shot and a menacing growl rose deep in his throat. He grasped Kenna's thin arms in his gloved hands and moved her to one side as he sat up. "'Tis more likely I should murder you, sprite!" He gently rubbed his chin with the back of his hand. "Couldn't you show a shade more concern in the face of such calamity? A modicum of remorse would not be amiss. As I recall, you used to cry when I left Dunnelly and now not so much as a tear for nearly cutting me down in my prime!"

Kenna laughed brightly as she looked into the rueful face of the highwayman massaging his tender chin. His outraged accents were without sting because his clear gray eyes danced as they met Kenna's. "I am not such a nuncheon that I cry at the least little thing any more," Kenna said tartly, removing his hand and giving him an affectionate kiss on the chin. "Is that better? No? Well, it is all you can expect in the way of a welcome! Nicholas did not even whisper that you were coming to the masque. That was very bad of him but you might have written to me."

Nicholas Dunne held out a hand for his sister. "It was Rhys's idea to surprise you, Kenna," he said quickly extricating himself from responsibility.

Rhys Canning sent his best friend a pained glance. "Steadfastness is not your strong suit, Nick. Now she's bound to give me another scold."

Kenna looked from one to the other, a smile playing about her wide mouth. It was difficult to stay angry at either one of them. Other than her father, these two were the men she loved best in the world.

In appearance Rhys and Nick were cut from the same cloth. Often as not they were mistaken for brothers but in truth were probably closer than if they had been siblings. They were of a similar height and build, both

14

possessed of handsome countenances that had caused more than a few hearts to flutter when they entered a room. This particular phenomenon amused Kenna but she knew it to be true because they told her it was so. She may have doubted their veracity if it hadn't coincided with a peculiar lurch Kenna felt in her chest when Rhys came to visit on occasion. It didn't occur to her to wonder why the same tingling didn't occur when Nick was around. If she had, she might have deduced the difference lay in the eyes—not hers, but theirs. While Nick's eyes were deep blue, sharp and gently teasing by turns, Rhys's gray eyes seemed infinitely more intriguing, subtly changing shades as his mood altered.

It did not surprise Kenna that Nick's costume was nearly identical to the one Rhys wore and she doubted they had consulted one another. It was exactly the sort of thing they would do independently and for their pains wind up looking like a coin with two heads.

To Kenna's knowledge they hadn't seen each other since leaving Oxford more than a year ago and while Nick divided his time between Dunnelly and London, Rhys had gone to the Continent for some purpose Kenna had never quite divined. Questioning Nick brought little satisfaction because he was unusually closed-mouth on the subject of Rhys's departure. She wondered why she thought of it now, when it no longer mattered that he had disappeared without a word. It was only important that he was back and Nick was looking happier than he had in months.

She tried her best to look severe as she shook off Nick's hand. Arms akimbo, she faced her brother. "And it is very like you to lay the blame at Rhys's door, but it won't serve."

Nicholas took a step backward, playfully holding out his arms as if to ward her off. "Don't fly into the boughs, sprite. And lower your voice. Father is certain to hear

15

you and then you'll be back in your room—this time with a keeper."

Kenna was ready to take offense for being called sprite again. It was an absurd name given the fact that she was only a few inches shy of attaining her brother's or Rhys's height. She thought better of it when Rhys reminded her of her real predicament.

"What's this, Kenna?" Rhys demanded, rising to his feet and brushing off his coat. "Another scrape?" He stopped his haphazard grooming and grinned genially at Yvonne, noticing her for the first time. "And who are you?" He swept her a courtly bow as grand as either girl had ever seen, picking up his tricorne in a single motion and holding it to his heart. "Dare I hope my most recent brush with Kenna has not addled my brain? I'm not imagining you, am I?"

Yvonne blushed beautifully, avoiding Rhys's mischievous eyes as she looked first to Kenna then Nicholas for help.

Kenna snorted at Rhys's banter. "This is our new sister, which you would know well enough if you had not been on the Continent at the time of Papa's wedding. Yvonne, do not be taken in by this rascal's addresses. His name is Rhys Canning and he has been Nick's friend since—well, since forever. He is an abominable tease and up to every trick and I think he is something of a rake, though I am not certain what that is. I suspect it has something to do with lightskirts and gambling."

"Kenna!" Two voices, Nick's and Yvonne's, rose in alarm at this unseemly announcement. Rhys then clapped his hand over Kenna's mouth and held it, and her, while he serenely addressed Nicholas.

"Perhaps we should escort the young lady and this bit of baggage back to their rooms."

"My thoughts exactly," Nick replied, giving Kenna a look that would have turned her to stone had she been

16

aware of it. He held out his arm to Yvonne. "This way, m'dear."

Only when they were safely in Kenna's bedchamber did Rhys remove his hand and his hold. "Here we are, Miss Scapegrace."

Kenna flounced over to her bed and sat on it so hard the snowy white canopy billowed. She crossed her arms in front of her and thrust out her lower lip. "That was very ill-mannered, Rhys Canning! It is common knowledge you are a rake and I shouldn't think you'd mind if I said so. You do know actresses, don't you?"

"Several," Rhys said dryly, "but none so skilled as you. I vow I shall ring a maid to dust your lower lip if you insist on pouting so."

Kenna drew in her lip and gave Rhys a saucy smile. "Didn't I say you were up to every trick?"

"Just so." He turned a wing chair away from the fireplace and seated himself, leaning back comfortably and crossing his Hessians at the ankle. He waited, imperturbably calm, while Yvonne and Nicholas took seats near him on the divan. "Now suppose you tell us what is toward?"

Kenna fidgeted, staring at the apple green walls of her room and wondering if she were on trial. She plucked a bit of the coverlet between her fingers and twisted it.

"I can wait all evening if necessary."

Kenna knew he could. Unlike Nicholas, who was rhythmically tapping his foot on the carpet, Rhys was infinitely patient. Taking a deep breath, Kenna plunged into her explanation. "Yvonne and I are not allowed to attend the masque. Even for a few minutes," she added earnestly. "It is my fault completely, for I persuaded Yvonne to abandon our fishing outing and explore the tower room. It would have come to naught if we hadn't had the misfortune of being locked in. The door blew shut and the key was in the door—on the wrong side—

and—well, that story can wait. But it was a good adventure, Rhys. Only it reminded Yvonne of the Bastille. Did you know she was born in Paris? One can't know from her accent because she's spent so much time in England."

"I haven't had the pleasure of hearing her speak at all." A ghost of a smile lifted Rhys's full mouth. "But Yvonne's command of the language is hardly the issue, is it?"

"I only mention it because it was easy for me to forget that Yvonne and her mother fled the Terror in France. I wouldn't have insisted we go to the tower if I had really thought on it. I *am* sorry, Yvonne. You do believe me don't you."

"Of course I believe you," Yvonne said softly, a delicate pink coming to her cheeks. "You are the most kind-hearted—"

"Oh, but I'm not! I have just come to the realization that I am astonishingly selfish!" Kenna missed Rhys nearly choking in surprise and Nicholas swallowing his laughter. "I practically had to drag you to the stairs tonight to watch the party and I never gave a thought that you might hate the consequence." She turned to Rhys. "Yvonne says she will simply *expire* if she has to spend more time in the schoolroom. For myself I do not mind but it is unconscionable to cause her to suffer."

"So you came to this conclusion and decided to return to your room before you were discovered," Nicholas said. "That was very wise of you."

Kenna looked uncomfortable.

"I think there is more to this," said Rhys. "Isn't that so, Kenna?"

"Well, yes, there is," Kenna admitted somewhat reluctantly. "I began to think how much this masque meant to Yvonne. She won't have her season for another year or two and this is a great *event,* an *opportunity.*

18

And I took it away from her. So of course I thought I could make things right again."

"Of course," Rhys and Nick said together, identical inflections in their voices.

Kenna ignored them. "It came to me that Yvonne is everything angelic. She *is* beautiful, don't you think? Everyone remarks on her nose," she added as if it explained everything.

At that moment acute embarrassment prevented them from seeing any part of Yvonne's face as she had buried it in her hands.

Rhys raised one dark eyebrow. "Whereas remarks on your nose make some mention of other people's business."

Kenna was unperturbed. "Exactly. So it came to me that she must not miss her chance to attend this evening's masque. You *will* help, won't you? It's not as if we shall ever be found out. It's a masque after all. I know I can find some sort of costume and her face will be hidden."

"Even the nose?" Nick asked, giving Yvonne a fond hug as she remained hidden behind her hands.

"Especially the nose," Kenna answered with assurance. "Will you help?"

Nick shrugged and looked at Rhys. "What do you think? Has a year on the Continent jaded you or are you up to Kenna's intrigues?"

Rhys studied the toes of his polished Hessians for a long moment while Kenna held her breath and Yvonne dared to peep between her fingers. Finally an enigmatic smile lifted the corners of his mouth. He scanned Kenna's expectant features slowly and when he responded his voice held a touch of something very young. "I never tire of Kenna's intrigues."

Kenna laughed brightly and bounded from her bed, throwing her arms about Rhys's neck. The wing chair teetered uneasily under the force of her enthusiasm but Rhys managed to keep it righted and returned the affectionate embrace. "It is so good to have you home again!"

As soon as she said the words Kenna wished she could have taken them back. She lifted her head in time to catch the flash of pain that paled Rhys's strong features.

"It's all right, sprite," Rhys said softly. "This has always been my home."

That was true enough, Kenna thought, but it didn't make it right. Rhys had relatives, but no family. He had a home, but no homeland. And the glimpse of aloneness that Kenna had surprised in his eyes reminded her that it still had the power to cause terrible hurt. Rhys's father was Roland Canning, a shipping magnate of no small influence and greater wealth in America, and though Kenna had never met him, indeed, had no desire to meet him, she knew from Rhys that he was regarded well by Boston society. Mr. Canning was a political noteworthy in his own country and had once served as ambassador to England. Kenna had learned from listening to her father speak that Roland Canning was raising his son to follow his lead and Kenna found nothing objectionable about a father's desire to see his son successful. But the powerful Mr. Canning had two sons and Rhys was not the one oft remembered and adored.

Roland Canning could forgive his heir anything and his younger son nothing, beginning with the death of his beloved wife at Rhys's birth. So it was that while Richard was raised in America under the doting eye of his father, Rhys was sent to his maternal great-grandmother's stately home in England. The duchess of Pelham made no secret she had no patience and little affection for a lad she considered too brash and rebellious, too thoroughly American for her tastes, and promptly discharged Rhys to boarding school. Her duty done, she forgot all about him and her man of affairs saw to Rhys's allowance and needs. Kenna had overheard her father once say that it must have been a relief for the headmaster when Nicholas had befriended Rhys at school. Until that time it fell on the poor fellow's shoulders to find excuses to keep Rhys in school during the holidays. Once Rhys became Nick's fast friend they were into so many scrapes the man no longer needed excuses, he had reasons. But Nick, ever the finder of stray pups and blessed with a quick mind that usually relieved him of all responsibility for their care, managed to bring himself and Rhys to Dunnelly Manor one Christmas ten years ago. It then fell to Kenna and her father to make it a home for him.

It was an easy enough matter for each of them. Lord Dunne had a fondness for all children. He loved their enthusiasm and courage and noise, above all, their laughter. It had been his wish, as well as his wife's, to have a dozen in his home and until Catherine's untimely death it had seemed possible. It was a doubly cruel blow that Lady Cathy had been carrying their third child when a carriage accident ended her life. Dunnelly Manor was still in mourning for her ladyship when Nicholas brought Rhys Canning home, but Lord Dunne made him welcome, ready to take Rhys under his wing as if he had been his own. He never mentioned that on that first acquaintance Rhys's solemn gray eyes were so like his Cathy's that it ached for him to look at the child.

Kenna was only three when Rhys first visited Dunnelly and she had no inhibitions about crawling onto his lap when he was introduced to her in the nursery. Rhys was eleven at the time and had no experience with persistent, curious, and adoring urchins. He held her rather awkwardly and took much good-natured teasing from Nick that he had made a conquest, but Lord Dunne saw it was more likely Rhys had been conquered by his flame-haired daughter. Had they but known it, when Kenna startled Rhys with an affection-ate, if somewhat wet, kiss on his cheek they were witness to the first spontaneous smile that had lighted Rhys's face in years. From that moment on Nick and Rhys were rarely seen about Dunnelly Manor without Kenna in tow. If Nick chafed a bit at having his sister dog their every footstep he never voiced his objections. If Rhys didn't mind having her in his pocket, he reasoned, then why should he?

Kenna glanced over at her brother and smiled at the path of her thoughts. Poor Nicky and Rhys! At some point over the years they had become her keepers and her champions, ready to assist her in any piece of work and take the consequences upon their own heads. She knew of no one else, save perhaps her father, who would have taken the assignment without a costly bribe.

Kenna gave Rhys a brief hug and straightened, smoothing her well-worn dressing gown. "You don't have to worry that I'll land you in the suds this time," she said earnestly. "No one ever has to know that Yvonne was at the masque."

Rhys grimaced at Nick. "I felt better about this thing until she mentioned not landing us in the suds," he said wryly. "Have you noticed events rarely go as she plans them?"

"Rarely?" Nick asked. "I should think it's never. Do you remember—"

Kenna stamped her foot. "If you are going to recount ancient history I am going to ask you both to leave. Faith! Yvonne would think me a hapless wretch if I let you two go on."

"She is not very discerning if she hasn't discovered that on her own," Nick said. "She can't have forgotten the tower incident so soon."

Yvonne came out from behind her hands and nudged Nick's ribs gently. "Kenna, I know you mean well. You always do, but I'm not certain this is such a good idea. If I were found out Mama would be most distressed and your father would feel obliged to punish us."

Kenna waved her hand airily. "You are defeated before we begin, Yvonne! I tell you, there is no one who will know save the four of us. Nick and Ryhs would never give you away. You do want to go to the masque, don't you?"

"Above all else, but—"

Kenna clapped her hands together as if all was settled. Nick leaned his head close to Yvonne's and confided, "In time you will learn to state your objections first. Kenna has little patience to hear them out once you've admitted a desire for her outcome."

"Would she have listened?" Yvonne asked as Nick helped her to her feet.

"Probably not. But at least you have voiced the folly of the venture one more time." Nick patted her hand. "Don't give it another thought. Rhys and I won't. Damnable waste of gray matter. It'll be a great lark, you'll see. Kenna's schemes always are."

Kenna was fairly dancing with excitement. She urged Rhys out of his chair and pushed him in the direction of the door. "We'll go to the attic. There's bound to be something suitable in one of the trunks. None of you are going to be the least sorry! Yvonne will be *radiant*."

And in less than one hour she was. They all agreed upon it. If anything, Kenna thought Yvonne very nearly blossomed when flanked by her two swarthy and disreputable escorts. Her rose satin gown had once belonged to Lord Dunne's grandmother and though its wide panniers and off the shoulder neckline made it sadly out of fashion, it was perfect for a masquerade. It recalled another time when Dunnelly Manor had been host to gay parties and was equal to this occasion. The same trunk had yielded matching slippers and splendid lace petticoats, but the only wig they could find had been home for a family of moths for decades. Undaunted, Kenna had arranged most of Yvonne's splendid hair high on her head. Three thick sausage curls dangled elegantly at the nape of her neck and every strand was dusted liberally with white powder and sprinkled with glitter. Kenna had no beauty patch but she improvised by painting a tiny black mark on one of Yvonne's high cheekbones and the half mask that Nick found set it off beautifully in addition to hiding most of Yvonne's nose. Her bare throat was adorned with a string of matched pearls that now belonged to Kenna but had been Lady Catherine's. Yvonne fretted a bit over the pearls, but when no one else thought Lord Dunne would recognize the necklace, she let the matter drop.

"You look like a princess," Kenna exclaimed happily, well pleased with her work. "Rhys. Nicky. You will keep an eye on her, won't you? I shouldn't want her accosted by some rake."

"Other than Rhys," Nick said, reaching around Yvonne to give his friend a good-natured poke.

"Especially Rhys. Or you, Nicholas. I vow I have heard Father remark that you are the true libertine and Rhys is but a foil for your games." Kenna frowned, puzzled briefly by the odd exchange of glances between her brother and Rhys. She told herself she had imagined Nick's guilty start and Rhys's quickly veiled warning. It was difficult to discern their meaning when their faces were nearly covered by their black masks and shadowed by their hats. "Yvonne, you shan't have a moment's worry with these highwaymen to guard you," she said, shrugging off the moment's unease. "They make most excellent brigands, don't you think?"

Yvonne nodded happily and held out her hands to Kenna. "Thank you for this, dear Kenna! I don't know how I will repay you."

"Just remember everything. I'll be waiting up and I want to hear it all."

"Won't you watch from the stairs?"

Kenna shook her head and saw Rhys's eyes grow skeptical beneath his mask. She wrinkled her unremarkable nose at him. "No. I think it best if I simply stay in my room."

"I hardly know if such wisdom becomes you, sprite, but I shall think on it," Rhys said, winking broadly at Nick. Before Kenna could object to the odious nickname, he ushered Nick and Yvonne into the hall. Their animated laughter nearly silenced the door slamming behind them.

"Horrid man!" Kenna announced to her empty bedchamber as she leaned against the door. "He should have stayed on the Continent. He and Napoleon deserve one another." But a moment later, when she was stoking the fire in her hearth, Kenna was smiling. It really was lovely to have Rhys at Dunnelly again.

Kenna fully expected Yvonne to return within the hour so she seated herself by the hearth and read while she waited. *The History of Tom Jones* was not precisely the sort of book Lord Dunne relished his daughter reading, which is why he had placed it on one of the library shelves at exactly eye level. Knowing Kenna as he did, he correctly assumed she would be interested in literature that was out of her reach, surmising it to be forbidden. But Kenna, finding the reading on the upper shelves to be rather dull stuff, though terribly edifying, eventually saw through her father's game and began to take books from the shelf at eye level. These books were also terribly edifying but the nature of the information had changed.

It did not take her long to become immersed in Tom Jones's misadventures and when she glanced at the ormolu clock on the mantel she was surprised to see more than an hour and a half had passed. Curiosity ate at her insides for another ten minutes while she tried to imagine what Yvonne was doing. Was she dancing with Nicholas? Or had her brother passed her along to some other young buck? Kenna chided herself for thinking ill of Nick but it could not change the truth. He and Rhys, for all that they looked alike, were not so similar under the skin. Nick was irrepressible and on occasion irresponsible. Rhys was so—she searched for the right word—wise. Kenna had the feeling that Rhys, whether he joined a scatter-brained escapade or initiated one, was always watchful, naturally cautious. She admitted that Rhys invariably made her feel protected, no matter what the consequences. No doubt he was with Yvonne and she would come to no harm in his care. That thought satisfied Kenna for another five minutes, then she could not tolerate the not knowing another second.

Coming to a decision, Kenna tossed aside her book. She rummaged through her mahogany chiffonier, pulling out the drawers and never quite pushing them back in when she didn't find what she wanted. A waterfall of lingerie covered the front of the chiffonier by the time Kenna found the clothing that would transform her. In a matter of minutes she was no longer a young lady, but a rogue every bit the equal of the two highwaymen who had preceded her to the masquerade.

Granted, she told herself, critically surveying her image in the cheval glass, it was not a particularly original idea, and certainly it was a far cry from the Cleopatra costume she had discussed with Yvonne prior to the tower room incident, but it served her purpose well. The more she looked at her reflection the more it seemed reasonable that not even Yvonne would recognize her. The lower half of her face was buried beneath a black wool scarf and the black cocked hat, similar to the ones Nick and Rhys sported, cast her eyes in a shadow. She wore a black velvet jacket from an old riding habit over a white linen nightshirt that had once been her father's. The hem of the shirt was tucked into a pair of dark breeches which were in turn tucked into a pair of riding boots. The breeches and jacket were a bit snug and the boots pinched her feet but Kenna congratulated herself for not throwing any of them away. The outfit she now wore had been an almost forgotten part of her wardrobe, relegated to the back of her drawers and her memory when she had vowed to give up riding hellbent across the contryside. The clothes might have been resurrected sooner, for she had reconsidered her rash promise to her father the very next day, but Kenna found that her new riding habit was not as restrictive as she thought it would be. In no time at all she was riding again at a breakneck speed, and Lord Dunne had to be thankful his daughter had a very fine seat.

Behind the rough scarf Kenna smiled impishly as she considered what a lark it would be to steal Yvonne away from the care of her brother and Rhys. Tucking a loose strand of fiery red hair beneath her hat, she turned away from the mirror and sauntered out of her room.

Kenna told herself it was not lack of courage, but simply good sense, that made her choose the enclosed servants' passageway rather than the main staircase. The deserted corridor served to reaffirm Kenna's intentions. Considering the number of footmen, chambermaids, grooms, gamekeepers, gardeners, stableboys, coachmen, housemaids, cooks, and laundry maids employed at Dunnelly, she thought it a miracle of sorts her path did not cross that of one servant.

The section of the manor that was the domain of the servants was a veritable maze of rooms. Had Kenna not explored the warren when she was a child she could have been forgiven for thinking that all work at Dunnelly was accomplished by magic. There were rooms for pressing linen, polishing shoes, cleaning and sharpening knives, washing, drying, ironing, and folding. There were separate larders off the main kitchen for meat, game, and fish. There were two sculleries, one for the kitchen and one for the dairy, a pantry and a wine cellar.

Staying clear of the kitchen and wine cellar, a certain hub of activity, Kenna slipped from the hallway into the lamp room which she knew would be deserted, the lamps having been filled and trimmed earlier in the day. From there she entered the main hallway and walked briskly toward the strains of music in the ballroom, narrowly avoiding a collision with a running footman. Kenna nearly laughed as he hurried on his way, never looking up and never knowing that his single-minded determination to deliver a silver salver laden with crystal wine glasses had prevented her discovery yet again.

It was not difficult to become part of the squeeze of guests at the ballroom's entrance. While searching the room for some sign of her father in the hope that she would then avoid him, Kenna mingled with an armored knight and his fair damsel, a red-caped devil, a Roman senator, and two of the four shepherdesses. Looking past the gold leaf medallion on the senator's shoulder which held his toga in place, Kenna spied her father and sighed with relief. She wasn't certain how much longer she could have looked at Squire Bitterpenney and maintained her composure. Really, she thought, he would have done better to hide his girth in something less revealing than a toga and sandals. Excusing herself from the squire's side with a deeply mumbled apology, Kenna moved to the edge of the crowd circling the floor and watched her father take up the next dance with his wife.

Even if Kenna had not helped Lord Dunne decide upon his costume she would have been able to find him. Her father had a certain presence that made other people seem less significant when he was in the room. It was not simply his commanding height, which Kenna had inherited, nor his serene composure, which Kenna had not, that made his peers look at Robert Dunne with respect and perhaps a shade of envy. It was rumored that his lordship possessed the most uncommon sort of luck; that whatever came to his attention flourished beneath his regard. As a result, the gossips had it, Lord Dunne's estates were free of debt, his lands were producing, his tenants and servants were loyal to a man, and the bills he sponsored in Parliament were passed nearly without a dissenting voice. The truth, Kenna knew, had nothing to do with luck, uncommon or otherwise, but lay in her father's brilliance. If he had good fortune he was its own architect, a dedicated planner of his own happiness.

Kenna glanced about the crowd and saw there were those few who would begrudge her father his beautiful new wife, thinking it was unconscionable for one man to be so graced, but Kenna imagined there were also those who thought the lovely French emigré, Comtesse Victorine Dussault, was the one most smiled upon by Lady Luck.

Nowhere in the room was there a more handsome or romantic couple, Kenna thought proudly, if a trifle subjectively. Although her father had scoffed at Victorine's suggestion that he should dress as a dashing Elizabethan privateer, he held up his hands in good-natured defeat when Kenna and Yvonne approved her plan. Now, in his blue velvet doublet and thigh-high boots, with his silver-handled sword at his side, he might have been Sir Francis Drake himself, escorting the lady of his choice on the deck of the *Golden Hind*.

Kenna tipped her hat a shade lower as she watched Victorine follow her father's lead. In light of their youthful expressions, it hardly seemed possible that either of them had grown children. Victorine was innately graceful, poised, and confident on the dance floor, her steps neatly matching her husband's so they appeared to be as one. Kenna was entranced by Victorine's splendid elegance. Wearing a gown she had copied from a portrait in Dunnelly's long gallery, she looked more Elizabethan than the ancestor who had worn the original. The stiff white ruff about her neck somehow made her skin seem porcelain and her honey hair more golden. The tapering waistline of the emerald dress drew in her tiny waist and the sleeves, billowing at the shoulders and tight at the elbow and wrist, accented her delicate slenderness. The gown was shot through with threads of gold and Victorine fairly shimmered as she went through the steps of the country dance.

Kenna did not remember her own mother, but she liked to think Lady Catherine had been as gracious and loving as Victorine. How could it be otherwise, she reasoned, else her father would not have proposed marriage to either. All things considered, and Kenna believed she had considered them all, she was very lucky to have a stepmother who was the antithesis of those portrayed in fairy tales.

Kenna blinked, startled when Victorine faltered in her steps. Then she saw her father's eyes, teasing his wife in a way that Kenna was beginning to understand bespoke of intimate matters, and she turned away, unaccountably embarrassed by their actions.

"She's quite something, isn't she?"

Kenna pulled up sharply, belatedly realizing it was the devil speaking to her. She had nearly impaled herself on his trident. "What?" she stammered. "Oh, you mean Lady Dunne. Yes, she's quite something. A diamond."

"Indeed. Pursued her myself once," the devil went on, leaning on his trident. "She would have none of me. A pity. For me, that is. Robert's a damn lucky fellow."

Eager to leave this particular conversation, Kenna made some unintelligible reply beneath her scarf. Unfortunately for her the devil took it as an assent.

"Course she's lucky herself. It couldn't have been easy for her, seeing her first husband lose his head to Madame Guillotine as well as her father and mother. Bloodthirsty race, the French. It's a miracle she was able to flee the country. I understand she and her daughter were nearly victims of the blade."

Kenna shrugged, unwilling to discuss Victorine's escape from France with a stranger, let alone one dressed in a ridiculous crimson leotard and blood red cape. Besides, this man was not so well informed. Kenna could have told him that Yvonne had never been in any real danger, having been secreted out of terror-ridden Paris when she was a child. It was Victorine's refusal to accompany her daughter to England, to the home of distant relatives of the Comte Dussault, that had nearly cost Victorine her life. She followed her husband and her parents to prison when the nobility were jailed and almost followed them in death. The devil was correct in one thing: it was a miracle that Victorine had been able to escape. While Yvonne had been cocooned in England for the better part of her life, Victorine had known hunger and cold, foul living conditions and the constant threat of death until two years ago. The safety and tranquility, the unhurried pattern of country life at Dunnelly's coastal shore was still new to Victorine and Kenna, sensing her mother's reserve, never broached the subject of her imprisonment or her escape.

"One has to wonder how she feels about our victory at Trafalgar," the devil said idly. "It's hard to grasp what these emigrés think when they hear Napoleon has been so soundly defeated."

Kenna felt herself bristle. Three weeks earlier the battle of Trafalgar and Admiral Nelson's death had thrown the nation into a state of celebration and mourning in one stunning blow. Victorine had no reason to feel any differently. Napoleon's rise to power had not

31

saved her husband or her parents. She relished his defeat as much as any Englishman, perhaps more. Kenna could not believe this man questioned her mother's allegiance, yet she was at a loss as to how to respond.

"As you say, sir," she murmured huskily. "If you'll excuse me." Giving Satan no choice, Kenna brushed by him and moved to a less crowded part of the room. She scanned the dancers again and those guests on the edge of floor, sighing with relief when she found Yvonne taking refreshment with a man wearing a forest green domino. The hood, cape, and mask hid his identity from Kenna but he appeared harmless enough and Yvonne was smiling up at him, patently enjoying his company. Deciding it would be cruel to take her away, especially since Rhys and Nick were nowhere to be found, Kenna thought it best to wait elsewhere.

The gallery afforded the most comfortable place to hide and it was one of Kenna's favorite rooms at Dunnelly. Lined with massive tapestries depicting medieval myths and commissioned oil paintings of Dunne ancestors, the gallery was imbued with fantasy and history. Kenna rubbed her hands together briskly as she nudged the massive door shut behind her. Obviously no one had thought the guests would find this room because the sculpted white marble fireplace was stone cold. She poked at the ashes for a few minutes, before shrugging philosophically and settling for a lap robe that had been carefully folded over the back of one of the chairs.

The gallery was nearly fifty feet long and the furniture had been arranged in three distinct settings. When a fire was laid Kenna always sat in the middle section, closest to the hearth. Realizing she was going to be chilled no matter where she sat, she chose the end of the room furthest from the door and huddled on the settee beneath the rug. Checking the time, she promised to give Yvonne thirty more minutes at the masque before venturing back to the ballroom. Perhaps by then Rhys and Nick would remember that Yvonne could not stay past midnight when the masks were traditionally removed.

"It was very bad of them to say they would take care of Yvonne, then disappear," she muttered softly. "I won't forgive them easily for this." Ten minutes ticked by, an eternity to Kenna as she was hard pressed to keep her eyes open. She slid lower on the settee and yawned sleepily. Comfortably aware that no exploring guest was likely to surprise her, hidden as she was by the rounded back of the sofa, Kenna closed her eyes.

She had no idea of how much time had passed when frantic, whispering voices brought her awake. Disoriented, Kenna nearly forgot where she was and only just managed to stop herself from sitting straight up and revealing her presence. She knew it was wicked to maintain silence when the intruders thought they were alone, but she told herself since she couldn't really hear what they were saying it wasn't as if she were truly an eavesdropper.

The conversation, which she now discerned was between a man and a woman, was conducted in tones rife with urgency and showed no signs of being over quickly. Biting her lip, Kenna worried about the time and wished the man and woman gone. Because she could not see the mantel clock from where she lay Kenna decided there was nothing for it but to take a peek above the settee's back. She removed her hat and held it to her breast then carefully lifted her head, stealing a look toward the fireplace. At the same moment, the gallery fell silent.

Thinking she had been seen, Kenna held her breath and cast a cautious, guilty glance toward the far end of the room. In the blink of an eye a myriad of emotion assailed her. Relief that the lovers had not seen her, caught as they were in an embrace that allowed for no intrusion upon their senses, was replaced by rage when Victorine stood on tiptoe to reach Rhys's mouth with her own.

Kenna's stomach gave a violent turn and she brought up her hand to stem the harsh gasp that was caught in her throat. She was not witness to an affectionate kiss between acquaintances, but a lover's kiss, and she wished she were too young to know the difference. Victorine's small hands were buried in Rhys's dark hair and his long fingers were running the length of her spine. Had the couple been any other two people, Kenna would have watched unabashedly, perhaps even finding an answer as to how the kiss was accomplished without bumping noses. But this display of infidelity shocked her so that she closed her eyes tightly and forgot all about noses. Falling back on the settee, Kenna buried her face in her hands, weeping without sound until the gallery door was opened and closed and she knew herself to be alone again.

Sniffing loudly, Kenna wiped her nose on her sleeve and sat up. How could Victorine betray her father so vilely? How could Rhys? If she hadn't seen their tryst she could not have been convinced they were capable of such a thing. Even now she wondered if her eyes had somehow deceived her. Admittedly she was tired; mayhap it was a horrible dream. But it wasn't, a tiny voice told her. You weren't dreaming. Victorine was kissing Rhys and Rhys was returning it measure for measure. Though she did not understand its nature, Kenna recognized a hurt beyond the pain she felt for her father.

Jamming her hat on her head, Kenna threw off the lap robe and rose on shaky feet. Uncertain of where she wanted to go or what she intended to do, Kenna knew only that she had to leave the gallery. She glanced at the clock and saw it was ten minutes past midnight. Rhys and Victorine had left in time to be part of the unmasking and if Yvonne had not thought to take safety in her bedchamber by now, it was too late to help her.

Practically running from the gallery, Kenna did not spare another thought for anyone but herself. She strode right by the ballroom without a glance in the direction of the laughter and music. None of it sounded as bright and engaging as it had a mere hour ago. She pushed past Henderson without acknowledging his inquiry about her cape or her coach and walked outside. She kept walking, past the curricles and barouches lining the driveway, past the carefully clipped boxwood hedges, past the colored lanterns strung along the main gate. As if in a trance, Kenna saw all of it and remembered little of it.

Once, she stopped and looked over her shoulder at Dunnelly Manor. As if liquid, more than fifty lighted windows, shimmered and danced before her eyes, yet she knew it was her vision causing the face of her home to blur alarmingly. Icy air swept up from the Channel, tore at her thin coat and stung her eyes, reminding Kenna she was ill-prepared to spend much time out in the cold, no matter how numb she had been to the elements when she first stepped out of doors. Cursing under her breath, Kenna turned away and changed her direction. She was not ready to return to the house but neither was she prepared to walk forever without purpose.

Retracing part of her path, Kenna circled around the manor and went directly to the summerhouse. Some of Kenna's clearest childhood memories were of playing there, pretending she was the grand lady of the pristine white cottage. The gardener's son tended the roses on the lattice for her and the head groom's young nephew kept her pony by the apple tree which was designated as the stable. And when the three of them tired of the play, which was not long because Kenna found it dull to be in the house with her dolls, they explored the slippery trail of rocks that led from the summerhouse's back door to the narrow beach nearly a hundred feet below.

For hours they played at being smugglers or pirates, hiding among the jagged boulders and searching out treasure in the deep caves that dotted this section of the beach. They carried on one entire sumer in such a manner, blithely unaware of the danger of their game until Lord Dunne surprised them by waiting in one of the caves. Kenna would have liked to discover how her father was able to get there without passing them or why his feet and clothes, unlike theirs, were suspiciously dry. She never had a chance to voice her question, since she was hauled without explanation onto her father's lap and spanked soundly right in front of the gardener's son and the head groom's nephew. Pride made her remain silent while the slaps echoed eerily around the cavern's damp walls. After it was over she was hugged within an inch of her life and carried out of the cave. Her two playmates, much subdued by the sharp look in Lord Dunne's eyes, followed at ten paces. As far as Kenna knew it was the last time any of them had ventured on the rocky coast.

Fully expecting the summerhouse to be locked, Kenna automatically reached for the key that was always kept lying atop the door frame. In spite of her height it was still a stretch and when she gave a little hop to get it she was surprised to see the door swing open of its own accord. Curious now and not a little wary, she forgot the key and walked inside.

Kenna did not require a light to find her way around the house. There were only two rooms: one for sitting and one for sleeping. Neither were extravagantly appointed and Kenna knew the location of every stick of furniture. Even before she bumped into the walnut table Kenna knew someone had been using the summerhouse. The furniture that should have been shrouded in muslin covers for the winter season was uncovered. There was a hint of perfume in the air and none of the mustiness that Kenna would have taken for granted.

Feeling as if she had been delivered another blow to her midsection, Kenna forced herself to examine the sleeping chamber, knowing what she would find but unable to prevent having her suspicions confirmed. The scent in here was heavier, perfumed yet somehow more heady than Victorine's familiar fragrance. Kenna's hand trembled as she ran it along the bed, knowing her worst fears were real ones when she found it unmade. At least they had not been together recently, she thought bitterly, for the sheets were cool to the touch.

Kenna could not leave the bedchamber quickly enough. Careless of injury to herself from the rearranged furniture, she ran to the back door of the summerhouse and threw it open. She managed to descend three steps of the sharp incline before tearing off her scarf and heaving the contents of her dinner on the rocks. When she was done she sat down on the stairs, head between her knees, and waited for the sick weakness to pass. By slow degrees she became aware of how cold it was again. The sharp sea air stung her exposed face like so many nettles and dissolved on her clothes until she felt as if she were wearing a damp blanket. Although she felt the cold she made no move to return to the relative warmth of the summerhouse.

I shall die of exposure here, she decided, and they'll know what I've discovered and they'll be sorry they ever played my family such a trick. For all of thirty seconds it seemed like a splendid plan then the ridiculousness of her notion set Kenna laughing. That her laughter was sad and a trifle hysterical she failed to notice.

Kenna's laughter eventually turned to tiny dry hiccoughs and she smothered them by wrapping the woolly scarf about her face and throat. Waiting for them to pass, her mind curiously vacant of all thought, Kenna focused her blank attention on the rhythmic wash of waves below. White crests of water broke ever nearer to

37

the wall of rocks as high tide approached. In a few hours the beach would disappear and the caves would fill and by morning the strip of land would be swept clean.

When her hiccoughs were gone, Kenna started to rise. Just then a beacon of light in the distance caught her eye. It disappeared almost immediately and Kenna wondered if she had imagined it. But just as she turned to go the flash of light came again and a moment later it was joined by another. Curious now, she sat down and waited to see if the twin beacons would be extinguished. They were— only to be lighted again less than a minute later.

Kenna knew full well that light, unhindered by rocky terrains and the curve of the earth, could be seen from great distances over water. It occurred to her that perhaps the light originated from France's northern coast. Then after reflecting upon the nature of the light and its signaling effect, Kenna decided she was witnessing the work of smugglers. It was by far the more exciting explanation, she thought.

There didn't seem to have been a time when she was unaware of the smuggling that went on up and down the Channel. For many years Kenna thought it was a profession just like any other. Some men were farmers, statesmen, landowners, merchants, and some were smugglers. About the same time she began to understand that smuggling was illegal, she also understood that her father turned his head from it. While he did not condone smuggling he was sympathetic to the plight of the men involved in it. In Parliament Lord Dunne fought the high tariffs and restrictions on trade that made smuggling a dangerous necessity for some men as well as a lucrative operation.

But Kenna knew her father's sympathies did not extend to permitting smugglers to use his property for a distribution point. That is why she questioned her own eyesight when the beacon of light over the water was

38

answered by a swinging lantern on the beach not a hundred feet from where she sat. Though she strained her eyes she could make out neither the ship in the Channel nor the man signaling from the shore. She thought it deuced clever of the smugglers to choose the night of the masque to visit Dunnelly. If she hadn't caught sight of them they might have finished their business with no one the wiser. With characteristic lack of caution, Kenna concluded this havey-cavey affair bore investigating.

Kenna's descent to the beach was slow. She took each of the narrow steps on her bottom, keeping a careful watch on the flickering lantern and the spots of light over the water. Clambering among the slippery rocks required all her concentration and she narrowly missed the lantern disappearing into the mouth of the cave she had explored as a child. The lights in the Channel had also vanished and though Kenna paused in her climbing to watch the water, they did not reappear. Supposing an end to the signaling meant the smugglers would soon come ashore, Kenna scrambled for better position at the entrance to the cave. She waited there, as patiently as she was able given the circumstances, worrying her lower lip and squeezing her cold hands into fists. Just when it seemed nothing would come of her vigil she heard the slapping of oars in the water. A few minutes later two dark figures dragged a rowboat onto the beach and secured it out of reach of the encroaching tide. Kenna expected them to unload their boat and carry their goods into the cave, but they went into the opening in the rocks empty-handed.

When they did not return with help for their cargo Kenna slipped from her hiding place and went to the boat. She did not know what to think when she found the boat empty save for its oars. What sort of smugglers didn't transport so much as a dram of French wine or a bolt of French linen?

Curious for an answer to this new mystery, Kenna approached the cave. From deep within she heard voices. Venturing inside, she kept her back against the slick walls as if to become invisible. Crediting herself with a certain amount of stealth, she crept closer to the origin of the voices, raised now in argument. The thought of overhearing a disagreement among the smugglers, a falling out between thieves, made her giddy with fear and excitement.

To one unfamiliar with the cave it was deceptively small, appearing to have only one main room. Kenna knew better and was quite pleased that her memory of its twists and turns was serving her so well. What looked like a corridor through the rock on the left actually was a dead end. Kenna took the right passage, halting when she reached the entrance to the cave's interior chamber. The lantern that had signaled the ship sat unattended on a shelf of stone and cast the room in a yellowish glow. Crouching low, Kenna pressed her face between a narrow fault in the rock and peered in.

The two men from the boat stood with their backs to Kenna, blocking her view of the one they confronted. Then one of the men bent over to brush at something on his leg and before he straightened and stepped to the side Kenna saw he had been hiding not one, but two people from her view. Kenna was too numb from this night's events to do more than blink owlishly when she recognized the Elizabethan lady and her highwayman escort.

"Why did you answer our signal if you had nothing to tell us?" one of the men demanded to know. Only after he asked the question did Kenna realize he was repeating himself impatiently.

Victorine's reply was soft and somehow weary. "I thought you may have something to tell me."

The man cursed in rapid French and continued to make demands of Victorine in the same language. Kenna's knowledge of the language was limited to drawing room conversation but she could catch enough to understand that he was berating Victorine for her stupidity. Kenna almost felt sorry for her and wondered why Rhys did not defend her. Abruptly the man switched to English. "You haven't forgotten why you are here? You recall what hangs in the balance, do you not?"

"I cannot forget," Victorine admitted. "But a word, just a word from you would—"

"Would mean nothing, m'dear."

Kenna gasped but it was swallowed by Victorine's. It was not Rhys who answered, but Lord Dunne. Somehow he had managed to enter the cave as easily as he had years ago, and still Kenna had no idea how it was accomplished. She glanced at the hem of Victorine's dress and saw it was not muddy or wet. Rhys's boots glistened a bit but he had been outside with the lantern. Kenna understood their path to the cave was undoubtedly the same as her father's.

"Robert—"

Lord Dunne brought his hands away from his side and showed everyone in the chamber that he had not come unprepared. In each hand he carried a primed pistol. "Victorine. Come here."

Victorine looked fearfully at the men in front of her and glanced uncertainly at Rhys's shadowed face before she stepped to her husband's side.

"Couldn't you trust me, Victorine?" Lord Dunne's voice was sad. "These men are naught but liars, including, to my everlasting regret, the one you looked to for help."

Kenna held her breath while her father steadied his pistol on Rhys. "Would you have her betray us all so that you might venture into some new scheme? I had not

41

thought you could be capable of this—not betraying your country for some notion of world peace designed by Napoleon. And that is what you intended, is it not? Don't bother to answer." He waved one pistol in the direction of the two men from the boat. "Their presence here is all the proof I required. I should kill you, you know. But I can't. At the very least I should bring you before the courts but I find my pride too great to allow you to shame my house. I will grant you the opportunity to leave Dunnelly and England. It is better than you deserve."

Kenna placed her hands over her ears, unwilling to hear another word. It was nonsensical talk, all of it, and she was better off not knowing what it meant. Rhys opened his mouth and made some reply but Kenna did not know what he said. Victorine was crying now and Kenna thought she looked pathetically wretched as she buried her face in her hands. Her father must have thought so too, for his face softened and his attention was diverted long enough to allow one of the Frenchmen to dive for the lantern, knock it over, and plunge the dank chamber into complete darkness.

Kenna's hands dropped away from her ears as shouting and shots reverberated about the cave. There were pained grunts as fists flew, striking out blindly in the hopes that knuckles would connect with flesh. There was another shot, then silence, aching and deep. A hard knot filled Kenna's middle and closed her throat as Victorine screamed Robert's name. The necessity of reaching her father spurred Kenna into action. Under cover of the unrelieved blackness of the cave, she crawled into the chamber and narrowly missed being trampled by a pair of feet fighting for their balance in the aftermath of the scuffle. There was a rustle of skirts and protests from Victorine as she was dragged from her husband's side.

"Find the lantern," one of the Frenchmen ordered.

Kenna froze as her fingers touched the lantern glass.

Someone was crawling toward her, arms sweeping the ground to find the misplaced light. She held her breath, immobile, until one of the hands touched her arm.

"Diable! Comment—"

Kenna grasped the lantern's iron ring and swung it for all she was worth in the direction of the surprised voice. The Frenchman screamed in pain as the glass shattered against his face. Kenna's victory was short-lived as she scrambled away from his flailing arms and was jerked back when he caught the ends of her scarf.

"His lordship brought assistance," he grunted, wrapping the scarf about one fist and bringing Kenna closer to him.

Kenna thought he would strangle her and she waited for the breath to be choked from her body. The last thing she expected was that her captor would use his free fist to break her unremarkable nose.

Something cold and wet tickled Kenna's fingers and she drew them into her palm as if to protect them. A moment later the wetness engulfed her hand. She stirred uneasily and slowly, not knowing what to make of her surroundings. It occurred to her she may have gone blind, for it was just as dark upon opening her eyes as it was when they were closed. Gradually awareness gathered at the corners of her mind and she could find no reason to give thanks for it.

The chamber was quiet save for her own labored breathing and the gentle lapping of water at her feet. "Papa?" There was no answer, nor had Kenna expected one. "Victorine?" Again the silence.

It was when Kenna tried to stand that she discovered her hands and feet were bound. She struggled with the ropes but they held her securely. Water swept over her hands again and this time it did not retreat more than a

43

few inches. When it made another pass her hands remained covered. Kenna struggled to her knees and crawled awkwardly for higher ground. Water lapped at her boots, soaked her breeches, and followed her progress across the cave floor. She slipped once and nearly fainted again as her broken and swollen nose bumped her forearm.

Fighting for air through her mouth, Kenna slid a few feet forward on her belly. Her harsh intake of breath became a keening cry as her fingers curled around the ruffled edging of a linen shirt. She had found her father's body.

She screamed . . .

Chapter One

January 1815

. . . Kenna woke up screaming, with the metallic taste of fear still in her mouth. Her skin was cold, clammy. The sheets tangled about her legs, trapping her, were also wet. She kicked at them impatiently while reaching for her dressing gown. She had only managed to shrug into it when her bedchamber door was thrown open.

Nick stood on the threshold, endearingly tousled and sleepy-eyed, but with a face made grave by concern. He belted his robe and nodded to the maid who stood hovering at his shoulder, dismissing her when he saw Kenna was sitting up and appeared to be over the worst of her nightmare.

He shut the door quietly behind him and crossed the room swiftly. "Kenna?" Nicholas enveloped her damp hands in both of his as he sat down beside her.

Kenna laughed uneasily as Nick massaged her numb and trembling fingers. "You should be used to this by now." She pulled her hands away and hugged herself, tucking her feet beneath her. "You could have stayed in bed. There was no need—"

"There was every need and I doubt I shall ever get used to it. I had hoped . . . it's been so long since the last one . . ." His voice trailed off, regret filling the silence.

"Nearly six months," she murmured. "I had reason to hope it was over." She shivered.

"You're cold. Here, get under the covers." He shifted and moved the blankets. When he felt the damp sheets he stopped. "My God! They're soaked! Go sit by the fire while I ring for one of the maids."

Kenna did not argue. She rarely argued any more. It was only one of the changes experience and time had wrought. She did not care to think about the others.

The bed changing was accomplished quickly. Kenna barely remembered warming her hands and feet by the hearth before Nick had her back in bed. She stirred listlessly against the pillows. Strands of red-gold hair, a far cry from the flaming tresses of her youth, escaped her thick braid and lay like rays of sunshine upon the lace sham.

"Do you want to talk about it?" Nick asked, concerned by the dull sheen in her brown eyes.

"It was much the same as always." She closed her eyes but a tear pushed through her thick lashes.

Nick brushed away the tear with a gentle touch. "But? I can hear it in your voice. You've remembered something else."

It was true though she wasn't certain she wanted to discuss it with Nick until she had the events of her nightmare more firmly in place. Upon waking nothing seemed clear. Kenna had no recollection of the night of the masquerade beyond watching the parade of shepherd-esses from the stairs with Yvonne. Her next firm memory was of the family physician and Rhys arguing in her chamber over the merits of bleeding her. Doctor Elliot was in favor of the method to release the bad blood and Rhys was adamantly against it. Nicholas, having no

46

informed opinion, sat at her bedside and awaited the outcome. It was Kenna herself who settled the disagreement. Coming to awareness and seeing Rhys in her room, she screamed for him to be gone. When she could not be calmed, Rhys left, and the physician, seeing she was alert though clearly distraught, decided there was no reason to bleed her after all.

She found out later the argument had taken place nearly two weeks after the masque. In all that time she had not been conscious.

"Does it matter what I remember?" she asked at last, opening her eyes to search Nick's dear face. He was older now, as was she, but there was still something boyish in the curve of his mouth, at the corners of his bright blue eyes. He had carried the responsibility for all of Dunnelly nearly ten years now and nothing indicated it had ever been a strain. "None of it seems to be true . . . except for Papa dying."

"He was murdered, Kenna," Nick said harshly. "And you nearly died in the cave. That much is true. If there is something in your memory which would help us identify the murderer then I could almost—almost—believe these nightmares have some merit. They certainly have taken their toll on your peace of mind."

And yours, Kenna wanted to apologize. She said nothing because Nick would dismiss it as unimportant. He knew how she felt about being a burden to him. "Victorine was there."

Nick shook his head. "We've been over that before. Six months ago by your recollection. Oh, Kenna, I wish your dreams served you better. Victorine was with me when father was killed."

"She was kissing Rhys in the gallery. I'm certain of it."

"The gallery?" Nicks' eyebrows knotted. "You've never mentioned the gallery before. What has that to do with anything?"

"I don't know." She passed a hand over her eyes as if to clear them. "Probably nothing. It just seemed so real. They were arguing . . . then kissing. And the summer-house . . ."

"What about the summerhouse?"

"In my dream they had been there. The bed . . . it was mussed."

"An erotic dream, sprite?" he teased, touching his finger to the small bump on the bridge of her nose, the only physical scar of her experience. "Mayhap there is hope for you yet. Victorine will be happy. She has all but given up seeing you wed."

Kenna made a face. "At twenty-three one's prospects dwindle dramatically. I am firmly on the shelf."

"Only because you refused a London Season."

"If you say so," she said, yawning sleepily. She wondered if Nicholas would recognize the ruse. She wasn't tired in the least, but her London Season, or rather the lack of it, was a subject she refused to discuss. Nick's generosity had made it possible for Yvonne to have a splendid season and she had accepted the marriage proposal of a young viscount. Now she was Lady Parker, living in a picturesque country home in the north and dividing her time between a half dozen committees dedicated to good works and her three lively children. No surprises there, Kenna thought a shade wistfully. Yvonne certainly had taken the proper course. Though they corresponded frequently Kenna had not even seen her youngest nephew. A visit to Cherry Hill was long overdue. When Nick left she would compose a letter and invite herself to visit the Parkers.

"Will you be able to sleep now?" Nick asked.

"Mmmm."

"I take that to mean yes." He kissed her warm cheek. "You haven't forgotten that Rhys is due to arrive on the morrow?"

48

Kenna bit her lip to keep from asking Nick what had he thought prompted the nightmare. He would only tell her her fears were unfounded, reminding her that Rhys had been the one who rescued her from the cave, had been the one who carried her to safety, eschewing help from the servants. Rhys was the one who kept a vigil by her bed when even Nicholas and Victorine had succumbed to exhaustion and the one who had been bitterly hurt when Kenna practically threw him from her room upon awakening. Nick never believed the part Rhys played in Kenna's dreams had any basis in reality. Rhys was like a son to Robert Dunne, he told Kenna. It was inconceivable that Rhys could be guilty of murder. Besides, Rhys was seeing Yvonne safely to her room during the time Kenna was exploring the cave. Kenna had, perforce, to accept it, but the explanation did nothing to ease her mind.

Why then, she wondered, did Rhys Canning frighten her so?

"Nick?"

Nicholas halted in his progress to the door and turned to face Kenna. "Is there something else, Kenna?"

Impulsively she asked, "What were you wearing the night of the masque?"

Nick looked at her strangely. "Why on earth do you want to know that now? It can be of no account."

"Humor me."

"I was the devil himself. Everyone remarked on the cleverness of my guise. Old Nick, you know. Never say you don't remember?"

Kenna frowned. "I suppose I didn't. I thought . . . oh, never mind. You're right. It can hardly be of any account now."

Nick watched Kenna's eyes close sleepily again. When her frown vanished, composing her face into the trusting serenity of a child, he left.

Kenna waited until Nick's footsteps receded in the hallway before she threw back her covers and got out of bed. At her writing desk she began composing a letter to Yvonne. If Nick knew what she was planning he would be put out with her, so Kenna explained in her missive that Yvonne must never mention Kenna had invited herself. She didn't have any worries that Yvonne would not understand the urgency she felt to be gone from Dunnelly. She had only to mention Rhys's name and Yvonne would command her to come to Cherry Hill. Even though Yvonne did not truly comprehend Kenna's aversion to Rhys, she would extend the invitation for Kenna's sake.

Of course Yvonne knew of her nightmares, had even shared Kenna's bed in the early days when the dreams came frequently and with an intensity that woke most of the house. They were vague, nebulous dreams then, more frightening because upon waking Kenna could remember almost nothing of them. Yet Rhys's presence had provided a common thread of sorts and Kenna's sleeping fears had transformed into a conscious repugnance of the man she had once considered a brother. While Yvonne had come to love Rhys for his unstinting devotion to the Dunne family, Kenna resented the way he had made himself invaluable during the period following her father's death.

According to Yvonne, Rhys had taken charge of everything. Nicholas was shattered by his father's murder and could think of nothing but revenge, though whom it should be directed to eluded him. Victorine, though she tried to nurse Kenna, was finally bedridden with shock and no one was certain Kenna would recover. It was left to Rhys to see to the arrangements and offer comfort to those who could appreciate it. Kenna could not help the cynical smile that touched her generous mouth. Rhys's comfort to Nick and Yvonne may have

50

been of the purest motives, but in light of her most recent dreams she questioned his response toward Victorine.

As Kenna cursed the confusing nightmares that plagued her, a drop of ink spattered her signature. She blotted it and fanned the vellum in disgust. Yvonne was certain to know the letter was penned in haste and her thoughts had been elsewhere. After Kenna folded the missive she placed it on a salver for the maid to post in the morning and returned to her bed. Satisfied that she would receive an answer in a few days and sure she could suffer Rhys's presence for that short while, Kenna fell into a blessedly peaceful sleep.

As was her custon, Kenna woke early and dressed for her morning ride. Her gray gelding was waiting anxiously in the stables, nosing the groom who was adjusting his bridle.

"I'm certain that's fine, Adams," Kenna said, coming up behind the groom and stroking the white star on Pyramid's nose. "Pyramid is ready to go, aren't you, boy?"

"As you say, Lady Kenna, but I don't want any accidents like the last one." Adams ran a hand over his sparse crop of silver hair. "Like as not that piece of work took ten years off my life."

Kenna smiled, patting the groom on his shoulder. "Then you'll only live to be one hundred."

Adams straightened and adjusted the saddle, giving it a sharp tug to make certain it was secure. "And don't you make light of it," he said sternly though there was a distinct twinkle in his eyes. "I'll never forgive myself for not seeing you off myself that morning." He gave Kenna a leg up.

"You refine upon it too much. It happened months ago, almost six to be exact, and yet you have remarked upon it nearly every day since then. It would be more remarkable if I were the only rider to have never taken a spill. I appreciate your concern, but I do wish you would cease speaking of it. You will shatter my confidence."

"Hmmpf. 'Tis a lucky thing your stepmama was riding with you, else you could have laid by the brook for hours. You took that spill and nearly broke your neck because the girth was worn through. I would have seen it."

"I'm certain you would have, but I could hardly ask you to saddle my horse when you were laid low with stomach trouble."

"And that's another thing," Adams went on grumpily. "I never had a bit of trouble with my breadbasket before or after."

Kenna's brows drew together and she quieted her restless horse. "Just what are you saying, Adams?"

Adams looked away, uncomfortable under Kenna's direct gaze and questioning. "Don't mind me, Lady Kenna. I'm just an old man what sometimes gets a notion in his head and can't shake it. Go on with you." He slapped Pyramid on the rump and called out to her to be careful as she rode away. When Kenna was out of sight he sat down on a bale of hay and plucked a stem of dry grass to pick at a bit of last night's stew still lodged between his molars. Heaven knew if Nicholas got wind of what he had said to Kenna he would be looking for other employment and it was not something Donald Adams relished. Yet today he had come as close as he had ever dared to letting Kenna suspect the truth. Damn! He knew that strap had been sawed clear through and he had taken it straight away to Nick when he discovered it. Nicholas dismissed the man who had saddled Kenna's horse that morning and made Adams promise not to mention his findings to Kenna. She would never understand that someone had deliberately tried to hurt her. Knowing the frail state of Kenna's mind—her nightmares were common knowledge among the staff—Adams agreed. Yet his promise bothered him. Didn't Lady Kenna have a right to know that her fall had been a calculated attempt to cause her grievous injury, perhaps even kill her?

Kenna rode Pyramid at a sedate pace until she was out of sight of the stables then she urged her mount to a gallop and jumped the stone wall that bounded Dunnelly to the north. Circling round she tempted fate and jumped the wall again, then guided Pyramid through the shallow icy brook and into the woods. Their progress was nearly silent as Pyramid's hooves settled in the light layer of snow covering the ground. Kenna breathed in the serenity of the winter wood and the crisp clear air that was a balm to her senses. Her conversation with Donald Adams was firmly relegated to the back of her mind.

Just when she thought nothing could spoil her enjoyment of the morning she heard a loud snap and the keening cry of a wounded animal. Weaving Pyramid through the thick grove of trees she headed toward the sound and dismounted as soon as she found the steel trap that had closed around the hind leg of a fox. Her first thought was for rescuing the animal and she located a sturdy fallen branch to pry open the metal jaws. It was a difficult task because the fox was frightened and twice sank his sharp little teeth into her velvet riding coat.

"You're not helping me, poor thing," Kenna said soothingly, tears coming to her eyes. "If you'd just stay still a moment I'd get you loose."

"What the hell do you think you're doing?"

Startled by the thundering voice behind her, Kenna fell back on her posterior and dropped her stick. She cried out as the fox nipped at her stockinged leg above her boot. She started to scramble out of the animal's reach, an action that was much aided by the unwelcome assistance ot two strong hands beneath her arms. When she was pulled to her feet she spun around, hands on her

53

hips, a militant look in her eyes, and faced Rhys Canning.

It galled her further that he should be one of the few men she still had to look up to. "I thought my actions were self-explanatory. It would please me greatly if you would help or leave." She turned away and bent over for the branch only to have Rhys take it from her hand. When his gloved hand touched Kenna's, she abruptly pulled back and a swift, almost pained expression came to his face. "I'll help. Stand away. There's no need for you to be bitten again."

Kenna moved back, watching Rhys insert the stick for leverage and pry the trap open. Fascinated by the capable, graceful strength of his hands, Kenna's eyes strayed from the fox. She looked away hurriedly when the animal was free so Rhys would not guess she had been wondering how his hands might feel touching her body in an intimate caress. She was shocked and angry that she could think of him in such a light.

"Thank you," she bit out sharply then reddened at the harshness of her voice.

Rhys brushed some snow from his knees as he got to his feet. "You're welcome. I think." He motioned in the direction the fox had gone. "I believe he'll recover. He was fortunate his leg wasn't broken and equally lucky you stumbled upon him."

"Yes, wasn't he." She was impatient for Rhys to be gone and refused to be drawn into conversation. She'd walk on hot coals before she admitted the fox had Rhys to thank for his reprieve.

"He didn't hurt you?"

"A scratch. It's nothing." There was a rivulet of blood running down her leg but she was not likely to lift her skirt and let Rhys Canning see it. She would attend to it in the privacy of her room. Kenna glanced at the coal black stallion tethered restlessly beside Pyramid. "Beelzebub is anxious to leave."

Rhys laughed. "His name is Higgins as you well know."

"Well, it is a singularly sorry name for an animal who looks like Satan."

"Perhaps." Rhys shrugged, a glimmer of a smile edging his mouth.

Kenna supposed it was too much to ask Rhys not to smile. She could not bear it if he knew how it bothered her when his handsome face split into a grin. "Aren't you going to ride him to the house?" she asked, tapping a small mound of snow with the toe of her boot.

"Yes, of course."

He was being deliberately obtuse. She refused to allow him to penetrate her mantle of distant reserve any more than he already had. "I am going to continue my ride. Don't let me keep you. I'm certain they're waiting for you at the house." She turned away.

Damn her, Rhys thought. She had retreated again. For a moment it seemed she would argue with him, fire off a spark of something other than ice. The morning was cold enough without her lowering the temperature. He followed her, eyeing the stiff set of her narrow shoulders and back and offered her a leg up.

Kenna took Rhys's help, wishing she could tread upon his face. She and Pyramid had only gone a few yards when Rhys caught up with her.

"I sent my valet on ahead in the coach. I knew you would be out riding. Nick will know where I am. I thought I would join you."

So that was how he had come upon her. She had become predictable. Somehow the thought brought an ache to her throat. "As you will."

Rhys knew that was as close to an invitation as he was going to get and he supposed he should feel pleased she hadn't flatly refused to have him trailing her side. She had done that before. Rhys was too astute, though, to congratulate himself that any progress had been made in their relationship. She seemed intent on proving to him that she could tolerate his presence and the fact he was being merely tolerated took most of the joy away.

Several times his eyes strayed from the path ahead to Kenna. She had grown into a beauty, a fact that seemed to astonish her brother, but not Rhys. Kenna was still careless of her looks, as if she were unaware of the subtle changes that had transformed her from a loose-limbed schoolgirl into the profound symmetry of womanhood. Rhys missed the fire of her hair but admitted the red-gold suited the quiet demeanor she had acquired since her father's death.

Seated as she was on a proper lady's saddle, Kenna's face was partially hidden from Rhys. It didn't matter in the least for he knew every contour of her face from the high arch of her cheekbones to the sensuous curve of her wide mouth. He knew the shape of her winged brows, the tilt of her dark chocolate eyes, and the nose that had been made slightly aquiline by the fist that had broken it. He felt as if he had actually touched the slender stem of her neck countless times, feeling the pulse in her throat come to life beneath his hands. In truth, for years he had not touched more than Kenna's hand.

She wore her hair in a thick braid more suited to the child she had been than the adult she was. It swung across her back in time to Pyramid's movements. Rhys subdued the urge to pull it by curling his fingers into his palms and reminding himself that if Kenna was older, then so was he. She would not appreciate antics that would tug at her memories of a happier time. It maddened Rhys that Kenna was unwilling to put the tragedy of ten years ago behind her and get on with her life. She might look a woman, with her sweetly rounded curves and elegant poise, but she carried a certain innocence about her that Rhys was as weary of seeing as he was the icy reserve that protected it.

In his mind he warned her: My patience is at end, Lady Kenna Dunne. I am through being your whipping boy.

"I wouldn't have thought Nicholas would put up with poachers," he said to break the silence.

Deep in her own thoughts, it took Kenna a moment to realize Rhys had spoken. "What? Oh, he doesn't. I can't think what possessed old Tom Allen to set that thing on Dunne land."

"Tom Allen? You know the poacher?" Rhys wouldn't have been surprised if the old Kenna had offered the information, for she had made it her business to know everyone on or around Dunnelly, but that this new Kenna knew caused his dark brows to raise in thoughtful regard.

Kenna twisted her head a bit to level a hard stare at Rhys. "If you insist upon talking I would rather you came around. I'm not going to strain my neck to speak."

Rhys let Pyramid move ahead then guided his horse to Kenna's other side. "Tom Allen?" he repeated, trying not to show his impatience with her mood.

"Why shouldn't I know him? His family has been poaching in this area for as long as anyone can remember. Though it's not his way to use traps. I'll have to speak to him about that."

"Then you don't intend to tell Nick?"

"No." She did not want to expound upon her answer but she recognized Rhys's probing mood. "It's no secret that Nicholas takes his position as lord of the manor very seriously. He rather likes to think the locals respect him too much to poach on his land. Every Christmas he gives the Allens a smoked ham and deer meat. They accept it but—"

Rhys chuckled. "But Old Tom has his own respect to think of."

"Exactly." Kenna allowed herself a brief smile which

faded as she shot Rhys an earnest look. "You won't mention it to Nick, will you?"

Rhys pretended to consider her request. "No, not if you promise to speak to Allen about the trap. If that fox hadn't found it first it could have been Pyramid's leg that was caught. You might have been thrown and trampled."

Kenna had already thought of that and she had not been as kind to herself as Rhys had been. She definitely *would* have been thrown and only the most unusual piece of luck would have kept Pyramid from crushing her in his mad frenzy to escape the trap.

"I'll speak to him this afternoon. His home is only a few miles from here." It will give me a reason to leave the house and you, she told herself. "Tom will have to hear from me that I won't sanction his use of traps. It's too cruel."

"So there is a soft spot in your heart after all." Rhys hadn't meant to speak the words aloud but when he saw Kenna give a start he knew he had done just that.

"For some of God's creatures," she said pointedly.

"Another well-aimed arrow, Kenna. I should have learned to duck them by now."

"You should have learned not to provoke them. I can't imagine why you even want to spend time with me. Nick and Victorine would be most happy to have your company."

"Meaning you're not."

Kenna shrugged and let him draw his own conclusions.

"I doubt Victorine is up at this hour and Nick is happily settled behind his paper in the breakfast room. Your brother isn't any company at all until he's read the gossip sheet and financial news. Never was."

Kenna reined in Pyramid abruptly and stared at Rhys, her chin raised a notch. "Why have you come, Rhys?"

"What do you mean?"

"Exactly what I asked. Why have you come to

Dunnelly now? Your last visit was nearly two years ago, when you returned from the fighting in Spain. You never come without some purpose in mind so I am asking: What is the purpose of your visit now?"

"Pray, tell me, Kenna. What was the nature of my visit the last time?"

"To regale my brother and Victorine with you heroics on the battlefield."

Rhys's eyes narrowed and his voice hardened. "Is that what you thought?"

Kenna averted her eyes and felt herself weakening under his glowering. She felt like a child jumping at shadows but there was no escaping the fact that she did not want to be alone with Rhys in the woods a moment longer. With Rhys and his mount crowding her on the path it was too narrow for her to change directions comfortably, but there was a clearing up ahead and Kenna nudged Pyramid forward, turning him around and heading back the way they came.

Rhys had not followed Kenna but when she returned he was waiting for her, Higgins facing the path out of the woods. When she attempted to pass him he reached out and took Pyramid's reins.

Kenna shied away immediately, dropping the ribbons. "What are you—"

"I asked you a question. I intend to receive an answer."

"Yes. That's why I thought you came. Didn't you want to prove that you were one of Wellington's favorites? Does my memory serve me? Was it two horses that were shot out beneath you in one battle? Didn't you then lead men against Napoleon's armies on the Peninsula on foot? You were part of that bloody war for five years and you and I both know why."

Rhys went very still. "Why?" he asked softly.

Kenna pitched caution to the four winds. "Because

you wanted to prove to Nicholas that you were not the traitor my father accused you of being!" She paused and said scathingly, "But how could you be otherwise you . . . *American!* Every story you told was carefully calculated to make you sound the modest hero. Damn you, Rhys Canning! You may have convinced Nick you had nothing to do with my father's murder, but all the heroics in the world won't convince me! No doubt the fighting could have been finished in half those years if Wellington had known one of his officers was a spy, a traitor, and a murderer!"

Had last night's dream not still been so vivid in her mind Kenna doubted she could have spoken as she just had. Those memories, preserved in her head in the same vibrant colors as the tapestries in the gallery, goaded her on.

Rhys caught his breath and his leather gloves were pulled taut around his clenched fists. His jaw ached from the stiff way he held it, biting back the words he wanted to use to flay her. "Dreams haunting you again Kenna?" he asked in a tight voice. "Permit me to give you something to dream about."

But Rhys did not wait for permission to be granted. Without any more warning he yanked the ribbons from Kenna's hands and tossed them aside, hauling Kenna onto the saddle in front of him.

Kenna was too startled to fight and when she gathered her wits she also recognized the futility of such a gesture. She sat rigidly, her hip and shoulder nestled intimately against Rhys's unyielding thighs and chest. "What are you doing?" she asked between clenched teeth.

Kenna felt her hat slide from her head as one of Rhys's hands clutched her thick braid, pulling back and lifting her face to him. A small space of wintry air separated Rhys's mouth from hers. Then it was gone, replaced by a warm, sweet, impatient sigh as Rhys studied her mouth with eyes that had lost their pewter softness and darkened dramatically.

The sweep of changes in Rhys's face frightened Kenna. She blinked, her expressive eyes shaded for a moment by the sweep of her long lashes. Her features paled as she awaited his retribution and the mutinous line of her mouth vanished as her lower lip trembled. What was he thinking, she wondered. She nervously touched the corner of her mouth with her tongue and heard Rhys's sharp intake of breath and felt his body stiffen against her.

"You are still a child, Kenna," he said harshly, looking away from her mouth to her eyes. "You don't deserve the retaliation I had in mind."

She would have asked him what he meant but there was no time. Without pause Rhys twisted her around in the saddle so that she was lying belly down in front of him, her wrists caught neatly behind her in one of his hands and the back of her legs trapped beneath one riding boot. Higgins moved restlessly, jolting Kenna uncomfortably until Rhys also brought him under control. Kenna was uncertain if her face flamed because of the ignominy of her position or because of the blood rushing to her head. She stared at her rakish little hat lying on the ground below her and continued to eye it through a wash of tears as the flat of Rhys's gloved hand came down hard on her bottom.

Though he did not spare her his strength his slaps did not hurt overmuch. Her heavy wool riding skirt saw her well protected against the sharpness of his punishment but there was no protection for the humiliation that assailed her. Kenna had no idea how many times Rhys lifted his hand against her and to her mind it was of no consequence. That he raised his hand once was one time too many. She was unsatisfied by the tortures she designed for him in her mind. There was no method of suffering she knew that was not too quick for him. She wanted his agony to last for years. If it were in her power she would consign him to hell. Tonight, she vowed, she would pray for it.

Kenna's whimper stayed Rhys's hand, penetrating the red haze of anger that had blinded his reason. "Damn you, Kenna Dunne," he swore deeply. "And damn me as well." Rhys released his hold over Kenna, slid his hands beneath her arms and aided her descent from his horse. He steadied her, leaning over Higgins as her knees buckled slightly when her feet touched the ground.

Light-headed, but retaining a measure of pride, Kenna pushed away from his loathsome touch and stood on her own. "How dare you damn me!" she said, swiping at the tears sparkling in her eyes. "You are without conscience! But we knew that already, you and I. If ever a finer feeling crossed your mind you would not have come to Dunnelly! You are not welcome here, Rhys Canning! Why not go back to the place that spawned you?"

"Boston?"

"Hell!"

Rhys's eyes swept Kenna. Without seeming to settle anywhere his eyes took in all of her. He saw the mottled color of her face, the uneven blush that revealed her rage before she spoke one word. Her mouth no longer trembled but her chin quivered slightly, betraying her emotions. Her heavy braid fell over one shoulder, the red-gold tip curving gently beneath her heaving breasts. The hem of her dark skirt was dusted with snow and caught between her slender legs, revealing their coltish lines and the narrow turn of her ankles.

Sighing heavily, Rhys turned away, a grimace tightening his mouth, and kicked Higgins into a walk.

Behind him Kenna's mouth fell open but no sound came out. She could not believe he was leaving her, ignoring her as if she were of no import. She stamped her foot, angered further because it made no sound on the powdery snow and called after him. "I hate you, Rhys Canning! Do you hear? I hate you!"

Rhys heard. Indeed, how could he not? Kenna's voice was raised like the veriest fishwife. So she hated him, did she? It was no more than he expected, no more than he thought he deserved for being unable to give her the truth. His handsome features were twisted by a bitter smile. The truth? How he wished he knew it! The tenth anniversary of Robert Dunne's death would be upon them this year and he knew little more about the identity of the murderer now than he did then. The suspicions he had carefully guarded over the years were without foundation. The proof lay somewhere in Kenna's mind, in her dreams, of that he was certain, but for too many painful years those dreams had done nothing but damn him. His broad shoulders slumped as he approached the stables. Lord, but he was tired of it all.

Kenna dallied overlong in her bath, hoping that Rhys would have left the breakfast room by the time she came downstairs. She arranged her unfashinably long hair on her head and dressed in a simple day dress of soft gray wool suitable for Dunnelly's drafty corridors and chilly rooms. As added protection she threw a deep maroon shawl over her shoulders. Her personal maid clucked her tongue chidingly at Kenna's chosen attire.

"It clashes with your hair, Lady Kenna," Janet said as Kenna glanced in the mirror and arranged the shawl's end into a neat knot.

"That hardly matters. It will keep me warm."

Janet Gourley lifted her hands in a helpless gesture. She wished Kenna would not dress like a dowd for she felt it cast a reflection on her own fashion sense and worth as a lady's maid. It horrified her to think what

Rhys Canning's thoughts would be when he saw Kenna. He was a guest after all and to her mind Kenna owed him a proper presentation.

At the entrance to the breakfast room Kenna halted, hearing voices within. Her hand hovered over the door's handle as she considered speaking to Henderson and taking her breakfast in her room. Although she doubted she would enjoy any of her food if she had to eat it in Rhys's presence, the alternative seemed cowardly. He would hardly lift a hand against her in Nick's presence. Using that thought to bolster her flagging courage, Kenna entered the room.

Nick was laughing at some jest Rhys had made, his head thrown back and his blue eyes alight with mirth. Normally Kenna would have found his merriment infectious but now she barely smiled.

Nick lowered his head, pushing back his chair from the table as he caught sight of his sister. "Kenna! Good, you've come. I thought you might hide in your room in which case I would have no choice but to listen to Rhys's tales all morning. Now I can attend a business matter with my man and you can keep this poor excuse for a libertine company."

"I would hardly hide in my room," she said quietly, the lie nearly sticking in her throat. She ignored the skeptical lift of Rhys's brows and began to serve herself from the sideboard. "Please, take yourself off. Perhaps Rhys would prefer to join you."

Nick's fingers threaded through his dark hair, classically styled to affect a careless, wind-blown look. Unlike his sister, Nick was up to every vagary of the current mode. He even looked comfortable in his tailored dove gray coat though it was so tight it required the full assistance of his valet to put it on and take it off. "Rhys? Would you rather join me? I must warn you, it's dull stuff. Accounts and such."

Thank you for nothing, Kenna thought, piling her plate higher than was her wont simply to keep her back to Rhys as long as she was able.

"I've a mind to have another plate of eggs."

"Pig," Kenna muttered.

"Did you say something, Kenna?" Rhys asked blandly.

"I was thinking I'd like some bacon. There doesn't appear to be any." She turned away from the sideboard and blushed as both men eyed the mound of food on her plate.

Nick rose from his seat and held out a chair for Kenna, giving her an affectionate kiss on the cheek as she sat down. "Don't know where you'd put it, sprite," he whispered, laughter lurking on his lips. He straightened, touching her shoulder lightly. "I'm off. Don't let her badger you, Rhys."

"Wouldn't think of it," Rhys replied easily.

Following Nick's exit, a strained silence filled the room. Kenna concentrated on eating, a function she realized she had taken entirely for granted until she had to do it under Rhys's speculative gaze. The eggs seemed exceptionally slippery so that keeping them on her fork was difficult in its own right. Inside her mouth they tasted rubbery and she chewed the flavor out of them, wondering all the while if she could manage to swallow without choking. Even buttering her scone took an inordinate amount of skill.

Without looking at him Kenna asked, "Aren't you going to have your eggs?"

"Weren't you ever taught not to talk with your mouth full?"

Mortified, Kenna's jaw clamped down on the bit of biscuit in her mouth which resulted in biting the tender inner lining of her cheek. "Oh!" Her head jerked up and pain welled in her eyes. She pushed away her plate and looked at Rhys accusingly.

Rhys slid her plate across the table toward him. "Thank you," he said calmly, as if it had been her intention to share the better part of her breakfast with him.

Kenna watched incredulously and not a little enviously as Rhys coolly tucked into the remains of her meal. He smiled at her over a forkful of eggs. "Delicious."

Kenna nursed the inside of her cheek with her tongue. "I'm glad you like them," she said politely, refusing to be goaded by his complacency and amusement.

"What? You don't hope I choke on them? That surprises me."

I hope they give you indigestion. She said, "I am not so small-minded."

"Oh? I hadn't noticed. Dare I hope this morning's altercation is responsible for the change?"

"If it pleases you. I shall strive to be accommodating."

"I wonder," Rhys said enigmatically, his eyes on her mouth. Almost immediately he looked away, buttering the remnants of a scone and popped the biscuit in his mouth.

Kenna watched him chew, wondering why it did not unnerve him as it did her when he stared. She added a generous dollop of milk to her tea and sipped it, refusing to let on the drink was so bland now as to be tasteless.

"My father is in London," Rhys said quietly.

Kenna was not certain she had heard correctly. She raised her brows in question.

"Earlier you asked why I came to Dunnelly," he explained. "My father is in London, staying at the duchess's townhouse." It was not necessary to add this was only part of the reason for his presence. Kenna would draw her own conclusions, accurate ones as far as they went.

"Have you spoken with him?"

"Briefly. It was enough."

Kenna sensed his bitterness but chose not to remark upon it. "Your brother?"

"Richard is with him. They were part of President Madison's diplomatic mission to work out the terms of peace between the United States and England. It was finished last month. They'll be leaving soon. I understand Father's business suffered great losses during the war."

"And you? Will you go to Boston with them?"

"No." He did not mention he had not been asked. "Neither has forgiven me for staying in London while the British and Americans fought. They were of the opinion I should rush across the Atlantic and make their cause mine."

"Why didn't you? There are many people here who say that war was avoidable, brought on by our single-mindedness. I believe the Americans took exception to our Orders in Council, barring their right to trade freely." She paused as Rhys's amused smile caught her attention. "Why are you laughing at me? I am not some whey-faced miss who knows nothing of what goes on in the world!"

Rhys's expression sobered immediately. "Then you will recall the Orders in Council were adopted to stop the United States from trading with, and therefore supporting, Napoleon's empire. England was at war with France."

"How generous of you to defend your adopted land."

Rhys shook his head. "Let us say I understand England's position, but I don't applaud it. For instance, I could never sanction the Royal Navy boarding American ships and impressing free men. There is a matter I could have fought for. It was that blatant infringement of those rights which rallied the Americans to war. The Orders of Council angered men in trade like my father. Impressment outraged a nation."

"But you didn't join the Americans," Kenna pointed out.

"It was 1812," Rhys sighed heavily. "I had just returned from the Peninsula, Kenna." There was an ache, a weariness in his voice. "I was tired of the atrocities of war."

Silence settled between them and Kenna looked away, unable to face the raw pain in his gray eyes. Rhys was more complex than she had suspected, loyal not to any one country, but to himself, to the principle he believed in. She wished she did not find him intriguing.

"The things you said to me in the woods," Rhys said. "They're not true, Kenna."

She put her cup down sharply at his abrupt change of subject and the serious tone of his voice. "You've always said so."

"And you've always refused to believe me. Why is that?"

"Why is it important that I believe you, Rhys? Everyone else does. Nick has defended you from the beginning. Victorine has never given any credence to my memory of that night. Yvonne worshipped you. If you had given her any encouragement she would have fallen in love with you. Can it matter so much that I alone think of you in a different light?"

"It matters," Rhys said tightly. "Would any man like to stand accused of murder? Where is your proof, Kenna?"

"My dreams—"

"Damn those dreams! What can you remember from that night that has not come to you while you were in the throes of Morpheus."

"Nothing," she said softly and added, inadequately, "That is, it's confused."

"And yet you treat me as if I were guilty of causing

68

your father's death."

"I cannot help it," she said miserably.

"You can."

"I cannot! What is, *is!* Do you think I do not want to remember that night? Mayhap I would be free then, free of sleepless nights or ones that end abruptly because my own screaming wakes me. Can you believe I enjoy living like this, afraid every night to close my eyes?"

"Kenna." He reached across the table to take her hand.

Kenna withdrew it quickly and folded her hands in her lap, leaving Rhys with his arm outstretched. He looked at it for a helpless moment before he retracted it. "I don't want anything from you, Rhys. Certainly not your comfort. You are the one constant in all my worst nightmares. Your presence is the one thing that remains, no matter how the dreams differ. I know you were with my father in the cave. The lead ball that killed him may not have come from your pistol, but you were the reason he was there that night."

Rhys leaned back in his chair. He would have given almost anything to be able to deny her words. The fact that they were true kept him silent. If he spoke and she detected the lie she would never begin to question the faith she put in her dreams.

"Have you nothing to say?" she asked.

He shook his head. "It does not seem I can make you see things differently. There is nothing for it but to go on as we do." You are determined to lie to her yet, Rhys told himself.

"That, at least, is something. If you'll excuse me, there are things that require my attention."

He stood as she rose from her chair. "By all means," he said genially. "I'd like to accompany you this afternoon when you speak to Tom Allen."

Kenna looked at him uncertainly. "I don't think so,"

69

she said at last. "It is all very well that we have achieved a truce of sorts, but I don't think I can suffer you in my pockets."

Rhys's face showed none of his disappointment. "As you wish. Mayhap Victorine will go for a ride with me in the curricle."

"I'm certain she will." Kenna tried not to think of the painful knot forming in her middle as she left the room.

Kenna had not spun a complete tale to Rhys when she excused herself. She *did* have some things that required her attention. There was the matter of this evening's meal as well as the menu for the remainder of the week. Usually Kenna did not care for this task because it demanded a lengthy conversation with Dunnelly's temperamental, but excellent, French chef. Today, however, she silently thanked Victorine for relinquishing the duty. Kenna also promised herself she would find Mrs. Parfitt and ask the seamstress to repair the uneven hem on her yellow muslin dress. Kenna had kept putting Parfitt off because she despised standing in one spot, turning by slow degrees, while the seamstress carried on an unintelligible monologue, mumbling her harangue through a mouthful of straight pins.

She decided the dress was the most distressing thing facing her and opted to be done with it first. She was on her way to her room when she met Victorine in the hallway.

"Good morning," Kenna said, giving her stepmother a kiss on her proffered cheek.

"Good morning, darling. You seem exceptionally bright-eyed though that shawl is perfectly dreadful with your hair."

Kenna laughed. Victorine would never stop trying to change her. At a glance she saw that not so much as a hair was out of place on Victorine's small head. She was wearing a pale blue empire dress with a white fichu and

70

carrying a sapphire shawl in one hand. Kenna was quite content to have Nicholas and Victorine follow the dictates of fashion. For herself she did not recognize the need. "Janet said much the same to me when I chose it."

"You should listen to her then," Victorine chided. The gentle teasing expression faded from her face as she suddenly remembered something. The look she gave Kenna now was more thoughtful, even concerned. "Nick interrupted my breakfast this morning with some disturbing news."

"Oh. You mean Rhys, of course. I left him in the breakfast room. He arrived quite early this morning."

Victorine waved her shawl in a graceful gesture. "No. I don't meant Rhys. Nicholas said you had an exceptionally bad nightmare last evening."

"I wish he hadn't. It was nothing." Kenna wondered at her own words as she spoke them. Even though Victorine had figured largely in her dream Kenna was moved to protect her by making light of her sleepless night. There was something innocent, even vulnerable, about her stepmother that made Kenna loath to burden her.

Victorine's beautiful face softened with a touch of sadness. "Mayhap one day you'll share the whole with me, Kenna. I'll not press you now." She touched Kenna's arm lightly in a reassuring gesture, then left her alone in the hallway.

Kenna held Victorine's hurt expressing in her mind's eye as she went about the tasks that kept her from Rhys's side. If she gave full credence to her dreams, she reasoned, then it did not make sense to treat Victorine as if she were a porcelain figurine and Rhys as if he were the devil himself. Yet her father had been moved to protect his wife and vilify Rhys. Kenna believed she could do no less.

On the pretext of going to town Kenna asked that the curricle be readied for her in the afternoon. Kenna enjoyed driving and she handled the ribbons with skill so no one thought anything of it when she left Dunnelly by herself. The snow-covered road forked a mile beyond her home and Kenna took the less traveled road on her left, the one that did not go to the village.

Kenna could see Tom Allen's cottage from the road but she did not dare take the curricle closer for fear of breaking an axle on the deeply rutted path to his home. After securing her horses to a tree Kenna walked toward the cottage, waving a friendly hello as Tom stepped out to greet her.

"What brings you here, Lady Kenna?" he asked as he ushered her into his small home. The cottage had one main room and a loft for sleeping, yet Kenna knew Old Tom had managed to raise five children in its tiny confines. Now, as then, everything was neat and lovingly cared for. The children were grown but living close by, and Tom was still the undisputed head of the scattered family. Kenna was surprised not to find one of his grandchildren in evidence. "Surely you don't bring another offering from your brother?"

Kenna warmed her hands and feet at the hearth before she took a seat at the ancient oak table which was the largest piece of furniture in the room. "No, Tom, no offerings. I've come about another matter." Tom looked disappointed and Kenna laughed, looking pointedly at the well fed belly that strained his brown worsted vest. "You don't appear ill fed. I would say the season's been good for you."

Tom's deeply lined face crinkled more as he smiled, tapping his middle. "You've got the way of it there." He turned away and began preparing tea for both of them. When he set the cups and pot on the table Kenna poured, serving Tom as if he were her honored guest.

She lifted the cracked cup to her lips with the same care she would have given delicate china. "I'm glad to see

72

you're well. The children?"

"They're fine. Jean is going to present me with another grandchild in the spring."

"That's wonderful. I believe that will make an even dozen."

"A baker's dozen," Tom said proudly. "Young Tom and Cathy had a boy just before Christmas."

"I didn't know." She hesitated, not knowing how to pose her concern. Tom's ability to provide for his family was not a thing to question without giving thought to the matter. "Everyone is doing well then? There isn't anything you need?"

Tom bristled slightly then laughed at himself. Young Kenna meant nothing by it. "Aye, well enough." He winked at her. "If his lordship could part with a bit of venison it would not be turned away."

"I'll see to it. And something for the babies also. A toy perhaps."

"Now don't go spoiling them. It's better they learn life's hard at the outset." He put down his cup. "What's this matter that's brought you here? An old man can't flatter himself that you've come because you've missed his company. Enough of this roundaboutation. You used to be more direct."

"I've come about the trap on Dunnelly land," she said, looking at him squarely. "I had to release a fox from it this morning."

"A trap? On your land, you say? Did you think I put it there then?"

Kenna nodded but she knew already her suspicions were ill-founded. Tom's disbelief was not feigned. "I'm sorry I offended you, Tom. I know traps are not your way, but I didn't know who else might be responsible."

"Hhmmpf. Not likely. Can't abide traps. I shoot clean and for the kill."

"I said I was sorry."

"I heard you," he said gruffly, not ready to forgive her yet. "I'd like to see this trap. Is it still there?"

"I didn't move it. I don't think Rhys did."

"Who is Rhys?"

"A friend of Nick's. He came early this morning. He is actually the one who freed the fox. I doubt I would have been able to."

"Ach, you would have found a way."

Kenna knew then that Tom was going to forgive her insult. "Will you know who set the trap if you see it?"

Tom shrugged his sloping shoulders. "Might. It's a puzzle why anyone in these parts would set a trap where you might stumble upon it. Everyone knows where you ride in the morning."

This was a surprise to Kenna. "I hadn't realized," she said thoughtfully. "It has been pointed out to me that I am frighteningly predictable. It is rather annoying."

Tom wasn't really listening to her. "That damnable trap could have caught your horse. Sorry business, that."

"Rhys said so, too."

"Then he's got a good head on his shoulders." Tom stood and began gathering his coat, gloves, and scarf. "Can you take me to the trap? I'm going to have someone's guts for garters before this day is out."

Kenna slipped on her own gloves. "Do not do violence on my account, Tom. I wasn't injured. If the poor soul set the trap is in need of food mayhap I can help."

"You're too tender-hearted, young Kenna," Tom admonished her as they left the cottage.

After leaving the curricle on the road Kenna found it difficult to keep up with Tom's long strides as they tramped through the woods. Her breath frosted in front of her and the only sounds she could hear were their feet crunching the snow beneath them and her own labored breathing.

"I think it's over here, Tom." She pointed to a circle of tall pines. Dusk was already upon them and the deepening forest shadows made it hard for Kenna to orient herself.

Tom found the trap by stubbing his toe on it. His vociferous cursing obliterated all other sounds as he bent over to examine the trap. Neither he nor Kenna heard the warning click of the shotgun being aimed in their direction. It seemed to Kenna that Tom collapsed at her side in the same moment she heard the explosion.

Her screams faded and she heard the fleeing steps of the hunter as he pushed his way through the underbrush in which he had hidden. Hardly knowing which way to turn, half expecting a lead ball to pierce her, Kenna dropped to her knees beside Tom. He was clutching his shoulder and breathing hard but his eyes were clear.

"Tis a scratch, nothing more."

"Are you certain, Tom? I think our poacher must not want finding out. He meant to kill you. My screaming frightened him off."

Tom's eyes clouded and an odd, faintly alarmed expression etched his leathery features. "I wonder."

"What?" Kenna had been frowning at the blood seeping through Tom's fingers as he held his wound and had not heard him.

"Help me up."

Tom wobbled precariously once he was standing. It was obvious to both of them that he could not walk without assistance. "I'm going to Dunnelly for help," Kenna said as Tom leaned against a tree. "I'll bring some servants and a litter."

Tom eased himself down the trunk until he was sitting at its base. "No, don't go to Dunnelly. Bring Young Tom and Jack. Their cottages aren't far."

"But Dunnelly is closer! I can't leave you for the time it would take to find your sons."

75

"Do as I say," Tom ordered roughly. "I want no help from Dunnelly. D'you ken?"

Kenna didn't understand but neither was she going to let him bleed to death while they argued. She reached under her dress and tore her slip, wadding up the linen and gave it to Tom to hold on his wound. "I won't be long."

"I know you won't." He closed his eyes wearily and when he opened them Kenna had disappeared from his sight.

By the time Kenna returned with Tom's sons in tow it was necessary to carry a torch. The light wavered eerily in the dark wood, casting shadows on the grim, sturdy faces of Young Tom and Jack. She had told her breathless story, first to Jack, then to his brother, while pulling at their coat sleeves, urging them to hurry. Kenna held the torch and led the way while Jack carried a hastily improvised litter under one arm and blankets in the other. Young Tom had the presence of mind to take a flask of liquor which he had helped himself to twice.

Nearing Tom, Kenna's steps faltered and she raised the torch higher, scarcely believing what she was seeing. Rhys Canning was bending over Tom, his caped greatcoat partially concealing the wounded man from her view. His gloved hands were on Tom's shoulders and she saw them slide toward the old man's throat.

Fear seized her. "Get away from him!" Kenna called, rushing forward. "Don't you dare touch him!"

Rhys looked up, surprise in his clear eyes and a grim slant about his mouth. "Kenna. Stay where you are." When she did not heed his words Rhys stepped in front of Tom and caught Kenna in his arms then wrested the torch from her hand. "Just once can't you listen to me?"

Kenna struggled, bobbing and weaving in Rhys's hold so that she could have a look at Tom. Rhys's anger made no impact even though she felt it in the hardness of his grip. "Let me go! I need to see him! Why won't you let

76

me help Tom?"

Rhys handed the torch to Jack and dragged Kenna a few feet away while Young Tom knelt beside his father. "It's too late. He's dead, Kenna," Rhys said softly. At first he thought she hadn't heard, then she sagged against him, burying her face in his shoulder. Before he thought better of it Rhys slid his hands around Kenna's waist and held her close, offering her comfort as he had ached to offer it for years. Over her shoulder he watched Jack and Young Tom lay their father on the crude litter and he kept Kenna's face averted until Jack covered the body with a blanket.

"It was only a shoulder wound," she mumbled against his coat. "Tom said it was nothing." She sobbed jerkily. "He wouldn't let me go to Dunnelly for help." Even in her misery she could feel Rhys stiffen. "What is it? What's wrong?"

"Your friend did not die from his wound," Rhys gritted.

"What?" She tried to push away from Rhys but he would not let her go.

"Tom Allen was strangled."

"No! It can't be! You're lying to me!" This time she did manage to get away from Rhys and ran to where Tom and Jack were standing over their father's body. Blind to everything but her own horror and grief, Kenna yanked at Jack's rough sleeve. "Rhys says your father was—"

"Murdered," Jack said between clenched teeth. "His lordship is right. It weren't any lead shot that killed me dad."

Kenna pressed the back of her hand to her eyes, impatiently clearing away the tears that would not stop. "But how . . . who would do . . .? Not Old Tom! He never hurt anyone!" She felt Rhys at her back, his hands resting lightly on her arms.

"Come away, Kenna. Let these men see to their father.

77

I'll send someone from Dunnelly for the authorities."

Kenna shook off Rhys's touch and began searching the area, kicking up snow with her feet. "Where is the trap?"

"Kenna."

"No, dammit! Don't patronize me! Where is the trap? Tom came here to catch the poacher and I owe it to him to find the thing. Jack or Young Tom may be able to identify it."

There was nothing for it but to assist her search, though none of the men had much hope of finding it. After a few minutes they stopped.

"We can't find it now, Lady Kenna," Young Tom said heavily, taking a swallow from his flask then offering it to his brother. "Jack and I will look again in the morning. If it's around, we'll get it. Do as his lordship says and go back to Dunnelly. We'll send your curricle around in the morning."

Kenna nodded wearily, not bothering to correct Young Tom's assumption that Rhys was titled. "I'm so sorry," she said, hating the inadequate words. "I wish—"

Jack reached out and touched her hand. "We know, m'lady. We'll find the poacher and when we do, well, hangin's too good for his kind."

Rhys put one arm about Kenna's back, nodding to Jack and Young Tom. "I'll talk with you both tomorrow. Mayhap we can make some sense of it." Gently he led Kenna away before she could see them lift Tom's lifeless body on the litter. "Higgins is waiting on the edge of the wood."

Kenna made no reply and allowed herself to be seated on Rhys's saddle in front of him. The chill she felt had nothing to do with the dropping temperature. The closeness of Rhys's body did little to assuage the cold and she bit her lip to keep her teeth from chattering. Rhys's arms slid around her to gather the reins and she shifted uneasily, not wanting him to touch her. She doubted she would ever forget the humiliation she had suffered at his hands this morning. Before they had gone very far her body ached because of the stiff way she held it. A vague fear kept her still as surely as Rhys's arms beneath her breasts.

"What were you doing there?" she asked. The belligerence of her tone surprised her.

It was the question Rhys had been waiting for and dreading. The way she asked it told him she had already reached her own conclusions. He sighed, feeling a headache begin to develop behind his eyes. "Victorine decided she did not want to ride this afternoon so I went alone."

"There are many places you could have ridden. Why there?"

"I wanted to get rid of the trap. It was dangerous."

"I don't understand," she persisted. "It had already been sprung. There was little danger in it."

"I didn't want the poacher resetting it."

"You have an answer for everything, Rhys." Kenna twisted her head to look at him.

Rhys kept his eyes straight ahead, refusing to meet her questioning, accusing glance. "And you never believe anything I say. Why ask?"

"Tell me you didn't kill Old Tom."

Rhys felt as if the breath had been knocked from his lungs. His eyes closed for a moment, shuttering his pain. "Believe what you will, Kenna."

As if to prove her wrong he gave her what was, in effect, no answer at all. The vision of Rhys bending over Tom, his hands on the old man's shoulders slowly gliding toward his throat, stayed with Kenna long after she had retired to her room for the night. She left Rhys to seek out Nick and Victorine and do the explanations. It occurred to her once again that he was good at them. No doubt he would convince the authorities he had chanced upon Tom's body while out for a leisurely ride. She would be the only one to doubt him.

Sitting at her vanity, brushing her hair with hard, impatient strokes, Kenna stared critically at her reflection and wondered where she had found the temerity to confront Rhys with Tom's murder. Her face seemed singularly lacking in the character that had marked it in its youth. What made her believe she could talk to Rhys in such a fashion and be spared his retribution? She admitted she had no proof that Rhys was doing anything but trying to help Old Tom, yet it struck her as odd that he was in the wood in the first place. She didn't believe for one moment he was there to remove the trap. More likely he had followed her for some unnamed reason of his own.

The longer she thought about it the more convinced she became that Rhys was bent on hounding her. Hadn't he met her on her morning ride? Kenna slowly set her brush on the vanity as a thought that would not be contained came to her. If her own horse had found the trap instead of the unfortunate fox, would Rhys have been so eager to help? Mayhap he would have stayed long enough to watch Pyramid trample her. A frisson of alarm touched her and she shivered as she imagined Rhys touching her broken body only to be certain she was dead. Kenna tightened the belt of her dressing gown and the action seemed to ease the hollowness in her stomach though her knuckles remained white against the red velvet knot. She looked once more at her pale reflection in the glass, taking in the bruised shadows under her eyes and the colorless curve of her mouth. Why would Rhys try to kill her now? Didn't he understand she had died inside the night he murdered her father?

It occurred to Kenna that she should tell him what she suspected. Nicky or Victorine would not believe her; they would humor her and invent excuses for Rhys. But if she confronted Rhys directly, told him that she knew what he was attempting to do, then perhaps he would be startled into a confession. Not that he would actually say anything, but an unguarded look, a movement born of surprise, might give him away. She had no idea what she would do then, or for that matter, what he would do. A sad, ironic smile touched her lips as she thought of offering him her throat and him taking it.

She heard Victorine's light footsteps in the hallway. There was a brief pause at her door as if her stepmother were debating the wisdom of coming in to offer some comfort to Kenna for her part in this night's work. The steps continued and Kenna realized she was glad. Victorine would not have truly understood how Kenna felt about Old Tom's death. It was a tragedy, to be sure, but not something that should have affected Kenna deeply. Who was Tom Allen after all?

When Victorine's presence faded as she continued toward her own suite of rooms Kenna marshalled her courage and slipped from her chamber before she could think better of it. Her bare feet made virtually no sound as she padded down the carpeted hallway to Rhys's room. At the door she hesitated, cautiously listening for sounds that would indicate Rhys's valet was inside. Hearing nothing, she quickly went in, her heart hammering as she shut the door behind her.

Once she was in Rhys's chamber the enormity of what she was doing struck her. If one of the servants had seen her, or God forbid, Nicholas or Victorine, she would have hopelessly compromised herself. It wouldn't matter that Rhys himself was not in the room yet. Her intent, or rather the meaning they would have placed upon her intent, would have been clear. At the moment, dying at Rhys's hands seemed infinitely preferable to falling into them.

The chamber was dark save for the glow of coals in the

grate. Kenna scanned the room rapidly, looking for a place to hide until Rhys dismissed his valet. The only item in the room that offered some protection was an empty copper tub behind the silk dressing screen. Kenna climbed into the tub and waited for Rhys. Somewhere in the room a clock ticked off the passing seconds and for want of something better to do, Kenna counted them until much against her will her eyes drifted closed.

She had no idea how long she slept, indeed, it seemed impossible to her that she could have slept at all, given the discomfort of her hiding place and the pounding of her breast. It took several seconds to clear her muzzy mind as the door to the chamber was jerked open and Rhys entered the room, followed by the shuffling steps of his valet. With some sense of self-preservation Kenna slid more deeply into the tub, tucking her head beneath its copper rim and folding her arms awkwardly about her knees.

"Just help me out of this damn coat, Powell, and you can be off to the comforts of your own bed." Rhys was carefully enunciating every word as drunks often do when they want to prove sobriety.

Powell had been with his employer too long to be fooled. He helped Rhys shrug out of his tight-fitting garment. "You and his lordship tipped quite a few this evening. You'll be wanting my remedy for a swollen head in the morning."

Rhys's stomach curled as he thought of the foul-tasting concoction Powell swore by. He thanked God he did not often have cause to take it. Rhys normally despised men who sought to ease their troubles in a cup of blue ruin. But Nick had offered him fine Scotch whiskey and Kenna's accusing words this evening had been provocation enough to indulge in an excess of drinking. "Keep your remedy," Rhys said. "I vow it is worse than the sickness itself."

Powell shrugged goodnaturedly as he folded Rhys's coat over his arm. "I'll take this for pressing. Will you be wanting a bath?"

Kenna's breath caught.

"No."

Her breath eased out slowly.

"Oh, what the hell." He pulled off his boots clumsily and dropped them on the floor. They thudded loudly in the quiet room. He took off one stocking and waved it like a flag of surrender, laughing at his own foolishness. "Mayhap it will bring me out of this slow-witted stupor."

Kenna ground her teeth together to keep from screaming, hoping if she maintained her silence Rhys would change his mind again.

"A hot bath's just the thing," Powell said. "I'll send for a maid and we'll have you fixed right and tight in no time."

"I'm already tight," Rhys said dryly. "Just fix me right."

Powell chuckled appreciatively and left the room to rouse a chambermaid from her slumbers. Kenna was ready to lurch from the tub and make a dash for the door when Rhys stepped behind the screen, three-quarters turned away from her, and began undressing. Instinctively Kenna closed her eyes tightly as if it would make her invisible while Rhys muttered under his breath about the resistance of buttons and buttonholes being proportional to number of drinks one had consumed. Cautiously she opened one eye and saw him slip out of his shirt and toss it carelessly on the chair in front of him.

She told herself she shouldn't watch, that it was wrong and faintly immoral not to make her presence known. But instead of closing her eye the other one came open and she stared unabashedly at her first glimpse of a naked man. Once, a few years ago, she had helped Victorine nurse Nicholas when he had come down with a high fever, but even when she had bathed him he had been covered by a sheet. She had had to slip the sponge beneath the linen to cool his feverish body. This was infinitely different, decidedly wicked, she thought, but there was a greater possibility of stopping time than there was of looking away.

Though she had no way of making a comparison, Kenna decided Rhys had a beautiful back. It was smooth, tautly muscled, broad at the shoulders and narrow at his waist. Of its own accord her mind wandered and she could see herself running her fingers down the length of his spine, making him shiver, making him want her intimate touch. She felt a certain heat begin to rise within her as his hands fumbled with the buttons of his trousers and finally dipped his fingers inside the waistband and pushed them off with his undergarments. He kicked them in the air and caught them, tossing them in the same chair as his shirt. Kenna thought the move was surprisingly graceful considering the foxed state of his mind.

Her eyes flickered down the solid length of his legs and she understood of a sudden why Rhys had no difficulty controlling that unruly beast he rode. Even that son of Satan had to be able to feel the strength in Rhys's powerful thighs. His buttocks were taut, curving slightly inward at the sides, and Kenna had a barely contained urge to touch him there. Sometimes at night, just before she drifted off to sleep, Kenna would imagine her husband was beside her in the bed. She would turn on her side and curl against the warmth of his back, touch his bare shoulder with her mouth. Her arm would ring his waist and his flat belly would contract slightly beneath her fingers. He would turn over then, drawing her close, but she never saw his face in the dark room. His elegant hand would seek her breast, caress the swollen tip just so, and then . . . Kenna did not know what happened then and her imaginings always faded with the not knowing.

Rhys reached for his dressing gown and Kenna knew it was unseemly to be disappointed that he was going to cover himself, yet she found herself wishing he would not. His body, any man's body, was a mystery to her, and she was quite unable to deny her curiosity even if it meant burning in hell for it. If she was consigned to Hades at least she would not go ignorant.

Without looking in her direction Rhys rounded the screen again as Powell returned with a chambermaid. They were both carrying two large buckets of water.

"That was quick," Rhys commented, taking one of the buckets from the maid as she was in danger of slopping its contents on herself and the floor. His face was wry with amusement as she did not seem to know where to put her eyes.

"Aye," Powell said. "Her ladyship supposed you'd be wanting to bathe and the water was already being prepared."

"Kenna?" His voice held an odd inflection.

Powell shook his head and saw the light die in Rhys's eyes. "Lady Victorine."

"Ever the thoughtful hostess. Kenna could learn something from her stepmother."

Behind the screen Kenna gritted her teeth. How dare he!

"I don't know. Lady Kenna's a right'un." Powell turned to the maid. "Go on with you, girl. You're practically asleep on your feet." The maid curtsied briefly, put her bucket on the floor, and left the room in a flurry. "Skittish bit, ain't she? I think she was wonderin' what manner of man you are beneath that robe."

Rhys shrugged. He had already forgotten what she looked like. He dipped his fingers into the bucket and found the water was not too hot for his purposes.

He stepped in front of Powell, blocking his manservant's path to the tub and with an unholy grin touching his lips he poured the contents of the bucket on Kenna's upturned face. He coughed to cover her sputtering then turned his back on her and addressed Powell. "Just leave the water there. I'll see to the bath myself."

Powell looked at him oddly, his brow furrowed. "It will only take a moment," he protested.

"No. Leave it. I've had enough of your cosseting for one evening."

Powell bristled, mildly hurt at Rhys's tone. Young pup, he thought, and made a note to throw open the drapes on the morrow when he roused Rhys. All that harsh winter sunlight should set off an aching head nicely. "Hmmpf," was what he said though and when he left he shut the door very quietly.

Rhys pushed aside the screen with an impatient movement as soon as Powell was out of the room. Kenna was still crouched in the tub, pushing ineffactually at the strands of wet hair clinging to her face and neck and gulping back air in pitiful sobs. "There'll be hell for me because of that, Kenna Dunne. I hope you're happy I saved your miserable skin, to say nothing of your reputation. Get out of there. I've seen sewer rats in the worst alleyways in London that look better than you."

Kenna could not even take offense at his remark, for she knew he spoke the truth. Gripping the sides of the tub she pulled herself upright and finally managed to stand in her sodden garments. The water made a funny little pinging sound as it dripped from the hem of her robe and her hair and hit the bottom of the tub.

If Kenna had been thirteen Rhys would have laughed at the forlorn expression on her face, knowing it was part of her winsome charm to garner his sympathy and sidetrack him from his lecture on ladylike behavior. She would have joined him, laughing at herself, earnestly relating how this madcapped scheme had gone awry and how she didn't care a fig about being a lady anyway. He saw something flash in her eyes, as if she were thinking how simply she could have managed him and this situation if they could only roll back the years. The look was shuttered an instant later, hidden by her thick lashes as she studied her bare feet and hugged her arms to her breasts, covering them where the sodden robe and gown were outlining her every curve.

"What are you doing here?" he asked roughly as he picked up a towel and threw it at her. "And what possessed you to hide in my tub? Couldn't you have chosen a better place? Under the bed, perhaps. Or in the wardrobe."

Kenna mopped her face with the towel. "I didn't think of it," she said into the depths of the towel.

Rhys simply looked at her incredulously, shaking his head. "You obviously weren't thinking when you came into this room. You're not a child any longer, Kenna. No one would believe you came here just to talk."

"But I did," she said quietly. She squeezed water from her hair and wrapped it in the towel. Her arms immediately came up to cover her breasts again. "I did," she said with greater force. She looked at him then, to will him to see the truth in her eyes, but his stony gray glance had dropped and he was eyeing the upward thrust of her breasts.

"*I* know you did. No doubt it will shock you that I wish it were otherwise."

It did shock her and she could not hide it. She looked away, uneasy beneath his regard.

Rhys sighed. "Get out of the tub, Kenna. I am not going to force myself on you. Credit me with a modicum of chivalry. Here, take this." He gave her his wrinkled shirt and she looked at it stupidly for a moment before she realized he meant her to put it on. "Go ahead," he

87

ordered. "Take off that wet robe and gown and put the shirt on. It's more modest than your present dishabille. Don't worry," he said wickedly, intent on goading her. "*I'll* shut *my* eyes."

She felt heat flower in her chest and creep over her face. "You knew all the time I was here?"

"Not until I stepped behind the screen. Did you really believe I didn't see you?"

Kenna clutched the shirt to her, the flimsy protection giving her an inordinate amount of courage that faltered as soon as she saw the devilish glint in his eyes. "But . . . but you could have said something," she stammered. "Instead you . . . you—"

"Took off my clothes? Is that what you're trying to say? Tell me, why didn't you stop me?"

"Because . . . because I thought I still could get away unseen."

"You were always a horrible liar, Kenna," Rhys admonished her, clicking his tongue. "Why didn't you close your eyes then?"

"I did! At least . . . at least for a little while I did."

"And I shall do the same." He crossed his arms in front of him and shut his eyes. "Come on. In my present condition the room is spinning madly."

"Turn your back," Kenna said stubbornly. That Rhys did so without protest amazed her. She quickly pulled off her robe and nightgown and put on his shirt, finding that she too had some difficulty with the buttons and nothing to blame it on but the state of her nerves and her own foolishness. Occasionally she glanced at Rhys while she fumbled with her clothes but he stood the whole while with his back to her. It wasn't until she stepped out of the tub, wishing she had some sort of covering for her bare legs, that she saw why he had been more than happy to keep his back turned. In the cheval glass beyond him her every movement was mirrored. "You were watching the entire time!" she accused.

Rhys turned around. "I was."

His easy admission startled her and she looked at him, not understanding why he didn't lie. Something of what she was thinking must have shown in her face for Rhys answered her as if she had spoken aloud.

"I've never lied to you, Kenna." He watched confusion register on her face then he walked over to the bed and sat down on the edge. "Now what is so important that you would beard the lion in his den?"

"Do you have another dressing gown?" She laughed nervously. "That isn't why I came. But I can't, you know, talk to you dressed in this fashion."

"A pity. It's a lovely fashion." His eyes swept the gentle curves of her coltish legs. His shirt drooped comically about her shoulders and the cuffs covered the backs of her hands, but her legs were so long that the hem only reached mid-thigh. He felt another stirring inside him, stronger than one he had felt as he watched her undress, and he fought to tamp it down. "I think there's another in the wardrobe."

Kenna shot him a grateful look and crossed the room to get it before she refined too long on the cause of the huskiness in his voice. She huddled on the padded window seat, curling her feet under her and wrapping her toes beneath the hem of Rhys's robe. The robe, like his shirt, had the faint odor of the tobacco he occasionally smoked and something else she could only identify as Rhys. To keep from thinking about it she unwrapped her hair, threading her fingers through it to untangle the knotted strands.

"It's cold by the window," Rhys said when Kenna seemed lost in her thoughts, far away from him. He wanted to draw her out, understand her purpose in coming to see him, though he doubted he would like what he heard. "Why don't you sit by the fire?"

"No. No, I'm fine here."

"Kenna," Rhys said gently as she looked anywhere but at him. "Let's have done with this. Tell me why you're here or take yourself back to your own room. I pray you can manage it without tripping over your brother on his way upstairs."

"Nick hasn't gone to bed yet?"

"No. When last I saw him he was passed out in his favorite chair in the study."

"Drank him under the table, did you? Do you remember the time—"

Rhys shook his head. It was not the time for memories. "I won't ask again, Kenna. What do you want?"

It didn't seem real to her any more, not the questions she was going to ask, not the half-formed thoughts that had tumbled about her head since she had seen Rhys beside Old Tom's body. She couldn't remember why she thought the things she did, couldn't concentrate on anything when she was this close to Rhys and he was searching her face with his smoky eyes. "Did you send for the authorities?" she asked finally.

It was a beginning, Rhys thought, and he went along with it. "Yes, Nick and I talked to them. McNulty and Wilver. I believe those were their names. They seemed like good men. They certainly asked a lot of questions. They wanted to talk to you, but Nick wouldn't let them. They'll probably be back in the morning after they talk to Tom Allen's sons."

"I'd like to speak to them," Kenna said. "I want to help."

"I know you do. I think there is every chance they'll find the poacher. If they don't, Nick will. He was livid when I told him about the trap on his land and your own narrow miss of it."

"He's going to be angry with me for not telling him right away."

"I think he's calmed down. In the morning his head will be throbbing too hard to give you proper scold."

"Is that why you're being kind to me now? Your head's throbbing, too?"

"I never mean to be unkind to you, Kenna. Sometimes—well, too often you strike a nerve and I say things I regret. But then you are not so different from other women there. You always knew you could hurt me."

But I didn't know that at all, she wanted to say. Of late Rhys's mind seemed impenetrable to her. She never could guess what he was thinking or feeling. She had concluded he thought overmuch and felt not at all. She could not find the words to express what she was thinking and perhaps it was just as well. She did not know what to make of this softening, this new vulnerability, she felt toward Rhys. She steered the conversation back to her original intention.

"Do you really think Old Tom was killed by a poacher, Rhys?"

"No." He couldn't find it in himself to lie to her now, no matter what she would make of it.

"I don't either," she said slowly.

"Do you still think I did it?"

Kenna's fingers curled around the belt of her robe and she toyed with the knot. "I did. Earlier. I don't know any more."

"Yet you came here. Why? Did you think I might confess?"

He had caught her out so neatly that she gave a little start.

"Don't bother to answer. I can see that you did," he said mostly to himself. It was no more than he expected but it still had the power to disappoint him. He reached his innermost soul for calm when all he could feel was a rising anger. "Let us suppose I did kill Tom—"

"I said I wasn't certain any longer."

He waved aside her hasty reminder. "For the sake of argument, let us say I did kill Tom. Why?"

"Why what?"

"Do not play the scatter-brain for me now. Why would I kill Old Tom? You must have some theory."

"I thought he could have identified the trap."

"As mine?" Rhys asked, clearly incredulous. "Kenna, be serious."

"I didn't think he would know it was yours," she said quickly. "But mayhap he would have know if it was purchased or handmade and if it was bought it could be traced to the purchaser."

"Supposing it came from a local forge," Rhys said dryly.

"I didn't think you'd have carried the thing the whole way from London so, of course, I thought you bought it locally."

"Why would I be carrying the damnable contraption in the first place? I can hunt on Dunnelly lands freely if I have a mind to. Why must I resort to a trap?"

Kenna drew in a deep breath and said in a rush, "Because it had to look like an accident, you see. You knew where I rode every morning, you said so yourself. And if Pyramid had found the trap who would suspect it was you who had laid it? Who would have considered you set the trap before you announced your arrival and that you came to ride with me only to steer me and my horse toward the trap. I would have been thrown and trampled and no one would have thought of you." Her hands were trembling now. "It would have been some poor poacher who would have been held for the blame. Perhaps even Tom Allen."

"My God!" Rhys breathed heavily. He got up from the bed, shoving his hands in his pockets to keep from making Kenna's words come true. At that moment there was little that would have given him more pleasure than strangling her. He sat down beside her and when she recoiled from what she saw in his face, the terrible anger that had hovered near the surface finally broke through. His hands came out of his pockets and he grasped her shoulders, shaking her first then doing the only thing that would give him more pleasure that strangling her.

He kissed her.

Chapter Two

Kenna's eyes opened wide and her lips closed in a mutinous line as Rhys's mouth met her own. She recoiled from the hard, angry pressure of his mouth and tried to push at his chest with her palms. Rhys was having none of her resistance. He caught her wrists in his hands and held them at her side. At the same time he gave her a little jerk and moved Kenna so her back was flush to the ice-flowered window panes.

A small whimpering sound came from her throat as Rhys began to deepen the kiss. It was as though her heart was being wounded, then healed in the same moment. The feel of the rough, wet edge of his tongue outlining her lips was more startling than it was unpleasant. Some part of her wished it were otherwise. She did not want to feel anything but contempt for his brutal, silencing kiss. This was not the loving, gentle kiss she had once hoped to receive, not the infinitely tender, intimate caress she had believed she could reciprocate. It did not seem that Rhys wanted anything from her.

She was wrong.

"Open your mouth," Rhys said against her lips.

Kenna gave a small negative shake of her head, then ruined the effect by whispering her refusal. Rhys's mouth captured the small puff of air and drew the breath from her lungs.

She tasted sweetly innocent, a little like chocolate, and Rhys realized she must have had a cup of hot cocoa in her room. He knew there was nothing remotely innocent about the way he touched her, tasting of whiskey and tobacco. This was not the kiss he had wanted to give, not for her first kiss, and Rhys knew it was that. It occurred to him that she did not deserve an initiation to intimacy that was conceived of anger and despair but he did not want to stop. His tongue swept the slightly uneven line of her teeth, pushing deeper when she gave a tiny gasp that was part shock, part surrender.

Rhys released her wrists and there was an instant when only their mouths were touching, when Kenna could have renewed the battle, but didn't. Encouraged, Rhys's fingers tugged at the knotted sash of her dressing gown and when it fell open he slid his arms around her, supported her back and drew her closer. Her breasts were crushed to his chest and he could feel them swelling, hardening with the contact. He ached to touch them with his hands, cup their firm roundness, arouse the tender, sensitive tips, but he held back, instinctively knowing the liberty would force her to fight him again.

Rhys softened the kiss when he felt her first tentative response, the wider opening of her mouth to accommodate his hunger. He drew back slightly, a breath away, and searched her eyes for the permission his body craved. He saw bewilderment, even fear, but he also saw the evidence of the need she could not name.

His anger faded. He touched his mouth to hers lightly. Then again. Again. Her head swayed weakly to one side as if too heavy to be supported by the slender column of her throat. His lips grazed her cheek, the telling pulse in her neck. He buried his face in her damp hair and whispered her name against her ear. His mouth hovered near her eyes and when she closed them he kissed the pale lids and fan of dark lashes.

Kenna's hand rested lightly on his shoulders, fluttered there like uneasy songbirds, then were still. She did not know what was happening to her. She could not reconcile within herself that she was experiencing desire for someone she professed to fear and despise. Yet Kenna could not deny the peculiar drugged sensation she felt in her arms and legs, nor could she ignore the uneven beat of her own heart and the warm, oddly liquid feeling that seemed to radiate within her.

"Rhys?" She choked on his name as his mouth was evoking pleasant sensations on the cord in her neck. Kenna wanted to make him stop; he was confusing her with his experienced mouth and hands. "Please. No more. Don't . . ." Her voice was silenced by the return of his lips to hers. She felt herself helpless under the sweet pressure of his mouth and tongue. His fingers were spread across her back, his thumbs just narrowly brushing the underside of her breasts. One of his hands moved, sliding along the length of her spine and in that instant Kenna became detached, moved outside of herself and saw another couple similarly entwined. The man's strong hands were gloved and the woman's were petite and elegant. He was wearing black and she was as bright as sunrise. The highwayman was slipping his hand along the Elizabethan lady's back, crushing her to him.

Kenna pushed with all her might against Rhys's shoulders, shoving him sideways so that she could bolt across the window seat. She huddled in the corner, drawing her robe together and wiping her swollen, cherry-red mouth with the back of one hand. Her dark eyes were awash with tears that would not fall and they glistened in the firelight like twin stars.

Rhys leaned forward, reaching for her hand, but she drew up her knees and hid her face in shadow. He looked at his hand in disgust, saw the slight trembling, and withdrew it, busying himself with the belt of his own robe. He got up from the window bench but did not walk away. Instead he stared at the frosted panes and imagined the great expanse of Dunnelly land beyond his vision, blanketed by the falling virgin snow. Someone was moving out there, he could make out the path of swinging lantern light and he tensed. The light was not moving toward the stables as he had first thought, but away, toward the summerhouse and the sea.

He wished he had not seen it, even now he wished he could ignore it. But it was, in part, the reason he had returned to Dunnelly and for the moment it was more pressing than the woman at his side.

"Kenna, I want you to leave," he said, turning away from the window. He drew the heavy velvet drapes so the night walker could not see in. It was a risk in itself, for the man might easily notice one of the lights winking out from the manor. It was the slim possibility that Kenna might be seen from the yard that made him take it.

Kenna was too numb to bristle at the rude dismissal. No apology. No comfort. Just, "I want you to leave." She was afraid to say anything that would arouse his anger and cause a repetition of events just passed. She nodded dumbly and edged off the seat, careful not to call attention to her legs by keeping them covered. Head bowed to hide her shame, her face curtained by the heavy fall of her red-gold hair, she began to gather her own belongings. The nightgown and robe were still damp and had watermarked the back of the chair they lay on. She rubbed at the stain.

"Leave it," Rhys ordered. Nothing in his hard and finely etched features gave away the ache he felt for her.

Without a word her hand dropped away, falling uselessly to her side. She glided like a wraith toward the door, silent, graceful. She touched the brass handle just as Rhys called her name, giving it a pained little sound, but she did not turn.

"Kenna. I . . . we'll talk in the morning."

She turned then, finding strength in the nearness of her escape. "I doubt if we shall talk again, Rhys. About anything. Ever." She had no idea whether Rhys intended to protest her statement or not. She was shutting the door behind her in the next moment and in her room a little later, crying herself to sleep.

Before Kenna's head touched the pillow Rhys was dressed and pulling on his boots. His greatcoat was downstairs but he knew where he was going his jacket would serve him just as well. He checked the corridor before he left his room and walked quietly down the hallway until he reached the south wing. It would have been easier for him if he had been given a room here, but the wing was seldom used except when Dunnelly was receiving great numbers of guests. On his left he counted down three doors, cursing his luck as he found it locked. Nothing he was ever commissioned to do was simple and he intended to let the Foreign Office hear directly that he was through with these cloak and dagger matters. Rhys had opened enough locks in his years of service for the crown that this one posed few problems. From an inside pocket in his jacket he extracted a slim leather pouch which held the finely crafted implements of the vocation he had once volunteered for and now could not escape. He selected a thin pick and inserted it into the lock, twisted it twice until he heard the tell-tale click, then tested the door handle. It opened without a creak in protest.

Rhys ducked inside quickly, locking the door behind him. He paused, waiting for his eyes to adjust to the dark and put away his pick. The room was much the way it had been when he first discovered it the night of the tragic masque. The furniture, even in this unused wing, was cared for with the same attention given to the rooms occupied by the Dunnes. Still, Rhys was careful not to touch anything in case the maids had been less than conscientious about their duties and he left incriminating dust-free fingermarks behind him. He immediately walked to the window and drew back the drapes just enough so he had a view of the sea. The lantern light was gone but Rhys had not really expected it to be within his sight. The curtain fell back and Rhys moved to the dark walnut panels on the right side of the fireplace. He touched the base of one of them with the toe of his boot, applying pressure gently while he pressed the upper two corners with his thumbs. There was a faint noise as a catch was released and the panel gave way in front of him. He caught the panel before it fell, for it was not hinged like a door, and stepped inside. A cobweb brushed his face as he replaced the panel. It was an annoyance, but also a good sign. It meant the passageway had not been used for some time, perhaps not since his last visit two years ago. That in itself struck him as odd, for he was certain he was not the only one at Dunnelly who knew of its existence.

Rhys groped in the dark to find the lantern that he had left behind on a previous trip. He swung it gently, swishing the oil around, then struck a match against the stone wall and touched it to the wick. He took a moment to adjust the light then began the steep descent of the dusty stairs in front of him. The steps were narrow and creaked ominously beneath his weight. He paid no attention to the noise and concentrated on not falling. The staircase was an economical spiral, taking up very limited space between the walls of the manor. He had never counted the steps but he knew there were well over one hundred and as he neared the bottom their edges were slippery, covered with sprinklings of moss as were the damp stone walls he used for support.

When the staircase ended, well underground of the

manor cellars, Rhys's environment changed. The stone walls, constructed by laborers hundreds of years earlier, vanished. On either side of him and beneath his feet was smooth, sheer rock. The passageway he walked through was cut by a natural underground water source eons before the builders of Dunnelly found it and connected it to the house. Having seen the Dunne ancestral portraits in the gallery Rhys could well imagine any one of them in the role of patron to the smugglers. It was easy to think of a ship, laden with booty from a pirate vessel or with treasure from the New World, anchoring off Dunnelly's shore and bringing the best of the prizes to the family, *then* paying tribute to the queen. He wondered if Kenna knew of her family's less than honest past.

He grimaced, tucking the thought of Kenna away. He would not, could not, think of her now. The passageway widened as it wended its way closer to the sea and eventually opened to a small antechamber. Rhys walked through four such chambers, each increasingly larger, until he came to the one in which Robert Dunne had been murdered. He did not enter it, indeed he could not, without attracting attention. There was a heavy stone that blocked his entrance and it could only be moved with the aid of the fulcrum and the steel bar lying near it. The stone could be edged up a narrow ramp so only the slightest touch from the other side was required to make it fall back, blocking the exit. It was not possible to reenter the corridors once the stone was in place. Rhys had tried it several times; even with tools he failed to budge it. The carefully constructed ramp on the other side kept it secured.

He was unafraid his lantern light would be seen. There was not even the tiniest crack through which light could escape to the chamber beyond. There was in one place, however, a pocket in the rock, making part of the natural wall thinner than in other places, allowing some sounds

101

to carry to Rhys's waiting ear. Unfortunately, though he could make out enough words to grasp the import of the conversation, the rock and the cave distorted voices.

Ever since he had seen the night walker heading toward the summerhouse Rhys had known the man would eventually come here. Even if he did not suspect anyone had seen him, common sense would have told him not to risk a conversation with his contact on the beach. The inner recesses of the cave were much safer, unless one knew about the pocket, and Rhys did not believe that was the case. He had only stumbled upon it after an extensive search of the chamber.

Rhys could make out at least two different speakers beyond the wall only because one of them tangled his speech with English and French while another spoke only English. There may have been more men in the room, it was difficult to know for certain but there seemed to be only two main speakers. If there had been any pleasantries they were well behind the men now, for they were arguing over a matter at the moment which struck Rhys like a blow to his midsection.

At first Rhys wanted to believe he hadn't heard correctly. Perhaps they *were* talking about an elbow. But it was silly and he knew it, knew in his gut they were discussing Elba, knew as surely as he knew Kenna Dunne hated him that they were talking about an escape for Napoleon from his island exile. Rhys remembered how he had complained bitterly about his present assignment. After nearly a year of peace, while the terms of the truce were being painstakingly drawn up in Vienna, it seemed absurd to suppose that Napoleon had a prayer of upsetting the delicate balance of power and borders on the Continent. Now it was clear to Rhys his superiors had every reason to be concerned. It bothered him not a little that they were correct about a plot to free Napoleon, but he admitted his greater fear, purely selfish in nature, concerned the involvement of Dunnelly lands as a meeting place for the traitors.

Rhys had to breathe deeply to calm himself and the pounding in his chest. For a few seconds it was all he could hear. Later he could make out the argument seemed to be about details. The Englishman wanted them and the Frenchy was merely repeating he had no more to give. Rhys realized he had missed the important beginning of the conversation. He caught the words "finance" and "backers." He felt sure he had not mistaken the meaning. Someone in England, supported with the money of others, was going to help Napoleon leave Elba and regain France, perhaps all of the Continent.

It seemed too improbable to be true, too evil an undertaking to have any foundation in reality, yet Napoleon's reign and conquest seemed equally incredible. Rhys listened intently for another ten minutes while money exchanged hands and his patience wore thin. Just when he thought he would hear nothing more of any import, the Englishman asked when he could expect to hear of their success. The Frenchy replied, *"Sept années."* Seven weeks! Rhys ticked them off on his fingers. The Frenchman expected Napoleon to be free sometime during the first week of March!

The time line was everything to Rhys. Seven weeks was long enough for the Foreign Office to formulate some measure to stop the escape, perhaps even long enough for him to put names to the characters in the international drama he had uncovered.

To be certain the men did not return to discuss anything of import, Rhys waited a few minutes after he heard the last sound in the cave before he retraced his steps to the south wing bedroom. Rhys took a minute at the top of the stairs to catch his breath, then slipped off his boots. He had been cautious thus far and was not about to track dirt across the bedchamber floor. Once Rhys was in his own room he immediately went to the window to see if he could catch sight of the night walker heading toward the stables. As he suspected would be the case, the man had already disappeared. Rhys reflected that if he had taken this assignment more seriously he would not have entered the passageway unarmed. Confrontation with the traitor was useless without a weapon and even then it was a risky proposition. If he were killed, and Rhys was not so naive as to dismiss the possibility, then there would be no one to relate the information to the Foreign Office.

Rhys was a long time falling to sleep but with Powell's help he woke early. "Close those blasted drapes, man!" Rhys muttered, burying his head in his pillow.

Powell felt vindicated for Rhys's rude behavior the night before but he did nothing about the drapes. "I thought you'd want to go riding with Lady Kenna," he said innocently.

Rhys sat up and threw the pillow to one side. "Has she gone yet?"

"Just. I saw her leave as I was coming up from breakfast."

Rhys's desire was to ride with Kenna, but last night's events meant there were new considerations to deal with. It was imperative that he speak to Nicholas first and it would be better if Kenna did not get wind of the conversation until he was prepared to share it with her. He glanced over at Powell who was examininng the three buckets of water which had never been used. The bewilderment on his craggy face was priceless. Rhys rose from the bed, dragging a sheet with him and put an arm around the man who had been as valuable as his right arm during the years of fighting on the Peninsula. First things first, he thought. "You would not believe the night I had," he said, and began his explanation.

Powell was leaving Dunnelly Manor for London by the time Rhys sat down to breakfast with Nicholas. His absence would go unremarked, indeed, it was unlikely anyone would really note it. It was a far safer course for Powell to relate the plot than for Rhys to make excuses and leave Dunnelly himself. Rhys had every confidence in his valet who had proved on many occasions he was a soldier first, a servant second.

Rhys flicked Nicholas's newspaper to get his attention. "Have you finished with the scandal sheet?"

Nick laughed good-naturedly as he lowered the paper and made a production of folding it. He put it to one side and picked up his cup of coffee. "You're a nuisance, Rhys. More trouble than a wife, I'd wager. At least I'd have her trained not to bother me while I'm reading."

"Then it's no mystery why you've never married," Rhys said dryly. "I don't know many women who will lend themselves to training."

"Then you haven't known the right women. I can introduce you to several who would be most accommodating for a few baubles."

"No, thank you. If you recall, I'm merely the younger son. I don't have trifles to squander." It was not precisely true because Rhys had a very adequate allowance from his father and great-grandmother and a fashionable townhouse in London, but it amused him to play at having empty pockets because he knew it goaded the duchess and in turn, his father. The Duchess of Pelham, well into her nineties, had become Roland Canning's eyes and ears once Rhys finished at Oxford. She wrote dutifully to Boston once a month detailing Rhys's scrapes and bemoaning his lack of convention and demeanor. At Rhys's request she used her influence to secure him a commission with Wellington's troops. That Rhys distinguished himself in battle mollified her only a little. Rhys knew the tenor of her correspondence because she once summoned him to an audience at Pelham and read her latest letter before she sent if off. Rhys had placed a smacking kiss on her wrinkled cheek and taken his leave while the bewildered, sputtering duchess threw up her hands in despair. He did nothing to correct the impression that he used his allowance to honor gambling debts he had accrued the quarter before, though in truth he won more often that he lost. Rhys decided his father should take some comfort in thinking his younger son had turned out no better than he ever thought he would. Above all, Roland Canning liked being in the right of things and Rhys felt a certain perverse pleasure in not disappointing his father.

"Hah!" Nicholas scoffed. "Then the rumors I hear about you and that actress—what's her name?"

"I haven't the vaguest idea."

Nick snapped his fingers. "Miss Polly Dawn Rose! Quaint name, that. A chorine from the country, no doubt. Are you saying you haven't set her up in her own house?"

"It never ceases to surprise me how you hear these things at Dunnelly," Rhys said, neither confirming or denying the bit of gossip. His business arrangement with P.D. Rose was a private matter and he intended to keep it that way. "Enough of this prattle about my affairs, or the lack of them. I am concerned about your sister at the moment."

Nick sat up straighter in his chair and gave Rhys his full attention. "What about Kenna?"

"That havey-cavey business yesterday, for one thing, and her attitude toward me for another." Rhys buttered a slice of toast. "Have you talked with her about Tom Allen?"

Nick nodded. "I managed to catch her as she was going out the door. It wasn't a satisfactory conversation but I think she heard my displeasure well enough. She's taking

Old Tom's death to heart and blaming herself. Nothing's to be served by that and I'm afraid it will complicate matters with McNulty and that other fellow."

"Wilver."

"Yes. She told me twice this morning that it could have been her in the trap, or shot, and of course it could have been, but the way she said it made me think she believed it was *meant* to be her. I don't like that at all. Furthermore, I don't know what I make of it nor do I have any idea what the authorities will think. God forbid Kenna should hear the truth about her riding accident! She would not be able to sleep for a month of Sundays!"

"Riding accident?" Rhys asked, a note of caution in his voice.

"What? Oh, yes. You couldn't know, could you? She fell from her horse some six months ago, I believe. Nothing noteworthy about that. All riders take a spill now and again. But the head groom brought a girth strap to me that had been maliciously sawed through. I dismissed the man who saddled Pyramid for her that morning though he vowed he knew nothing about it. I've forbidden Adams to talk to Kenna about it. I won't have her upset by that affair." He waved a hand in front of Rhys when he saw his friend was about to protest his decision. "No. I did the correct thing. That accident occurred shortly after one of Kenna's worst nightmares and I was not going to risk a string of them. As it happened she went until two nights ago without another. That's the longest ever. There is no telling what will happen now that her imagination is in full swing again."

"I think you'll agree it is not a matter of her imagination any longer, Nick. She has the right to be worried. I believe someone is trying to harm her. You can't protect her if you can't at least admit the possibility."

Nick put a hand to his forehead and massaged it,

closing his eyes briefly. "I can't believe someone would want to hurt Kenna," he said after a moment. "Why? She's never done anything but get up to mischief. And Father's death changed that."

Rhys thought of Kenna crouching in his copper tub and nearly smiled. If he had caused her to "get up to mischief" then he counted his visit as a success of sorts. She had become far too retiring and genteel since Lord Dunne died. "I have a theory," Rhys said quietly.

"Then share it! Don't keep it to yourself!"

"I think someone is afraid Kenna's nightmares will eventually name her father's murderer."

Nick laughed but there was nothing amusing in the sound. "Then that would make you the prime suspect. Kenna has never stopped saying it was you with Father that night."

"I know. But I did *not* kill him, Nick."

"I wasn't saying that!"

"No. I know you weren't," Rhys said wearily. "The fact remains that Kenna is. She has already accused me of laying the trap and strangling Old Tom. If she knew that Pyramid's girth had been tampered with she would find a way to lay that at my door also."

"But you weren't even here then."

"I could have hired someone," Rhys said, to play the devil's advocate.

"You tied the attempts on her life to her nightmares. How could you have known about the one six months ago, or even the most recent one?"

"Someone on your staff is in my employ. Kenna's restless nights are no secret among the servants."

"This is ridiculous," Nick said heavily.

"I agree. But there it is."

Nick frowned, his sharp blue eyes leveled on Rhys. "There what is?"

"I have reason to believe someone on your staff is

108

collecting a salary from your father's murderer." Rhys thought of the night walker, but held his tongue. There was no way he could tell Nick of last evening's rendezvous on Dunnelly land. He was certain there was a connection between the attempts on Kenna's life and the business in the cave, but the proof would be long in coming, if it ever did. "If Kenna comes too close to remembering the details of the night of the masquerade, I'm certain he has orders to kill her."

"But Kenna only discusses her nightmares with me," Nick protested. "And I only discuss them with Victorine."

Rhys could see that Nick was being swayed. His protest lacked conviction. "Are you certain Victorine has never mentioned them to a servant? Or Kenna?"

"Victorine? No, she would never discuss such a personal matter with one of the staff. You know her well enough to know that is true. She would never think of it. But Kenna . . ." He paused thoughtfully. "Kenna has never been particularly discreet with her personal maid or those servants she counts as friends. I never considered before that she might share something with any one of them."

"Then you admit she may."

"As you said, it's possible. Poor Kenna. She will be so hurt if she finds out someone she trusts is not her friend."

"I don't want her to know," Rhys said quickly. "Not yet. It's imperative that we do not allow this person, whoever he is, to get his guard up. Kenna would give herself away. Can you promise not to say anything to her about my suspicions?"

"Is that what you really want, Rhys?" Nick asked with insight. "She'll continue to hold you responsible. That can't be easy for you."

"It's what I want . . . for now. I can deal with Kenna."

He smiled ruefully as he took a bite of buttered toast, now stone cold. "At least I think I can. What I need from you is patience and no small amount of cooperation."

"You have the latter. The former will take some doing."

Rhys nodded, expecting the answer he got. "I want a list of all the people who attended the masque. Can you make me one?"

"I suppose," Nick said slowly, "though my memory may not serve me. It *was* nearly ten years ago. If I may speak to Victorine of this matter, she can assist me. After all, she helped my father draw up the guest list."

"By all means, speak to Victorine," Rhys said easily. "But no one else. Victorine will want to help and it's important she knows what is happening to Kenna. Until I can find a satisfactory way to protect your sister, it remains for the three of us to be watchful."

At that moment the door opened and Victorine glided into the breakfast room. She looked radiant in a pale rose morning gown and matching kid slippers. She gave Nick and Rhys an arch look before she turned to serve herself from the sideboard. "It is in the worst possible taste to stop talking when a woman enters the room. It is bound to make her think you were discussing her."

Rhys rose and held out a chair for Victorine, giving her a kiss on her smooth, unlined cheek as she sat down.

"Rogue," she said teasingly, patting the hand that rested on the back of her chair. "But don't think I'll be put off. Now what exactly *were* you men discussing?"

Rhys smiled, looking over Victorine at Nicholas. "I'll leave this very lovely lady in your hands, Nick. I've no strength to withstand her interrogation."

Nick nodded. "Where are you going now?"

"To find Kenna."

Victorine raised an eyebrow. "And you say you haven't the strength to face me?"

Nick laughed at her dry poser, but Rhys had already left the room.

Certain that Kenna was not likely to ride in the wood where Tom Allen had been murdered, Rhys waited for her in the stables. He passed the time by rubbing down his own horse and talking to Donald Adams about Kenna's riding accident. Learning of Donald's mysterious illness the morning of the accident only served to confirm Rhys's suspicions. At the same time he was unable to learn anything at all about last evening's visitor to the stables. Although he was not direct in his questioning, he talked long enough with Donald to know the man hadn't seen anything the night before.

He had heard a lot more than he ever wanted to about Donald Adams's life by the time Kenna led Pyramid into the stables. Rhys saw the head groom being given the full force of her smile until she looked past Donald's face and saw him standing there.

Kenna's smile froze. She gave the reins to Adams and nodded slightly at Rhys. It was only the head groom's presence that kept her from running from the stables.

"Did you have a good ride, Lady Kenna?" Donald asked, patting Pyramid's neck.

"Very nice," Kenna replied, her voice not much above a whisper. "Very nice," she repeated louder.

Rhys saw Donald give Kenna a questioning look, then glance in his direction as if sensing something amiss. "Walk with me, Kenna," he said.

"I . . . I don't . . ." She saw Donald's furrowed brow and interested gaze. "Very well," she said as graciously as she was able. "Where would you like to walk?"

Rhys took Kenna's arm, knowing she would hardly fight him off in front of the groom. "The summerhouse, I think," he said as he led her from the stables.

Kenna walked quietly by Rhys's side until she was sure Donald could not hear them. "Let go of my arm," she said stiffly.

"Not yet, Kenna," Rhys said genially. "In the summerhouse, perhaps."

Kenna tried to pull away but he held her fast, with very little effort, she noted miserably. "In the summerhouse, you most certainly will." She thought she heard him say, "We'll see," but she knew he was trying to goad her and she refused to give him the satisfaction.

Rhys took the key from the door frame ledge and unlocked the door. He gave Kenna a courtly bow and ushered her inside, releasing her arm when he shut the door behind them. He watched her quickly put some distance between them as he casually leaned against the wall. "So eager to be out of my reach?" he chided.

"Do you blame me? I have suffered enough at your hands."

Pain clouded Rhys's eyes when he thought Kenna was once again taking him to task for her father's death. When he saw her hands drift unconsciously to her backside he realized she was referring to the spanking. "That still rankles, does it?"

"To be treated as a child when one is nothing less than a lady?" she asked sarcastically. "I would say I have cause to take exception to your methods."

"Point taken," Rhys said dryly. "In the future I will simply call you out."

Did the man feel no remorse, she wondered. His smug riposte was insufferable! Deciding to behave better than he, Kenna ignored Rhys's taunt, rubbing her arms briskly as she glanced about at the sheet-shrouded furniture. "Couldn't we have talked at the manor? It's quite cold here."

"I think you can appreciate the need for complete privacy." He looked at her significantly and a brief smile touched his eyes as Kenna's cheeks pinkened. "Anyway, I doubt we'll freeze."

"Then say what you will."

Rhys would not be hurried. "You are looking well."

She shrugged.

"McNulty and Wilver will be here in a few hours to talk to you."

"Yes, I know. It is precisely the reason I would like to go back to my room and prepare for their visit."

Rhys pushed away from the wall and took a few steps closer to Kenna. He felt a niggling of admiration that she did not move away from him though it was clearly written in her dark eyes that she wanted to. "I wish that you would not mention to either of the men your suspicions about the attempt on your life."

Kenna nearly choked on her surprise. "You cannot be serious!"

"I am. Deadly so."

Kenna blinked widely. "Are you threatening me, Rhys?"

"No. At least not in the way you think. Will you do as I ask?"

"Why should I?"

"Because your suspicions are wrong and it would serve nothing but to confuse matters, even delay the men in finding Tom's real murderer."

"Am I to say nothing then about the trap being meant for me?" she demanded. "Even if I don't mention you? Last night you said you did not believe Old Tom was killed by a poacher. Who then?"

"I don't know, but I believe it would be unwise for you to say anything until we have proof."

"Isn't that the job of the authorities?" she asked coolly, watching Rhys carefully. "To find proof, I mean?"

"Yes, of course, but that doesn't mean I can't find it also."

"You?" she scoffed. "I would say that is very much

113

like asking a cobra to prove his venom is harmless. He simply doesn't bite anyone for a while."

"Then you're safe, aren't you . . . for a while."

The piercing, knowing look he gave Kenna made her blood go cold, then hot. She remembered his kiss and knew her face gave away her thoughts. "Am I?" she challenged weakly, feeling light and off balance.

"Yes, Kenna, you are." He would have liked to take her in his arms. Instead he pressed for a commitment. "Will you do as I ask?"

Kenna hesitated, feeling his eyes bore into her. There was something faintly pleading in his expression and Kenna called herself every bit a fool for being moved by it. "I'll do as you asked."

Rhys felt as if the proverbial weight had been lifted. "You won't be sorry, Kenna. I promise."

"That remains to be seen, Rhys. I hope I do not pay with my life for trusting you."

"Kenna." He said her name patiently, affectionately. "You never told me why you suspect me in the first place."

"I thought it was obvious. I'm the only one who knows you killed my father." She held her breath, waiting for him to breathe fire or walk away from her at the very least. He did neither. In fact, he seemed uncommonly amused.

"You are nothing if not tenacious, m'lady. Hasn't it occurred to you that though you've believed the worst of me for nigh on a decade, no one else believes it? If I thought anyone accepted your story, surely the time to kill you was when you were still a child and unable to protect yourself. I have not the least interest in killing you, save when you try my patience. I came as close to it last night as I ever have."

Kenna looked away. "You didn't though," she said in a low voice. "Instead you . . . you—"

114

Rhys took a step closer, an indulgent smile touching the curve of his mouth. "I what?" he teased.

"Kissed me." She faced him again, tipping her head back to look up at him. His eyes were on her lips. "You kissed me."

"So I did." His head bent a little nearer. "As you pointed out minutes ago, you are not a child. I regret turning you over my knee, Kenna. I wished I had kissed you then as I did last night." Rhys nearly laughed at Kenna's startled confusion as she considered his statement. "I can see you are having difficulty deciding which action is preferable. Was my kiss so awful?"

"Yes," she said quickly. "No," she said a moment later.

"You used to be more certain of yourself, sprite."

His breath was sweet. He was looking at her as she had sometimes dreamed of a man looking at her, dark-eyed and searching. She scarcely noticed the nickname. "You hurt me," she said.

A shuttered look came over Rhys's features. "I know. I was rough. I didn't mean . . ."

Kenna's lips parted. It was on the tip of her tongue to say it didn't matter, but it did. She said nothing.

Rhys watched her lips part, saw her tongue peep up to wet one corner in a nervous gesture. It undid him.

Somewhere in the back of her mind Kenna could hear herself telling Rhys they would not talk again. Ever. And now she was waiting for the touch of his mouth on hers. She could not move away or avert her face. She thought herself weak and hated it. And when his lips met hers she reveled in it.

Rhys made certain this kiss was everything Kenna had a right to expect. His touch was gentle, lightly insistent. He merely tasted her lips, applying only a tentative pressure. Rhys's hands remained at his side, ready to take Kenna in his arms but not without some sign it was what she wanted. He found it when she leaned into him and touched the back of his hands briefly to find her balance. Rhys pulled Kenna close but held her loosely, one hand cupping her face, the other at the base of her spine.

Kenna felt a certain heady excitement as Rhys deepened the kiss with the probing edge of his tongue. Not only did she not deny his entrance, she met the first stirrings of passion by returning the kiss in kind. It vaguely occurred to her that she was being reckless, even licentious, but she pushed that bit of conscience to the back of her mind. She would do nothing to deny herself the liquid pleasure that was coursing her veins as Rhys gave her a little jerk and pulled her flush to him.

Rhys could not get Kenna close enough to him. Her riding jacket and his great coat were unwanted barriers. He ached to feel her swelling breasts against his chest. Carefully he stepped backward until the back of his knees made contact with the divan, then he sat down, never breaking the kiss, and pulled Kenna with him. She fell on his lap with an awkward little "ooof" and tried to scramble off, looking everywhere but at him. Rhys smiled serenely, shaking his head, and pushed her gently backward until she lay cornered against the divan's single arm rest. He shrugged out of his coat as he shifted, trapping Kenna with one of his legs.

"You'll be cold," she said in a throaty whisper. Her eyes widened as one of his eyebrows lifted in tender mockery.

"Innocent," he said as his head bent closer.

He didn't kiss her on the mouth this time. His lips touched her eyes first, closing them, then traced the smooth arch of her cheekbones, the downy soft line of her jaw. She turned toward him, trying to capture his mouth, but he teased her and moved to her ear. Pushing away the tendrils of red-gold hair that had escaped her braid, Rhys nibbled at Kenna's lobe and was rewarded for

116

his efforts by a tiny gasp that seemed to brand his cheek.

Knowing what he risked, Rhys brought his mouth back to Kenna's in a relentlessly searching kiss while one of his hands insinuated itself between their bodies and unbuttoned her jacket. His fingers brushed her ripening breast through her thin linen blouse and she tried to move away in protest. Rhys let his hand fall immediately to her waist and rested it there until he felt her relax against him.

Kenna opened her eyes when he broke the kiss, frowning ever so slightly when she saw a hint of amusement about Rhys's beautiful mouth.

Rhys saw the question in her eyes and put a finger to her lips, quieting her. "Sssh. I'm not laughing at you. Only myself."

She was not surprised that he had read her mind. In that respect he was not so different from the young man she had admired and loved who was up to her every trick. For a while, when his mouth held hers and his hands and body kept her captive, it was easy to forget her nightmares and instead, remember her dreams. "Why?" she asked on a thread of sound.

"I doubt you would find it amusing." When Kenna gave no reply but continued to look at him expectantly, Rhys gave in. "Very well. I was thinking that seducing you requires more strategy than this soldier ever learned in Wellington's camp."

Kenna realized she probably shouldn't have found it the least bit amusing but after a moment's reflection her lips twitched. At Rhys's look of amazement she could not hold back the bubble of laughter that hovered about her mouth. "Is that what you're doing? Seducing me?" It was a novel idea that she was the object of a seduction. She wondered if she should be flattered that Rhys found her more difficult than his usual conquests.

Rhys nodded, smiling with roguish charm. "At least I

thought I was. Mayhap you're seducing me."

"I don't think so. I wouldn't know what to do."

"I could show you. I wouldn't prove at all difficult."

Kenna shifted a trifle uncomfortably as Rhys's smoky eyes searched her face. "I don't think so . . . this isn't . . . isn't a good idea. I don't know why I let—" Her voice drifted off as Rhys's hand drifted across her ribcage until he touched the underside of her breast.

"Don't you?" he asked. "Touch me, Kenna. Touch *me.*" He drew her hand to his face.

Her fingers were uncertain as they slid along Rhys's cheek and strong jawline. They became more sure as she investigated the tiny dimple at the base of his chin. She drew her fingers upward then, tracing his lips with a whisper-light touch. His mouth parted and she could feel the edge of his tongue sweep across the soft pads of her fingers. His eyes held hers, making the contact intimate and knowing. Kenna tried not to show her fear because she wasn't sure what it was she feared, but it was there, in her eyes, and she withdrew her hand.

Rhys caught Kenna's hand in his and held it to his chest, over the uneven pounding of his heart. "Has there been no one, Kenna?"

"No. No one."

Rhys had known she was innocent, but surely there had been some suitor over the years who had held her hand or taken the liberty of kissing her cheek. "Why didn't you have a London Season?"

Kenna's fingers curled into a fist against Rhys's chest. "What would it have served? In the unlikely event someone offered for me I would have been bound to refuse. I can never marry," she finished simply.

Rhys was confused by Kenna's sincerity. She obviously meant every word she said. "I don't think I understand, Kenna. What is there to keep you from

118

marrying? Surely Nick and Victorine would—"

She shook her head quickly. "No. It has nothing to do with them. Don't you see? It's because of the nightmares." She smiled, trying to make light of the matter. "I would make a poor sort of companion in the marriage bed."

"Oh, Kenna," Rhys sighed, hurting for her. Some day, when she trusted him more, he would pursue the content of her nightmares, but not now. He leaned back on the divan and pulled Kenna into his arms so that she lay softly against him. She came without protest and when he reached for his coat to cover them she laughed a little sadly.

"I told you you would be cold."

"So you did," Rhys said easily. "Are you always right?"

"About most things."

Rhys was thoughtfully silent. "I don't think so," he said after a moment. "Not about the marriage offers. You would have been deluged with proposals." He did not add that it had been his greatest fear while he was on the Peninsula.

"You still like to tease me."

"I do. But I'm not teasing now, Kenna. There would have been many offers for your hand. Do you doubt me?"

Kenna spoke into the curve of Rhys's shoulder. "I have a looking glass, Rhys," she said as if it explained everything.

"I don't think we see the same things, you and I."

"I'm frightfully tall."

"Not to me."

"My hair is unfashionably long."

"Who cares a fig for fashion?"

"I can see there is no use cataloging the remainder of

119

my faults."

"No, there's not." He squeezed her shoulder lightly. "Have you ever been in love, Kenna?"

Taken off guard, she spoke before she thought. "Once, I think. It was a long time ago."

Rhys stiffened. He had been so certain she had never loved any man save her father, her brother, and perhaps him. "What happened?"

"He went away," she said slowly. "It was nothing. He never knew how I felt, if it was love at all."

"Who was he?" Jealousy tugged at his insides.

Kenna sat up and Rhys let her go. Her head suddenly felt clearer and she felt a measure of sanity returning to her. "It's really none of your affair, Rhys. I didn't know him very well. He never made any promises so none were broken."

Rhys watched her fasten the buttons of her jacket with hands that trembled slightly. "Did he hurt you?"

Kenna met Rhys's probing gaze directly. She had never thought him particularly obtuse, but she could see he hadn't a clue. She would not have had it otherwise. "Desperately." She turned away while Rhys stood and put on his own coat.

Rhys came up behind Kenna and laid his hands on her shoulders. "I want you to know about last night, Kenna. About why I asked you to leave." She remained silent, waiting. "I could not trust myself with you any longer. I would have compromised you."

"Supposing I permitted you to," she said, pride asserting itself. "Don't worry, Rhys. I want neither of us compromised. I shan't say anything about last night or this morning to Nick."

"That isn't what I meant, Kenna."

"It's precisely what I meant," she said firmly, shrugging away from him and moving toward the door. "I don't know how I let myself be wrapped about your little finger, but it won't happen again." She turned briefly as she opened the door. "Stay away from me, Rhys. If you want to while away the hours at Dunnelly seducing someone, then try Victorine. Her feelings for you have not changed as dramatically as mine have." With that parting shot Kenna swept out of the summerhouse.

Rhys walked to the window and watched her cross the yard toward the manor, noting her regal carriage, the proud tilt of her head. What had she meant about Victorine? he wondered, pressing his forehead to the cool glass. What cork-brained notion had she got into her head this time? Rhys waited until Kenna had disappeared into one of the manor's side doors before he traced her footsteps back to the house.

Rhys did not even ask if he could be present when Kenna talked to the authorities. He knew she would view it as a lack of trust on his part if he sat with her. He spoke to McNulty and Wilver briefly as they were leaving but as he expected they had turned up nothing that would lead them to Tom Allen's killer. After they had gone Rhys went to the study to find Nick.

"I must talk to you, Nick," he said shutting the door firmly behind him. "I believe I have come upon a way to offer Kenna complete protection."

Twenty minutes later he slammed out of the study leaving a bemused and somewhat angered friend in his wake. His long, impatient strides covered the distance to the stables in no time at all and he ordered a young stable boy to ready his mount. Rider and horse were as one as Rhys slapped Higgins's haunches and headed out of the stable on what was to be a bruising gallop for both of them.

From her bedroom window Kenna saw Rhys tear across the yard on his horse. A shiver of fear shot

121

through her. It looked as if that devil of a mount was much more in control of things than Rhys. She could not recall ever seeing him ride so recklessly. She held her breath as he turned Higgins sharply, kicking up clumps of snow and dirt, and headed toward Dunnelly's main gate. She watched until he was out of sight on the road to town before she went downstairs to find out what had sent him off in such a fury.

Nicholas poured himself a few fingers of scotch and gulped them back. He made a face as the drink burned his throat but resolutely poured another.

"Must you drink, Nicholas?" Victorine asked softly. "Surely there is no solution in that. Tell me what has come between you and Rhys. He nearly knocked me over in his haste to be gone from here."

"Are you all right?" Nick took his drink and sat behind his desk, propping his feet on the polished surface. "If he hurt you . . ."

"I'm perfectly fine." She brushed aside his concern with a wave of her elegant hand. "I will not be put off. What has happened to make Rhys tear out of here and you drink scotch in the middle of the day?"

"He made an offer."

"An offer?"

"For Kenna's hand."

Victorine was visibly shaken. Her hands twisted in her lap. "Dear God! Was he serious?"

Nick's laugh held no amusement. "Quite."

Victorine drew in a breath and let it out gently. "Forgive me. It's such a shock to think of Kenna marrying. And to Rhys Canning of all people."

"I said he had made an offer, Victorine. I did not say she had accepted it."

"Then he's not broached the subject to Kenna?"

Nick took another swallow of scotch and set down the

tumbler sharply. "No. He hasn't. He wants me to speak to her."

"You? But why?"

"To force her hand. He wants Kenna to have no choice but to accept his proposal."

"You can't do that, Nick! She would never forgive you! You know she holds Rhys in abhorrence."

"I know it," Nick said heavily. "And Rhys knows it as well, else he would have asked for her hand himself."

"What prompted him to make the offer now?" Her smooth forehead wrinkled suddenly. "Does he love her, Nick? I mean, truly love her?"

"He loves her, of course. But the way you mean, I don't know. It never came up and I didn't ask. He wants to protect her, Victorine. You can understand that, surely. He knows no other way."

"But to sacrifice himself, his own future with the woman of his choice, to protect Kenna. There must be another way. He has not considered the consequences."

"When I said as much to him he nearly reached for my throat. I believe he has considered the matter as thoroughly as he wishes to."

"What did you tell him? Will you speak to Kenna?"

Nick shut his eyes and rubbed his temples in a weary gesture. "I told him I wouldn't interfere. Kenna has the right to make her own decisions. It's the way she was raised. That's when he slammed out of here. I don't know what I'll tell him when he returns."

"But Kenna must be allowed to make up her own mind," Victorine said earnestly, leaning forward in her chair. "Oh, there was a time when I thought she should marry, but she seems to be content now. She never cared about the things other girls do. Do you remember how she begged us not to put her through a London Season? She said she had no stomach for the marriage mart or marriage. Nick, I know I've not spoken of this to you before, but I fear Kenna is not as other women."

"What the bloody hell is that supposed to mean?" Nick asked, lifting his lids and glaring at his stepmother with eyes as cold as blue ice.

"No, no! You must have misunderstood," she said quickly. "I can see in your face that you have mistaken my meaning. I think she would not suit in the marriage bed. I think she would make Rhys, make any man, a cold wife. She has no understanding of passion nor the least inkling of what would be expected of her. Her husband would never be faithful. Heaven knows, it takes little enough provocation these days for men to seek out a mistress. Do Kenna a kindness and spare her certain humiliation."

"Let me think on it, Victorine. There is much here to consider. I don't want my sister humiliated but neither do I wish to see her dead."

"I never thought you did," Victorine said with dignity. "And neither do I." She came to her feet with a certain regal air. "I love Kenna. As much as I do my own daughter, perhaps more, because Yvonne never needed me the way Kenna does. It's important to feel needed, Nicholas."

"Victorine." Nick drew out her name warningly and saw by the flash of pain in her eyes that she understood. "Not now. Leave me and let me think. I will let you know later what I've decided."

Victorine gave Nick a small nod of assent and left him to his own troubled thoughts.

Kenna leaned against the gallery door, catching her breath, as she heard the soft fall of Victorine's steps along the hallway.

"Lady Kenna?"

Kenna jumped away from the door, suddenly realizing

she wasn't alone in the room. One of the young downstairs maids was running a feather duster over the gilt edges of the gallery's paintings.

"Are you all right, Lady Kenna?" the girl asked again. "Faith, it looks as if you've seen a ghost."

"I'm fine." She groped her memory for a name to put with the dark hair and heart shaped face of the maid. "Jean is it?"

Jean smiled widely. Not many ladies would have bothered to take note of her name and address her by it. "Yes, m'lady, it's Jean. Will you be wanting anything? A cup of tea? A tisane? Please pardon my impertinence, but you don't look well, m'lady."

Kenna touched her brow and felt tiny droplets of perspiration at her hairline. She must look a veritable fright to the girl. "No, really, there's no need for anything. I'd like to be alone right now. Can you finish your work later?"

"Of course, m'lady. As you wish. It was just a bit of dusting I was doing anyway." She saw Kenna was not paying attention to her any more and tiptoed quietly out of the gallery.

There was a fire in the hearth and Kenna went to warm herself in front of it though she doubted she would ever feel warm again. Taking a shawl from one of the chairs she wrapped it around her shoulders and sat on the marble apron of the fireplace. There was no comfort in telling herself she shouldn't have been listening at doors. She *had* listened. She had heard the entire exchange between her brother and Victorine though she wished with all her heart she had been elsewhere.

So Rhys Canning wanted to marry her, did he. He was going to—what had Victorine said?—oh yes, he was going to sacrifice himself to provide for her safety. It sounded so damn noble that Kenna wanted to vomit.

And who did Victorine think was going to protect her from Rhys? He was the only one she knew who presented the least bit of danger. She groaned softly at her own thoughts. Would she never be able to make up her mind about Rhys? This morning in the summerhouse she had been persuaded to believe he was innocent. Now she was not so certain that he hadn't proposed marriage to keep her under his thumb. A sacrifice, indeed. More likely he had stumbled upon some means of self-preservation. As his wife she could hardly testify against him. It was nearly as good as having her dead.

Tears swam in her eyes, spiking her thick lashes as she thought of the other things Victorine had said. Her stepmother hadn't meant to be cruel. Kenna knew that but found it did nothing to raise her spirits. She couldn't help but ask herself if Victorine was right. Was she a cold woman?

She had told Rhys she could never marry because of her nightmares, but perhaps it was not entirely true. Mayhap some instinct warned her she would offer very little pleasure to her husband in the marriage bed so she held fast to her nightmares, hoping they would protect her. She could not help but wonder if Rhys had thought her cold.

He said he had left her because he could not trust himself. Was it naught but a lie to set another trap? She recalled how she had been afraid of his angry kisses, how she had pushed him away when he had tried to touch her breast. Is that what made her cold? Was she then to accept whatever advances a man made toward her? It was not the sort of thing she had ever discussed with Victorine. There was never any need . . . until now. Kenna's shoulders heaved as she buried her face in her hands. She was twenty-three, a veritable spinster, and she was innocent as a babe.

Thinking of a babe reminded Kenna of the nephew she

had yet to see. She sniffed, taking a handkerchief from her sleeve, and blew her nose. Yvonne would explain everything to her, she was married after all and surely three children proved her husband did not find her a cold fish. Oh, please, Kenna prayed, please let her invitation arrive in the morning.

Chapter Three

Kenna spent the rest of the evening and all of the following day in her room, pleading a headache that became more of a blinding reality as time went on. Victorine swept in and out with cold compresses and words of comfort. Nick visited her twice and Kenna was hard-pressed to convince him she was not in need of a doctor. Her personal maid kept her company with a steady stream of conversation and saw to it that Kenna ate everything on her specially prepared trays. Rhys did not enter her room at all and since no one ever mentioned marriage, Kenna felt as if she had been given a reprieve. If she hadn't felt so awful she might have enjoyed the stay of execution.

"Was there nothing for me in the post?" Kenna asked Janet on the morning of the third day. She pushed the eggs around on her plate with a listless motion.

Janet eyed Kenna's uneaten breakfast, clucking her tongue in disapproval. "If you can't manage the eggs, then at least drink your cocoa. Lyin' abed like this, you need your strength. Liable to waste away, you will."

Kenna knew there was nothing for it but to drink the hot cocoa. Janet would go on and on until she got what she wanted. With a long-suffering sigh Kenna brought the warm mug to her lips and held back a grimace when she tasted the drink. Kenna thought it could have used a bit more sugar, but in the interest of peace in the kitchen she hesitated to tell Janet. Her maid would give Dunnelly's temperamental chef a lecture and no one would eat this evening.

Janet fairly beamed with satisfaction as Kenna drank. "I believe you asked about the post. I can check with Henderson again, of course, but he didn't give me anything for you. Such a long face!"

Kenna gave her maid a tiny smile. "I was hoping to hear from Yvonne."

"Aaah," Janet said knowingly. "And you're disappointed. I'm sorry. Mayhap there will be something in the next mail."

"Perhaps." But she was not hopeful. She finished the last of her drink and set the mug aside, pushing the tray toward Janet. "I really don't want another thing."

"Still not feeling all of one piece, are we? Shall I fetch another compress?"

Kenna laid her head back on her pillow as Janet took away the tray. What had begun as a dull throbbing in her temples had gradually become a violently sharp pain behind her eyes. The ache was so relentless that she was beginning to feel ill. "I think I'll just sleep a while," said Kenna. "I'm certain I'll be better this afternoon." She closed her eyes and slipped one hand beneath her pillow as she very gently turned on her side. "Shut the drapes, Janet. The light is bothersome."

A frown wrinkled Janet's brow as she looked at her mistress's pale face. After a moment she pulled the drapes closed and soundlessly left the room.

Kenna slept until midday when she was awakened by severe cramping in her stomach. Necessity made her push herself out of bed and stagger toward the chamber pot, making it just in time to heave what little she had

130

eaten for breakfast. Afterward she cooled her face and rinsed her mouth at the porcelain bowl on the wash stand, then stumbled back to bed. She lay on top of the comforter, too weak to crawl beneath it and too fatigued to care.

Victorine found Kenna still curled on the bed, hugging her knees to her chest, when she brought lunch. *"Dieu!* Kenna, what is wrong?" She hurried over to the bed, setting aside a tray of broth and warm bread. She felt Kenna's forehead with the back ot her hand. "You don't have a fever, *ma petite chou*. Here, let me help you under the covers. You're shivering."

Kenna allowed herself to be prodded and coaxed under the comforter. "My head aches abominably," she admitted wearily. "And I hurt everywhere."

Nick stepped into the room, followed by Rhys. "I'm sending for the doctor," he said. His tone clearly meant he would not be gainsaid.

"There's no need," Kenna protested, though she merely mouthed the sentiment out of habit.

"There's every need." It was Rhys who spoke with conviction as he stepped past Nick, taking in Kenna's white complexion and the pained glaze of her eyes.

Kenna shut her eyes so she would not have to see Rhys's thorough examination of her face. She snuggled deeper into the comforter to hide her flushed cheeks. "Go away," she said sharply, then, to take the sting from her words, she added lightly, "I want to expire in peace."

"That's not amusing," Rhys said. He touched Nick's shoulder. "I am going to send a servant for the doctor." He saw the tray on Kenna's bedside table. "I'll take this out. She doesn't look as if she could eat a thing."

Kenna was grateful for the removal of the tray. The cloying odor of the chicken broth was making her stomach churn.

"She must eat something," Victorine said, a frown

playing about her mouth. "You can see for yourself that she's as weak as a kitten."

"I couldn't possibly—" Kenna broke off as Rhys turned away from the stand with the tray in front of him and bumped directly into Nick who had moved closer to hear what she had to say. Rhys tried to balance the tray, then attempted to catch the bowl of broth, but his efforts came to naught. The hot, clear broth slid off the tray and splattered his shirt, his trousers, the toes of his boots, and the oriental rug. Nick had adroitly managed to miss most of the mess. Kenna hid a faint smile as Rhys swore softly but explicitly.

Victorine moved from Kenna's side, arms akimbo, and ready to do violence. "Out! Both of you! This is no place for either of you! I care little who sends for the physician, but one of you please do so. Immediately!" When they were gone from the room she turned to Kenna. "Graceless wretches. They do manage to get underfoot. I'll have someone clean up this mess. Are you certain you can't eat anything?"

Kenna nodded. "I'd rather not."

"As you wish." She gave Kenna a kiss on her forehead and tucked her in a little better, smoothing the blankets in a loving fashion. "I'll be here when the doctor arrives."

Kenna was deeply asleep when Janet came to clean up the mess left by Rhys and Nick. The maid stayed at her mistress's side and hovered in the background when Victorine showed the doctor in.

Kenna was nudged awake by Doctor Tipping's gentle hand. She looked up into his kindly brown eyes and smiled weakly. "Hello."

"M'lady. You've got Dunnelly in an uproar. What seems to be the problem?"

Kenna related her aches and pains but Tipping reserved judgment until he had conducted a thorough

132

examination. "I've seen this sort of thing before," he said to Kenna as he repacked his bag. "But I thought you had better sense. I wouldn't have taken you for one of the vain sillies I've treated in the past."

Kenna's brows wrinkled. "What do you mean?"

"Arsenic, m'lady. A pale complexion is all the rage, but taking a bit of poison to enhance it is foolhardy, and in some cases, deadly. You've been fortunate thus far, but I want you to cease its use."

"But I—"

"Now. Now. I won't listen to your objections. There's no excuse for tempting fate. I gave the same advice to Lady Blake and she scoffed also. In the pursuit of fashionably pale youth she did what she wanted. I will say, she was a remarkably lovely corpse." He shook his head in deep disgust. "If I could find the person who first recommended the use of arsenic for the complexion, I would cheerfully wring his, or her, neck. 'Tis insanity, that's what it is."

Kenna was simply too stunned to defend herself. She had never used arsenic in her life though she was well aware of the practice. Out of the corner of her eye she could see Victorine looking at her with sharp, disapproval and across the room Janet was clucking her tongue softly.

"I will speak to your brother about this matter and I want your promise not to use the stuff again. In fact, I would like your bottle to take with me."

"Of course she won't use it again," said Victorine. "Where is your bottle, Kenna? Your maid can get it."

Before Kenna could answer Janet was handing over a small green glass bottle that she had picked up on Kenna's dressing table. "You can see for yourself she's used the last of it," the maid said. "Good riddance to the stuff, I say."

Tipping echoed Janet's words while he briefly exam-

133

ined the nearly empty bottle then dropped it in his case. "Give it few days to work out of your system and you'll be feeling quite the thing. As long as you don't use it again. You can build some tolerance to the poison, then accidentally give yourself an overdose. No more. Is that understood?" He looked at all three women and saw them agree with varying degrees of conviction. Kenna appeared most reluctant but Tipping was confident neither her stepmother nor her maid would let her be so foolish again.

"Good day, ladies," he said, giving Victorine a brief bow.

"I'll walk with you downstairs," said Victorine.

"Why did you give the doctor that bottle?" Kenna asked Janet as soon as they were alone.

"I could see you were tired, m'lady. You don't mind, do you? He was going on and on and it shut him up."

Kenna rubbed her eyes and temples. "I don't mind. But he's going to discover sooner or later it held nothing but some bath salts."

"By that time I'm going to discover where the arsenic came from," Janet said with assurance. "Aren't you the least bit curious?"

Curious did not even begin to describe what Kenna was feeling. She was still reeling from the knowledge that someone had tried to poison her. Probably several times since she had taken to her room, she realized. The dosage was small, the effects cumulative, which is why she had been feeling steadily worse. She could not help but wonder what her state would be if she had been able to hold down her breakfast. "What will you do?" she asked slowly. The pounding in her head was almost unbearable. She should have asked the doctor for some powders.

"Do? I'm going to supervise the preparation of your meals myself, that's what I'm going to do. I never trusted that Frenchy cook your stepmother brought here. I

134

always said it's better if the staff speaks English. He stubbornly refused to learn more than a few words. No doubt he's filled the salt cellars with rat poison. Don't worry. I'll set him straight."

"Why didn't you tell Victorine and Doctor Tipping your suspicions?" The pounding in her head lessened. Janet thought it was an accident, nothing more, and Kenna conceded she could be right. She felt as if a weight was being lifted from her chest.

Janet flushed to the roots of her hair and she could not meet her mistress's eye. Her voice was soft, almost girlish. "I admit to a certain fondness for that temperamental fool. I thought to save his position."

"Oh, Janet," Kenna sighed. "But now Victorine and Nick have heard what the doctor said. They will think I'm so foolish."

Janet had the grace to look discomfited. "I'm sorry, m'lady. Please say you'll forgive me. I promise I'll speak to Claude. I'll have the kitchen searched from top to bottom, everything tested. It won't happen again."

Kenna felt herself softening as soon as Janet spoke of the chef as Claude. What did it matter if her family thought her vain and silly? Didn't she owe Janet some small measure of her trust and loyalty? Janet had taken care of Kenna since right before Lord Dunne's death and had never asked for any favor during all that time. "Of course I forgive you, Janet. But please talk to—Claude, was it?"

"Yes, m'lady."

"I never knew. I always thought of him as Monsieur Raillier. You must speak to him before he poisons the entire house. It's something of a miracle no one else has taken sick."

"That it is," Janet said hurriedly. "I'll speak to him. You have my word upon it." She made a deep curtsy. "Shall I bring you some tea? I'm sure the doctor would approve of something light."

"No. Nothing. I'd like to rest now." When she was alone her doubts returned. How was it she was the only one in the house to take ill if the poisoning was accidental? It was useless to think on it now when she couldn't concentrate on anything save the insistent ache in her temples. Another cramp seized her and she reached for the basin Janet had seen fit to leave on her nightstand. She held on to it, clutching it to her middle, but she had nothing to give up. The dry cramping was extremely painful and when it was over Kenna was exhausted. She pushed the empty basin away, buried her face in the pillow, and prayed for sleep.

It came effortlessly, but then so did the dream. There was nothing she could do to call back the moment when she caught Yvonne by the hand and dragged her toward the bedchamber so she could change for the masque. She saw her father and Victorine dancing in the ballroom and repeated her conversation with the mysterious devil. She hid in the gallery and witnessed Victorine kissing the highwayman and she took the same route to the summerhouse and to the cave as she had always taken. She crouched low in the antechamber, listened to the argument with growing wonderment, then, without warning, the threads of her dreams changed, creating a new tapestry of terror . . .

As Kenna watched from the crack in the rock Victorine began to cry, looking pathetically wretched as she buried her face in her hands. Kenna's stomach churned as her father comforted the wife who had betrayed him in the gallery and held off the Frenchman and Rhys with his pistols. She was afraid for him and afraid for herself. Her fear paralyzed her, made her incapable of acting on her instincts to help her father.

Kenna struggled to her feet, clawing at the rock for support, and edged closer to the entrance to the antechamber. One of the Frenchmen moved almost imperceptibly nearer to her father and his fingers curled for the pistol tucked in the waistband of his breeches. Kenna caught the movement and her breath caught as she waited for her father to respond. When he didn't, she stepped into the entranceway, in full view of Lord Dunne, Victorine, and Rhys. Though Kenna did not spare a glance for anyone save her father, she saw enough to know neither Rhys nor Victorine recognized her in her highwayman garb. Not so her father. His eyes widened and Kenna swore his face drained of color. Both Frenchmen twisted their heads to see what had caught the attention of the others and when they saw Kenna, they froze.

Their shocked stillness lasted until they realized the intruder was without a weapon, but it was Kenna who leaped first, tackling the Frenchman closest to her. The lantern was knocked over and the chamber was plunged into complete darkness. There were shots and Victorine's screams covered Kenna's pained grunt as her nose was broken.

She woke in the quiet darkness, heard the gentle rush of water, and knew what she would find. Her hand had not even touched her father's sleeve before Kenna began screaming . . .

Kenna sat straight up in her bed, heart hammering. It took her several moments to orient herself. Her fingers curled around the sheets and found them only slightly damp. She wondered if she had really screamed or if she had merely imagined she had. Glancing at the window she saw someone had opened the drapes but that it was already dark outside. A few logs had been added to the fireplace and they burned brightly, casting distorted shadows on the walls of her room. Nick was leaning against the mantel, half turned toward Kenna, his profile etched darkly against the orange flames. His shoulders were slumped forward and in one hand he held a drink which he kept turning in weary thoughtfulness.

He looks so tired, she thought, and her heart ached for him. She had never considered before how heavily her nightmares weighed on her brother and now it occurred to her that in some way they had affected Nick's decision not to marry. She had never meant to become a burden to Nicholas, but however unwittingly, it seemed she had. When she thought of how Nick had taken her side against Rhys, refusing to issue an ultimatum of marriage to her, her heart swelled with love.

"Nick?" She held out a hand to him. "Come here. See for yourself that I'm all of a piece." When he didn't move or respond in any way she retracted her hand and fingered the braid that hung over her shoulder. "I'm sorry about the nightmare, Nick. I wish it were different; wish I could control it. You're very good to me, to come like this when you know I'm frightened." Kenna took the ribbon from her hair and unwound the braid, threading her fingers through the damp tangles at her nape. "It was much the same dream," she said thoughtfully, reviewing it in her mind.

"But?" he asked.

She smiled. "You know me so well. I remember stepping into the antechamber this time. The Frenchmen turned toward me, ever so briefly. God, how I wish I could recall their faces! Everything happened too quickly. Victorine was there—and Rhys—but they didn't seem to recognize me. Papa did." Her smiled vanished. "I'm afraid it's why he didn't fire his weapon sooner. Oh, Nick! I think I may have caused it all to happen!"

"No. You didn't." He stepped away from the mantel.

Kenna was going to deny his words but as he approached the bed she couldn't find her voice. Her hand went from her hair to her throat. "Rhys!"

138

"Yes."

"But I thought—"

"I know. You thought I was Nick."

"You let me go on."

"I wanted to hear about your dream. You've never told me about it before."

Kenna pulled the comforter to her neck. "And I don't want to discuss it with you now. Why did you come here? What do you want?"

"I thought that was obvious," said Rhys. His steely gaze was partially shuttered by his lashes but he could see Kenna clearly and she looked incredibly lovely to him. He wanted the right to sit beside her, thread his fingers through her long fall of red-gold hair, and kiss the uncertain frown playing on her lips. He wanted to feel the fullness of her breasts in the palm of his hand and touch his mouth to the invitation of their hardened tips. It was too easy to imagine lying beside her, legs and arms twined in the aftermath of loving. Her head would rest on his shoulder and her slender, curious fingers would trace a narrow path across his chest, his abdomen, and finally lower where she would find him ready to love her again. His body responded to the tenor of his thoughts, swelling and tightening and aching. He would have given his soul for a like response from Kenna, but he saw only fear and quietly he cursed her and then himself.

Kenna shrank from the anger she saw in Rhys as he stepped nearer. His body was corded with tension and a muscle leaped in his clenched jaw. Though she wanted to escape, she felt drawn to him, powerless to look away.

"How can I convince you?" Rhys asked, drawing up a wing chair and sitting on its very edge. He leaned forward, folding his hands on his knees. "I mean no harm to you, Kenna."

She opened her mouth to tell him there was nothing he could do, yet the words she heard herself speak were vastly different. "If only you did not glower so. You are always so angry with me."

"Am I?" He smiled slightly and relaxed. "Perhaps I am. But then there is a measure of self-defense in that guise. You are always angry with me."

"I did not think it anger."

"What then? No, don't answer. You think it is hatred. Mayhap some day I will argue that hatred is not so deliberate as you practice it. I have never known anyone to use it as a shield the way you do. It makes one wonder what would happen if you were to discard it."

Kenna could think of no reply to make to that, so she returned the conversation to his purpose in her room. "Your presence here is not obvious to me. Does Nicky or Victorine know you're here?"

Rhys leaned back in the chair, stretching out his long legs and crossing them at the ankles. He took some small pleasure in seeing how his comfortable posture irked Kenna. "No. Neither know I came. It's been hours since everyone went to bed." He saw Kenna's eyes wander to the clock on the mantel and confirm his statement for herself. "You slept through dinner and the light repast Victorine brought you before she retired. Would you like me to bring something from the kitchen for you now?"

"You didn't come here to feed me," she said, shaking her head.

"No. I wanted to speak to you about what the doctor told us this afternoon."

"What of it?"

"Nicholas and Victorine were most distressed by your use of arsenic." He looked at her expectantly and when she made no reply he continued. "I understand you've agreed never to use it again."

"Of course I won't."

"Of course," Rhys said, a wry smile twisting his lips. "That won't be hard, will it? Since you've never used

140

it before."

Kenna was too startled to prevaricate. "How did you know?"

"Credit me with some sense, Kenna. You've never been vain about your appearance. I doubt you even know how rare your beauty is."

"Don't tease me," she said sharply. "It's unkind of you."

"I am not teasing," he replied easily. "But that you think I am proves my point. It would be out of character for you to try to enhance loveliness you don't believe exists in the first place."

Kenna smoothed the comforter over her lap, tracing its snowy pattern so she did not have to look at Rhys. "Please stop this talk. It is of no account."

"But it is," he continued resolutely. "If you did not use the arsenic, where did it come from? And why did you lie about it? The doctor showed Nick the bottle your maid gave him. What was in it, Kenna?"

"A few grains of bath salts."

Rhys sighed. It was much as he had expected. "I think you had better tell me the whole of it."

Kenna related everything then, not because she trusted him, an inner voice insisted, but because she wanted him gone and there seemed but one way to achieve that end. "And Janet said she would speak to Monsieur Raillier," she concluded a trifle breathlessly. "There is no need to alarm Nick. Everything will be taken care of."

Rhys said nothing and his face gave none of his thoughts away. It had never occurred to him that he would ever want to accuse Kenna of being too trusting. She gave him none of it, yet bestowed it indiscriminately on others. "You believe your maid's explanation?"

"I—yes, I believe her. Why shouldn't I?" she added a little defiantly. "Janet has taken care of me for years. Since just before my father died. She is more confidante

141

than servant."

"Powell is like that," said Rhys. "My valet. He rather inspires loyalty. Tell me, do you often mention your nightmares to Janet?"

A tiny frown lined Kenna's brow. "I fail to see—"

"Humor me."

"Yes, I talk with her about them, though surely that is my affair. She is a good listener, not at all critical," she said pointedly.

Rhys ignored the barb. "I see."

"I doubt you do. You cannot know what it is like, to ever be haunted by events of the past and powerless to make a difference."

"Don't I?" he replied enigmatically.

"What do you mean?"

Rhys shrugged. "It's of no import now." He rose from his chair, searching Kenna's face, and knew himself reluctant to leave. "Will you be able to go back to sleep?"

"I think so."

"I could stay a while."

"No. It's better that you go. Nick is a light sleeper. It is surprising he did not hear me scream."

"But you didn't." He could not help himself. He reached out to touch the brilliant wave of hair that fell across her shoulder.

Kenna watched his fingers curl in her hair. She could not breathe or move as he stroked the feather-soft ends.

"I was going to wake you when I came here. I had not meant to watch you sleep," Rhys said huskily. "But you seemed so peaceful. You didn't move or make a sound. I never knew until you sat up how tortured your thoughts were. Do you usually wake up screaming?"

She nodded, unable to speak as his hand stilled close to her breast. The comforter seemed no protection at all. She could feel the heat of his hand through it.

"I wish I could make it different for you, Kenna." His

hand dropped away abruptly. "I must leave." He turned to go and was halfway to the door when she called to him.

"Am I a cold woman, Rhys?"

Rhys stopped, uncertain he had heard correctly. At his side his fingers curled into white-knuckled fists but he did not face her. "What did you say?"

Kenna was already regretting her question and the mad impulse that made her voice it. It had been at the back of her mind since she discovered it was not her brother in her bedchamber, but she had never expected to speak the thought aloud. She looked at Rhys's back, the taut broad shoulders and still, expectant posture, and wanted to call back the words. It was obvious she had taken him by surprise, even embarrassed him, to say nothing of the humiliation she had heaped upon her own head. She worried her lower lip, saying nothing, and waited for him to continue on his way.

Kenna's silence forced Rhys to turn toward her bed as nothing else could have. He saw the way her teeth caught her lip, the uncertainty in eyes that seemed impossibly large for her face. "Kenna?" He spoke her name gently.

The question tumbled out again. "Am I a cold woman?"

Rhys covered the distance to her bed quickly and sat beside her, taking her hands in both of his. When she tried to pull away he would not let her. "What makes you ask such a thing?"

That he had not answered her question immediately made Kenna feel as if he were playing for time, searching for a way to spare her. "I don't know," she lied. "Sometimes I think I am not as other women," she said, echoing Victorine's words. "I don't think I would suit any man."

Not any man, Rhys thought. I don't want you to suit any man. Only me. "So you think you may be cold, is

143

that it?"

"Yes."

"I could tell you you're wrong, but then you rarely believe anything I tell you. Why should this be different?"

"You're right, of course. It was silly of me to ask you."

"I could show you. All you would have to do is feel."

"You mean—" But she had only to look at his darkening eyes to know what he meant. "It would be wrong."

"Would it?" He doubted anything would be more right but he refused to pressure her into something she would regret.

"Yes." But there was no certainty in her voice.

"Very well." Rhys released her hands and began to edge off the bed.

Kenna caught the sleeve of his jacket. "No. Don't leave. I want to know. I must know."

"Why ask me, Kenna?"

"There is no one else," she said simply.

Rhys had not thought the truth would cut him so deeply and he nearly winced with the pain Kenna unwittingly inflicted. He touched her chin with his hand, lifting her face to him. "You haven't so much as a sliver of ice in your body. Let us leave it at that."

"How can you be so sure?"

"I've kissed you, Kenna. I know. And so should you."

"But you left me."

"I am not such a libertine as you think. On occasion I have a gallant streak. I did not leave you because I found you cold. Quite the opposite, in fact."

"Then show me," she said. "Now." As an afterthough, she added, "I demand it."

Rhys's laughter was brilliant, softening the hard planes and angles of his face. "You are not so different from the girl I remember," he said when he caught his breath. "I had thought otherwise."

Kenna pushed the comforter aside as she leaned forward. Her white linen gown lay like a whisper against her skin. "I am not a girl any longer," she said earnestly, willing Rhys to look at her fully and see the truth for himself. "I know what I want." There was more, much more she could not say, and she could not let Rhys guess the gist of her thoughts. If he suspected how she was using him he would leave her and she would never know if Victorine spoke the truth. It had to be Rhys who introduced her to the rites of loving. If she could respond to him, a man she had reason to despise, then Kenna believed she could respond to anyone. She would not have to remain on the shelf, nor would she be trapped into accepting the only man who had offered for her. Rhys could give her the confidence to leave the cloister she had made of her home. In time, perhaps with the understanding of a loving husband, the nightmares would take care of themselves. "I know," she repeated, her large cinnamon eyes steady on his face.

"Do you? Do you really?" He could not lift his glance from her provocative mouth.

"Must I beg you, Rhys?"

He thought of the things he could say that would sober her. He could remind her that she considered him her father's murderer. If he asked her to marry him, what would she say? He could mention Nick, only a few rooms away, or Victorine in her nearby suite. But he knew he did not want to stop her, so he said nothing to make her reconsider her recklessness. "No," he said, his eyes dropping to the curve of her throat then her breasts. "No. You don't have to beg me. God knows it's what I've wanted, too."

Rhys's hand trembled as he cupped the side of Kenna's face. His thumb traced the line of her mouth, parting her lips with light insistence. "You have a beautiful mouth,

145

Kenna," he whispered as his head lowered to meet her lips. They were petal soft, deliciously moist, and one small taste was not enough. Her response was uncertain but she did not pull away; not when he deepened the kiss, nor when he eased her down on the pillows and stretched out beside her. Her mouth opened beneath his, allowing him to explore her sweetness at his leisure. His tongue caressed her and when she answered in the same way Rhys knew Kenna could shatter his precarious control.

He drew back, planting small, teasing kisses on the corner of her mouth. Kenna moved a shade restlessly beneath Rhys, wanting the return of the full pressure of his lips, the gentle stroking of the rough edge of his tongue. She had to be satisfied with his mouth traveling over her face, tracing the contours of her cheek and the smooth line of her jaw. His teeth caught her earlobe and tugged with sublime tenderness. He smiled as he heard her faint sigh of satisfaction.

"Cold? Don't even think it."

Rhys's breath tickled her ear as he spoke the words and a shiver rippled Kenna's flesh. She realized she was not thinking of anything save the splendid sensations flowing down her spine. Her arms eased around Rhys's shoulders, smoothing the material at his back but curious to touch what lay beneath it. Her fingers slipped under the lapels of his jacket and tugged.

Rhys sat up, his eyes as dark as coals, and eased out of his jacket. He tossed it to the foot of the bed then removed his shoes and stockings. The entire time he watched Kenna, waiting for her to make some protest. When she remained silent, her face expectant, Rhys knew she would not alter the course she had set. His body rejoiced in the knowledge and quieted the doubts in his mind.

He lay down beside her, propping himself on one elbow. He watched Kenna's lashes flutter closed as his fingers idly brushed the lacy neckline of her gown. Her breathing stilled when he dipped below it to touch the soft skin beneath. He pulled at the satin ribbon that kept the gown's modest neckline together and opened the virginal collar to bare Kenna's throat, touching his lips to the tempting pulse beating there.

He savored the taste of her fair skin, the honeyed warmth of the curve of her shoulder. "You're lovely," he said against her flesh. His head lifted and he said it again against her mouth.

Kenna found herself welcoming the return of Rhys's mouth and she answered his searching kiss with a depth of feeling that surprised her. "Oh my," she whispered when he broke the kiss.

"Indeed." He smiled.

"Indeed," she repeated, framing his face with her hands and bringing his mouth down to hers. She initiated the kiss, recalling what he had already taught her to give and receive pleasure. Her tongue peeped out, touching his lips, tasting them. She kissed the corners of his mouth, the slight dimple in his chin, then brushed her lips against his once more before her mouth pressed greedily on his. The comforter and sheets were pushed aside but their movement made little impact on Kenna's senses. It was the warmth of his hand through her thin linen gown that got her attention but the shock of it only lasted a moment. It was quickly replaced by another shock: she did not want him to remove his hand from her breast.

The way her flesh swelled to Rhys's light touch was faintly embarrassing to Kenna but the sensations he aroused when his thumb stroked her nipple were too exquisite to forego. Without thought she arched into the pressure and heat of his hand.

Feeling Kenna's response, Rhys moved closer to Kenna's slender frame and slid his mouth quickly over her throat. His tongue flicked over the tip of her breast, wetting her gown until her nipple was revealed provocatively by the clinging damp circle he created. His mouth wandered in fleeting little kisses to her other breast while he tugged at the hem of her gown, pushing it out of the way so he could touch her bare skin.

Kenna's fingers wound in Rhys's dark hair as his palms slid underneath her calves and stroked the length of her legs. His hands pressed against the back of her thighs and swept upward, pausing when they reached the curve of her buttocks. He sat up then and pulled Kenna with him.

"I think it is time we dispose of this gown," he said huskily. "Lift your arms."

Kenna shied away from Rhys's implacable eyes and looked past his shoulder, studying the patterned wallpaper as if she had never seen it before. "Must I?"

Rhys touched her chin with one finger and turned her face toward him. "Lift your arms."

Kenna's hands twisted in her lap a moment before she raised them overhead. There was not time to reconsider as she felt Rhys take the edge of her gown and draw it from her body in a single motion. Her arms dropped immediately to cover her breasts.

Rhys shook his head. "No. I want to see you," he said softly, grasping her wrists and pulling them downward. "You have beautiful breasts." His eyes lifted, meeting hers. "All of you is beautiful, Kenna." His fingers trailed the gentle slope of her breasts, nudging her pink nipples with the pads of his thumbs. "And none of you is cold."

A wisp of a smile touched Kenna's mouth. "I don't feel very warm," she said, eyeing Rhys from under the thick sweep of her lashes.

Rhys was hard pressed to keep the amusement he felt from showing on his face. Had Kenna but known it, a very warm blush had colored her features the moment she spoke with such innocent temerity. "I will have to do something about that, won't I?" He gave her a light kiss, pressing her shoulders back to the soft mattress. "Don't move," he said, adding a kiss to the tip of her nose. Rhys got off the bed and quickly stripped off his shirt and trousers and tossed them on the nearby chair. Naked, he slipped back in bed and pulled the sheet over them. He kissed her tightly closed lids. "You can open your eyes now." There was no hiding his amusement now. When she looked at him he said, "You know it would have been quite proper for you to look this time. I would have been flattered by a little maidenly interest on your part."

"I don't doubt that you've had more flatterers than you can count." Kenna was surprised by the niggling jealousy she felt and prayed Rhys had not heard it.

"That is not very complimentary to my skill with mathematics."

"That is not what I meant."

"I know what you meant and I should be devastated if your lovely brown eyes took on the traditional green of your emotion."

So he had heard. Well, she wouldn't admit it. Ever! "You flatter yourself. There is no need for me to do it as well."

"That's my Kenna."

"I'm not your anything," she said with asperity.

"Aren't you?" he asked, brushing her cheek with his mouth. "You should be." He kissed the bridge of her nose. "You *will* be." He kissed her deeply and felt her obligatory resistance give way to surrender.

Kenna's hands slid around Rhys's waist as his body covered hers. Her palms stroked his tautly muscled back and her fingers trailed over the length of his spine as she welcomed the weight and security of his lean frame flush to her skin. His hands were everywhere, feather-light, curiously reverent, as he caressed her arms, her waist,

149

the sensitive flesh of her inner thighs. His mouth moved over her face, then the gentle suck of it on her breast drew a sigh from deep inside Kenna. The sheet was pushed aside as his lips traveled lower, over the flat plane of her stomach and the arc of her hip. His mouth touched her once on the red-gold triangle between her legs but the contact was so brief she forced herself to believe she had imagined it. Surely he had not meant to kiss her there.

Kenna's fingers explored Rhys's hard chest when his mouth returned to hers. His flat male nipples hardened beneath her curious hands and she felt his abdomen tauten as her hands slipped lower. Something warned her that she could stop Rhys now and know very well that she was not as Victorine had said, yet she had no desire to heed the warning. She wanted to know everything that happened between a man and a woman; she wanted to be released from her schoolgirl ignorance at last.

When Rhys nudged her thighs with his knee Kenna opened to him. His hand slipped between her legs and the intimacy of his caress was as startling as it was pleasurable. Liquid sparks shot through her as his insistent fingers stroked her, fanning her desire. One hand fell to her side while the other reached down to tug at his wrist, intending to pull him away. Instead it rested there while her eyes sought his, naked save for the wonderment of what he was making her feel.

A gasp rose in her throat as the sensations spiraled and she turned her head into her shoulder to keep from crying out.

"No," he said, lifting the pressure of his hand slightly. "Look at me. I want to see your face . . . your eyes." When she still did not look at him he drew his hand away. "Give me your mouth, Kenna."

She turned her face to him and though her longing was clear she needed to say it aloud. "Don't stop," she said on a thread of sound. "I couldn't bear it." She thought she must be shameless.

Rhys did not think so as his mouth ground into her with an intensity that left them both breathless. His tongue stroked her in an intimate prelude to the loving he desired. When his hand returned to her thighs he felt Kenna arch her hips against him, searching for release from the web of sensation he had caught her in. Her hands lifted, fingers digging into the flesh of his shoulders as he touched the moist, velvet center of her pleasure. His mouth caught her incoherent murmurs as if they were nectar and his own need grew with hers until he realized he could not put off his own hunger another moment.

"Are you certain, Kenna?" he asked roughly.

She had only a vague sense of what he was asking. He had moved, leaving her mouth, her thighs, and was kneeling between her legs, tilting her hips toward him. Her eyes dropped from his face and his strangely ascetic features outlined in the firelight, to the more shadowy outline of his thrusting manhood poised to enter her.

Certain? she thought, panicking at the sight of him. She wasn't certain of anything, least of all how her body was going to accept his. It seemed quite impossible that she could accommodate him and she almost blurted her astonishment aloud, but when she found her voice she also found she wanted him. "Yes," she said simply. "Yes."

"There will be some pain this first time."

Since it would be the only time with him Kenna didn't care and told him so.

The sharp edge of self-denial vanished from Rhys's features as he eased himself into Kenna's warmth. He withdrew a little at her first distressed whimper as he encountered her maidenhead then thrust quickly forward, jerking her hips toward him and tearing the barrier to his entry. He was still for a moment, letting her

151

become accustomed to the feel of him inside her and then he moved slowly, acquainting her with the rhythm of his loving.

As Rhys filled her Kenna admitted her imagination had failed her miserably on this occasion. She had never dreamed her body could give her such delight, nor that a man's body could offer so much pleasure. It seemed the most natural thing in the world to give as she took and she caught the urgency of his motion as his thrusts deepened. Her hands caressed his chest and shoulders when he leaned over her and the sparks he had ignited earlier flickered through her limbs without pause.

Their strained voices mingled as Kenna felt her body being stretched taut like a bow. Her neck arched and her fingers stiffened on Rhys's arms as a cascade of bright light seemed to wash over her. She felt as if she were sparkling, brilliant with the fiery sensation that enfolded her. Her eyes closed and she bit her lip to hold back the sounds of her pleasure.

"I want to hear you, Kenna."

Rhys's voice tipped her over the edge and she cried out his name as his thrusts quickened. Her lashes fluttered open and she saw Rhys's beautiful face grow rigid and still, as if he had suddenly been cast in bronze, then felt him flood her with his seed.

For a while there was no sound beyond their breathing. Rhys shifted his weight from Kenna but lay close to her, one leg flung over hers to keep her near. He pulled the comforter over them, keeping the chill which seemed to seep into their bodies at bay. They both became aware of the rhythmic ticking of the clock on the mantel at the same time and glanced at it together.

"It's very late," Kenna said, not knowing what else to say. Her head was filled with clumsy thoughts that she could not express.

"Yes, it is."

"The servants will be up soon."

"Not that soon," Rhys disagreed. "We have a few hours before I must leave." He turned her face toward him and searched her dark eyes. "Are you so anxious for me to go?"

She wished she knew the answer to that and her confusion registered clearly on her flushed features. "You must leave. You can't be found here."

"Where was that reasoning when you asked me to make love to you?" Rhys questioned reasonably though he felt a surge of irritability that she was concerned with proprieties now. It had not taken reality long to set in.

"I didn't ask you to make—"

"Don't lie to yourself, Kenna. It does not become you."

"But I am not lying," she persisted, edging away from him only to find that some of her hair was trapped beneath his shoulder. It made her unaccountably angry that he was still holding onto her. "Release my hair, please," she said in frosty accents. "And kindly remove your leg."

"When you explain yourself," he answered easily, pressing down upon her legs just to show her he could keep her there all night if he had a mind to.

"Oh, very well. Though why you should need an explanation eludes me. It should be perfectly clear that love had nothing to do with what happened in this bed."

One of Rhys's dark brows slanted upward. "Didn't it?" he asked softly.

"You know it didn't. It was an experiment, nothing more. I posed a question and you gave me an answer. There is no need to puff the thing up with romantic balderdash."

"I see. Then what happened in this bed, as you euphemistically put it, was nothing more than the coupling of two animals. Perhaps the stable would have

153

suited your needs better; a stallion and a filly acting purely on their instincts as nature intended."

Kenna was only now becoming aware of how angry Rhys was with her. The gentle, inquiring tone of his voice had made her blind to his heat until he mentioned coupling and the stables. "There is no need for crudity. We are hardly animals."

"That is precisely what we are, Kenna Dunne, though mayhap I should have likened you to a brood mare."

She gasped and would have slapped his face if he had not anticipated her action and pinned her wrist to the bed. "What is that supposed to mean?" she bit out, frustrated in the extreme because she could not move.

"It means you could be *enceinte*. Have I put that delicately enough for your ears?"

Kenna felt the fight drain out of her and she went limp against him. "A child? It isn't possible."

"Of course it is," he scoffed. "Surely you know how a woman gets with child?" To Rhys's astonishment he saw all the color leave Kenna's face. "My God, you didn't know!"

"Of course I knew," she snapped. "Or rather I knew it had something to do with . . . something," she finished lamely, ignoring Rhys's hoot of sardonic laughter. "But it cannot happen from this one time. I forbid it!"

Rhys lifted his shoulder and removed his leg from Kenna's. "Tell that to my son or daughter nine months hence."

Kenna twisted away from Rhys and sat up, curling against the mahogany headboard. The comforter was pulled tautly across her breasts and her heavy hair tumbled about her face and shoulders. "You are teasing," she accused. "You wouldn't dare give me a babe. It would be the grandchild of the man you murdered."

"Seventy-five minutes," he said tersely after glancing

at the clock.

"What nonsense are you saying now?"

Rhys threw off the covers and slipped off the bed. With uninhibited grace he began gathering his clothes and putting them on. "By my reckoning it's been seventy-five minutes that we've been together and this is the first mention of your father. Who, by the way, happened to be the man I admired, not murdered."

He was leaving. That's what she wanted, wasn't it? Then why did she feel strangely bereft that she had chased him from her bed with her sharp tongue?

"As to a child," he continued roughly, "we shall have to wait and see, won't we?" He paused in buttoning his shirt and eyed her narrowly. "You could plan for that eventuality and marry me now."

"Marry you!" she sputtered, astonished. It was exactly this pass she had hoped to avoid and instead she had fallen neatly into his trap. If she didn't know better she would think he had planned the thing himself, even to putting the words in her mouth. She could never ask another man to accept Rhys's child any more than she could bring herself to marry Rhys. "I am not going to marry you!"

"You will if you are carrying my child!"

"Will you lower your voice?" she whispered harshly. "The entire house will be down upon us!"

"That would suit me though I can see you are plainly horrified by the prospect."

"If Nicky or Victorine . . ."

Kenna could not finish the sentence but Rhys had no such difficulty. "If they found you cowering in your bed, wearing nothing but your modesty, the banns would be posted on the morrow. Is that what you wanted to say?"

"More or less," she murmured.

Rhys's lips curled in derision. "The scenario will be much the same when they notice the thickening of

155

your waist."

"Stop it! I am not with child. You cannot know! It would ruin everything!"

Rhys sat on the edge of the bed and pulled on his boots. "Ruin everything? What sort of plot have you been hatching?"

"Do not make light of this, Rhys Canning!"

Making light of it was all that kept Rhys from throttling Kenna. He knew the risk he had taken by making love to her, knew that she was unprepared to allow a few moments of pleasure speak to her after years of nurturing hatred. He found no satisfaction in realizing he had anticipated her reaction correctly when he would have given almost anything to have been wrong. He sighed deeply and turned on her. "Tell me truly, Kenna. What was this evening in aid of?"

"I told you."

"I know what you told me. But why? Where did you get such a notion?"

She would not tell him what she had overheard in Nick's study. It seemed safer to share other truths. "I am twenty-three years old and no man has ever looked at me with anything but polite interest."

Rhys wondered if Kenna merely did not consider him a man or if she had been oblivious to his interest. "You don't know many men," he said. "You refused your season and shut yourself here at Dunnelly."

"Nick has friends who have visited," she persisted. "They scarcely noticed me."

"That only proves how blind they were, not that you are some sort of faerie snow queen. But why try to prove something to yourself now, Kenna? And why with me?"

"It had to be now. I cannot explain it any better than that. And you? I told you, there is no one else."

"There was more to your decision than that," Rhys said implacably. "What was it?"

"Rhys . . ."

"What was it?"

"I cannot believe you really want to know."

"I do."

"It had to be you. If I could respond to you, then . . ."

He put a finger to her lips. "I know the rest. It was an experiment then, just as you said." She nodded and he was thoughtful for a moment. "You would not object if I conducted an experiment of my own?"

Kenna did not know if she had even responded to his query when Rhys's mouth crushed hers. There was a hungry sort of passion in his touch, an element of something primitive that Kenna answered without thinking. Her breasts were still tender from their earlier arousal at Rhys's hands and when he touched them now, stroking them with less than gentle pressure, they swelled and hardened immediately. The comforter fell away as Rhys dragged her against him. A soft moan escaped her as his hand caressed her abdomen then her naked thigh and her arms stole around his neck. She pressed her body to him, reveling in the texture of his clothes against her skin.

Rhys's fingers caught a swatch of hair at Kenna's nape and tugged. Her head snapped backward and the kiss was broken. He looked at her for a long moment, his face expressionless.

"I must revise an earlier opinion, Kenna," he said, pushing her off his lap and getting to his feet. "Of those countless women I've known, you easily have the warmest body, Lady Dunne. And, without question, the coldest heart." He walked across the room and opened the door. "I bid you good night and dare we hope, pleasant dreams?"

Chapter Four

"But I want to ride this morning!"

Janet's expression was incredulous as she listened to her mistress demand to leave her room. "I have strict orders that you are to spend another day in your room."

Kenna felt mutinous. It had been two days since Doctor Tipping's visit and everyone was still treating her as if she had to be wrapped in cotton wool. It was the outside of enough. She felt fine; her headache was gone and she was able to keep food down now that Monsieur Raillier had been apprised of his mistake by Janet. According to her maid, the chef was nearly apopletic when he discovered arsenic in the salt and promptly boxed the ears of the kitchen boy who had been responsible for filling the cellars. The reason Kenna was the only person to have taken ill was because her meals were prepared separately at a small table where both the salt and sugar had been contaminated.

Kenna accepted her maid's explanation because there was no reoccurrence of her symptoms and because she did not want to believe the poisoning had been anything less than accidental. The alternative did not bear thinking about.

"How dare Rhys give you orders to keep me a prisoner

in my own home!" Kenna said. "He has no right!"

"I was not referring to Mr. Canning," Janet said. "Your brother gave me the instructions."

"Oh." She avoided her maid's speculative glance and wished she had not brought up Rhys's name. There was no telling what Janet would make of that. Kenna told herself she was glad Rhys had not bothered her with his odious presence. What could they possibly have to say to one another? It was much better that he kept his distance. "Well, Nick hasn't the right either," she said, putting a period to her thoughts of Rhys. "I am perfectly capable of knowing when I am well enough to leave this room."

Janet shrugged, a mischievous light in her hazel eyes. "I know what I was told, m'lady, but I suppose if you were to send me on an errand I couldn't be responsible if you weren't here when I returned."

An impish smile tugged at Kenna's mouth. "Then you wouldn't mind finding Herderson and asking him if there was a letter for me from my sister?"

"I wouldn't mind at all." She picked up Kenna's breakfast tray. "I'll take this to the kitchen first."

The door had barely clicked into place behind Janet when Kenna scrambled out of bed. She washed her face, gave her hair a few quick strokes with a brush and plaited it in a braid, then dressed for riding. Taking the servant's corridors to avoid meeting her family or Rhys, Kenna made it to the stables a full fifteen minutes before Janet returned to her bedchamber.

Pyramid was happy to see his mistress and quite anxious for her to give him full rein. Kenna was not so lacking in common sense that she gave in to her mount. She kept him to a comfortable pace the entire time and thoroughly enjoyed the peace of her trek around Dunnelly. A new, heavier snowfall had covered everything during the previous night and the leafless trees were shaded in white. The air felt surprisingly warm and Kenna welcomed the odd silence of winter. For the first time in days she felt free of Rhys Canning.

She did not give him any thought at all until she returned to the stables ninety minutes later and saw the stall beside Pyramid's was empty. "Has someone taken Higgins for exercising?" she asked Donald Adams as he helped her dismount.

The groom shook his head. "No, Mr. Canning's man arrived but a few minutes after you left and shortly after that he and the other were tearing out of here, hellbent on reaching London before nightfall. The boys and I barely had the tack off Powell's horse when we were putting it on again. Your brother offered a fresh mount but he didn't want one. Came down to the stables to see them off, he did. Looked a might out of sorts."

"Out of sorts how?"

"Can't say exactly. Sad, I think. Worried, for sure."

"Why did Rhys leave? Didn't you hear anything?"

"Not a word m'lady." Adams rubbed his chin with his hand. "They were here and gone. He didn't even take his luggage. Left his coach behind, too. Never saw such a rush."

"Thank you, Donald," Kenna called behind her as she hurried out of the stable. There was no sense in trying to pretend she hadn't gone anywhere so Kenna went straight to Dunnelly's front door. Henderson greeted her with an ominous, "They're waiting for you in the study," and Kenna went in before her courage failed her.

"Where have you been?" Nick demanded, ignoring Victorine's imploring look to lower his voice and show a little tolerance.

Kenna took a seat on the sofa beside her stepmother and accepted the comforting hand Victorine offered. "I was riding, Nick. I had to get out of that room else expire from boredom."

"I gave strict instructions that you were not to leave. Must you tempt fate at every turn?"

Kenna frowned. "What do you mean? I assure you I am feeling quite the thing."

Nick swore under his breath and looked at Victorine for help. He had nearly given Rhys's suspicions away after promising not to.

"Your brother is naturally concerned that you chose to go out alone, Kenna," Victorine said softly. "What if you had had a relapse?"

"But I didn't and I was not tempting fate. You exaggerate, Nick," said Kenna calmly. "Now tell me why Rhys left. I assume he came to say goodbye and found me gone."

"I came to tell you he was gone," Nick corrected. "And that's when I discovered you had taken off."

Kenna squelched her disappointment, refusing to credit that she could feel any such emotion because Rhys left without trying to say farewell personally. "So why has he left Dunnelly? Adams said something about his valet arriving? I didn't know his man had gone."

"Neither did I," said Nick, taking a seat behind his desk now that the greater part of his anger had fled. "Rhys apparently sent him to London on some sort of business. He rushed back today to tell Rhys there had been an accident involving Rhys's father and brother."

Kenna's hands went immediately to her paling cheeks. "What kind of accident? When? Are they seriously hurt?" The heavy silence which greeted her questions was answer enough. "Dear God! They're dead?"

"Richard is," Victorine said. "Rhys's father was still clinging to life when Powell left London. Rhys doesn't hold much hope that he'll still be alive when he gets there, but he had to try."

Even though Kenna knew there was no love lost between Roland Canning and his younger son, she could well imagine how much Rhys was hurting. "Of course he had to try," she said. "What happened, Nicky?"

"Roland was at the duchess's townhouse. Sometime during the night there was a fire. It took down three homes before it was contained. There were six other victims. Richard never had a chance. According to the reports the fire started in his room. Roland was quite badly burned when a staircase collapsed under him. He was trying to help get the servants out."

"Poor Roland. It seems odd he should be hurt helping others. I always thought him such an ogre."

"He was to Rhys," said Nick. "Richard was everything to him after his wife died. Rhys ranked a poor fifth behind politics, business, and the rest of humanity."

"It's so sad," Kenna said quietly, getting to her feet. "If you'll excuse me, I think I'll go to my room."

"And stay there," Victorine added.

"Yes, of course."

Kenna's thoughts were all for Rhys as she climbed the stairs to her room. It couldn't be easy for him, no matter that he and his father had never gotten on. And to lose his brother at the same time! How he must ache!

"Janet!" Kenna cried out, startled when she came out of her reverie and found her maid in the room. "What are you doing here?"

"I'm supposed to pass this on to you," she said, holding out an envelope.

"From Nicky? I just saw him. He didn't say anything."

"Not from your brother. From Mr. Canning. Oh, dear. Such a tragedy! I suppose he'll be going to Boston now."

Kenna took the letter, too weary to marvel at the speed with which news spread at Dunnelly. Rhys had not even reached his father's side yet and the gossip had him taking over the shipping firm already. She turned the letter over in her hand and saw the seal had been broken. "This has been opened."

163

"It was that way when he gave it to me," Janet defended herself.

Kenna flipped the letter again and noticed for the first time it was not a missive from Rhys that she was holding, but one from Yvonne. She hastened to her writing table and unfolded the letter, examining the date Yvonne had penned the thing. "Rhys gave this to you?" she asked Janet again.

"Yes, M'lady. Just before he rushed out of here. Caught me as he was leaving his room."

"Yvonne wrote this the same day she received my letter! It must have arrived here days ago. He had no right to keep my mail from me! And to read it! The man's nerve is not to be believed! How did he get it?"

"As to that, m'lady, I found out this morning when I spoke to Henderson that a letter had arrived from your sister the afternoon you took so ill. He was going to bring it to you personally but Mr. Canning was there when the post came and offered to deliver it. I was going to tell you about it when you came back from your ride, but then, well, you know what happened, and he gave me the letter himself. He said you should accept Lady Parker's offer now that he had to leave."

"Is that all he said?" she sighed.

"He was rather insistent upon it. Repeated himself twice as if I couldn't grasp the gist of it the first time," Janet said huffily. "'Tell your mistress,' he said, 'that she's to accept her sister's invitation to Cherry Hill now that I have to leave Dunnelly.' Those are his exact words. Said them twice, like I told you."

Kenna thought Rhys a singularly obtuse individual. Surely he must know there was no reason to run off to Cherry Hill once he was gone from her home. He had incredible gall to order her life as if she had naught but space between her ears. "I'd like to be alone, Janet." When her maid hesitated she added, "Don't worry. I'm staying here. Nick was livid that I left and I'll abide by his wishes. You aren't in any trouble.'' She thought she heard Janet's sigh of relief as she left the room.

Kenna took her time reading the letter, thoroughly enjoying Yvonne's rare and humorous descriptions of life at Cherry Hill. The invitation to join her family was wedged somewhere between a tale of how her oldest boy had rescued a nest of sparrows from certain death in the library fireplace and how his younger sister had lit a fire beneath him while he was curled in the chimney. The baby, thank heaven, was too young to be involved in the goings-on but he had a regrettable penchant for slapping at his porridge when the bowl was placed near him. It all sounded wonderful to Kenna and she admitted it was rather silly not to go simply because Rhys had said she should.

She folded the letter and stuck it in a drawer filled with correspondence. After a moment's more consideration she quickly penned a note to Yvonne telling her to clean up the children, their favorite aunt was on her way.

Kenna had not anticipated Victorine's resistance to her plan. While Nick was all for Kenna getting away from Dunnelly, her stepmother raised a number of concerns about Kenna's health, about her availability to the authorities should there be more questions on Tom Allen's death, and about the advisability in traveling when the winter storms were so uncertain. It was finally Nick who put his foot down and told Victorine that her cosseting was unnecessary; Kenna was no less than an adult and surely capable of withstanding the rigors of the journey to Cherry Hill. As for Old Tom's death, if the authorities had more questions they could visit her there. It was not as if she were going to the Continent.

''Perhaps she would like to go with me,'' Kenna told Nick a week later as she was going through her wardrobe and selecting gowns to take with her. She had delayed her trip long enough to stay with Victorine while Nick attended the Cannings' funeral in London. Her stepmother disliked funerals intensely and Kenna had no wish to see Rhys, even to offer her sympathies. It would hardly matter to him that she did not come, after all he believed her to be the most cold-hearted of women. That criticism still had the power to sting. He would never have to know how she had grieved for him when word came back from London that his father had also died. "Yvonne would probably like the surprise and I would be grateful for the company on the journey."

Nick laughed. "You are too kind-hearted, sprite. Yvonne would hate the surprise and you need a rest from Victorine's well-intentioned worrying."

"No doubt you're right. Yvonne once confided in me that her mother is a little critical of the children's playfulness and Yvonne's own desire to spend so much time with them. As I recall, Victorine never had much patience for the pranks we got up to before Papa died." She held up a day dress the color of Jonquils and saw Nick wrinkle his nose. With a shrug she put it back in the wardrobe. "Still, I don't like leaving her alone."

"Well thank you very much."

"You have to admit you aren't much company at times, Nick. Victorine needs to find someone she can dote on. She should remarry."

"I have said as much to her."

"Have you?" asked Kenna, much impressed her brother would broach the subject with Victorine. "What did she say?"

"She says she cannot leave Dunnelly."

"Why ever not?"

"She says you need her."

Kenna leaned against the wardrobe, hugging a blue silk dress to her middle, a sad, thoughtful smile playing on her lips. "Oh, Nick. I've become a veritable albatross about her neck. And yours. How awful for both of you!''

Nick shook his head, indicating the dress. Kenna stamped her foot and put it away. "You are nothing of the sort," he said. "I know it's shocking but I'm quite content with my life. I hardly live like a monk, you know."

"Yes, but actresses and opera singers are hardly proper marriage prospects. I hear stories, Nick," she added when he looked faintly shocked that she knew about his women. "A little bit of gossip always finds its way back to Dunnelly whenever you're in London. Most of it does not bear repeating."

Nick looked a little uncomfortable. "Most of it does not bear an element of truth, I'll wager." He hesitated, searching Kenna's face. "Kenna, there is something you should know, perhaps it will soften your feelings for Rhys and help you understand why I hold him with such affection and regard."

"Must we talk of Rhys?" she asked tiredly. "I thought we were speaking of your life."

"We still are." He went on rapidly before she could object. "There was something of scandal a number of years ago, before Papa married Victorine in fact. I doubt you remember it, you were so young yourself and it was mostly hushed up."

Kenna thought about that for a moment. "I know," she said, clicking her fingers. "When Rhys disappeared to the Continent! Is that it?"

"Yes."

"What did he do?"

"That's just it, Kenna. Rhys did nothing save take the blame for me. I had compromised a young woman from a good family and when I refused to marry her, she killed herself. You must believe me, I have nothing but disgust at the memory. I ill-used her and made promises that should never have been spoken. She was a beautiful girl,

Kenna, possessed of the loveliest laughter, totally without guile. Lara was an innocent in every sense of the word and I was bewitched by her. To my everlasting regret I also discovered she was quite mad."

"Oh, Nick," Kenna said, coming to sit beside him. She put a hand on his arm. "How did you know?"

"Rhys warned me that she was not always as she seemed. I think they had words once and she flew into a rage all out of proportion to the disagreement. I didn't believe him. I was too spellbound. But then I began to notice peculiarities in her behavior that could not be dismissed. I slowly came to realize that no matter what had happened between us, I could not marry her. When she killed herself her brother came to me and demanded satisfaction. That was when Rhys interfered. He said Lara had broken off with me some time ago and that they had been secretly meeting. He took responsibility for her depression and her death."

"And you let him? How could you?"

"I'm not proud of it, Kenna. I was young and foolish, though one does not justify the other. I let him do it because he convinced me I would only get myself killed in a duel. Rhys was always a better shot than me. He took to the field and I acted as his second. Lara's brother was seriously wounded and Rhys fled the country. He did not return until hours before the masque."

"I can hardly believe this."

"Believe it, Kenna. Rhys most probably saved my life and if I do not marry it has less to do with you and much more to do with the fact that I don't trust my judgment of women. There have been other mistakes with women of good birth and breeding I thought I could love. I find the occasional actress or opera singer much more to my tastes."

"Did Papa know what happened?"

"Yes. He bitterly disapproved of the way Rhys and I

168

handled the situation, but he loved us both, and I like to think he forgave us."

"I'm certain he did." She hugged her brother. "I'm glad you told me, Nick, Not for Rhys's sake, for I find that I cannot change my opinion of him because of one gallant moment, but because it explains so much about you. I do love you, Nicholas."

He returned her hug. "I wish you would reconsider about Rhys. I had hoped . . . Never mind, let's have another look at your pitiful wardrobe," he said, giving her shoulder a playful squeeze and putting the past behind them.

Even though Nick suggested discarding a full one third of her clothes, Kenna's coach was still loaded with two trunks, three leather cases, and a portmanteau which she carried inside. The arrival of Janet's bags meant the entire load had to be readjusted once and the two grooms accompanying them on the journey grumbled under their breath as they moved everything around and roped it all in again.

After a rather lengthy farewell to Victorine and Nick, during which Kenna was given instructions on how to deal with everything from Yvonne's children to the innkeeper who ran the hostelry where they planned to spend the night, Kenna's driver snapped his whip sharply and headed the coach down Dunnelly's wide entrance and out the main gate.

Kenna thoroughly enjoyed the ride though Janet complained mightily of the poor road conditions which gave them a painful jolt upon occasion. A spring-like thaw had settled in during the past week and while the warm weather was a pleasant change, according to Janet it had created conditions on the road only a pig could appreciate. In order to escape her maid's less than enthusiastic companionship Kenna asked the groom who was riding alongside on Pyramid to change places with her. He looked miserable at the prospect but Kenna remained adamant.

They stopped only long enough to change her mount's saddle. Kenna sometimes rode ahead of the coach, sometimes behind it, but she never let it get out of her sight. She had been warned it wasn't safe to be on these roads without an escort and Kenna knew Nick insisted her grooms and driver carry pistols.

It was approaching dusk when they reached Robinson's Ale House. Janet made it clear at the outset that she disapproved of their surroundings. Her dark eyebrows rose nearly to her hairline as she looked around the common room and passed judgment on the guests.

"Disreputable lot," Janet announced, pulling the hood of her cape more closely about her face.

"Calm yourself," Kenna told her. "Nick would not have arranged for us to stay here if he thought it was anything less than respectable." Kenna found the accommodations quite acceptable. The dining room was clean, the innkeeper and his wife were solicitous without groveling, and the aroma of stew from the kitchen was mouth-watering. If she and Janet were the only women present and if several of the patrons smelled strongly of spirits, well, it could not be helped. Kenna saw that most of the clientele appeared to be quality. How like Janet to dwell on the cloud and ignore the silver lining.

"Look at those two over there," Janet whispered when she and Kenna were seated in a private corner of the room. "No, not now! They're looking this way!"

Kenna smiled tolerantly. "Well, where should they be looking? No doubt they're struck by your great beauty."

Janet straightened her shoulders and sniffed disdainfully. "Mind your tongue, Young Kenna," she said, slipping into the tone she had adopted when Kenna was a child in need of a scold. "I'll have you know, in my youth my looks were often remarked upon. And kindly!"

Kenna lifted her hands in mock surrender. "It does not surprise me in the least, dear Janet. Now, won't you try some of this delicious stew and concern yourself less with the other patrons?" As Janet applied herself to her meal, Kenna glanced at the guests in question. When she caught them staring at her they turned away guiltily and Kenna was forced to agree with her maid. The two men swilling ale a few tables away were easily the most disreputable pair she had seen in ages. Their swarthy faces were shadowed by muddied hats and their clothes were rough farmer's garb, though Kenna doubted very much they were from that sturdy stock. Their thick fingers circled their mugs as if they were intent upon choking the drink from them.

"Now who's staring?" Janet observed as she buttered a slice of warm bread.

"Sorry," Kenna said.

"If your attention should wander again, mayhap you could notice that nice-looking gentleman sitting near the door. He's been trying to catch your eye since we came in here."

"Janet!" she laughed. "You shouldn't be encouraging me. What would my brother think?"

"Can't say as to that. Here, have some bread."

Kenna took the offered slice and broke off a piece, dipping it into the stew's thick gravy. Under cover of her thick lashes she stole a glance at the table by the door. The lone gentleman seated there was indeed handsome. His hair was fair, his features clearly defined like those of an Adonis, and his slender hands were both elegant and strong. He was wearing fashionable traveling clothes and a crystal knobbed walking stick rested at the side of his chair.

Kenna's interest turned to the other patrons in turn. There was a father and his two young sons, a group of men who could only be locals given the familiarity with

171

which they greeted the innkeeper, and a half dozen or so travelers from the public coach which had pulled up just before Kenna's arrival. The atmosphere of the ale house was lively, what with so many conversations taking place at once, and Kenna took more time with her meal than usual to prolong the illusion of being part of the activity.

When Kenna had had enough of Janet's reproachful look she motioned to Mrs. Robinson and the kindly woman showed them to the room they would share for the night. As they were standing in the hallway while Mrs. Robinson searched her oversized apron pocket for the key to the room, the handsome young lord from the common room passed them, tipping his hat politely as he went to his own chamber. Kenna's cheeks warmed at the polite gesture but she was careful not to give him any encouragement.

The room Mrs. Robinson had prepared for them was eminently satisfactory. Crisp, well-laundered sheets were turned down on the double bed and a heavy colorful quilt was folded at the foot. Kenna's portmanteau and Janet's bags rested beside a glowing fire and fresh water had been added to the basin on the nightstand and a pitcher filled with more of the same stood beside it.

Janet helped Kenna out of her drab but practical traveling clothes and hung everything up on hooks on the wall while Kenna washed at the basin. Afterwards she gave Kenna's hair a sturdy brushing and plaited it.

"Which side of the bed do you want?" Kenna asked as Janet changed into her voluminous nightdress.

"I prefer to be closer to the wall. I should warn you, my late husband said I snore a mite."

Kenna yawned sleepily, unperturbed. "'S quite all right," she said, slurring her words. "I sometimes scream."

"Don't I know it. We'll have none of that tonight, m'lady," she said teasingly as she climbed over Kenna to

172

get to her side of the bed. "Try thinking of something pleasant, like that young man you pretended not to notice in the common room."

Kenna wrinkled her nose at her maid. "I can't conjure my dreams to order." But as she fell asleep she found herself thinking of a fair, handsome face and the rest came surprisingly easy.

Kenna did not know how many hours had passed when some strange noise woke her, but when she opened her eyes sleepily the face that was staring down at her was so familair, so gentle that she thought she must be still dreaming. Her eyes drifted closed and she started to turn on her side. It was only when her movement was prevented by an insistent hand on her shoulder that she realized she was awake.

She opened her mouth to scream and immediately a gloved hand was clamped over it. Kenna kicked wildly, hoping to rouse Janet but the calm, handsome countenance above her warned her it was useless. He allowed Kenna to move her head slightly to one side, never releasing his hand. She paled as she saw the blood on Janet's temple mingle with a shock of silver hair.

"Jeb hit her a little too hard for my tastes."

The soft voice, very faintly accented, of the gentleman who was not at all what he seemed washed over Kenna and she ceased to struggle. She stared up at him, trying to still her panic. Upon closer examination the face above her was not as young as it first seemed. There were faint lines about his eyes and mouth, and at the temples his fair hair was actually a very light gray.

Another voice, rougher and uncultured came from across the room. "Now don't be usin' any names. We don't want her singin' any tunes to the authorities, mate. Anyway, it was you wot walloped the old one with yer cane."

"So I did, but this young lady won't be going within

173

miles of anyone who will listen to her," the man replied easily and to show his unconcern with the matter he introduced himself. "My name is Mason, lovely Kenna, and the two miscreants accompanying me are Jeb and Sweet."

Was she supposed to care? she wondered. She wanted to help Janet whose breathing was shockingly light and shallow. The pressure on her mouth was unrelenting and she pleaded for release with her eyes.

Mason ignored her and spoke to the others. "Sweet, get the bottle, Jeb, tie her wrists and ankles, then hold her down. I suspect she's not going to accept this easily."

Kenna began to struggle immediately and though it proved useless she did not quiet until the last of her energy was drained and her hands and legs were tightly bound.

"Now listen to me carefully, Kenna," Mason said, his eyes on her heaving breasts as she fought for air in the aftermath of her struggle. "We are not going to harm you. Do you believe me?"

Was he serious? Kenna shook her head.

"Good girl," he said. "In the same circumstances I wouldn't believe me either. No matter, it happens to be the truth. I was hired to do otherwise which explains the presence of Sweet and his friend." His voice was soft, hypnotic. "I've no real taste for murder, not when I can turn a profit."

Kenna frowned. Murder? Profit? What was he talking about?

"When I saw you in the common room an alternate plan formed in my mind, one of a decidedly less final nature. Rather fortunate for you, don't you think? Now, don't worry about answering," he grinned, showing a mouth full of white even teeth. "I don't really expect one. What I want you to do now is drink something I've specially prepared for you. It won't kill you," he added when he saw her look of pure terror. "Though at less skilled hands than mine it could. It will make you very drowsy and distort your perception a bit, but it will not harm you permanently. Sweet is going to hold your nose and I am going to pour a measure of it down your throat. I would suggest you not try screaming for the alternative to this is very painful. Look to your maid again if you doubt me."

Kenna didn't doubt him at all. Sweet's thick fingers pinched her nose and Mason lifted his hand just enough to pour a dram of liquid in her mouth as she opened it for air. She sputtered and coughed and tried to spit it out but another measure of the foul tasting stuff was poured in again. She saw Mason hold up the bottle to the firelight, roughly measuring how much he had given her. He did not slip the bottle into his inside vest pocket until it was a quarter empty. His hand remained on Kenna's mouth and he glanced at his companions with something akin to satisfaction on his beautiful face.

"Now we wait."

It was not long before Kenna's eyes closed much against her will and she dropped into a state of semi-consciousness. When Mason felt the stiffness vanish from her body he slowly removed his hand and motioned to Sweet. "Gag her, *mon ami,* then we are leaving."

Rhys lay back on the bed, fluffing a pillow under his head. The pale pink silk canopy billowed at his smallest movement. He imagined it must resemble a rushing tide when Polly Dawn was entertaining her clients. The fat little cherubs carved into the bed's headboard smiled serenely over Rhys's head and the gold threads running through the pink wallpaper glittered at him from across the room. The bedchamber was hardly to his liking but it suited Miss Rose.

Rhys watched her comb her hair and arrange it artfully about her head. Her tiny plump fingers flicked the platinum curls this way and that until she was satisfied with her reflection. She caught Rhys's eye in the mirror and silently asked the age-old question.

"You're beautiful," Rhys responded dutifully, though he realized it was also true. A few years younger than he, P.D. Rose displayed an excess of sensuality in every one of her petite curves. Her features were softly rounded and though she swore she wanted to lose a few pounds her weakness for chocolates made it a life battle. She wrinkled her upturned nose at Rhys as she reached for one now and plopped it into her tiny bow-shaped mouth.

"I have to return to Dunnelly soon," Rhys remarked, shaking his head as Polly got up from the vanity and offered him the box.

She put the box aside and sashayed over to the bed. Polly never walked when she could sashay. Her training had come very early and she was doing the only sort of work she had ever known. "How soon is soon?"

"A few days. Perhaps tomorrow. I'm not certain."

"You're awfully tense," she noted. "Are you sure you won't let me ease some of that for you?"

"That's not why I come here, P.D."

She laughed, a bright, tinkling sound. "Don't Oi know it, guv!" she said, slipping into the speech of her past. "One can't give up 'ope!"

He gave her arm a light squeeze as she sat beside him. "You're incorrigible." Rhys sighed. "I won't be back for a while. My name has been linked to yours."

"I should hope so. You're one of my regulars. Though hardly my usual sort. Most men want a tad more than conversation."

He smiled. "Nick thinks I've set you up."

"Lord Dunne?" She was thoughtful. "Now there's a man I wouldn't turn away from my establishment. He's a

176

looker. I've seen him once or twice. What does it matter if he thinks you've set me up? It's the truth."

"He thinks you're my mistress."

Polly clapped her hands together, her mouth opening in a delightful O of pleasure. "How lovely!"

"Polly," Rhys said warningly. "I don't know how the stories get turned by the time Nick hears them but I doubt he'd be pleased if he knew I helped you open this house. He could accept you as my mistress long before he could accept that you are a . . . professional business-woman. He would certainly think twice about the wisdom of having me for a brother-in-law."

"Brother-in-law!" she exclaimed. "Then you asked for Kenna's hand! How wonderful! When is the wedding?"

"I have no idea. Nick was not a great deal more receptive to the idea than his sister."

"She turned you down?" It was difficult to believe.

"Emphatically."

"Then she doesn't deserve you!"

"I think you mean that," said Rhys.

"I do! You're noble and kind and generous and . . . and I would have been dead years ago if you hadn't intervened! You're rather like my personal guardian angel," she finished smugly.

Rhys glanced at the cherubs overhead. "God forbid," he said feelingly.

"Be serious! It was as if heaven sent you the night you came to Mrs. Miller's place."

Rhys remembered the meeting well enough. It had been two years ago, shortly after his return from the Peninsula and his visit to Dunnelly. He was depressed and lonely and feeling rather sorry for himself. The Foreign Office was after him to spy for them in America, a request he found repugnant, and his father and brother wanted him to come to Boston and fight the English. While Victorine and Nick welcomed him to Dunnelly,

Kenna wanted nothing from him, and that knowledge cut more deeply than anything.

It was that realization that triggered his bout with several bottles of scotch and a wild gambling spree that cost him thousands of pounds. He had not understood how much Kenna's approval meant to him until he saw her again. Though he had thought of her often during the years he was away, and knew a little about her from his correspondence with Nick, he was unprepared to face the fact that he had truly come to love her with more than platonic affection. The promise of her fiery beauty had come true and though her spirit had dimmed and her playfulness had disappeared, she managed to hold his heart. The time he spent in her company during that visit was pure torture and if it had not been necessary to explore the caves of Dunnelly he would have left after only a few days.

When he did depart the world seemed to fold around him and, as quickly as some of his friends goodnaturedly suggested a sporting visit to Mrs. Miller's he took them up on it. Had he been sober at the time he doubted he would have done it, but upon reflection it had turned out to be a good thing because he met Miss Polly Dawn Rose.

He did not remember choosing Miss Rose as his partner that evening, but he found himself in her room nonetheless, and though she seemed to be enthusiastic about the encounter, Rhys found he was not. Instead of making love to the wriggling bundle of femininity in his arms he poured out his troubles in a somewhat drunken though perfectly coherent manner. He had no idea if Miss Rose was a good lover, but she was an excellent listener. He went back to visit her several times, just to talk, and though he knew she thought him peculiar, she seemed to enjoy his company.

It was on his fourth visit that he was told Polly was not available. When he said he would wait for her he was finally told she was ill. Demanding to see her caused more of an uproar than he expected and he was nearly ejected from the brothel by the madam's two footmen. In the end he had his way by holding a primed pistol to Mrs. Miller's head.

Polly was lying on her bed, her face vacant of its usual rosy glow and her features so sunken that her cheekbones stood out sharply. The sheet that covered her was as white as her neck and shoulders except where it covered her thighs. There it was blood red. It only took Rhys a moment to assess the situation which was confirmed by the madam at once. One of Mrs. Miller's physician clients had performed an abortion on Polly and she was hemorrhaging.

Rhys did not waste any time. He covered Polly in several blankets and carried her out of the brothel to his waiting carriage. He had to draw his pistol again when the physician he summoned did not want to care for Miss Rose. In the end he was also persuaded.

Polly recovered under the care of Rhys and his staff and he found he was possessed of some skill with listening also. Polly's entry into prostitution was nothing less than a horror story. She was sold into the profession when she was eighteen, much older than most other girls when they got started, she assured him. It was only because she appeared to be so young that she had been overlooked on a number of occasions by the pimp who frequented the street where she lived. When she was drugged and taken to Mrs. Miller's everyone assumed she was not more than fourteen.

Polly impressed upon Rhys that if she hadn't been sold to an establishment she would have died in the back alleys as the property of some pimp who procured girls for diseased gents. Mrs. Miller specialized in clean and comely girls and her clientele was of a better quality than most houses. Polly was numb in the beginning, too

179

drugged to make an escape from the house, and unresistant as men paraded through her room. But as the numbness passed she assessed her situation and decided she could be worse off. Rhys was not so easily convinced. When Polly was well he offered to set her up in a shop of some kind but she refused, saying she had no skill for any business save one. Rhys argued with her for weeks and it wasn't until she threatened to leave and return to Mrs. Miller's that he understood how serious she was about what she wanted to do with her life. He told her to unpack her things and they would work something out.

Rather than have her go back to Mrs. Miller and her butchers, Rhys agreed to help Polly invest her savings and establish her own house. It would have caused a roaring scandal if they had been less than discreet. As it was, the opening of Polly's house was a quiet success and the Canning name was never connected to the enterprise.

Rhys's interest in Polly extended beyond helping a friend. She could seek his advice on business ventures as long as she agreed that none of the women who worked for her were there through force. Furthermore, when the opportunity presented itself for her to purchase young girls she was to do so, then keep them safe until Rhys found more respectable and safer employment for them.

During the eighteen months that Polly's loving arms had been open she and Rhys had pulled twenty girls from the streets who would have otherwise been working them. Fifteen of the girls were given positions in the country homes of Rhys's friends, three returned to their own homes, and two asked to remain with Polly, one as her personal maid, the other as a cook's helper. Polly once complained that her good works were going to cause her financial ruin but when Rhys offered to pay the amount she had spent on the last three girls, she refused, more than a little hurt that he believed her.

She laughed at herself then, saying she was a lady of

the evening possessed of the proverbial heart of gold. Rhys had not laughed, finding the description more accurate than Polly was wont to believe.

"I appreciate everything you've done for me," said Miss Rose. She leaned to one side and gave Rhys a kiss on his smooth cheek.

"Little enough," Rhys said. "I can name twenty young women who think of you as their guardian angel." And several pimps now serving in his Majesty's service who would be less complimentary if they knew how a period was put to their operation.

Polly glanced at the dimpled little cherubs smiling sweetly from her headboard. She groaned dramatically, placing a hand over her heart. "You wound me, sirrah. The resemblance does not bear close examination."

Rhys laughed and swung his feet off the bed. "I must be going, P.D. If you need anything you can send a message in the usual way to my townhouse. I've left orders that anything carrying the little rose is to be sent on to me at Dunnelly."

"Your staff must wonder."

"I'm certain my staff knows and they wouldn't breathe a word. Weren't they everything solicitous when you recuperated at my home?"

Polly lifted one eyebrow in disbelief. "They were scandalized!"

"But they wouldn't let any of it touch me. I trust them."

"Very well. If I have news for you I won't hesitate to send a message." She helped Rhys into his tight-fitting jacket. "How long do you expect to be at Dunnelly?"

"A week, maybe two."

"You'll talk to Kenna again?"

"She isn't going to be there. She's gone to visit her sister. At least Nick told me those were her plans when I saw him at the funeral." He looked sad for a moment, but he wasn't thinking of his father or brother. "I rather think I've ruined what could have passed as a future with Kenna." A shutter came down over his bleak features and he smiled down into Polly's worried face. "Don't give it a thought, love." He kissed her upturned nose. "Take care."

He was out the door before Polly found her voice. "God's speed, Rhys."

"I don't know if I want her, Mason," said Mrs. Miller. Elizabeth Miller had never been married but she adopted the title to discourage people from calling her Betty. She despised the nickname as common and she tenaciously resisted anything that was not of a refined nature. She had given some thought to changing her last name some years ago but her business had been so firmly established by that time and her reputation made that it seemed unnecessarily confusing. She raised her quizzing glass, an affectation she thought gave her great presence, especially since it was normally used by men, and examined the woman propped between Mason's two thugs.

"She's a veritable Amazon," she sighed, glancing swiftly from Kenna's feet to the top of her head. "Still, she has some good features. Her skin is not bad and her bosom and legs are adequate."

Mason laughed. "Not bad? Adequate? My dear Mrs. Miller, by no stretch of the imagination can this girl be considered merely adequate. She's outside the common mode and well you know it."

Mrs. Miller refused to be swayed so easily. "She's hardly a girl in her first bloom, Mason. The other side of eighteen I would think. You know it is more difficult to break the older ones."

"But think of the challenge," he needled. "And the

182

rewards. She'll earn a nice sum for you."

"Perhaps."

"If it is breaking her that is keeping you from leaping at the purchase then you should know I will be most willing to supply the drugs you need. At a very reasonable cost, I hasten to add." He extracted the small bottle of liquid he had force-fed Kenna and showed it to Mrs. Miller. "There is more where this came from. Keep her on it for thirty days and by the end of that time she'll do anything you want in order to have more."

Mrs. Miller set her quizzing glass aside and looked at Mason shrewdly. "In effect you're telling me she is no good to me without the drug, that she can't be bent without it. I don't know if I like that. It is my experience that the drugged ones do not last long. A few years, perhaps. Never more. Then they die or I have to dismiss them because they can't work."

"So?"

"So? You're asking a great deal of the ready for a girl who can only work a few years at most. Who is she anyway? Where did you find her?"

"It is unimportant." He shrugged off her answer impatiently. "Are you interested or not?"

Mrs. Miller smiled slowly, refusing to be pushed. "I want the drug free for the first thirty days. Afterward you can charge whatever you like. She will be paying then."

"Done."

"I will pay half what you ask for her now, the other half when she is broken."

"*Non.* It is all now or I will look elsewhere. Amelia's place perhaps. Or the Flower House, the one run by Miss Rose."

The mention of Miss Rose's name did not sit well with Mrs. Miller. If she hadn't thought Rhys Canning would ruin her business she would have done something about Polly Dawn and her erstwhile knight a long time ago.

183

"Don't threaten me, Mason," she said tersely. "Two-thirds now and the rest after thirty days. It is better than you deserve. Just look at her! I suppose she'll clean up well enough but her hair is outrageous. It will take the full month for me to make something stylish of it. She's been sheared like a sheep."

"A necessary precaution," Mason said, glancing in Kenna's direction. Her head lolled to one side though he could see she fought to keep it upright. The bright red-gold braid was no longer in evidence and the remainder of her hair had been cropped close to her head. "A pity Sweet's knife was not sharper, but then he hardly pretends to be a barber." He turned back to the madam. "As you wish," he conceded. "Two-thirds now and the remainder in one month."

Mrs. Miller rose from behind her desk. "Have your men take her to the attic room. The chamber on the left is vacant. I'll get your money."

Mason directed Jeb and Sweet. "You heard what she wants. Use the back stairs."

Jeb hefted Kenna over his shoulder while Sweet opened the door. When they were gone Mrs. Miller unlocked the middle drawer of her desk and counted out the payment to Mason. He attached the leather pouch of gold and silver coins to his trousers.

"As always, Mrs. Miller, it has been a pleasure doing business with you." He gave her a little salute with his cane and turned to leave.

"How quickly you forget the terms of our agreement," she chided him. "I'll take the bottle you have on you now and expect more of the same in two days."

He gave her the bottle, cautioning her about its use. "This has not been diluted. Use it judiciously and it will last you a full week. She will only require a dram now and again to keep her pliant. I will send Sweet around with more of the same strength in forty-eight hours. Toward

184

the end of the thirty days withhold it several times to gauge her reaction. As I said, I am certain she will do anything for it." He heard Jeb and Sweet lumbering down the stairs. "I believe we're ready to leave. Good evening, Mrs. Miller."

"Good evening," she said pleasantly and showed them to the door.

After they were gone she went to the main lounge and signaled two of her girls who were not entertaining clients. "Linda. Katie. We have a new arrival. She's in Angela's old room. Take a look at her and see if you can't make something presentable out of her. I'd like to be able to give our gentleman callers something to anticipate until the day she is ready."

Albert Reilly opened the door to Rhys's library and announced his purpose with an officious air. "Lord Dunne is here to see you, sir."

Rhys looked up from his reading. "Nicholas? I wonder why."

"I'm certain I could not say," Reilly responded gravely.

Rhys hid a smile at his butler's solemnity. His staff was noticeably puffed up with their own importance since they were now serving the owner of Canning Shipping. Rhys only hoped things would settle into a less formal routine in a few weeks. He set a stack of papers aside, glad to have an excuse to put down the reports he had been given on his father's shipping business. He had begun reading them out of duty to his new position and responsibilities, and had been surprised that he felt interested and challenged. It was rather unsettling. "Well, have him come in then." He got to his feet as Nicholas brushed past Reilly. "Nick! Good to see you! Though something of a surprise. Did you forget I was coming to Dunnelly?" He would have chided his friend for his poor memory but the greyish cast to Nick's face stopped him. "What is it? You look terrible!"

Nicholas drew off his gloves and threw them on the spindle-legged table near the window. "It's Kenna. She's disappeared. I think she may be dead!"

Rhys felt the color drain from his face but he managed to ask for details with deadly calm.

Nick tossed his greatcoat aside and paced the floor as he spoke. "She left yesterday morning for Yvonne's with her maid, two grooms, and a driver. It was all arranged that she should stay at Robinson's for one night before going on to Cherry Hill. She arrived there safely but some time during the night she was abducted. Mrs. Robinson became curious when Kenna did not come down for breakfast and at the request of the driver she went to investigate. Kenna's maid was injured, bashed on the head with a brick from the looks of it, and Kenna was gone."

"You saw the maid for yourself, then?"

Nick shook his head. "Not yet. One of the grooms came back to Dunnelly on Pyramid to report what happened. Mrs. Robinson sent for a physician for the maid and the driver and groom are remaining to transport her back to Dunnelly when the doctor approves." He paused in his pacing long enough to accept the drink Rhys offered him, knocking it back in one swallow. "I came here on my way to the ale house. I thought you would want to be involved and I can use your help."

"I'll have a fresh horse made ready for you," Rhys said. "As soon as I change my clothes we can be off."

Nick nodded and his shoulders visibly straightened as he thought he would not have to face the ordeal alone. He put his hands in his jacket pockets to hide their trembling. His fingers touched something and he pulled it out. "Here, this is for you. I've been carrying it around since before the funerel. Forgot to give it to you."

Rhys took the paper, his brows lifted in question. "What is it?"

"That guest list you wanted from the night of the masque. Victorine drew it up. I really haven't looked at it myself."

Rhys merely glanced at it then tossed it aside. "The significance of it is as nothing if we cannot find Kenna."

Nick did not like hearing the words but he knew the possibility at least must be faced. He gathered his coat and gloves and followed Rhys out of the library.

Their horses were lathered by the time they reached the ale house some thirty miles north of London. Mrs. Robinson ushered them in and took them to Janet's room.

"My husband's beside himself with worry," she said as she opened the door. "Took to his bed right after we discovered that the young lady was gone. His heart's not good; don't know what's to become of him. Nothing like this has ever happened in our inn before."

"Ease yourself, Mrs. Robinson," Rhys said to her as Nick crossed the room to Janet's side. "His lordship doesn't hold you to blame."

Nick examined the livid mark on Janet's temple and spoke her name softly. When there was no reply he stepped away, shaking his head. "It's no use. She can't tell us anything now, perhaps not even when she's recovered." He turned to Mrs. Robinson. "Do you keep a ledger of sorts? Something that will tell us who stayed here last night?"

"I have it downstairs. There was a stage on its way to London. Six passengers in all. I put them three to a room." She continued on about the other guests as Rhys and Nick followed her downstairs. She gave the ledger to Nick then went behind the bar and drew them both a pint of ale.

Rhys asked for paper and pen to copy the names and she told him to tear out the page. He pointed to the first six names on the list. "These are from the stage?"

Mrs. Robinson tilted her head to see the writing. "No. The first three are that family I was telling you about. The widower and his two lads. They were gone at first light, headin' for Scotland."

"You saw them leave?"

"I did. They had but two horses between them. The boys rode together. Her ladyship was definitely not there."

"What of the next three names?" asked Nick.

"Well, Jeb Thompson and Jake Sweet came in together. But after they drank away their funds they didn't have the ready to get a room here. Slept out in the stables, the pair of them. I can tell you I was glad of that. I didn't want them muddying up my linens. Neither had taken a bath in a sennight as near as I could tell."

Rhys listened patiently. "Did they have breakfast before they left?"

"No. I think your grooms mentioned they were gone at sunup." She pointed a work-hardened finger at the name directly below Sweet's. "Now this gentleman came a while later. About an hour before the stage and her ladyship arrived. He was quiet, well-mannered, not like some of the quality we get in here, lookin' down their nose at everyone and fixin' to raise a little hell." She blushed to the roots of her dark hair as she remembered who she was speaking to. "Forgive my bluntness. Present company excluded, naturally."

"Naturally," Nick said dryly. "Was this," he looked at the name again, "Deverell person here for breakfast? Rhys, look at this. I can't make out the first initial. Is it an em?"

"It appears to be."

Mrs. Robinson agreed happily. "Such fine handwriting, don't you think? Yes, he was here for breakfast. Departed right before the stage."

"Did he have a conveyance of some sort or was he riding a mount?" asked Nick.

"He had a roan colored horse."

"Tell us about the people on the stage."

The proprietress did so in great detail. "I know your sister wasn't on that stage, m'lord. My husband helped load the baggage himself and saw them off."

Nick sighed heavily. "That pretty much narrows it to Thompson and Sweet, don't you think, Rhys?"

"It would appear so since Mrs. Robinson saw everyone else take their leave. What about your other customers, the ones who didn't spend the night?"

"I can give you their names, but I'll vouch for everyone of them. They'd not be involved in this havey-cavey affair. Besides, they left last night when I locked everything up. You can see the doors yourself. Nothing was jimmied or forced. Everything was right and tight when I opened up this morning. No one broke in here."

"Which means one of your guests was responsible," Nick said. "That rather puts a hole in the theory concerning this pair." He pointed to the names of Thompson and Sweet.

"Not necessarily." Rhys tore out the page and pocketed it, pulling Nick away from the bar so they could talk in private. "We know Kenna did not leave with anyone else this morning. Isn't it possible that someone allowed those two in? They took Kenna and left while their accomplice had a leisurely breakfast and departed, perhaps on the stage."

"But that would make this no simple abduction. From the woman's description of those two I was willing to believe this scheme began as a whim. An accomplice would make it premeditated."

"Precisely," Rhys agreed. "How many people knew of

189

Kenna's plans?"

"Who didn't would be easier to answer. It was no secret that she was going to Cherry Hill nor that she was going to be here for the night. I provided pistols for her escorts but not because I suspected trouble of this nature. I did caution Janet that Kenna was not to be out of her sight and you can see where that led."

"All right," Rhys said gently. "There is no need to blame yourself. So everyone knew where Kenna would be. This couldn't be anticipated. I urged her myself to visit Yvonne."

"So did I," Nick acknowledged bleakly. "Victorine was the one who didn't want her to go. Damn! I should have forced Kenna's hand when I had the chance."

"No more recriminations. I think we should start with the men on the stage. They slept three to a room and their alibis will be the easiest to verify. With some help from Powell and a few friends we should be able to locate them and discern something of the truth for ourselves."

"What about Thompson and Sweet?"

"They won't be so easy to find. We must start where we can, by eliminating all the others. Including Deverell. And I haven't forgotten the widower," he said as Nick began to speak. "It's entirely possible that his purpose was a mother for his children and his destination is Gretna Green."

Nick paled at the reference to the Scottish border town where eloping couples could be married. "Kenna would not stand for it!"

"I doubt she will be given any choice."

Though they began their search with a fair amount of optimism, by week's end it had disappeared. A likeness of Kenna was printed in the *Gazette* and leaflets were distributed throughout London. Some of the stage riders stepped forward before they were located by Rhys and Nick, saying they remembered Kenna, but were of no further use than that. Worse, they were as certain as they could be that no one had left their respective rooms. Sleeping three to a bed did not make for a particularly restful night, but neither had they heard anything out of the ordinary. The widower had no one with him save his two sons when he was stopped short of entering Scotland and he had no information about Thompson and Sweet that Mrs. Robinson had not already offered.

Of Deverell there was no news. Since he did not come forward as a gentleman would, Nick tried him in his own mind and found him guilty. Rhys thought it more likely that he was simply no longer in the country. When Janet Gourley recovered enough to talk she sided with Rhys. Deverell was too fine a man to have anything to do with Kenna's disappearance, but she would lay her life's wages that Thompson and Sweet were involved.

On the eighth day of their search, very close to the same time a package was being delivered to Dunnelly Manor, investigators from Bow Street brought some news to Nick at Rhys's residence. Jeb Thompson and Jake Sweet had been found . . . belly up in the Thames with their throats slit. They were going to drag the river for Kenna's body.

Three days later, with no results forthcoming, Rhys accompanied Nicholas back to Dunnelly.

Henderson met the weary riders at the door. "Very good you're home, m'lord. And you, Mr. Canning. Lady Dunne expressed her wish to see you immediately upon your arrival."

"My stepmother will have to wait, Henderson. I wish to soak the grime from my body and the cobwebs from my head."

"She was really most insistent, your lordship," Henderson added somewhat diffidently seeing the shadows beneath Nick's eyes and the drawn face of his companion.

"She can—" He halted abruptly as he saw for the first time the black armband his head of staff was wearing.

Rhys saw the direction of Nick's gaze and stepped in front of his friend just in time to keep him from lifting Henderson off the floor and shaking him.

"Why are you wearing that thing?" Nick cried out, his face livid. "She's not dead! Do you hear? She's not dead!"

"It was Lady Dunne's orders three days ago, m'lord," the butler replied, visibly shaken by his employer's wrath. "A package arrived and she opened it. Went straight to her chamber then and hasn't come out since. The only word we had from her was to observe mourning and that you come to see her immediately upon your return."

"I shall get to the bottom of this matter, by God," said Nick, taking the stairs two and three at a time, Rhys on his heels.

Nick shrugged off Rhys's restraining hand and flung open the door to Victorine's room. "I demand to know why you have given orders to the staff to observe mourning!"

Rhys stepped around Nick and went to Victorine's bedside. "Nick. You must see Victorine is in no state to be badgered."

Nick flushed a trifle guiltily as he looked at his stepmother. She had lost a full stone's weight since he had last seen her. Her cheeks were sunken and her eyelids were swollen and puffy from crying. Victorine's skin, always pale, was now nearly translucent, and her hair was dull and matted.

She patted Rhys's hand. "It's all right. Nicky is hurt as I am." She pointed to the box lying atop her cherrywood secretary. "Over there. It came a few days ago, addressed simply to the manor. I opened it. Dear God, I wish I had not!"

Nick went to the desk and lifted the lid of the nondescript box. He swore harshly and his hand trembled as he reached inside.

"Nick?" asked Rhys. "What is it?"

Nick lifted his hand and thrust what he held in Rhys's direction. "Kenna's hair. Those bastards cut my sister's hair!"

Rhys blanched at the sight of Kenna's red-gold braid swinging like a rope from Nick's fist.

Nick dropped the length of hair back in the box and sat down in the delicate chair beside the desk, his head in his hands. "It's over, Rhys. She's dead."

Rhys slammed his fist into wall above Victorine's bed, not feeling the pain or seeing the blood on his knuckles. "It's her hair, Nick! Her hair! Not her body! She's not dead!" He hesitated, his voice softening. "I would feel it. I know I would."

"Well, I *do* feel it! Just as Victorine does. Why would this be sent to us if she were not dead?"

Rhys had no answer. He walked to the window and stared out, straight into the late afternoon sun.

"You may as well return to London, Rhys," said Nick heavily. "There is nothing more to be done here."

In the end Rhys stayed on another ten days, grieving in the solitude of his room, offering what little comfort he could to Victorine and Nicholas. The news of Kenna's death reached London and was discussed in every conceivable social circle until it was replaced by news of a more threatening nature.

On March 1 Napoleon had escaped Elba.

Chapter Five

"Please," Kenna begged, holding out her hand to take the bottle from Mrs. Miller. "A little more."

Elizabeth Miller appeared to consider the request then shook her head, dropping the bottle into her apron pocket. "You've had enough for one morning, deary." A sly smile touched her thin mouth as she turned to go.

Kenna's pleading expression changed to one of stark hunger and hatred. Her craving was so great she was able to shrug off the languor that had kept her pliant and biddable during the last several weeks. She scrambled off the bed before Mrs. Miller had left the room and lunged at the woman, knocking her against the door and slamming it shut.

Kenna clawed at the madam's apron, tearing the pocket while Mrs. Miller screamed for help. Kenna lost interest in Mrs. Miller as soon as the bottle fell out of her pocket and dropped to the floor. Both women lunged at the same time, but Kenna came up with it and held it triumphantly over her head out of the madam's reach. Laughing somewhat hysterically as Mrs. Miller tried to drag her arms down, she uncorked the vial and tipped some of the liquid into her mouth. Most of it fell on her lips and chin but Kenna licked it eagerly with the tip of her tongue, the bitter taste of it bothering her not at all.

"Little bitch," Mrs. Miller swore as she managed to pry open Kenna's fingers and take the bottle from her hand. "We'll see who's laughing tomorrow when there's none at all for you."

But Kenna didn't care any more, smiling dreamily as she waited a few minutes for the potion to complete its work. Tomorrow would take care of itself. This moment, this feeling, was the only thing that mattered.

There was a rush of noise on the stairs and in the hallway and the door to Kenna's chamber was flung open.

"You took your own sweet time getting here," Mrs. Miller said nastily, observing the brawny footman's disheveled state with some distaste. "It's over now, as you can see for yourself." Kenna had dropped back on the bed, knees folded into her chest. She was smiling serenely. "Give her a few more minutes then tie her to the bed. I won't have her scratching and clawing at my girls when they come to prepare her. I have a young lord who has expressed an interest in seeing Diana this evening." Mrs. Miller swept out of the room, straightening her disarrayed coiffure. "In a few days I think she'll be most anxious to please him."

Kenna made not the slightest protest when the footman bound her wrists to the brass headboard with silk scarves, nor was there a murmur later when Linda and Katie came to style her hair, apply creams and rouge to her face and the tips of her breasts, and dress her in a whisper of silk that passed for a nightgown. She never noticed their pitying looks as they washed her or understood their comments that her fair skin might never recover after the visit from young Lord Tremont. Kenna merely accepted their attention quietly, content to stay in her world of drifting color and light.

"If you'll come this way, m'lord," Mrs. Miller said,

ushering Tremont up the narrow staircase to the top story of her establishment. "I'm confident our Diana is everything you could want."

He smiled faintly but none of it reached his eyes as they narrowed on the madam's back. "I've been disappointed before. Even you have shown me girls who could not address my needs." His quirt bumped gently against his thigh. "Tell me about Diana."

"She's been named after the goddess of the hunt, m'lord. A young woman of rare beauty and spirit."

"It is the latter in which I am most interested."

Mrs. Miller cleared her throat uneasily as she opened the door to Kenna's chamber. "You will find her a trifle lacking in it this evening. It is only a preview after all. If you should choose her, I can assure you, you will not be disappointed."

Tremont's thin lower lip quivered slightly as he looked past the madam's shoulder to the young woman bound to the bed. Her pale, shapely arms had been extended over her head and she lay in an attitude of supplication and submission. Short mahogany curls framed her face but her finely arched brows were of a lighter hue. Her dark eyes, fringed with ebony lashes, were open but unfocused. Her cheeks were flushed with color and her mouth was slightly parted, damp, as if she had just swept her tongue across it. Her breasts were plainly visible through the silk of her gown and it had been arranged to tie over one shoulder, baring the other, in the fashion Diana herself might have worn. A belt of beaten gold outlined the smallness of her waist and the gentle swell of her hips.

Tremont brushed past Mrs. Miller and walked slowly to the bed. Using the tip of his quirt he caught the hem of her gown and edged it over her ankles and calves. The silk became trapped at her knees but he had seen enough. He lifted the quirt and stroked Kenna's neck, her bare shoulder, and passed it lightly over the tip of her breast..

197

She made a little moué and tried to shift away from the feather-light touch. "Tickles," she murmured, her lips barely moving.

"Does it, m'dear?" Tremont's thin wrist gave an expert flick and the quirt's braided leather lash struck Kenna's hip sharply.

Kenna moaned and turned to the other side, biting her lip. The quirt descended again, this time on her thigh. Her protest was a soft mewling sound as tears sprang to her eyes.

Satisfied, Tremont backed away from the bed and addressed the madam. "She is no good to me so heavily drugged," he said, tapping his quirt against a small dressing table.

"I said this was but a preview. If she is as you desire I will have her sedated less."

"I want to hear her scream," he went on impatiently, whining much like a child. A lock of his fair hair fell on his forehead and he brushed it aside with a jerky motion.

Mrs. Miller strove to placate him, wearing her most ingratiating smile. "It will be as you wish, m'lord. I can have a private room prepared so the other gentlemen will not be disturbed and you may use Diana at your leisure."

"Very well," he said sulkily, glancing at Kenna again. "She's very tall, isn't she?"

The madam knew that young Tremont was sensitive about his height, or rather the lack of it. She trod very carefully. "I thought it would please you to master one such as she. Your skill is well known."

Tremont's chest puffed a little. "Yes. It will please me. Your Diana presents a certain challenge."

Mrs. Miller nodded eagerly. "Then I can expect you in three days?"

"So long?" he pouted.

"Only if you want to hear her scream," she reminded him.

He wet his lips and ceased tapping the quirt. "Very well. In three days." Tremont gave Kenna one last look before he exited the room.

Mrs. Miller paused before she closed the door. "Three days, Diana. You'll be sorry you ever crossed me."

Polly Dawn Rose fingered her water glass thoughtfully as she looked at the pinched and unsmiling faces of the eight women seated at her dining table. "Ladies," she said, tapping a spoon against her china plate. "Whatever is wrong? From the sad looks surrounding me I could well suspect someone was getting married." The attempt at teasing brought only a glimmer of response. She put down the spoon. "I insist you tell me what these long faces are about. We open our doors in but two hours and our clients pay well enough for our gaiety and not a halfpence for out troubles." Polly turned to the young woman on her left. "Sheila. You begin."

"It's about the new girl at Mrs. Miller's, P.D."

Polly sighed. "Her again. I thought it was settled. There is nothing I can do for her. Nor any of you," she added pointedly.

"You did ask," Sheila answered, pushing away her plate.

Polly watched as the other girls did the same, mutinous expressions on their faces. "Really, ladies. What is it you think we can do?"

At that moment the kitchen assistant set down a dish of hot peas in front of Polly. Hard. Some of the peas bounced out of the dish and rolled across the white table cloth. There were a few snickers along the table but they ceased as the young girl spoke up somewhat defiantly. "We think we can get her out of there, Miss Rose. Same as you helped me."

"It is hardly the same thing at all," Polly answered,

striving for calm. "You were brought here for purchase. She, on the other hand, was not. I help those I can but helping this girl is something else again."

At the far end of the table Loreta spoke up, tossing back her long black mane of hair. "I talked with Katie in the park this afternoon. Diana, that's what Mrs. Miller's named this girl, is going to be Lord Tremont's property tonight! You know what will happen to her, P.D.!"

"I've heard she's been drugged since she got there," Sheila added. "Even those witches at Betty's have some compassion for her. They say she won't survive Tremont. Betty's made him wait three days to have her. He'll be savage by the time he takes Diana."

Polly's hands twisted in her lap. She knew Tremont's requirements, having nursed two girls who felt the sting and slash of his crop when she was still working at Mrs. Miller's. She had counted herself among the fortunate that he never found her to his tastes. He was a young pup then, bent on proving himself someone to be reckoned with. And because he had not matured one whit, at Polly's own house he was barred from the door. "Betty's girls may be compassionate, but are they willing to help? Have any of them lifted a finger to get Diana out of that house?" Silence greeted her and several heads dropped to study the pattern in the white linen tablecloth. "As I thought. What, then, can we do?"

"We thought . . . perhaps . . . Mr. Canning would help," one of them ventured meekly.

Polly would not even consider it. "He has had enough laid at his door these past weeks. I cannot ask him. The woman who was murdered, Lady Kenna Dunne, was a close friend of his." A murmur of shock greeted her announcement.

"We didn't know," Sheila said softly.

Polly patted Sheila's hand. "I know you didn't. And this latest business with Napoleon. Well, you can imagine how he's taken it. Fighting so long on the Peninsula, and for what?" She pushed away from the table and stood up, tossing her napkin on her plate. "If it's help you want to offer Diana then we must come upon a plan ourselves."

"We?" Loreta asked uncertainly.

"Yes, we. All of you and me," she said staunchly as if there had never been any question. "And, everything considered, we don't have much time."

Kenna's hands trembled as Linda fussed with her hair and made nervous cooing sounds when she patted down curls. The face that was reflected in the glass was not her own, she thought somewhat fuzzily. Her cheeks were not so red, nor her lips. Her hair was darker and shorter than she remembered and her eyelids were painted a light blue. There was a chill in the room and her rouged nipples pressed provocatively against the gossamer gown she had been forced to put on. Beneath it was only her flesh and she felt as naked with the clothing as she had without it.

"I can't do this," she said, though in truth she hadn't any clear expectation of what was required of her. Mrs. Miller had explained it to her several times over the last three days, always holding the precious bottle at arm's length and giving Kenna just a taste before she whisked from the room.

Linda laid a comforting hand on Kenna's bare shoulder. "Of course you can," she said though the words stuck in her throat. "You want more of your medicine, don't you?"

Kenna nodded, touching her fingers to her temples, trying to still the throbbing so she could think. "I want it now," she said petulantly. "I need it. I don't feel well."

Linda knew that was certainly true. In the afternoon

201

Kenna had had severe cramping and a bout of nausea that dropped her to her knees. Mrs. Miller had been forced to give Kenna more of the drug than was her desire to keep the sickness of withdrawal at bay. Linda urged Kenna to her feet. "Over here, Diana. On the bed."

Kenna stumbled a little as they crossed the floor. "Don't call me Diana. 'S not my name."

"Of course it's not," Linda replied easily. "And Linda's not mine. We don't use our given names here unless they're very pretty."

"Oh." The explanation satisfied Kenna.

"That's it. Lie down." Linda arranged Kenna's gown prettily. The skirt had been split so the length of one bare leg could be seen.

Kenna fingered the soft material, little knowing in hours it would be in shreds about her body. "'S very nice."

"Yes. It is."

Katie came in the room somewhat breathless from her run up the stairs. She glanced about the walls, padded with heavy tapestries and grimaced. "God, how I hate this room! Mrs. Miller wants to know if Diana's ready. She's fairly frothing at the mouth to let Tremont at her. Diana shouldn't have attacked her."

"I hardly think she knew what she was doing." Linda bound Kenna's wrists together and tied them overhead. "Is that bastard waiting for her?"

"He hasn't arrived yet. Come on, let's leave here."

Linda bent over Kenna and brushed her forehead with her mouth. "I'm sorry. Forgive me."

Kenna smiled a trifle dreamily and said nothing at all.

Linda and Katie could not leave the chamber quickly enough. They nearly collided with the madam in the hallway.

"Everything is in readiness, girls?" They nodded simultaneously. "Good. His lordship will be here any moment. In fact, he's a little late. No matter, he's paying dearly for this evening. Everything I paid for our stubborn Amazon and more besides. Even if she doesn't make it through this evening I've recouped my loss." And my pride, she thought, paying no attention to the whitely drawn faces of her girls.

Linda and Katie exchanged pained glances. Mrs. Miller was as good as giving license to Tremont to kill Diana. The knowledge weighed heavily upon them but they were helpless.

Mrs. Miller opened her mouth to speak again when a commotion below stairs drew her attention. "What in God's name is going on down there?" She hurried to the top of the stairs and what she saw taking place in her drawing room had her rushing down them.

Katie and Linda bumped into her when she stopped abruptly at the foot of the stairs and she had to grasp the newel post to keep her balance. One of her carefully arranged curls came loose from the pins and flopped against her ear.

"She looks much like a basset hound I once had, don't you think, Lord Tremont?" Polly asked gaily, nudging the ribs of her companion. "That poor dog had but one ear also."

Lord Tremont chuckled appreciatively, leaning heavily on Polly's arm. Surrounding him were six other girls from the Flower House, all in a state of attractive dishabille in spite of the cold temperature outside. "Let down t'other curl, Betty, and you'll look like the basset *I* once had!"

Mrs. Miller cringed visibly at the familiar use of her name. She stamped her foot hard against the step, demanding quiet, and received for her efforts another gale of laughter as a sausage curl fell over her other ear. The humiliation was not to be borne. "What are *you* doing here?" she demanded, glaring at Polly.

Polly's eyes widened innocently as some of Mrs. Miller's customers deserted the corners of the room to be part of the revelry. They gathered around Polly's girls and were greeted with a great deal of billing and cooing. "Yer 'eart, Betty. Think of yer 'eart. We was only 'aving a bit o' fun with 'is lordship. Weren't we, luv? Quite lost his way, he did. The poor dear."

"Didn't," Lord Tremont said, lifting a glass of scotch to his lips.

"*Did*," Polly insisted sweetly between clenched teeth.

"S'all right. I did."

"There, you see, Betty, he did lose his way." She dropped her accent and picked up her aitches. "Quite thought my house was yours. Though how he could make such a mistake doesn't bear thinking. I shall have to do something about the trim and the fence. Look, I've brought him back to you. I wouldn't want you to think I was stealing your business."

"He's foxed," said Mrs. Miller tersely.

The young lord agreed. "Quite."

"I'm afraid he arrived this way, which possibly accounts for his confusion in the matter of establishments. He kept insisting he had an appointment with a young goddess."

"Diana," offered Tremont helpfully, taking an unsteady step toward the stairs. "Want to see Diana."

"Since I don't have anyone by that name I assumed he meant to come here. Have I the right place?"

"Yes," Mrs. Miller bit out. "Katie. Linda. Help his lordship upstairs. Get out of here, Polly. You're not welcome."

"Oh." She feigned disappointment. "How cruel of you. And after I extended myself." She waved to her girls. "I must be going, ladies. Don't be late."

"And take them with you."

Polly's ladies voiced their objections loudly, wrapping

204

their arms around the gentlemen within their reach.

"Girls!" Polly admonished them sternly. "Don't be greedy. You are not without your own guests this evening. They are bound to feel neglected by now."

With varying degrees of reluctance the girls let go of their gentleman friends and followed Polly out the door. The last thing any of them saw was Mrs. Miller hurrying up the stairs to assist the poor efforts of Linda and Katie as they attempted to help Lord Tremont make his drunken climb.

After waving away Tremont's driver, it was a silent group of partially clad women who walked briskly down the street toward their own home. There were no congratulations and none of them dared voice the question as to whether they were in order. They all were thinking along the same lines. Had they given enough time to Sheila and Loreta? What if they hadn't been able to come in the back entrance? Had they even found Diana, and if so, had she been cooperative?

The house was as silent as they were when they walked in. In spite of what Polly said there were no gentlemen waiting for their return. She had closed her house for the evening to entertain one guest.

A faint smile lifted the corners of her mouth as she remembered how overwhelmed Tremont and his driver had been when her girls diverted his barouche. The driver had offered only a token resistance after two of her ladies flagged him down and clambered aboard. Tremont had been harder to convince but four lovelies climbing in his carriage and all over him helped him see reason. Polly could see his mind spinning, thinking what harm would there be in a few drinks with these girls. They clearly had whetted his appetite as they allowed him to tease them with his quirt. Her smile faded as she pushed the door open to the kitchen, hoping it had not been for nothing.

Apparently it had not. The girls dogging her heels

gasped as they saw the state of the usually pristine kitchen and scullery. A keg of flour had been overturned and the white powder dusted the floor and the table. A bucket of water had been spilled, mixed with some of the flour, and gooey footprints led into the pantry. Dishes were broken. Three pots and a kettle littered the floor. The cook's chair was lying on its side.

Sheila was hopping on one foot, nursing a cut on the other and Loreta had her shoulder to the pantry door, bracing herself against it to keep it closed. She saw Polly and the others and pointed to the door, motioning to the noise inside. "She's in there."

Polly nodded and took command briskly. "Amanda, see to Sheila's foot. Pam, you and Renata, start to clean up this mess. We have to get Diana out of the pantry soon, before Betty comes looking for her. Deborah, get some linens from the closet and make a room for her of sorts in that large cupboard in your chamber. Pad it well. We'll hide her there until Betty's done with her search. The rest of you, prepare for battle."

"She was no trouble at all, quite docile in fact, until we got her outside in the cold. Then there was no controlling her. Sheila gave her a clip on the jaw and that settled her some, enough for us to drag her here anyway. The trouble began again when we were inside. She wants to go back for her medicine, she says."

Polly glanced over her shoulder. "One of you get the potion we laced Tremont's drink with. It will have to do for now. Hurry. We've got to bribe her with something. Step away from the door, Loreta."

As soon as she did so, Kenna, who was on her knees on the other side, fists raised against the door, fell forward. Momentarily stunned, she shook her head weakly and looked up. The number of faces staring down at her completed her disorientation and she began keening softly, curling into a ball to ease the cramping inside her.

206

"Poor thing's all but worn out," Polly said. "Let's take her upstairs while we can."

It was awkward carrying Kenna through the kitchen which had not completely been restored to order but they managed it. She was taken to Deborah's room on the second story and deposited on the bed. Polly took the vial of liquid when it was handed to her and showed it to Kenna.

"Just a little to help you sleep, Diana, until it is safe again. There's time enough to rid your body of this wicked stuff." She touched the tip of the bottle to Kenna's lips and measured the dose carefully. "That's enough, child."

Kenna moaned as the bottle was taken away but her tongue felt thick in her mouth and she could not form the words to ask for more.

"As soon as she's sleeping put her in the cupboard, pack some linens in front of her and lock it. We'll hope Betty does not investigate but if she does then we'll pray Diana does not make a shambles of her hiding place."

Mrs. Miller's arrival was not long in coming and though she railed at Polly, swore she would ruin her, and searched the Flower House with the aid of her footman and two of her girls, in the end she had to admit defeat. Polly considered her own performance as the wronged innocent in this affair to be worthy of Covent Garden—she had been truly magnificent and her supporting players no less so!

Polly pulled Mrs. Miller to one side as she was making ready to leave. "What has Tremont to say about the missing Diana?"

"That young sot doesn't even know. He passed out on the bed."

"Has he paid you for Diana's company?"

Mrs. Miller nodded, her eyes narrowing on Polly. "Handsomely. It was arranged days ago."

"Then you have lost nothing, have you?"

"But he'll demand his payment and if I want to keep my house open I'll have to give it to him."

"Not if he thinks he's had her." She smiled wickedly. "Tell him he whipped her to death. He'd like to believe that. No one need ever know your girl escaped . . . on her own, naturally."

"Naturally." Mrs. Miller pulled her cloak about her and stomped out the door followed by her retinue.

Rhys cushioned his head behind his arms and stretched out on Polly's bed. Polly sat at his side, brushing back a few strands of dark hair that had feathered his forehead. She frowned, noting his haggard appearance, the rough growth of beard he had not bothered to shave. His eyes had a bruised, vacant look and there were lines about his mouth that had not been there before.

He closed his eyes at the gentle touch of her hand. "You should come with me to America, P.D."

She teased to keep the tears in her own eyes at bay. "Wot? 'Ave they a shortage of 'ores there?"

Rhys held her wrist, keeping her cupped hand on his face. "Come as my wife, Polly."

"You're daft!"

"No!" His eyes opened and his expression was earnest. "Marry me, Polly, no one will ever know what you were here."

"It's what I am, Rhys, darling." Her tears spilled over. "There's no changing it. I'm doing what I want. Can you never accept that?"

"Can you never accept that it is possible to change?"

"If I wanted to," she said gently. "But I don't." She drew her hand back and wiped her eyes. "You honor me, Rhys. More than I can say, but it is better if I don't take you too seriously. We'd both be bitterly hurt in the end."

"I love you, P.D."

She sniffed. "I know you do. But not like you loved her. And that's the only kind of love that could change my life." She bent over him and kissed the single tear that trickled down his temple. Before he could hold her to him and she could take back her refusal Polly moved off the bed and sat at her vanity. "So when do you leave?"

"In three days. I've put it off as long as I could. I received another packet of letters in yesterday's post, asking when I was returning to take over the property and the business. The lawyer's hands are powerless to dispose of anything or make any changes without my approval. What do I know of shipping? I'm a soldier!"

"Aah," she said knowingly. "You're frightened."

"You have your countrymen's gift of understatement. Bluntly put, I am bloody well terrified." He drew in a deep breath. "I'm expected to put my father's shipping concern back in order after it's been made a shambles by that stupid war."

"To which stupid war are you referring?"

"The one the Americans call the War of 1812," he said impatiently. "The one that just ended in December and they were still fighting it in New Orleans in January. That stupid war! President Madison's embargoes ruined trade in New England and now I'm to make it right again. I doubt a tenth of the Americans are even aware that Napoleon's in Paris now, amassing his army. For them it is back to their shops and businesses and their peculiar notions of free trade. How free will their trade be if they are only dealing with Napoleon?"

"Then it's up to you to explain it to them," Polly said reasonably, unruffled by Rhys's tone. "And you cannot do it from London. You're an American after all. They might listen to one of their own."

Rhys was not convinced. "They may not accept me.

My own father didn't."

"Your father was a fool. Until now I thought you had nothing in common. But here you are, judging your own people without proof, and damning your own abilities without making any attempt to discover the breadth of them."

Rhys turned on his side and smiled a trifle sheepishly. "Are you certain you won't marry me?"

Polly fluttered her lashes playfully. "Me, sir? You'd not get a welcome reception with me dangling from your arm. Better you should find a sturdy young American lass." She would have expanded on her theme, describing the attributes his intended should possess, but a shrill scream from down the hall interrupted her. Polly's hand flew to her throat and she stood up.

Rhys stiffened at the cry and jumped off the bed. "What was that?"

"It's Diana, the one I sent a message about."

"I received no message, unless I overlooked it."

"No matter." She rushed into the hall and explained as she went. "Can you help us with her? We stole her from Betty before Tremont could use her and we haven't been able to free her from the drugs yet. We've only had two days with her, but it's going very slowly. She has terrible nightmares and . . ." She threw open the door to Kenna's chamber and ceased to talk.

Kenna's hands had been wrapped in thick batting to keep her from scratching her face or hurting those who assisted her. At the moment she was trying to wrest the bottle from Sheila who had her hand in Kenna's short curls and was attempting to pull her away.

Rhys stood in the doorway, paralyzed. He watched as if outside of himself, incapable of movement or thought. The bottle was squeezed from Sheila's fingers and flew in an arc across the room, splintering against the floor. Kenna screamed as its precious contents flowed outward

210

and she pulled away from Sheila, dropped to her knees, and began dipping her wrapped hands in the wetness then sucking on the ends greedily, never minding the shards of glass that cut her lips.

Polly and Sheila moved at the same time to pull Kenna back but Rhys reached her first, slapping her hands away from her mouth then gripping her wrists and yanking her to her feet. Kenna pounded on his chest and shoulders and when that brought no results she folded like a rag doll in his arms and began weeping.

"Sheila," said Rhys as he held Kenna tightly to him. "Polly and I can take care of her now. She's exhausted herself."

Sheila hesitated until Polly motioned to her that it was indeed all right to leave.

When Sheila was gone Rhys lifted Kenna in his arms and carried her to the bed. When he laid her on it she immediately curled in a ball, her eyes tightly shut while tears squeezed through her lashes. Rhys touched the beads of perspiration on her forehead and asked Polly for a cool, damp cloth. He wiped Kenna's face and throat gently then laid the cloth across her brow.

"You know her, don't you?" asked Polly. "I can tell."

"This is Kenna Dunne." Very carefully, as if she were as delicate as crystal, Rhys helped Kenna unfold her cramping body. He drew up the blanket from the foot of the bed and covered her, then rubbed her abdomen in slow, soothing circles with the palm of his hand.

Polly's eyes became even rounder in astonishment. "Good Lord."

"Exactly. Her hair's been shorn and the color changed, but this undoubtedly is Kenna. Tell me again how she came to be here."

Polly told him everything of Kenna's rescue from Mrs. Miller's while Rhys listened, giving nothing away of his thoughts.

211

Kenna's piteous weeping had stopped and Rhys realized she had fallen asleep. "She didn't recognize me."

"It's to be expected," Polly assured him. "She had only one thing on her mind—her medicine, as she was taught to call it. She doesn't know what is happening to her. She leaps at shadows and cowers from things only she can see. She can be quiet or violent by turns. The poor dear can't help herself. It will take time, Rhys."

"How much?"

"Weeks, perhaps months. Mrs. Miller used a heavy hand when she applied the drug. It might have killed her."

"She's out of danger now, isn't she?"

"I think so. With proper care and eventually some cooperation on her part, she will be fine."

Rhys stood up, pacing the floor as he came to a decision. "I'm taking her with me, Polly. To Boston. She'll have those weeks she needs to recover on board ship."

"Oh, Rhys, how can you do that? Shouldn't she go to Dunnelly? What of her family?"

Rhys shook his head quickly. "You don't understand. She's safer with me. Someone at Dunnelly has been trying to kill her. There is no one I can trust. No one."

"Surely her brother . . ."

"No one," he repeated. "I can be certain of nothing any more. Everyone thinks she is dead. If I tell them otherwise there may very well be another attempt on her life. I must go to the United States, Polly, and I can't protect her with an ocean between us. I couldn't do it when she was nearly in my pocket. I have to take Kenna out of England."

"It seems so cruel to her family," Polly said softly.

"It would be cruel to Kenna if I left her behind."

Polly nodded. "I understand."

"You must never mention what I'm going to do to anyone."

"I wouldn't," she gasped, hurt by his lack of trust.

"I'm sorry, but not even your girls can know. They must think Diana died. It is the only way to insure her safety. You will be the only person left in England who knows where she is. It has to be that way."

"How will we get her out of here? And where will she go until you're ready to leave? You can't take her to your townhouse if you want this kept secret."

"No, you're right. But the ship I am taking to Boston is one of my father's . . . one of mine now, I suppose. I can put her aboard the evening before I sail. The crew will not know who she is."

"Suppose she tells them?"

Rhys was skeptical. "Do you really think in two more days she'll be able to tell them anything?"

Polly understood his reasoning. "Probably not."

"Then it's settled." He kissed Polly affectionately on the lips. "Can we go to your room? I'd like you to explain everything I must do to assist her recovery."

Later that afternoon, armed with Polly's instructions if not her whole-hearted blessing, Rhys began scouring the London shops for the things Kenna would need on the voyage. Clothing was difficult to find. The modistes were anxious to please and nodded gleefully as Rhys described Kenna's figure. Yes, they had something that would fit such a svelte woman they said. Then Rhys described her height and they blanched. At the end of a long day he had but three changes of clothes for her. To supplement her wardrobe and help her pass the time when she was well, Rhys purchased yards of material. The modistes smiled happily as he chose bolts of silks and satins, velvets and wools, in colors that would compliment Kenna's fair complexion and her red-gold hair when the dye had faded. He picked out a book that pictured the latest fashions and added ribbons, lace, needles, and threads of every conceivable color. He chose stockings and chemises, beautifully fashioned kid slippers and walking shoes, riding boots, shawls, nightgowns and a redingote trimmed with sable, perfect for the cold ocean voyage.

He bought books he thought she would enjoy in the event she wanted nothing to do with him and a chess set in the event she did. He had everything placed in trunks and sent to the *Carasea*. Exhausted from his tour of London shops, Rhys returned to his townhouse and slept better that night than he had in months.

He visited the Flower House the following day and stayed with Kenna until after midnight. He bathed and fed her, read to her from the *Gazette*, and told her stories from his own imagination. He fought with her, swore at her, and cried when she did. He held her in his arms and stroked her back, teased her curls, and paced the floor when she slept. He thought he had been through everything with her but when he returned in the morning he discovered he had underestimated Kenna Dunne.

Rhys carefully measured out a teaspoon of the drug and pocketed the bottle inside his jacket before he brought the liquid to Kenna's lips. He wished he could simply give her none of it but when he suggested it to Polly she cautioned him against that plan. She had no experience with anything but gradual withdrawal and she did not know what would happen. Polly had unwrapped Kenna's hands as she had become less violent and they trembled now as Rhys brought the liquid to her lips. She grabbed his wrists to make certain he wouldn't withdraw the spoon before she had licked every drop, then she fell back on the pillow and waited for the drift of sweet pleasure.

"You're very kind to me, Rhys," she said.

The spoon clattered to the floor. "Kenna!"

She smiled serenely and motioned him to sit beside her. "Mmmm. I like it better than Diana."

He would have had to sit even if she hadn't invited

214

him. "You remember then?"

Kenna nodded. "Most everything. It's like a dream, still." She touched the sleeve of his jacket and ran her hand across his forearm. "I've wronged you, Rhys."

"Sssh. Doesn't matter. Not now."

"It does." She sat up and a rush of bittersweet pleasure made her dizzy. She held onto Rhys for support. "I'm fine, Rhys. Jus' fine."

Rhys drew her onto his lap and she relaxed against him. It was agony for him to hold her but he could not have set her aside if his life depended upon it.

Kenna's hands stole inside Rhys's open jacket and she felt his sharp intake of breath as her fingers massaged his back, then his chest. She nuzzled the curve of his shoulder sleepily, teasing the side of his face with the feather-light touch of her hair. "I like it when you hold me."

"I like it, too." He spoke against her hair.

Kenna lifted her face. "Kiss me, Rhys."

"Kenna." It was an uncertain warning at best.

Her pupils were widely dilated, making her eyes nearly black with only a slim ring of their dark chocolate color visible. "Kiss me." Her mouth parted.

Rhys hesitated a moment longer then gave in to the desire he thought he saw in her eyes. He said her name again, but this time he surrendered to it. There was a faintly bitter taste to her lips and he realized it was the drug that had robbed her of the heady sweetness he was used to. His hands slipped to her sides, then cupped her breasts as he deepened the kiss. She accepted his touch with a disarming languor, moving sinuously against him, until his body tightened in response. It was Kenna who broke the kiss and teased his ear, his jaw, and the smooth plane of his cheeks with her mouth.

Her fingers fumbled with the buttons of his shirt and slipped inside to touch his bare flesh. She ran her hand

215

over the hard ridges of his flat belly and felt him suck in his breath. She pressed a siren's smile into the curve of his neck then trailed kisses along his warm skin.

Kenna's breasts filled Rhys's hands and the tips hardened as he teased them with the pads of his thumbs. Her nightgown added a delicious friction to his teasing. The tiny moan of pleasaure that parted her lips was swallowed by Rhys's mouth.

Kenna's hands clutched his sides as she felt the hard proof of his desire press against her thigh. Her movements became more frantic, exploring, touching, intent.

Caught up in Kenna's seduction Rhys did not notice she had lifted the vial from his inside pocket until he saw it flash in her hand as she pushed him away and ran across the room.

In one corner of the chamber Kenna turned her back on Rhys and with frantic, desperate movements began trying to uncork the vial. She had just managed to loosen the cork when she felt Rhys's hands on her elbows. She shrugged away from him and crouched in the corner, shoulders hunched and head bowed to protect herself from his interference.

"Go away!" she gritted between clenched teeth.

"Give me the bottle, Kenna."

She didn't waste effort on a reply as she tugged the cork free. Rhys's arms surrounded her as she began lifting the bottle to her mouth. His fingers were painfully tight on her wrists. Kenna kicked backward, surprising Rhys as her heel connected with his shin, and his grip slackened slightly, enough for her to reach her lips with the tip of the bottle.

Rhys's large hand closed over hers and with hard, implacable force pulled her arm behind her back, jerking it upward until she cried out. Her numbed fingers twitched, then flowered open. Rhys caught the bottle as it started to fall, holding it out of her reach when she turned on him.

"Give it to me, Rhys!" she screamed, lunging for him. Although her nails had been clipped short she still managed to cut a furrow on his cheek when she clawed at him.

Rhys put his index finger over the narrow opening of the bottle to keep the contents from spilling while he pushed Kenna away with his other hand. She staggered backward, stiffened her shoulders as well as her resolve and came at him again. Rhys put the bottle behind his back and though Kenna tried to get at it from a dozen different angles she could not reach it.

What she had been able to do was maneuver Rhys against the wall and when he could move no further she dropped to her knees in front of him. "Please, Rhys. I beg you. Give it to me. I need it! Can't you see I need it?"

What Rhys saw churned his gut. She was without pride, her soul ravaged by the craving of her body and mind. Everything she had done with him had been in aid of getting the drug. She had no thoughts of her brother or Victorine. She had not asked about Janet. All her concerns had disappeared save one and he held it behind his back.

"I cannot give it to you, Kenna."

"You can!" She pounded once on the floor with her fists. "You can! I'll do anything, Rhys! Anything!" Kenna lifted her hands and ran them over his thighs. She could feel the muscles in his legs grow taut beneath her palms. Her fingers dipped into the waistband of his trousers and she pulled herself up. She leaned into him, pressing the warm curves of her body against the unyielding planes and angles of his own.

Rhys would have had to be cut from stone in order not to feel something. And he was not cut from stone. Kenna moved against him with feline grace, her caresses

217

intimate, and he lost control of his body's response. She rolled her hips against his arousal, sliding her arms about Rhys's neck so he could not push her away.

"We can make love," she whispered. "I want to. I know you do." Her head shot back from the curve of his shoulder as Rhys began laughing.

"Do you know where we are? If I want to make love I can have P.D. or Sheila or Pam or Loreta or Deborah . . ."

"Damn you!" Tears sprang to her eyes.

"And damn you, Kenna Dunne!" Rhys responded feelingly.

"Please, Rhys!" she begged again. "I must have my medicine. I hurt so badly. Please! Nothing is right without it!" She sobbed against his chest. "I'll do whatever you want. Just give me the bottle."

Rhys made no move to hold her, afraid to trust her tears. "Marry me."

Kenna did not hesitate. "Yes."

"Now. Today."

"Yes. Of course." She wiped away her tears with the back of her hand. "Now give me the bottle."

He shook his head. "After we're married."

"But—"

"After." He saw her resist for a moment, then it faded as she listened to her greedy addiction speak. "Go back to bed, Kenna. Try to sleep. When I return we'll be married."

Polly was shocked by Rhys's plan but was persuaded to help him. "She'll be furious when you don't give her more of the drug," she told him as she cleaned the scratch on his cheek.

"I'm willing to face that."

"Very well. There is a priest I know who will perform the rites."

One of Rhys's eyebrows kicked up. "A visitor to the Flower House?"

"Frequently." She winked at him. "But he comes to save our damned souls. I think he would be most cooperative if he thought he was helping one of the fallen angels give up her profession."

"Then arrange it for this evening. I will meet him at his church with Kenna. I'd like you to be there as a witness."

"You couldn't keep me away, Rhys."

"I will take Kenna immediately to the ship afterward. You will have to explain her death to your girls alone."

"I can manage the thing. I only hope you do as well."

Rhys came back for Kenna after midnight. Polly made certain her girls were all occupied with clients and would be for several hours. Kenna was drowsy from another small dose of the drug which Polly had administered an hour earlier and therefore cooperative. She allowed herself to be dressed in a peach dress with a garland of flowers embroidered at the hem. An ivory fichu was draped over her shoulders and gloves of the same color covered her arms from the tips of her fingers to several inches past her elbows. Polly fastened the redingote at Kenna's throat and lifted the collar so the fur trim framed her neck and brushed the curling tips of her hair. Rhys carried her out the back of the Flower House and placed her in his coach. He held out a hand for Polly and helped her in. She supported Kenna's head in her lap as Rhys took the driver's seat and wound the carriage through narrow London alleys and streets to get to the church.

The Anglican priest was waiting for them in his private rooms affixed to the church. He had prepared an altar and wore his vestments. The necessary papers were waiting for signatures on his desk. He made a few token protests about the impropriety of the situation but when

219

Polly gave him her cherub's smile he ceased complaining and cleared his throat, looking at the participants expectantly.

Kenna stood to one side of Rhys and a little in front of him so he could support her. He whispered in her ear. "Do you know what you are doing?"

"Yes. We made a bargain."

Rhys was satisfied it was what she wanted, even if it was for the wrong reasons. He told the priest they were ready.

The ceremony was brief. Polly shed a few tears and had to nudge Kenna to make her respond to her fictitious name. The ring Rhys placed on Kenna's finger was a fraction too large and it kept slipping down to her first knuckle. Rhys recited his vows in clear tones; Kenna stumbled a bit over the words. The kiss that sealed their promises was brief. Rhys helped Kenna sign her name to the registry while Polly occupied the priest with conversation. Though she wrote her own name, with Rhys's assistance it was nearly illegible and the priest would never think it said anything but Diana Dome. Rhys kept a record of the ceremony for himself which he quickly put out of Kenna's reach. Signaling to Polly that everything was accomplished they took their leave a few minutes later.

On the way back to the Flower House Kenna became more alert and the empty ache she felt inside warned her it was time for more of her medicine. It tore at Polly's heart to see Kenna beg but she remained unyielding. When Rhys helped her down from the carriage she told him Kenna was sick for it again.

Rhys glanced inside the coach and saw Kenna curled on the padded seat, her knees to her chest. He took Polly's hand and led her away. "I have your instructions. I know what to do. She's going to be fine, P.D."

"She has to want to get well, Rhys," Polly said with

some urgency, taking his hands in hers. "You cannot force her recovery on her. At the moment she wants no part of your good sense. It is my experience that some of the girls who stay on the drug do so because life with it is infinitely preferable to life without. It dulls the hard edges of reality. I would not have thought it would be true in Kenna's case, her being quality and all, used to every luxury. But I think I erred in judging her life. She has been fighting us tooth and nail because she does not want to return to the way things were. I don't think she was a very happy woman, Rhys. She can forget it with the drug."

Rhys knew Polly was right. Kenna had been unhappy and frightened and more alone than she ever would have admitted. Her life at Dunnelly had taken on a sameness that had been eroding her spirit and when events began to change the catalyst was betrayal. She had been powerless, confused, and defeated. It was small wonder that she clung to the solace of the drug that had been forced upon her.

Rhys squeezed Polly's hands gently. "Kenna and I will manage, P.D. I thank you for all you have done, not simply for Kenna, but everything. I'll write to you."

There was an ache in Polly's throat. She stood on tiptoe and kissed Rhys full on the mouth. His arms closed around her and they held each other for a long moment. Finally she broke away. "I want to hear about everything. You must describe it all to me. The voyage, your home, the business. Everything."

"I will."

She nodded, blinking back tears. "Farewell, Rhys. God bless you."

"And you, Miss Rose." But he spoke to Polly's retreating back as she hurried up the walk to her home.

Kenna was sleeping by the time Rhys stopped the coach on the wharf. Thanking heaven for this favor, he

221

lifted her from the carriage and carried her up the gangplank of the *Carasea*. He spoke to the man on watch, then took Kenna to his cabin.

He had no trouble finding the bed in the dark but he bumped into a few things when he went searching for a lantern. After a few tries he was able to light it and then placed it back in its secured holder on the massive oak desk. Looking around him, he wondered if Kenna would appreciate the luxury of her accommodations. His father might have appeared synonymous to the thrifty New Englander, but he traveled with every comfort available to him.

The bed was of three-quarter width, its mattress stuffed thick with goosedown. The trunk secured to the floor at its foot was filled with heavy blankets and other fresh linens. In one corner of the cabin there was a small Franklin stove for warmth on the cold ocean crossing and Rhys counted twenty individual panes of leaded glass that made up the large bowed window at the cabin's stern end. At least Kenna could see where she had been if she did not want to see where she was going. Crossing the length of the window at its base was a bench padded in red velvet with drawers built below it for storage.

The large cabin had its own dining table that could seat six with ease, two shelves anchored to the wall that held a selection of books limited to shipping, sermons, and science, and an oak wardrobe which was filled with Rhys's and Kenna's clothes. A full-length mirror was attached to one side of it and there was a commode with a basin built into its counter and a cupboard beneath it which held a chamber pot. Most of the hardwood floor had been covered with an expensive Oriental carpet and the incidental fixtures such as the lantern holder, knobs, and handles were polished brass. Rhys thought if he sold the contents of this room he might well be able to put Canning Shipping back on its feet.

Kenna continued to sleep deeply while Rhys changed her clothes and dressed her in one of the more modest nightgowns he had purchased for her. It proved something of a struggle to manage the change without her help but he knew if she had been awake it would have been nothing less than a battle. When he was certain she was as comfortable and warm as he could make her he left the cabin, locking the door behind him.

The watch had not changed. "My wife is sleeping in our cabin this evening. I trust she will not be disturbed in any way while I see to what remains of our belongings at the townhouse."

"I'll make certain the others know, Mr. Canning," the man replied. "No one will wake her." He hesitated. "Speakin' for myself, sir, it was a terrible thing about your father and Mr. Richard. Good men, both of 'em. Please accept my sympathies."

"Thank you." Rhys struggled not to show his unease with the sailor's condolences. During the funeral he had had to come to terms with the fact that the man who was lauded, respected, and eulogized, was a stranger to him. Only Nick had suspected how uncomfortable it had been for him to hear tributes from the other diplomats to his father's genius and to accept sympathy for his passing. Roland Canning had never really been alive to Rhys. "It's kind of you to say so." Before the sailor could speak again Rhys slipped away into the foggy London night.

Rhys did not sleep at all. He finished writing the glowing characters for his staff who would all be seeking new employment and signed papers that would permit his solicitors to sell the townhouse. He attached a codicil forbidding the sale until every one of his employees had found a position equal to or better than what they had with him. He left a large payment to be distributed to the staff after he was gone and another envelope filled with markers he had accepted from his fellow gamblers which was to go to Polly. She could choose to collect on them if she wanted.

Just before daybreak Powell came to his study and saved him from nodding off and literally missing the boat.

"Thank you, Powell," he said, accepting the steaming cup of tea that was set in front of him. "Have you reconsidered coming with me?"

"I can't, sir. There's much to do here."

Rhys had known the answer. It was really too much to expect Powell to join him. The man's services were going to be needed while Napoleon was contemplating the regaining of an empire. Rhys regretted he was going to have no part in it. Something of his thoughts must have shown on his face, or perhaps it was that Powell knew him so well, for his friend spoke up.

"You did more than your share, sir, uncovering the plot to free the little corporal. It was a bloody shame those blokes in the Foreign Office discussed it to death before acting on your information."

"They are not given to hasty action."

"Well, they've got their hands full now."

"They do indeed." He sipped his tea, looking at Powell over the rim of his cup. "Do you have any questions about the layout of the caves and passages at Dunnelly?"

Powell touched a finger to his forehead. "All up here, sir. Every word. I'll be starting my post at the manor in two days and I'll have access to everything."

"Good. I suspect there will be more money changing hands as Napoleon masses his army. You must discover who his supporters are. I regret most deeply I was unable to."

"No one thinks you did less than you could."

Rhys smiled briefly at the reference to the men who ran the Foreign Office. "I'm glad they're going to have a chance to discover your full worth, Powell."

"I appreciate your confidence, sir."

Rhys set down his drink. "Now that that's settled, perhaps you can tell me who I am going to turn to when I've gone too deep in my cups?"

"As to that," Powell said, grinning from ear to ear, "I've left you my special recipe. You'll find it amongst your papers."

"Thank you," Rhys said gravely. "I think."

Chapter Six

Rhys was not the only man to make his farewells as the bright morning sun burned off the shroud of fog in London and all along the coast. Mason Deverell stood on the narrow strip of shore near the entrance to Dunnelly's caves and waited for his contact to make an appearance. He leaned against an oar and observed the steps leading down from the summerhouse.

"Why do you never use the cave passage?" he asked as he was approached.

"I don't like it," was the terse reply.

Mason laughed mockingly. "Not after that one night, eh? What a debacle that was!"

"What do you want?" The question was offered impatiently. "I could not believe it when I saw your signal. You're clearly mad. The fog is all but gone. Anyone could see you."

"It matters not." He pointed down the rocky coast. Where it took a twist the tips of a mast could be seen. His ship waited beyond, out of sight of the manor. "I'll be gone from here and the explanations will be yours to make."

"Bastard."

"Most likely. I came to tell you how she died."

"I don't want to know."

"It doesn't matter. You will listen. You proved you were incompetent to take care of her yourself and I had to intervene. Now you will know how it was done."

"I did not want her dead."

"*Mon Dieu!* Do you think we didn't know that? But you were trusted to do what was necessary so you would not be exposed. Kenna was coming painfully close to recalling the truth and yet you were ignoring it. Do you think I give one *sou* if she remembers you killed her father or that I broke her nose? *Non!* It is the sanctity of my mission for the emperor which must be preserved. Her recollection would have removed you from Dunnelly and compromised everything that I have worked for."

"I cannot be compromised now. You've seen to that."

"Yes, I have." One corner of his handsome mouth lifted in a sneer. "Do you know of the young Lord Tremont?"

"His reputation, yes."

"I wonder if you know his reputation with women. I wonder if you know he enjoys a bit of slap and tickle in the seedier sections of London. Place the emphasis on slap."

"What has this to do with Kenna?"

"She was the last woman he enjoyed. He flogged her to death in his excitement." He took pleasure in seeing the face across from him blanch but when he read the intent in those eyes he dropped the oar and pulled his pistol. "Think twice before you lunge."

"You are one of Satan's own."

"I shall take that as a compliment." Seeing the threat was gone he tucked the pistol away. "Kenna's death changes nothing of our arrangement. You will still come to the cave when you see the signal and continue to provide the funds as requested. Your refusal would mean death." His mouth lifted again. "Not yours, but that of

228

those around you."

There was a short nod to indicate understanding.

"*Bien.* This is farewell for us then. I am leaving for the United States today. There are sympathizers there, especially among the Creoles in New Orleans. I hope to increase their numbers and lighten their pockets." Mason did not wait for a reply, knowing none was forthcoming. He picked up the oar and tossed it into the rowboat, glancing over his shoulder. "Care to help me put this in the water?"

"Go to hell."

Mason shrugged, pushed off and jumped in the boat. As he rowed away he kept his eyes on the caped figure making the long climb to the summerhouse.

Kenna woke up sick. Her temples throbbed and she could taste bile at the back of her throat. Sliding her feet over the side of the bed, she sat up and put her head between her knees. The room was doing more than merely spinning, it was rocking. "Stop it!" she cried out, lifting her head and opening her eyes. This last action had the effect of completing her disorientation. Nothing was familiar to her and the panic that seized her made it impossible for her to catch her breath. She began to hyperventilate.

Rhys swore his head had only touched the pillow when Kenna's cry of alarm reached him. The sound of her strained and rapid breathing sent a frission of fear through him. Without thinking he grabbed the back of her nightgown and pulled her down next to him, flinging an arm over her heaving chest. One hand cupped her face.

"Slowly, Kenna." His voice was gentle. "Slowly." He stroked her cheek with the tips of his fingers. "A deep breath. That's it. Let it out slowly." Rhys held his own breath a beat then let it out to a count of ten, showing Kenna what he wanted her to do.

She watched his face, a certain distance in her wide eyes as if she didn't really know him. Gradually she was able to pattern her breathing after his. At her sides her fingers trembled and she dug them into the mattress.

"Better?" asked Rhys.

Kenna's eyes closed. Very quietly she told him she was going to be sick.

Rhys fairly dove over her to get off the bed and retrieve the empty chamber pot. He managed to return with it just as Kenna pushed herself to the side of the bed and leaned her head over the edge. He shoved the chamber pot under her and held her heaving shoulders while she was sick. Afterwards he poured a cup of water and let her rinse out her mouth.

Kenna moved away from bed's edge and Rhys covered her with a blanket. "I need my medicine," she said weakly.

"I'll get it for you."

As was his custom Rhys measured out some on a spoon and lifted her head as he fed it to her.

After she licked the taste of it from her lips Kenna eyed the bottle. "More. I remember. You promised."

"I did." He poured a spoonful, then another. "Enough?"

She nodded.

He hid his smug smile as he locked the bottle with its diluted contents inside the oak desk. Several other bottles mixed with exactly the same proportions, lay beside it. Three teaspoons was still not the equal to the amount she had been receiving in one dose at Polly's. Rhys returned the key to a slim gold chain he wore around his neck. If Kenna wanted the key badly enough she could always break the chain, but not without him knowing it.

"Better now?" he asked, standing beside the bed.

She nodded, a serene smile touching her mouth.

"Good. Move over."

Kenna obligingly did as she was asked until she was against the paneled wall of the cabin.

Rhys slipped between the covers. "Not that far, sweet." He pulled her close and curled his body against hers. She murmured something he did not catch. "What was that, Kenna?"

"S'lovely."

"It is." Rhys closed his eyes. In his own dreams Kenna said those words and knew what she was saying.

For the following ten days Rhys battled on and off with Kenna. She was frequently sick which he attributed more to the motion of the ship and less to her dependency upon the drug. He often entered the cabin in the middle of the day and found her sleeping. At night she kept Rhys awake, begging him to give her more medicine. She was a stranger to the crew. Rhys was afraid to let her out of the cabin for fear of what she would do. There were times when he did not think she knew she was on a ship at all. He had to care for her, washing her hair, bathing her, and feeding her. When their meals were prepared he had the cook's assistant leave them in the companionway outside their door, then made certain the young man was gone before he went to get them. Rhys did it, not because he was ashamed of anything Kenna might do or say, but to protect her. The captain of the *Carasea* accepted his explanation that Kenna was unused to ocean travel and therefore indisposed.

When Rhys was not with Kenna he spent his time on deck or quartered with Captain Johnson, learning about the shipping line he had inherited. Johnson was a brusque man, unable to tolerate ceremony for its own sake. He told Rhys bluntly that while he may be the new owner of the line he, Johnson, was in command of the

Carasea and that's the way it would be until he drew his last. Rhys replied he would not have it differently and proceeded to grill the captain for all the information and expertise he had from his twenty years with the line.

Johnson was impressed that Rhys was not merely interested in the profit and cargo side of the trade. He asked about ship maintenance, trade routes, winds, navigation, the men's food and sleeping quarters, their salaries, construction, and maritime laws. The captain was similarly impressed by Rhys's quick mind and his grasp of what was important to the men trusted with the line's cargo.

Rhys was not satisfied with simply listening to Johnson answer his questions. He wanted experience as part of the crew so he knew what he was asking others to do for him.

Johnson balked at the request. "Your father never asked to climb the rigging in his life," he said. "Or to take a watch, hold the wheel, or plot a course."

Rhys leaned forward in his chair then, his gray eyes as sharp as winter frost. "I am not my father."

Johnson was thoughtful, rubbing one sandy eyebrow between his thumb and forefinger. "No, you're not. Or your brother either."

His voice was noncommittal and Rhys could not divine whether the captain thought it was a good or a bad thing, but it hardly mattered, for he saw that Johnson had relented. Rhys hurried back to his cabin to change his clothes before Johnson changed his mind.

He flung open the door to the cabin and in the brief moment he stood poised in the doorway he was transported to a time two years earlier when he had braved Mrs. Miller's wrath and found Polly Rose very nearly bleeding to death.

Kenna was lying on the floor near the window bench, doubled up in pain. Her hands were covered with blood and below her waist her nightgown was crimson. A pool of dark blood stained the deck and the fringe of the carpet.

A young man was walking down the companionway toward the upper deck. Rhys grabbed him by his shirt and barked out orders. "Get the ship's doctor! My wife has had a miscarriage." He practically flung the startled man away from him, then ran to Kenna's side.

She was moaning softly, unaware of anything save her pain, when Rhys tore the gown from her body and wiped her thighs and hands. He tossed the gown aside and carried her to the bed. The man who arrived to help Rhys carried the title of doctor because he had set a few bones, knew how to bring down a raging fever, and could stop the flow of blood from a wound. McKillop had no experience with miscarriages, having been at sea when his wife had two as well as when she had birthed his five sons, so he improvised as he went along.

He told Rhys to tear a sheet in quarters and fold the sections in pads. While this was being done, McKillop washed the stain of blood from Kenna's body. He took the pillow from her head and stuck it under her feet, then placed the pad between her thighs and quickly covered her with a blanket. The pinched look on Kenna's face was already fading and a measure of color was returning to her cheeks. McKillop wet a cloth and bathed her face. Mercifully she had either fallen asleep or passed out.

"Puir lassie," he said in his pronounced brogue. "She dinna ken what happened to her."

"Is it over?" asked Rhys.

"Aye. The worst of it is." He hoped it was true. "She dinna know about the bairn, did she?"

"No. Neither did I,"

McKillop nodded, observing Rhys's strained features. "Then it's a shock to you as well." He left Kenna's side and began cleaning the pool of blood by the window.

"She needs to lie abed a day or so."

"Will there be more pain?"

"Canna say, but I think not."

Rhys wondered how long she had suffered before he found her. He called himself a fool and much worse for never suspecting she might be pregnant. He knew from Polly that no man at Mrs. Miller's had touched her. It was their own child she had been carrying.

For two days Kenna lay in bed, sleeping long hours, eating little, and talking not at all. Never once did she mention her medicine and Rhys gave her none of it. On the third day she got up and moved about the cabin, touching things thoughtfully as if they were unfamiliar to her and she wanted to learn their identity. Rhys woke the moment he felt her stir from the bed. Curious, he turned on his side, propping his head on his elbow, and watched her.

She ran her hand along the length of the oak desk, fingered the brass handle of the lantern. Standing in front of the book shelves, she appeared to read the title of every one of the volumes before she moved away. The mirror on the side of the wardrobe held her interest for long minutes as she explored her face by touching the glass. An uncertain frown drew her brows together as her hand lifted to her hair and ruffled the short mahogany curls then found the red-gold roots. She sat at the window seat, her slender back to Rhys, and watched the sun's early morning rise on the horizon. Finally she turned to him as if she had expected him to be watching her, and spoke.

"I think you had better tell me the whole of it, Rhys." Her eyes were more brown than black now, less vacant and glazed. They touched his face from across the room.

Rhys sat up, hitching a sheet around his waist, and leaned his naked shoulders against the wall. He noticed the color that came to her cheeks when she realized he

234

hadn't any clothes on. He did not take it as a good sign and wondered what she remembered.

"Tell me where to begin," he said.

Kenna cut right to the heart. "Were you responsible for my abduction from the ale house?"

A muscle jumped in Rhys's jaw. "No." He held his breath, searching her face for some sign that she believed him, but refusing to beg for her trust. Tears welled in her eyes suddenly and her shoulders sagged as a tiny choked sob escaped her throat. He knew then she had accepted his word and that her grief was for the betrayal of someone she had never suspected.

Rhys edged off the bed and crossed the cabin to Kenna. He stood in front of her, studying her bowed head, the hands that twisted in her lap, before he caught her chin and lifted her face.

She blinked at him, stemming the flow of tears briefly. Her bottom lip trembled. "Why are these things happening to me, Rhys?" Then his face dissolved again as bitter tears streaked her face.

Rhys sat beside her, sliding an arm around her back, and wiped her face with a corner of his sheet. "I only have a suspicion, Kenna. Are you certain you want to hear it?"

She sniffled. "Yes."

"It has to do with your father's death and your memory of that night."

Kenna turned to him. "I want to know."

"All right." He let out his breath slowly. "I believe that someone living at Dunnelly murdered Robert, or is employed by the person who killed him. The only person who can identify the killer is you, Kenna. For years you have accused me and though no one believed you, your uncompromising position that I had done it kept the real murderer safe."

"But it was you in the cave. I saw you!"

Rhys smiled faintly. "Do you remember the night I came to your room and stood by the mantel? Who did you mistake me for then?"

She gasped softly. "Nick! Oh, but it couldn't have been Nick! It couldn't have been!"

"I'm not saying it was. Only that you have confused us before. Mightn't you have made a similar error the night of the masque? There were so many people there, all costumed, many of them alike. There may have been dozens dressed as I was that evening. I don't know. I didn't spend a great deal of time at the ball itself, but by your own admission you watched scores of people enter the ballroom from your vantage point on the staircase."

"I remember the four shepherdesses."

He nodded, satisfied. "And in time you may remember more. At least someone else believes you will."

"It's been nearly ten years, Rhys. I doubt if I shall."

"I think it is because you have not wanted to."

"That's ridiculous."

"Perhaps. You can be very strong-willed, Kenna. It does not strike me as odd that you could be hiding what you know from yourself, especially if the truth were particularly painful."

"Let us agree to disagree," she said.

"Very well. Can you concede that you have erred in judging me guilty of your father's death?"

"Yes."

He squeezed her hand. "Good. That is something at least. And can you admit that this past year your dreams have altered slightly, introducing new people, new events, into them?"

Kenna's brows drew together as she thought hard on the matter. "Well, yes, they have, but how could you know? I've only discussed my nightmares with you once, and that was when I thought you were Nick." Her expression lightened. "Nick told you, then?"

"No. It wasn't Nick, though years ago he discussed them with me."

"Then Victorine. I know Nick told her everything and sometimes I shared things with her."

"No. Not Victorine, nor your maid. I knew you told her, too. There was someone else you described everything to and she, in turn, told me."

Kenna was puzzled. "I can't imagine . . . Good Lord! It has to be Yvonne! I always wrote her!"

"And she wrote me," he confirmed her suspicion a trifle triumphantly.

"The beast! She had no right. They were confidences!"

Rhys gave Kenna a shake. "She is the best friend you ever had, Kenna Dunne!" He said her name out of habit, quite forgetting for the moment that she was Kenna Canning now. "Yvonne loves you dearly and she wrote to me for help when she became unsettled by the accident you had."

"What accident?"

"When you fell from your horse."

"That?" she scoffed. "It was nothing."

Rhys shook his head, his mouth tightened in a grim line. "As it turned out it was hardly nothing."

"I don't understand. It was a spill, nothing more. Victorine was with me and she rode for help. I almost didn't mention it to Yvonne."

Thank God she had, Rhys thought, and thank God again for Yvonne's fertile imagination, for it was she who introduced Rhys to the idea of Kenna's changing dreams being the cause of the trouble at Dunnelly. Rhys had been skeptical at first and soothed Yvonne's worries in a return letter, telling her that a fall from a horse was all part of being a rider, that it had nothing to do with the nightmare which Kenna had had the evening before. But Yvonne had persevered, pointing out other things that did not sit well with her any longer. Like the time Kenna had fallen down the stairs and bruised her back or the time before that when she had nearly caught her death of cold because her rowboat had tipped in the pond. Each perfectly explicable accident had occurred following a nightmare.

He mentioned these occasions and continued. "Do you remember writing to Yvonne—I think these were the words you used—my dreams are making me regrettably graceless?"

"I suppose I could have written some such nonsense, but I only meant that I was not getting enough sleep and was therefore clumsy."

"That is the interpretation I put upon it also. Yvonne, however, thought there was some merit in looking into the matter."

"So you came to Dunnelly," she said. "You told me it was because of your father's presence in London."

"That was also true, just not the entire truth." Later he thought he could tell her about his work for the Foreign Office, but it was too soon yet. "And when I arrived at Dunnelly I found you trying to free a fox from a trap that could easily have been meant for you."

"I had a nightmare the evening before," she said slowly, hardly able to take in the possibility he was presenting.

"So I discovered later that day. And Nick also told me the riding accident had been no such thing. Pyramid's girth had been tampered with and the head groom had—"

"Had been ill the morning I took Pyramid out," she finished for him. "Why did Nick say nothing to me?"

"He did not want to worry you and have the dreams go on night after endless night."

Kenna nodded in understanding. "Sometimes I think they were more terrible on him than they were on me." Lost in her thoughts, she failed to notice that Rhys withheld comment. She shook herself out of her reverie.

"Still, it seems absurd that someone would think I could happen upon the truth after so much time. Why did the accidents occur so far apart? And why were there so many after you arrived at Dunnelly?" Her tone almost dared him to offer an explanation.

"I have guesses at best," he told her. He walked over to the wardrobe and began pulling out the clothes he wished to wear. "But first, let us have done with calling them accidents. They were deliberate attempts on your life." He tossed a pair of buff riding breeches onto the bed. "I think your assailant became afraid after each arranged accident, giving up, not because they failed, but because he clung to the hope there would be no more dreams. Then, without warning, you would have another and he was forced to make the attempt again. As to why there was no end to them while I was at Dunnelly? It is simple. The killer knew my presence there would disturb you and cause a succession of nightmares. He was through taking chances."

"Then Old Tom's death—"

"Began as a mistake, I think. The shot that wounded him was probably meant for you. When the killer realized his error, he ran. But he became frightened, maybe when he realized who Tom Allen was and why you had brought him to the woods. He went back, strangled Tom, and took the trap as a precaution. It is probably at the bottom of the Channel by now. Later your assailant tried poison."

"Monseiur Raillier!"

Rhys shrugged into a shirt and began fastening it. "The chef," he nodded. "He is as much a suspect as anyone. Then there is your maid who conveniently passed on bath salts to the doctor to cover for Raillier. And Nick who bumped me when I was trying to carry out your soup to test it myself. And Victorine who brought it—"

Kenna put her hands over her ears and shut her eyes.

"Stop it! I don't want to hear any more! You're wrong! You must be!"

Rhys tore off the sheet, yanked on his breeches, and went on relentlessly. "Think, Kenna! Think! You are resisting the possibilities. It is safer to believe I must be wrong than to face the truth. You are fighting yourself again. Surely you can see that! Do you realize that you asked *why* these things were happening to you, never once did you ask *who* was responsible?" He pulled on his stockings and boots and brushed his hair, observing Kenna's confusion in the mirror. He dropped the brush on the table as he went to her again. Rhys took her by the arms and brought her to her feet. "Listen to me, Kenna. I know it will take time for you to become accustomed to the idea that I am not the villain in this piece, but it remains true nonetheless. I don't know who is responsible for this sleeping and waking nightmare you have been trapped in, but *you* do!" He sighed, pulling her close, and cradled her in his arms. "I'm sorry. Forgive me." He ruffled her hair as she nestled against him. "These things no longer matter. While you are with me, no one is going to harm you. Ever."

Rhys pressed a kiss in her soft hair. "There is much we still must discuss but I think enough has been said for now."

Kenna agreed. She drew back from Rhys, letting her hands slide down his arms, held his hands briefly, then let go reluctantly. "I would enjoy some time alone," she admitted. "May I join you later?"

His heart lightened at her request. Everything was going to be all right. "Whenever you wish."

After Rhys had gone, Kenna stood for several minutes in exactly the position he had left her. She felt curiously empty of all thought, all emotion. Slowly she sat back down on the window bench as her legs folded beneath her. Her eyes wandered to the one part of the room she had avoided since getting out of bed. Perhaps Rhys spoke more than a little truth when he said there were things she did not want to face. Kenna stared at the faint brownish-tinged stain on the hardwood floor and the darkened tips of the carpet fringe. Burying her face in her hands, she wept, mourning the loss of her innocence and the loss of her child.

When her tears were finally spent Kenna reviewed the choices open to her. She could save her would-be assassin a great deal of trouble and simply throw herself overboard. She could pry open the drawer where Rhys kept her drugs and lose herself in sleep and rose-colored dreams as long as the supply lasted. Or she could begin living again. Only one of those choices made sense to her any more.

Kenna opened the wardrobe and though it was crowded with Rhys's clothes she found several dresses. Something tugged at her memory as she chose an empire cut peach gown with a garland of flowers embroidered on the hem, but she shrugged it off, laying the gown on the bed. She found undergarments and hose, slippers, and a pastel yellow fichu to cover her shoulders, and laid these out also. After washing at the basin, she dressed, brushed her hair, and straightened the covers on the bed. As she was tidying the cabin she heard a noise in the companionway and went to investigate. She found the kitchen assistant in the process of leaving her breakfast tray.

"Oh, please, bring it in," she said, slightly bewildered by the young man's surprise. He nearly spilled the entire tray by looking wide-eyed at her instead of where he was going. "Just put it on the table." He set her meal down, blushing to the roots of his yellow hair. "Have I a smut on my nose?" she asked when he continued to stare at her. She hadn't thought it possible but the sailor blushed even deeper.

241

"No, ma'am," he stammered. "It's just that Mr. Canning, he told us you were . . . but he didn't say . . ."

"I'm afraid I can't make out what you're saying."

"Beautiful!" the sailor blurted out.

"Oh!" It was Kenna's turn to blush as the young man hurried from the room. There was still a measure of heat in her cheeks as she carried the tray to the oak desk. Between bites of her biscuits and eggs, Kenna jiggled the drawer containing the bottles. With the aid of the butter knife provided with her meal, Kenna managed to jimmy the drawer's catch. She set the five vials she found inside on the desk top, lining them up like soldiers at attention at the back of her tray, and stared at them while she finished her meal.

After she was done eating she gathered the bottles in her arms and left the cabin.

Rhys was in the rigging, taking some good-natured ribbing about his clumsy first ascent, when he saw Kenna step on deck. She hesitated a moment, looking around, then walked purposefully toward the taffrail. His companions noticed the direction of Rhys's gaze and stopped working at the same time to watch Kenna. Below them the rough chatter and activity ceased. Captain Johnson stepped away from the wheel, his sandy brows pulled in a single line over his eyes, as Kenna approached the ship's port rail.

Rhys's face paled as he watched Kenna from the dizzying height of his perch. He knew a gut-wrenching helplessness that he could not reach her in time to prevent her leap overboard. He screamed her name but she did not turn and he realized the sound had been carried away by the rush of wind rippling the sails. Not knowing what else to do, Rhys began a reckless rapid descent that burned the skin from his palms. Halfway down he stopped as Kenna's right arm drew back and heaved a bottle over the side. The others followed and by

242

the time Rhys reached the deck her hands were empty and she had stepped away from the rail.

"Kenna!" He called to her again.

She turned, smiling happily now that her decision to carry on living had been affirmed by such a grand gesture. "Did you see, Rhys?" she asked, eyes shining.

"I saw." She was simply beautiful. He held out his arms and Kenna ran to him, filling their emptiness with her spirit.

The noise and activity around them resumed and neither heard a bit of it. It took the rough, gravel sound of a throat clearing itself nearby to penetrate their senses.

Rhys loosened his hold on Kenna and glanced over his shoulder. "This is Captain Amos Johnson, Kenna," he said. "Captain Johnson, my wife, Kenna Canning."

Kenna's smile froze on her face as she extended her hand to the captain. Her mind worked furiously, reasoning that Rhys could have hardly introduced her as the sister of his friend after they had shared a cabin these past weeks. He had done it to save her reputation, of course. It made perfect sense. "How do you do, Captain Johnson. I am very pleased to meet you at last."

"Thank you, Mrs. Canning. For myself and the crew, may I say it's a pleasure to have you with us. The *Carasea* is brighter for your presence."

Rhys was quite amazed by Johnson's smooth tongue. The old salt hadn't been so ingratiating toward him. But then, he reflected, he hardly had Kenna's stunning appearance. Damned if the ship *wasn't* brighter for her presence! "I'd like to take my wife on a tour of the ship, Captain."

Johnson shook his head and said gruffly, "There's work to be done." He pointed overhead to the post Rhys had left. "I'll take your wife on the tour." He raised his elbow for Kenna to hold and stopped the protest that was rising in Rhys's throat with a hard glance. "You were the

243

one who wanted to know how the men worked. Escorting a lady is a captain's pleasure."

At Rhys's chagrined expression a bubble of laughter touched Kenna's lips. She patted his forearm sympathetically, her dark brown eyes dancing, as Captain Johnson led her away.

The sun was bright, but the air chilly and Kenna and the captain returned to her cabin to get her spencer. Johnson took Kenna into the belly of the ship first, showing her with no little pride the rooms filled with the line's precious cargo of colorful Indian fabrics, barrels of tea from the Far East, and furniture crafted by some of England's best known artisans. Though much of what the *Carasea* carried had come from all over the world, Johnson had picked up his share in London, still the largest center of trade anywhere. Not that Boston couldn't hold its own, he assured Mrs. Canning. Now that the war with England was over he looked for an increase in America's fortunes.

Kenna listened politely and withheld comment, deciding it was not the time to mention that if Napoleon succeeded in his second conquest there would be another stranglehold on trade. She followed Johnson into the galley where the afternoon meal was being prepared. The cook's assistant looked up from where he was chopping onions for a stew and smiled. A trifle teary-eyed from his task he accidentally brought down his knife on his index finger and muttered a sharp imprecation. Kenna was hustled out of the galley as the cook gave his helper's ears a sound boxing.

"Why is this floor painted red?" she asked when Johnson showed her the gun deck. Wheeled gun carriages lined both sides of the large room. He had already explained the guns were going to be removed in Boston, their necessity vanishing with the end of the war.

Johnson cleared his throat uneasily. "It softens the

shock during battle, Mrs. Canning. The men don't notice the blood so much." When he saw Kenna pale slightly he quickly moved her toward an upper deck.

She had some tea with him in his cabin before returning topside and Kenna kept the conversation centered on the captain, finding his experiences entertaining and instructive. They strolled about the upper deck once, then Johnson called Rhys to come down from the rigging. Kenna held her breath as she watched Rhys make his descent. Beside her, the captain chuckled.

"You can ease yourself now, Mrs. Canning," he said when Rhys's feet touched the deck. "As you can see, he's managed the thing as if he'd been born to it."

He had indeed, Kenna thought, awed again by Rhys's grace and strength.

"Did you enjoy your tour?" asked Rhys, blithely unaware of the state of Kenna's mind.

"Must you go up there?" she demanded as Captain Johnson slipped away.

Rhys's brows shot up at her tone. He held up his hands as if to ward her off. Almost immediately he realized it had been the wrong tack to take because he unwittingly showed Kenna the raw skin on his palms.

A salty breeze ruffled Kenna's hair as she reached forward and took Rhys's wrists. She examined them in the stern manner of her former governess, turning them over while she shook her head, clearly shocked by their appearance. "Your beautiful hands, Rhys," she said, sighing. "How could you?"

Rhys's mouth opened slightly, then snapped shut. He looked at his hands in astonishment, wondering what she could possibly have seen in them to call them beautiful. "There were things to be done," he offered somewhat diffidently.

"Well, no longer. Come with me, for I shall have to patch them up. They're bound to blister."

Rhys reddened a bit when he saw some of the men poking each other in the ribs as they listened unabashedly to his exchange with Kenna. Then he saw them study their own hands and glance at his wife wistfully as if hoping she would offer to do the same for them. "Let's go below before everyone wants your attention," he said a shade impatiently.

"Don't use that tone with me, Rhys Canning," said Kenna, but there was no sting in her words.

Kenna led Rhys straight to the ship's sick bay where she found bandages and alcohol. She cleaned his raw hands, wincing herself when Rhys gritted his teeth as she poured alcohol on the open cuts.

"I can see the tour was helpful," he said while she wrapped his hands. "You seem to know where everything is."

"It was enlightening. Did you know there is a red deck where the guns are kept?"

"Yes."

"Do you know why it's red?"

"Yes."

"Oh, Rhys. War is appalling. How could you have spent so many years fighting in Portugal and Spain?"

"How could I not? I was needed."

His simple explanation only lodged the lump in her throat more firmly. She remembered the cruel words she had spoken to him at Dunnelly, accusing him of trading on his heroism to gain the affections of Nick and Victorine, and worse, she had called him a traitor. She lifted his bandaged hands and pressed a kiss into each palm.

Rhys felt as if she had touched his soul. "Kenna."

She shook her head, begging him not to say anything. It was too soon and she didn't know her mind, or trust herself. "Will you have lunch with me?"

He held up his bandaged hands and wiggled the tips of

his free thumbs. "I'll have to. I wouldn't dare ask anyone else to feed me."

Actually Rhys managed quite well with a spoon. Kenna was glad. Feeding Rhys would have been . . . intimate, she thought, and she was ill-prepared to do such a task. He seemed to sense her discomfort in sitting directly opposite him at the table because after a few bites of stew he declared he wanted to put his feet up. He moved to one end of the table so that now they were seated at a right angle and promptly rested his feet on another chair. Kenna enjoyed her meal after that.

"Do you know," she asked, "I didn't realize we were going to the United States until this morning?" She pointed toward the window seat. "I sat there and watched the sun come up and it slowly came to me there was but one direction we could be going."

"What did you think?"

She broke a chunk of bread from the loaf on the cutting board between them and offered him some. "I don't know that I thought anything. I was confused, a little frightened, and perhaps angry with you."

He nodded. "And now?"

She dipped her bread into the stew. "I'm numb."

Rhys almost wished she would lie to him. "That's understandable."

"How long will we be staying in Boston?"

He nearly dropped his spoon in surprise. Didn't she know? Rhys thought to avoid the truth, then decided against it. "For the rest of our lives, I suspect."

Kenna's spoon did clatter to the table top. Her astonishment was complete. "You don't mean that," she said, even while the implacable expression in his eyes told her he did.

"I am the head of Canning Shipping now, Kenna. There are many people who are depending on me for their livelihood. I have to be in Boston."

"But what about me? You, at least, are American. My home is in England!"

There were probably more tactful ways to approach this issue but Rhys wanted to have done with it. "Your home is with me now. You're my wife, Kenna."

"Let us finish with that piece of fiction, Rhys. It is all very well to tell the others we are married to save my reputation, but it is of no account between us."

Rhys's loss of appetite was immediate. He pushed away his bowl of stew. "It is no fiction," he said, gauging her reaction watchfully. "We *are* married. Don't you remember?"

"If I remembered I wouldn't be saying such stupid things, would I?" She picked up the napkin on her lap and tossed it on the table, her mind working furiously as she tried to recall the event.

"I have our license."

She further surprised him by saying, "I don't require proof, Rhys. I believe you. I simply don't know how I allowed such a thing to happen."

"You had your reasons," Rhys said. "You tossed them overboard this morning."

"I see," she said thoughtfully. She looked down at her dress. "Was I wearing this when we were married?"

"Yes."

"This morning . . . it seemed familiar," she told him slowly. "Did I want to marry you?"

It was an odd question but Rhys answered it honestly. "You wanted your medicine, as you called it. You would have done anything to get it. You offered your body. I offered marriage."

"And I accepted."

"Without hesitation," he said deliberately.

"You used my illness to get what you wanted."

"Yes."

Kenna searched Rhys's face. "Why was it so important we marry? Did you know I was carrying your child?"

Rhys paled slightly. "No. I didn't know."

"Then why?"

"Because it seemed the best way to protect you," he said after a brief pause. He could not lay himself open to more hurt at Kenna's hands. "When I found you at Polly's, everyone at Dunnelly was already mourning your death. Taking you back there would have only meant another attempt on your life. I had to come to America and it struck me that your safety depended upon your coming with me."

Kenna felt a heaviness in her breast as she listened. He talked of protection and safety, never once of love. It was as Victorine suspected, Rhys was sacrificing his own happiness. An image came to Kenna of another woman. She was petite, with platinum curls and an abundance of feminine curves, not so different from Victorine. Vaguely she could recall Rhys holding this woman in his arms, kissing her full on the mouth. There was a sadness in their parting and Kenna wondered about her, wondered if this perhaps was the woman Rhys loved.

Suddenly Kenna wanted to be alone, to think, to plan. She could not bear a marriage to Rhys that was prompted out of some misguided noble kindness. "Could we speak of this another time?" she asked. "It is all something of a shock."

Rhys supposed that it was, but he hardly rejoiced at Kenna's withdrawal. He stood and pushed his ladder-backed chair, placing his hands firmly on the top rung. "Before I go topside, Kenna, there is something else you must know."

She raised her face to him. "What?" Surely everything had been said.

"There will be no divorce." Before she had time to respond to his announcement Rhys left the cabin.

How could he have known the direction of her thoughts and then put a period to them? What sort of marriage could they possibly have? It was hardly one of convenience, for it convenienced no one. Kenna thought rather forlornly that she was bringing nothing save trouble to this union. She stared at her naked hands. Rhys had not even given her a ring. If she had been drugged when she accepted his offer, he must have been foxed when he made it.

Dinner was a very quiet affair. Neither of them mentioned what had passed at lunch. Kenna could not recall feeling more miserable and Rhys took her reticence as a sign that she was not happy.

"I see you found the material and fashion book," he said, lifting his chin in the direction of the bed. A bolt of pale yellow muslin lay on top. Scattered next to it were scissors, needles, pins, and thread.

"Yes. It was kind of you to think of me."

Her stilted reply bothered Rhys and he cursed himself for being so sensitive to her every word. A simple thank you on her part would have sufficed just as well. She had a way of expressing herself that made him feel as if his thoughtfulness surprised her.

"The material is lovely," she added a moment later when he made no response.

"I'm glad you like it. The modistes were certain they could not fail to please you."

Kenna felt deflated. She had hoped he had chosen the fabric himself. What a pea-goose she was being! She came out of her self-pitying reverie when Rhys's chair scraped jerkily against the carpet.

"I'm going to find Captain Johnson," he said. "There are some matters I must attend."

Kenna gave him a brief nod, biting down the questions that came to her lips. Was he going to climb the rigging again? Could she walk with him on deck? Why was he seeing the captain? What sort of matters did he concern himself with? Could she help? Above all, where did she fit into his life?

After the kitchen assistant cleared away the remains of their dinner, Kenna laid out the yellow muslin again and began cutting the pattern she had chosen. She worked on the dress for two hours before the confinement of the cabin became more than she could bear. Taking out her redingote, she draped it over her shoulders and went on deck.

The night was very clear and colder than she first imagined, but she was determined to stay topside even if her fingers and nose turned blue. She glanced around, looking for Rhys, and when she couldn't find him she decided to stroll the deck on her own. It was not long before she had two escorts, one on each arm, and several seamen following her at a respectful distance. Her entourage was unfailingly polite and Kenna realized they were starving to hear a woman's voice and share her company. She chatted gaily with them, forgetting her own concerns as they let her hold the great wheel of the ship and teased her about sailing the ship into the treacherous North Atlantic icebergs. She asked about their families and their homes, about life in Boston, and she listened thoughtfully to their replies. Without consciously setting out to do so, Kenna conquered the men with her genuine interest in everything that touched their lives in America. When she finally insisted she had to return to her cabin their long faces told her clearly how much the time she had spent with them meant.

The companionway outside her cabin was crowded with men bidding her good evening and Kenna had to slip quickly through the doorway before she found herself inviting them in for tea. She turned away from the door when she heard them shuffling off and smiled to herself.

"I take it you've finished holding court," Rhys said dryly. The secretive, dreamy smile on her face taunted him.

Kenna gasped softly at the sound of his voice, never suspecting until he spoke that he was even in the cabin. Rhys was sitting in a copper hip bath near the stove calmly soaping his chest and shoulders while his head rested against the rim of the tub. His eyes were nearly closed though Kenna could see he was watching her. She wondered what he was thinking. There was a weariness inherent in his posture that tugged at Kenna and she walked over to the tub while the mood to offer some small comfort was upon her. She took off her coat and set it on the back of the chair, then knelt beside the bath.

She held out her hand for the sponge. "I'll do your back," she said.

Rhys's expression turned wary. Could he stand it if she touched him? Could he stand it if she didn't? He gave her the sponge and sat up a little, leaning forward so she could reach his back.

Kenna inched forward on her knees, avoiding Rhys's eyes as she took the sponge. She dipped it in the water then squeezed it over his shoulders, watching the rivulets of warm water run over his smooth back. "I wasn't holding court, you know," she said as she touched the sponge to the top of his spine. "I went on deck to look for you."

"I was in the captain's cabin."

"I realized that later. The men . . . they were very kind. I didn't think it would be wrong to speak with them."

The gentle circles she drew on his back were sweet torture. His eyes closed completely. "It wasn't wrong."

Kenna let out her breath slowly. "I'm glad. I thought

252

you were angry."

Jealous as hell, he thought. Didn't she know? "No, I'm not angry. I shouldn't have left you alone for so long."

"It's all right," she lied, not wanting to be demanding of his time. "I understand you have responsibilities."

Did she have to be so gracious? The muscles in his back bunched and he realized he was in danger of instigating a fight with her simply to ease his tension. "Give me the sponge," he said abruptly. "I can wash myself."

Kenna tried not to show her hurt. What had she done wrong? She gave Rhys the sponge and scooted back from the tub, curling her legs beneath her. Out of habit she reached for her hair, trying to draw a strand of it through her mouth as she had done as a child when she was worried or upset. The cropped curls thwarted her and she sighed.

"It will grow back," Rhys said.

"I suppose so." Her hand dropped to her side. "I do not mind the shortness of it as much as I mind the color. Mason ordered Sweet to chop it but it was Mrs. Miller who dyed it. I couldn't stop them."

"Of course you couldn't," he replied. "But I'll wager you gave them pause about doing it to someone else."

Kenna smiled faintly. "I hope so. I fought as much as I was able. I like to think they could not have done it without the drug."

Rhys lifted one leg and began soaping his calf. "Tell me," he said casually. "I know Sweet and Mrs. Miller, but who is Mason?"

Kenna stared at Rhys's leg unabashedly until she saw the amusement in the lift of his lips. She dropped her gaze quickly and studied the pattern in the carpet instead. "He's the man who abducted me from Robinson's. Didn't you know?"

"Mason Deverell," Rhys said slowly, tasting the name

on his tongue. "It must be." He rinsed one leg and began on the other. "No, I didn't know his full name. I knew of Sweet. There was another one who helped, wasn't there? Jeb Thompson?"

"Yes. I suppose that's the one. I only heard his first name mentioned."

Rhys was thoughtful. "They were very certain of themselves, weren't they? It didn't occur to them that you could ever name your abductors."

Kenna nodded. "Mason was the one who was certain. He was the leader. It was his idea, I think, to take me to Mrs. Miller's." She shivered slightly at the fleeting memories of her time there. "Who do you think sent Mason and the others to the ale house?"

"I don't know, Kenna."

"Do you really think that somehow I know the answer?"

"Yes." He stretched out an arm and touched her face, willing her to look at him. "Yes, I really think you do. But as long as you are with me, as long as those at Dunnelly think you're dead, you're safe. It doesn't matter if you ever stumble upon the truth, or even if you believe me. The only thing of importance is that you are protected now."

Kenna wanted to hold his hand to her face but she was afraid he would pull away. She leaned away from his touch and got to her feet, not realizing that it was she who had pulled away instead. She hung up her coat in the wardrobe and found her nightgown. "I hadn't realized everyone thinks I'm dead. It doesn't seem right somehow. Not everyone at Dunnelly is guilty in this."

While Kenna's back was turned Rhys got out of the bath and toweled himself dry quickly. "It cannot be helped," he said, shrugging into his robe. "It would be dangerous to trust any one person."

254

Kenna turned just as Rhys was belting his robe and a warm flush spread across her cheeks. "But Nick . . ." Her voice died as Rhys shook his head firmly and his mouth thinned warningly.

"Not even Nick must know."

"It couldn't be Nick," she said, more to herself than to Rhys. "He's my brother. He loves me."

Rhys crossed the room and stood in front of Kenna. His large hands gripped her upper arms as if he would shake her, then there was a hesitation and they simply glided to her wrists and held her loosely. "He is my dearest friend, Kenna. It is not that I don't want to trust him, but simply that I cannot. Love is no indicator of innocence here. Someone wants you dead."

"Please, just hold me," she said, a catch in her voice. "Hold me. I have never been so alone. I may as well be dead."

This time he did shake her, then held her so tightly he could feel the beat of her heart against his chest. "Don't say that. Don't even think it!"

She shuddered against him, caught in his warm embrace, and tried to think of nothing save the security of his arms as he rocked her gently and murmured her name in her ear. Her hands were trapped between their bodies and as his strength seeped into her she gradually pushed him away. "I'm sorry," she said, recovering a measure of her reserve. "I feel silly. I don't mean to burden you."

Rhys's hands slipped inside his dressing gown's pockets. In the left one he felt the gold band he had given Kenna and pocketed when it fell off her finger once too often. He wondered if this was the time to give it to her. "You're no burden, Kenna, and I never want you to feel you can't turn to me. You're not alone in this." Rhys decided to wait to return the ring to her.

"I know. And I thank you." She picked up her nightgown from the bed and twisted it uncertainly in her hands. "If it weren't for you I would still be at Mrs. Miller's."

He had no desire to pursue that topic. She obviously did not realize what had waited for her in Tremont's bed. Rhys watched her turn the nightgown over in her hands and a brief smile touched his face. "Turn around so I can play the lady's maid. How did you manage to dress yourself?"

Kenna turned obligingly, bending her head forward so he could reach the uppermost fasteners. "It was difficult. I merely persevered." She felt Rhys's fingers touch her bare skin, pause, then begin working on the back of her gown with brisk efficiency. She would not allow herself to dwell on how many times he had performed a similar service for other women. "Thank you," she said politely when he had finished.

"Would you like me to ask for fresh bath water? It's salt water, but it serves the purpose well enough." He pointed to the copper tub. "I confess that was meant for you, but since you weren't here when it arrived I was not going to let it go to waste."

Kenna was touched by his thoughtfulness. "I'm sorry I wasn't here, but there is no need to bother anyone now. I'll wash at the basin."

"As you wish." He walked over to the desk and began pulling out charts, a log book, and the ship's manifest. "I can look over these things now."

Kenna glanced over her shoulder as she slipped out of her gown, concern knitting her brows. "Should you? I mean, you seemed so tired when I came in. Shouldn't you try to go to sleep?"

Rhys did not look up from the things he laid in front of him. "I doubt that I can," he muttered. More clearly he

256

said, "This won't take long."

Shrugging, Kenna put away her gown then went to the basin. Unaware that Rhys was watching her now she sighed happily as she took off her shoes and wriggled her pinched toes. She dipped a cloth into the clear basin water and cooled her face with it, letting drops of the water trickle down her neck and dampen the lacy edge of her chemise. A sliver of lavender soap lay near the washbowl. Kenna used it to lather the cloth and washed her face and throat.

Eyes forward, Rhys commanded himself, then disobeyed his own edict. He watched Kenna slip the chemise over her shoulders until it rested around her waist, baring the tantalizing curve of her back to him. She soaped her breasts and shoulders, drew the cloth along the inside length of her arms, then rinsed. His eyes fell on the manifest in front of him but his vision blurred. The lines on the paper merged and formed the slender outline of Kenna's body. It took no effort to imagine the narrow curve of her waist, the smooth contours of her incredibly long legs, or the arched thrust of her buttocks. The vision in front of him turned and though he held her gaze, his fingertips traced the column of her throat then the vulnerable flare of her collarbone. He cupped her breasts and they swelled at his touch. Her flesh grew warm as he brushed her abdomen. There was a hushed intake of air when he cradled her hips and brought her flush against him and . . .

"Did you say something, Rhys?" asked Kenna as she turned away from the basin and fastened the buttons at the neck of her nightgown.

Rhys blinked at the paper and the picture in his mind dissolved. He looked up at Kenna, saw that she had completed her bathing and was dressed for bed, and he guiltily wondered if she could guess the direction of his

257

thoughts. Her expressive eyes were curious. "No. I didn't say anything." He pushed back the papers. "You're ready for bed?" Stupid, he thought. It was obvious she was ready.

She nodded slightly and stifled a weak yawn with the back of her hand. "I'm more tired than I thought." Kenna went to the bed and pulled back the blankets. She sat down on the edge and fiddled with the lace cuffs of her sleeves. "Rhys . . ."

"I won't bother you, Kenna," Rhys said quickly, believing he understood the reason for her hesitation. That her head lifted sharply at his words seemed to confirm his suspicions. "I know you have not had the time to become accustomed to our marriage. I don't want you to worry that I shall force imtimacy upon you. In fact, I was thinking that I could sleep on the windowseat. It's long enough and I should be quite comfortable."

Kenna was mortified at this turn of conversation. She had only been going to ask him to put away his charts and books and come to bed. It seemed as if he wanted nothing to do with her. She glanced past him to the windowseat. "You'll be miserable there," she said quietly, color staining her cheeks. "It will be cold and you'll probably fall off the ledge before morning."

Rhys shrugged. "I'll take my chances."

"All right." She put a pillow and two blankets at the foot of the bed then slipped beneath the remaining covers, turning on her side to face the wall so he would not see the tears that misted her eyes.

Rhys stared at the stiff set of her shoulders for a moment before he got up from the desk. Telling himself he was doing the only sensible thing, he took the pillow and blankets, threw them on the window seat, then blew out the lantern.

Kenna found little satisfaction in hearing Rhys toss

and turn as he tried to make himself comfortable on the padded seat. Darkness and distance gave her courage. "If you do not intend this to be a real marriage, then why did you say there will be no divorce?"

Rhys thumped his pillow. "Pardon. What did you say?"

Would talking to him never be easy? Kenna repeated her question in a rush, stumbling over the words. She swore if he didn't understand her this time he would go to his grave without hearing the words again. He was silent for so long that Kenna thought this was indeed going to be the case.

"What do you mean by a real marriage?" he asked finally.

"You know."

"Oh. Well, yes, I intend ours to be a true marriage. You shall be in charge of all the staff, oversee the running of our home. I doubt you need my permission, but you may harangue me at your leisure over any trifle I've forgotten, or complain bitterly that I've spent far too many hours immersed in matters of trade. We shall go out together and make a polite show of being a most loving couple, leaving our differences behind us. I will endeavor not to flirt overmuch if you will promise the same. An affair for either of us in our first year of marriage would be in bad taste, I think." Rhys was lying on his back, fingers locked behind his head, and for all that his tone was serious, he was smiling broadly. "Have I got the way of it? Is this the real marriage you spoke of? Pray tell me if there is something I've forgotten."

Rhys was so pleased with himself as he developed his speech that he never heard Kenna getting out of bed. His first indication that she had done so was when her pillow thudded into his chest and effectively wiped the smile from his face. He grabbed the pillow, intending to pull her down, but she had already released it. In the blue moonlit shadows of the cabin he could see the pale outline of her gown as she stalked back to bed. He took aim and the pillow thumped unerringly on her derriere.

Kenna paused, not quite believing he had retaliated in kind, then a wicked smile lifted the corners of her mouth. She turned, picked up the pillow at the ends, shook it so the feathers clumped together, and advanced on Rhys. He held up his hands to ward off the blow but Kenna was giving no quarter. She walloped him over the head.

The pillow exploded. A puff of featheres rose above Rhys's face then drifted downward, settling on his cheeks, eyelilds, and in his open mouth. He sat up slowly and deliberately, giving Kenna time to run but knowing there was no place she could hide. He brushed the feathers off his face as Kenna backed away. He heard her give a nervous little laugh as he stood and picked up his own pillow.

Now it was Kenna who held out her arms to keep Rhys at bay. She retreated until she felt the back of her knees connect with the bed frame then she sat down abruptly and scooted to the far side of the bed. "Unfair, Rhys!" she pleaded, choking down her laughter. "I have no weapons left."

That gave Rhys pause and he shook his head slowly. "Oh, Kenna, you have not even begun to tap your arsenal."

In her innocence she looked around frantically for something she might hurl at him. Her search lowered her guard and Rhys hit her shoulder with the pillow, knocking her to one side. She made a grab for it, missed, and prepared herself for another soft blow. When it didn't come she peeked at him through her fingers. His shoulders were shaking, an unmistakable sign that he was laughing at her. She supposed she did look rather funny, curled up with her face in her hands and her backside an obliging target.

"Please, just hit me and get it over with," she said.

"Anything to oblige my wife," said Rhys. The pillow connected with her rump.

With cat-like quickness Kenna caught it from behind and yanked hard, pulling Rhys off balance so he fell on the bed. His fingers lost their grip and though he waited to be clobbered again Kenna merely busied herself fluffing and smoothing the pillow. His eyes widened as she laid it down at the head of the bed and promptly rested her own head upon it. The final straw was when she pulled a blanket over her shoulder and serenely closed her eyes. Her smile was terribly complacent.

"Oh, no," said Rhys, giving her a shake. "You are not going to get away with it. That's my pillow."

"Wife-beater," Kenna murmured, not unkindly.

"Thief!"

"Wretched man."

"Robber!"

"Poor, abused Rhys Canning."

"Sleep-snatcher!"

"Sleep-snatcher?" Kenna's eyes opened. "I take offense to that remark. It's a horrid sort of man who would dare call me a sleep-snatcher. Especially when I'm quite willing to share."

"Share?"

Kenna closed her eyes again and a wisp of smile touched her mouth. "Hmm-mmm. Share my pillow."

"It's *my* pillow."

"A moot point, don't you think, since it's in *my* possession."

Rhys grinned as he stretched out beside her, propping himself on an elbow. "Kenna, are you trying to seduce me?"

"Seduce you?" she asked sleepily. "I think I mentioned once before that I haven't the least idea how to go about it."

Rhys gave her an arch look. "I wonder," he said under his breath.

"Mmmm?"

He slipped down further, pillowing his head on his arm. "No idea at all?"

Kenna touched her cheek where his warm, sweet breath had caressed it. "None."

"Oh."

Was it disappointment she heard? She peeked at him through her lashes. His face was very close, his mouth hovered near her own. "I would kiss you good night, but I fear you may misinterpret the gesture."

"I wouldn't," he said earnestly.

"You're certain?"

"Absolutely."

"Very well," She moved her head a fraction and brushed his lips with hers. "Good night."

"Kenna." His exasperation was obvious.

"What?"

"Aren't you going to give me part of the pillow?" he asked innocently.

It was Kenna's turn to grin. "Beast." She slid the pillow over a little and felt Rhys lay his head close to hers. Though her eyes were still shut she could sense Rhys looking at her. "Go to sleep, Rhys."

He sighed, pulling part of her blanket over him, and closed his eyes. "So you really weren't trying to seduce me."

"Only trying to give you a comfortable bed."

"Thank you." He meant it. The windowseat offered questionable comfort. "Good night, Kenna."

She murmured something in reply and in a few minutes they were both asleep.

When Kenna woke it was still dark. She stretched slightly, feeling a confining ribbon of heat beneath her breasts. It took her a moment to understand it was Rhys's arm that held her and that it was his bare leg that lay between her own. She was lying with her back against his chest, her hips cradled against his thighs. The warmth of him felt delicious next to her and she wondered if it was wicked to find it enjoyable.

She lifted her arm and laid it on his, matching the length and breadth of his hand with her own. Though her fingers were nearly as long as Rhys's, her hand looked impossibly delicate against his. Very lightly she let the tips of her tapered nails trace the length of his lean fingers, drawing gently over his knuckles. Holding her breath, hardly believing the direction of her own thoughts, she lifted his hand and pressed it to her breast. She remembered how it felt when his hands had touched her breast of their own accord, the fine damp heat of his mouth when it replaced his hand and suckled her, arousing slender threads of fire that tugged at her loins. That memory, and the desire to make it more than a memory, gave Kenna courage.

Careful not to wake Rhys, Kenna turned in his arms. She listened to the sound of his even breathing, laid her palm against his chest and felt the steady beat of his heart. It did not matter that the room was dark or that she could only make out the curve of Rhys's shoulder and the beautiful shape of his head. Even if her eyes had been closed she would have seen the firm thrust of his jaw and the hint of vulnerability in his chin. She knew the breadth of his shoulders, the strong column of his throat, the aquiline slant of his nose. These things she remembered in her mind's eye.

While one of Rhys's arms rested on the curve of her waist, the other supported his head. She realized that sometime during the night she had confiscated the pillow. Kenna raised her hand and touched Rhys's forehead, brushing back a lock of his dark hair. Her fingers crept lower, caressing his temple and tracing the outline of his ear. The soft pad of her thumb touched his jaw.

She wondered what Rhys expected from her. How had he thought she would react to the news of their marriage? Had he anticipated she would be uncooperative of his plan, demand a divorce and return to Dunnelly? Had he believed she was so small-minded that she could not appreciate what Rhys was doing to protect her?

Kenna drew one fingertip along Rhys's nose and smiled to herself when he wrinkled it. He was a kind man, she thought, and she had been perfectly horrid to him on more occasions than she could count. That he should want to help her in spite of all she had done to him moved her more deeply than she could express in mere words. She touched his lips, feeling the soft cadence of his breathing, and knew she wanted to feel his breath against her cheek as he whispered her name. No one had ever said her name the way Rhys did, invoking a specialness that often gave her pause. Kenna wondered if she loved him.

The sash that held Rhys's robe together came undone beneath Kenna's fingers. She edged the satin lapels apart, baring his chest. Her hand slipped inside and her palm stroked his warm skin. Nestling closer, she breathed in the clean scent of him, masculine and faintly musky. Kenna's fingers trembled as they glided over the ridge of his ribs and dipped lower, fanning out over his hip. Her knee nudged his and she insinuated her calf between his legs, delighting in the texture of his skin flush to hers. Sighing softly, she wondered if she dared kiss him. Her mouth hovered near his chest but the fraction of an inch that she had to move to touch him seemed a distance too fraught with danger to risk.

Suddenly Rhys's chest began to shake and before Kenna understood that he was laughing, she found herself turned on her back and pinned to the bed. Rhys's hands had snaked around Kenna's wrists and now held them above her head. Most of his weight lay against her, one thigh trapping both her legs and his chest flattening her breasts. She blinked up at him, eyes widening at the wicked grin that outlined two rows of even teeth.

"The truth, madam," he said huskily. "Were you trying to seduce me?"

Kenna shook her head solemnly. "Torture could not wring an admission from me, sir."

"I wasn't thinking of using torture . . . exactly." His lips brushed her mouth and his thighs pressed against her hip so she could not mistake his arousal. "Have you rethought your position?"

"I think my position speaks for itself," she said cheekily though she blushed at her response.

Rhys growled, nipping her earlobe with his teeth. "Let me rephrase my question."

"Please."

"Do you want to make love with me, Kenna?" There was no smile in his voice now, no jest. The silence between them was thick and still as he waited for her reply.

"Yes," she said softly.

"Why?"

Kenna could only stare at him blankly.

"Is it because we're married?"

She could answer that with some assurance. "No."

"Then because I happen to be the man in your bed."

Kenna bristled. Did he think she would behave so wantonly with any man? "No!"

His smile was bleak. "Good. I won't be used again."

Kenna had the grace to be ashamed. "The last time . . . those things I said . . . I didn't mean—"

Rhys gave her a shake. "Don't lie to me now. I found your honesty admirable. You meant what you said. You used me for your own purposes. You hated me, remember?"

She nodded. "I'm sorry. You're right. I did mean those things, but I don't hate you now."

"What do you feel, I wonder?"

The question defeated her. "I don't know."

He sighed, easing the grip on her wrists. "That, at least, is honest."

"Is it enough?"

"It's enough. For now." He kissed her cheek lightly, released her, and turned over on his back. "You may carry on."

Kenna was plainly bewildered. "Carry on?"

"You know, seducing me."

"Oh." She was thoughtful. "Mayhap you would instruct me." She was already turning on her side, fitting the curves of her body to his.

Rhys cleared his throat as Kenna's knee nudged his groin. "I think instructions would be superfluous." His wicked grin returned. "Give me your mouth, Kenna."

"Anything to shut you up."

"I was thinking the same thi—" He did not finish his thought. Kenna's mouth covered his own very sweetly.

Rhys could have drowned in that kiss. Kenna's lips were soft and moist, searching the contours of his mouth for an opening. His abdomen contracted as her palm slid along his ribcage and a husky sigh gave Kenna what she sought. Her tongue slipped in Rhys's mouth at the same time his hand cupped her breast. She moaned her satisfaction against his lips as she relished the pressure of the rough edge of his tongue. Caught in the erotic spell of his touch, Kenna murmured Rhys's name when his fingers tugged at the tip of her breast. The nipple swelled, hardened, while Kenna ached for more than the touch of his hands.

As if Rhys sensed her need he pulled back from the kiss. "Tell me what you want, Kenna."

"You know." Her slender fingers held the side of his face.

"Perhaps," he acknowledged. "But tell me anyway. I want to hear it from you."

The words stuck in her throat. It was one thing to admit to herself that she wanted his mouth on her, quite another to say the words aloud. "I don't think . . ."

"Tell me."

"Kiss my breasts . . . the way you did before. It was . . . it was like fire."

"Was it?" he asked, prolonging the moment.

"Yes."

"Take off your nightgown."

Kenna sat up on her knees, took the hem of her gown, and raised it over her head. Rhys shrugged out of his robe. Both articles of clothing were carelessly relegated to the floor. Rhys touched Kenna's shoulders and pulled her down beside him. He placed teasing, biting kisses on her jaw, the pulsing cord of her neck, and across her collarbone. Kenna moved restlessly beneath him, anticipating the moment his mouth would move over her sensitive, aching breasts.

Rhys spiraled kisses on one breast until he heard Kenna's soft moan of frustration, then his tongue flicked across the tip and she was silenced. The suck of his mouth tugged at Kenna's nerve endings, showering her body in sensation. One of her hands made a fist in his hair, holding him to her, while the other stroked his shoulder. Rhys took the same care with the other breast while the palms of his hands caressed Kenna's hips and thighs. As his fingers dipped intimately Kenna's legs parted. Against her thigh she could feel the hot proof of his arousal and she wondered if she was shameless

267

because she wanted him inside her, filling her, stroking her with pleasure's steady rhythm.

Rhys's mouth left her breasts and moved lower. Kenna sucked in her breath as his lips glided across her abdomen. Without ever knowing quite how it happened Kenna felt Rhys move between her thighs and cup her buttocks in his strong hands. A tremor of shock rippled through Kenna as Rhys bent his head and placed his mouth against her. Mortified, she went rigid and tears sprang unexpectedly to her eyes.

Rhys felt her tension and he stopped. He lowered her hips and stretched out beside her, keeping one leg between hers and caressing her waist with his fingertips. "Kenna? What is it?"

"Why did you do that?"

Rhys resisted asking what *that* was. "All of you is beautiful," he said simply. He lowered his head and kissed her mouth with infinite gentleness. "But until you believe me I will go carefully." He kissed her again, this time with more pressure and felt her respond to his insistence.

Kenna suddenly felt very foolish. She kissed him hard while her palms smoothed the corded muscles of his back. One of her hands slipped between their bodies and sought Rhys's arousal. Rhys required no further encouragement, whispering her name huskily as he thrust into her.

Kenna gasped at the force of his entry and quieted as Rhys stilled, letting her feel the fullness of him inside her. He whispered half-formed words against her skin that made her feel peculiarly alive and desirable. In turn she gave sound to the thoughts that trembled on her lips. When he began to move she moved with him, letting her hands glide over his back until she clutched at his shoulders when a torrent of sensation washed over her. Rhys's thrusts quickened as Kenna lost herself in the purity of pleasure. He tensed above her, gritting her name as he found release.

Kenna touched her mouth to the sheen of perspiration glistening on Rhys's shoulder. Their breathing grew quiet together as Kenna was drawn close to the contours of his body. They fell asleep, neither missing the pillow that had slid to the floor beside their clothes.

Chapter Seven

When Kenna woke it was midmorning. Rhys was no longer beside her and she rose from the bed somewhat self-consciously, bemused that she could have slept so soundly while he prepared to leave the cabin. Memories of being loved by Rhys folded in upon her. Kenna picked up the pillow and hugged it to her breast, burying her smile in its softness. Everything was going to be all right between them. She would not let him regret his decision to marry her!

Kenna washed and dressed hurriedly, anxious to go on deck and see Rhys. Her hair was still damp at her nape and temples when she stepped topside and the cool ocean breeze ruffled it dry. Rhys was standing at the wheel with Captain Johnson. They were watching the man at the helm of the *Carasea*. She suddenly felt shy as Rhys turned when Johnson greeted her, but the welcoming smile that touched his eyes propelled her forward. She took his outstretched hand and allowed herself to be drawn close beside him. One of his arms fell protectively across her shoulders.

"Good morning, sprite," Rhys said softly.

Kenna stiffened a little at the use of her nickname. It was rather deflating that after last night he could call her by a name that was more suited to a child. She was not so certain of herself that his address did not sting her pride. "Good morning."

Rhys frowned slightly, observing her. "Have you had breakfast?"

She shook her head and smiled warmly at the captain. "I trust you are feeling well this morning."

"The day just got a touch brighter, Mrs. Canning. I'd be honored if you'd let me escort you around the ship, then perhaps breakfast with me in my cabin. I've not yet taken my morning meal."

Kenna looked at Rhys, hoping he would tell the captain that he wanted to be with his wife. When he said nothing and merely dropped his arm from around her shoulder Kenna wanted to scream in frustration. Instead she gave him a coolly polite smile and took Johnson's arm. "I'd be delighted, Captain." She glanced over her shoulder as the captain led her away, but Rhys had already turned his back on them and was discussing something with the sailor who held the ship's wheel.

By afternoon Kenna's mood was as gray as the skies. Rhys was busy in the ship's hold when Johnson and she finished their meal and she realized there was no reason for her to stay on deck. She returned to her cabin and read for a while. When that could not hold her interest she began working on her dress. Rain lashed a steady staccato beat against the windowpanes as Kenna sewed. She told herself that she did not expect Rhys to entertain her, but neither did she think he would be so eager to ignore her, passing her off to the captain and finding more work to do simply to avoid her. He did not join her for lunch and when dinner arrived she had given up hope of seeing him. When he came through the door, shivering like a wet pup, Kenna nearly tipped back her chair in surprise.

She stood up quickly. All the sharp, self-pitying

thoughts she had been thinking vanished in the face of her concern. "Rhys? Are you all right?"

Rhys nodded jerkily, stripping off his soaked shirt. "Just wet and cold." He rifled the wardrobe for something to put on while Kenna picked up the wet shirt and wrung it out over the empty copper tub. He sat on one of the chairs and started to take off his boots. His fingers were so stiff with cold that after a few false starts he gave up and sagged against the back of the chair, clearly exhausted.

Kenna draped the shirt over the edge of the tub and smiled at Rhys's abandoned efforts. Shaking her head gently from side to side she knelt in front of him and lifted one of his feet onto her lap.

"Kenna! You don't have to do that! I'll get them off in a few minutes."

"And catch your death in the meantime," she said briskly. She managed the first boot well enough but pulling on the second one sent her to the floor on her backside. "Ooof!" She rubbed her bruised posterior and gave Rhys a quelling look when a smile tugged at the corners of his lips. "Not a word, do you hear? Not a word! Now, get out of those wet trousers while I pour a warm drink for you and serve up a plate of stew."

Rhys wisely tamped down the urge to salute and dutifully followed Kenna's instructions. He put on a pair of warm trousers and a heavy pair of socks and sat back down at the table. Kenna placed a warm mug of tea in his hands and pushed a plate of steaming stew in front of him.

"Why are you smiling?" she asked as she seated herself across from him.

Rhys sipped his drink, feigning ignorance. "Was I?"

"You know you were. Am I so amusing?"

"Amusing?" His dark eyebrows lifted. "Mayhap I do find your efforts to mother me a trifle amusing."

273

"Mother you? Is that what you thought I was doing?"

"Wasn't it?" He put down his cup and began tucking into the stew. "Now don't get your hackles up. It was not so long ago that you would have thrown water over me, pushed me out in the cold, and hoped I froze to death. I can tell you, I infinitely prefer this treatment."

A ghost of a smile touched Kenna's chocolate eyes. "It is not too late to throw you out yet," she reminded him. "Keep smiling and I could be tempted."

Rhys managed a remarkably grave face which brought a bubble of laughter to Kenna's lips. "Am I so amusing?" he asked.

"Yes. Yes, you are."

"Well, that's all right then."

Of a sudden Kenna felt very good. "Yes," she said, looking straight into his soft pewter eyes. "It is."

Rhys doubted he would ever completely understand her moods. She confounded him by seeming to be very pleased with herself. He shrugged philosophically and continued eating.

"You were very busy today," she said. She spread some preserves on a slice of bread and handed it to him.

Rhys took it, thanking her. "You cannot believe how much there is to learn, sprite. I've asked Captain Johnson to teach me everything about ship maintainance, building, and sailing. I confess I find it all more fascinating than I thought possible."

"But surely you do not expect to sail yourself."

"No. That will remain in the capable hands of men like Johnson, but I think it's important that I know how every facet of the business operates. There will be much more to learn once we are in Boston. So many people are depending on Canning Shipping. I won't let them down, Kenna. I am going to make this work."

Kenna believed him. When Rhys spoke with such conviction she could do no less. "Let me help you, Rhys.

I want to. Please."

"Help me? How?" He realized how that sounded and apologized immediately. "I'm sorry. I didn't mean—"

She waved away his concern. "You have every right to be skeptical. I'm not certain that I even know what I mean, but I want to learn with you, Rhys. I don't want to be left behind while you study all manner of wonderful things."

"Wouldn't it bore you?"

"That remark was condescending and not worthy of you. If you find this business fascinating, who is to say I won't? Let me at least have the opportunity to discover it for myself."

It has been years since Rhys had seen so much fire in Kenna's eyes. As much as he enjoyed it he still felt compelled to warn her. "I can't let you disrupt things by getting up to mischief. This isn't some lark, sprite."

There it was again, that odious nickname. He was bent on remembering her as a rattle-brained child. "I know that. I have every intention of applying myself to the best of my abilities. Please, Rhys. Let me learn. I'm starving for it." Only now did she realize how much she missed challenging her mind.

"This isn't the schoolroom," Rhys said gently.

"But it is," she insisted. "In a way it still is. I cannot be a conventional wife, Rhys. It would bore me beyond all reason. Why as quick as that"—she snapped her fingers—"you would find cause to send me to an asylum!"

Rhys grinned at her dramatic announcement. "No doubt I should send myself to one of those places," he muttered under his breath. He glanced at the scraps of fabric that littered the windowseat. The haphazard pile of material bore mute testimony to the fact that while Kenna was a capable seamstress, she disliked the activity. "I think I have always known that you would not suit

275

convention, though these last few years gave me pause. You were fairly drowning in the miserable stuff by the time I returned from the Peninsula."

"It is cruel of you to remind me what a prig I was."

"I doubt I would have phrased it just so."

"Well, it matters not, for it is all behind me now." She leaned forward in her chair. "You must feel it, Rhys. The excitement of a new beginning in America. For me it is like being reborn. Don't raise your eyebrows! I am not overstating what I feel!" she said passionately. "I have left everything behind in England, left everyone but you. You forced this new life upon me but have the kindness to permit me to live it as I wish. I cannot fill my hours with good works as Yvonne does or wait on you as Victorine would want to do. I—"

Rhys held up his hands, cutting her off. "A moment, if you please. I am not married to Yvonne or Victorine. I have no desire for you to emulate either of those lovely women if it goes against your grain. I want you to be happy."

Kenna realized it was rather small of her, but she would have been happy if he had left out the word lovely. "They you'll let me learn with you?"

"As long as you wish," he said easily as if he had never considered otherwise.

Kenna stood and skirted the edge of the table. Her arms came around Rhys from behind, hugging his neck and shoulders. She dropped a kiss on his cheek. "Thank you, Rhys! You won't regret this! I promise I won't interfere with your work! Oh, thank you!" She would have pulled away then but Rhys had taken hold of her slender wrists and was drawing her around the chair. "What are—"

"Come here." He slid back his chair and in the same motion pulled Kenna onto his lap. "If you are of a mind to thank me, do it properly."

Kenna pressed her forehead to his and said softly, "I haven't the vaguest notion what you mean."

"You are the most lamentable liar. Kiss me."

Kenna kissed the tip of his nose.

"On the mouth."

She obliged enthusiastically. When she thought she had responded properly, Kenna drew back and laid her head against the curve of Rhys's shoulder. She felt a rumble of laughter stirring in his chest and she had to smile herself.

"You are rather more obedient than I would have thought possible," he said.

"When it suits me."

"Just as I thought. I wish you had been so affectionate when you came on deck this morning. It seemed you couldn't wait to be gone from my presence."

"You have interpreted the situation badly. It was you who wanted me gone."

Rhys shook his head. "I didn't want you to go, but neither could I offer you an escort around the deck or companionship at breakfast. I may be the head of Canning Shipping when I am in Boston but I made it quite clear to Johnson that while I am on board I work for him. I had not expected him to take such delight in stealing you away." Rhys bent his head and touched her forehead with his lips. "In truth, I did not expect you to find my company worth seeking."

Kenna could not blame him for that and she told him so. "I have not always been kind to you, but you have invariably been tolerant of me. Why?"

Rhys knew himself to be a coward then. He could not bring himself to lay bare the entire truth. "Do you remember when we first met, sprite? You were a guileless four-year-old and I was a very solemn eleven. As I recall you climbed onto my lap much as you have now and proceeded to greet me with a very wet, affectionate kiss."

His voice was soft with the memory. "That innocent overture was the first time in my life anyone had touched me with feeling. I suppose that's why I've never forgotten it. You changed me that day, Kenna. You gave me reason to hope that I could be loved. How could I banish you from my pockets after that, or not take part in your every scrape, or refuse to help even when you wanted none of me? You make me feel alive. That is far more than I have ever done for you."

Kenna's hands slid around him, hugging Rhys to her. "You're wrong, you know. You saved my life."

"Pure selfishness on my part. I only had to ask myself how things would be different without you."

"Then I thank you for being so selfish." Kenna brought her head up and searched Rhys's face. "I'm going to be a very good wife to you, Rhys. I know why you married me and I promise I'll do everything in my power to make sure you don't regret it."

Rhys's brows drew together. She knew why he married her? She knew he loved her? He hesitated a moment, hoping she would say she loved him. When she said nothing else he realized his expectations were too great. He was already regretting that she knew how he felt. Nothing would be served if she made promises because she was grateful to him. He wanted more than that from her. He said the only thing he could. "Just be you, sprite, and I doubt I shall regret anything."

Sprite! He was ridiculous! She was talking about being his wife and he was treating her like a four-year-old again. It was not to be borne! Kenna could not get off his lap quickly enough. She walked away from him, her arms hugging her middle, and missed the look of pure bewilderment crossing Rhys's features.

"Kenna?"

She spun around, hands on her hips and tears glistening in her eyes. "I'm Kenna now, am I?"

278

Rhys shook his head as if to clear it. "What in the devil's name are you talking about?"

She stamped her foot. "Do not be clever!" she snapped. "The devil's name has nothing to do with this. It is my name that is in question."

Rhys's eyes widened. He could not make any sense of her anger but he saw that it was real enough. "Perhaps if you repeat the question," he suggested.

"There isn't any question, at least in my mind. I do not pretend to understand what goes on in yours."

Before Rhys could form a response there was a knock at the door. "Thank God," he said feelingly, welcoming the interruption. He told the knocker to come in as Kenna sat down on the windowseat and picked up her sewing.

The cook's assistant came into the cabin carrying a large tray. "O'Malley sent me to clear the table if you've finished."

Rhys motioned to the remains of their meal. "All done, Hank."

The room was very quiet except for the occasional clatter of the dishes as the helper stacked them on the tray. Kenna was stabbing at the hem of her gown and Rhys was leaning back in his chair, deep in thought. Hank could not get out of the cabin quickly enough.

"Cap'n says to tell you to secure everything, Mr. Canning," he said in a rush as he backed out the door. "This squall is going to get worse afore it gets better."

Rhys nodded shortly and looked past Kenna to the darkening sky outside. His glance returned to Kenna. "What about *this* squall? Is it going to get worse before it gets better?"

She shrugged. "I'm sure I couldn't say."

Rhys pushed himself out of his chair and crossed the room to stand in front of Kenna. Without any warning he took the material from her hand and threw it on the seat.

He grasped her upper arms and pulled her to her feet, then put one arm beneath her thighs and swung her in his arms.

Kenna had no choice but to grasp Rhys's shoulders else risk being dropped to the floor. "What are you doing?" she demanded as Rhys carried her over to the bed.

"You heard Hank. The captain says to secure everything. And you, my dear Kenna, are the only thing worth securing." He tipped her out of his arms onto the bed. While Kenna struggled to sit up and sputtered some sort of unintelligible protest, Rhys locked the cabin door and turned back the wicks on the lantern lights. The cabin, the furniture, even Rhys, dimmed into shadow.

Kenna watched Rhys warily as he approached the bed. She noticed that though the ship was rolling with greater force than it had even minutes before, Rhys's steps were sure, his balance faultless. "Rhys?" Her voice had lost its confident quality. "What are you doing now?" His brief laugh, totally lacking in humor, unnerved her. She scrambled back toward the wall.

"Even in this poor light it should be obvious. I'm taking off my clothes." He drew his linen shirt over his head and carelessly tossed it on a chair.

"But why? It is not much past eight. You surely don't intend to go to sleep now."

"You're right. I don't intend to go to sleep."

"But . . ." Her thoughts faded to nothingness as Rhys bent closer and she caught the flinty gleam in his eyes. His trousers and socks went the way of his shirt and when he sat down on the bed he was naked.

"Come here, Kenna."

She didn't, couldn't, move.

Rhys could, and did. He caught Kenna's arm and pulled her away from the wall while he moved backward on the bed. His hand made a fist in her hair, tightened, and drew her head up so that her parted lips were near his mouth. She was breathing shallowly, clearly frightened by what she did not understand. He laid one palm between her breasts and felt the wild fluttering of her heart.

"Why are you so angry with me?" she whispered.

"I could ask you the same thing."

"But I'm not angry. Not any longer." It was true, she thought. Her anger had vanished the moment he held her again. She wondered at the power he had over her, wondered anew if loving him gave him that power.

"Then it's the same for me. But I find I want you very, very much." His mouth descended hungrily on hers.

Kenna discovered her desire matched his own and returned his kiss measure for measure. Rhys's grip on her hair lessened as her arms slid around his neck and she pressed herself to his naked chest. She felt Rhys's fingers on the back of her gown, loosening it enough so he could drag it over her shoulders and free her breasts. Her soft gasp rent the air as his mouth touched the aching tips of her nipples. When he would have returned his lips to hers she stopped him.

"Help me out of this dress." The neckline of the gown was bunched about her waist and the skirt had ridden up her thighs.

"Turn around." When she had done so Rhys fiddled with her gown, teasing her bare shoulders with kisses. "I think you can get out of it now," he said huskily. She had better be able to because he was within seconds of tearing it off her.

Kenna scooted off the bed and stepped out of the dress, then quickly discarded her undergarments. She tumbled back onto the bed when the ship shifted beneath her feet. Rhys caught her and pulled her over him as they both fell back on the thick feather tick. Kenna laughed a trifle breathlessly, looking down into his face. "I have yet to cultivate my sea legs."

Rhys's palms glided along the backs of her thighs.
"Graceless wench. I love your legs." His hands cupped
her buttocks and gave her a little jerk. Her thighs,
slipping over him, and Kenna found herself straddling
Rhys. She placed her hands on his shoulders and raised
her torso, feeling his hardness pressing against her flat
belly. Rhys's arms stretched in front of him, fondling her
swollen, sensitive breasts. "Ride me, Kenna."

She required no further instructions, understanding
full well what he wanted. Kenna raised herself slightly
and with Rhys's help and throaty encouragement, guided
herself onto him. She bit back a small cry of wonderment
as she adjusted to the feel of him deep inside her.

"It's all right, Kenna. I want to hear you. Don't hold
anything back." He rocked his hips once to give her the
rhythm then caught his breath as she began to move.

Kenna gloried in the control she had. She teased him
with her slow thrusts in much the manner he had taunted
her. She ached for release yet did all that was in her
power to prolong its moment. Most of all she watched his
face, loving the tension and desire she brought to his
mouth, his eyes, the set of his jaw. "Yes," she said when
one of his hands slipped from her breast and probed
gently between her thighs. "Please," she murmured on a
thread of sound as his fingers sought and found and
stroked the moist bud of her pleasure. "I want—" she
began, but she could not complete the thought as a force
more powerful for the moment than her will took over.
Her hips moved more quickly and then it seemed as if
every muscle in her body tensed in anticipation of what
would follow. Kenna's head was flung backward, her
neck and back arched in an abandoned posture that was
the most beautiful thing Rhys had ever seen. His fingers
pressed against Kenna's thighs as he felt the nearness of
his own release. He arched into her, bringing a soft cry to

her lips, then she fell forward and moved with him again until she felt the astonishing strength of his climax.

Her head rested very close to his while his hands massaged her back and buttocks, quieting her. After a few moments he turned them on their side and withdrew from her. Even his gentle movement was more than Kenna could bear. She clutched his shoulders, her fingers digging into his taut flesh as another river of sensation swelled within her.

"Rhys!" She cried out his name, panicked at the return of the sweet frisson of pleasure. She didn't think she could bear it again, not so soon, not so unexpectedly. Kenna buried her face in his shoulder, mortified that seemingly against her will her hips were pressing hard at his thighs.

"It's all right," he whispered. "More than all right." He cradled her buttocks and urged her closer until the intense, relentless pressure of their contact brought Kenna the end she sought.

"My God!" she breathed against his neck.

"Mmmm." Rhys pressed a smile to her forehead and brushed a few damp tendrils of hair from her nape.

"What happened to me?"

"Nothing out of the extraordinary."

"So you say. From where I am it was extraordinary indeed."

"It is not so uncommon for a woman to reach her pleasure more than once during lovemaking."

It would have been unfair to ask him how he knew, so Kenna held her jealous question. She didn't think she wanted to know the answer even if he had deigned to tell her. She shivered slightly in his arms and he drew one of the blankets that had been kicked aside over them.

"Kenna," he said after a moment when he could still feel the heat from her cheeks burning his shoulder. "I found it incredibly beautiful. More to the point, I find you incredibly beautiful." When she didn't say anything Rhys gave her a gentle shake, "Kenna?" Rhys laughed ruefully when he still received no response. She was sound asleep.

It took Kenna more than a few seconds to orient herself when she awoke. She was lying on the floor, tangled in a sheet and two blankets, and the ship's roll had increased to nauseating proportions. She groped for the edge of the bed and tried to find some humor in the fact she had fallen out of it. "You really are a graceless wench," she said aloud. The sound of her own voice was muted by the waves crashing against the hull of the ship and the shouting she could hear from the men above her. She patted the bed, searching for Rhys but knowing too well that he was gone. He must have been summoned on deck to help the others manage the *Carasea* in the storm. "Now is as good a time as any to earn your sea legs," she decided, reasoning she may as well be terrified on deck as below it.

Kenna freed herself from the tangle of blankets and stood, balancing herself the way she had seen Rhys do. Still, the short walk to the wardrobe was an uphill, then downhill, battle. Kenna rifled the wardrobe until she found a pair of Rhys's breeches and a shirt. To keep the breeches around her waist she improvised a sash from the material he bought her. She had no suitable shoes and no illusions that she could manage barefoot as many of the men did. She stuffed a pair of shoes belonging to Rhys with scraps of material and put on several pairs of woolen stockings for good measure. The shoes were still no more than an adequate fit.

As soon as she shuffled her way topside she questioned the wisdom of her actions. One of her shoulders was already bruised from banging it against the wall of the companionway and the moment she stepped on deck her hair was plastered to her head by the lashing rain. She had to squint to see more than a few yards in front of her.

"You there!" The rough voice came from behind her and Kenna nearly jumped out of her shoes. "This is no time to be standin' around. Didn't you hear the cap'n say we've got to haul in those sails?"

Kenna held up her hand to shield her eyes and glanced overhead. Some of the sails had come loose from the yardarms and were beating vainly against the wind like moths with broken wings. On deck men were struggling with the lines to haul them up but the ropes had become hopelessly tangled and the pulleys so clogged that it would require men in the rigging to finish the task. Kenna's protest that she was not up to such work died in the wind. Her elbow was grabbed and she was pulled across the heaving deck with some force.

"Up you go, laddie," came the order. "I'm right behind you."

Kenna grabbed the rigging in both her hands and heaved herself up, clutching the slick ropes for dear life. Her feet slid almost immediately on the lines and she kicked off her shoes. Her toes curled on the ropes and once she felt confident of her footing she scrambled a few yards higher. As the gale force winds buffeted her and whistled past her ears the *Carasea* leaped on the crest of a breaking wave and listed at a sickening angle. "I am no hothouse flower. I am no hothouse flower." She repeated the litany in her head as she continued to climb. "Kenna Canning is no hothouse flower." Her heart thumped in her chest to the rhythm of her words. In front of her the sail flapped, trying to knock her off the ropes. Below her the deck tilted alarmingly. And behind her was an endless expanse of angry ocean. Kenna drew in a deep breath and struggled on gamely. She was going to live through this, she told herself, if only to give Rhys the pleasure of killing her for her foolishness.

Several other men had joined her on the rigging and

one of them took charge, yelling orders in such thunderous tones that even the shrieking wind could not silence him. "Wait for the lull! Steady on the downbeat when she shakes the wind from her sail! Heave!"

Kenna followed the lead of the men around her although in her heart she doubted if the thrashing sail could ever be tamed. But it was just as the self-appointed leader said. When the *Carasea* shifted downward she shook off the wind as if brushing aside a bothersome pest and her sails flattened. Kenna reached with the others and grasped the lines.

"Heave again!"

Their combined efforts rolled the sail less than a yard before the ship swung upward and wind filled the canvas again. Kenna thought she would suffocate as the billowing sail enfolded her body. She held onto the line with white-knuckled determination and no small amount of strength born of fear. At the next lull the order came again and she heaved with all of her might. It seemed an eternity before the final demand on her strength was made.

"Once more! Heave lively, men!"

Kenna pulled on the wet line with everything she had and the sail was furled. Quickly, before they lost it again, five pairs of hands tore at the sail and lashed it to the yardarm. Euphoria lent Kenna the stamina to scramble down the rigging behind the others. On the mizzenmast and foremast more sails were being lashed and the *Carasea* put her shoulder to the sea, riding in the trough between the waves as secure as a babe in arms.

Kenna jumped down on the deck, amazed at the difference in the ship's motion now that the sails were secured. Someone slapped her on the back, nearly knocking her to her knees.

"Damn good job, laddie."

Kenna grinned rather stupidly as she faltered on her

feet. Her shirt was molded to her breasts and she pulled it away as she straightened. "You too," she said hoarsely. Rain continued to blind her, stinging her face and shoulders. Someone else brushed past her and gave her a congratulating shake on her arm.

A familiar voice rose above the lashing wind. "We can go below now! There's nothing else to be done. She'll ride this out!"

Kenna looked up, startled to hear Rhys beside her. "Rhys!"

Rhys slid a little on the slippery deck before he was able to halt his forward motion. "Kenna!" He turned and astonishment etched his taut features as he came face to face with his wife. "What the hell are you doing up here?"

"I fell out of bed!" she shouted back as if it explained everything. "Did you see, Rhys?" She pointed at the mainsail secured on the yardarm. "I helped do that!" Her eyes traveled upward to the spot on the rigging where she had been perched. How was it that the height seemed more dizzying now than when she had been clutching at the lines? When she faced Rhys again she felt light-headed. "Oh my!" she said giddily.

"Kenna?" Rhys stepped forward.

Kenna was not certain if the ship pitched or if her knees buckled. It mattered not. She fell into Rhys's strong arms in a dead faint. . . .

. . . Kenna was in the gallery at Dunnelly again but this time she was not hiding behind the sofa, nor was she thirteen any longer. She spun around as the door opened and her beloved highwayman entered the room. When he shut the door and leaned against it Kenna ran to him. Rhys did not hesitate to fold her in his embrace. He touched her upturned face with his fingertips and

287

caressed the length of her back before he kissed her full on the mouth.

"You make a lovely Cleopatra," he said, teasing the blunt black ends of her shoulder-length wig. "But I prefer your own hair. This is rather too dark for your fairness."

"Silly! I am not Cleo. I'm a highwayman, as you are."

"Look again. It is an odd sort of rogue who shimmers when he walks."

Kenna drew back and looked down at herself. Amazement struck her every feature. She was indeed wearing a close-fitting, narrow gown of spangled gold and sandals on her feet. She touched her forehead and could feel the gold leaf circlet that held her coal black wig in place. On her bare arms were bracelets, fashioned like snakes, that were fitted above her elbows. She glanced up at Rhys and bewilderment etched her smile. "How odd," she said slowly. "I am certain I intended to be a highwayman this evening."

Rhys's eyes crinkled at the corners as he laughed. "No matter. I much prefer this guise. Come. How may this rogue be of service to the Egyptian queen?"

Kenna slid her regal arms about Rhys's neck. "You may kiss me, sir. And go on kissing me until I call a halt."

"My pleasure," he murmured as his lips sought hers.

Kenna was pulled against his hard body and clutched his shoulders for support. His kiss was demanding and hungry. His chest offered her breasts all the comfort of sheer rock. Kenna closed her eyes and pressed against him, trying to make him yield to her softer contours.

When her eyes fluttered open she was no longer in the gallery, but had been magically transported to the cave. She lay flat against a damp stone wall, gripping its sheer face so that she might hear everything going on in the chamber beyond. Kenna wanted to leave the cave and return to the safety of the gallery but she could not turn away. She was compelled against her will to go through the same motions she always had . . .

Rhys touched Kenna's forehead, brushing back a wayward curl that had fallen over her brow. She moved restlessly beside him, tossing and turning, finding no comfort in any position. Rhys wrung out the damp cloth he had in the basin on his right and bathed her perspiring face.

Kenna had come out of the faint shortly after Rhys had put her in bed. She was so pale and appeared so vulnerable that he hadn't the heart to upbraid her for this latest escapade. She was safe, all of a piece, and it was enough for now. She fell asleep shortly after Rhys helped her strip off her wet clothes. He slipped in beside her and the *Carasea* rocked him to sleep with Kenna curled securely against his length. When he shut his eyes he was certain a veritable tidal wave couldn't wake him, but he hadn't counted on Kenna clawing at his chest or kneeing him in the groin. Pain brought him sharply awake and his initial effort to rouse Kenna was unsuccessful. That was when he grabbed the basin and began bathing her face. Now he wondered if he should try to wake her again.

He touched her shoulder and said her name with gentle insistence. She said something but Rhys could neither make out the words nor be sure she was really responding to him.

"It's a dream, Kenna. A dream." He drew the cloth over her neck. "Wake up, darling." Droplets of water trickled on her flushed cheeks, mixing with the tears that were squeezing out from under her closed lids. Rhys put the basin on the floor and dropped the cloth in it. He picked Kenna up and embraced her as she began to sob uncontrollably. Repeating her name in a soft litany, he rocked her in his arms.

Kenna's scream was muffled against Rhys's damp shoulder. She opened her eyes, blinking several times to clear them. "Dear God," she husked jerkily. "Oh, Rhys, it was awful!"

"Sssh! It's over. It was the dream, nothing more."

She nodded. "I'm sorry I woke you. Did I scream?"

"Only at the end, just before you woke. Do you want to talk about it?"

"I think I must. Mayhap I can put it straight in my own mind."

"Here. Lie down." Rhys shifted so Kenna could lie back. He stretched out at her side and propped himself on an elbow. Her nightgown had tucked up about her thighs and Rhys smoothed it, then tucked a blanket about both of them. "Better?"

"Mmmm. I can hardly think how to begin."

"Wherever you like." He reached for her hand and squeezed it for assurance.

Kenna smiled faintly. "It began differently this time. I was in the gallery."

"What were you doing there?"

"In most of the dreams I am waiting for Yvonne. She is still at the masque, you see, and I hide in there until there is an opportunity to get her out of the ballroom. Only this time it was different. I wasn't dressed as a highwayman, but as Cleopatra, and I was waiting for you, not my sister. The Cleopatra disguise is easy enough to explain. It is how I intended to dress before I coerced Yvonne into the tower room."

"But you never wore it. When we found you in the cavern you had on the highwayman guise."

"Yes, I know." She hesitated, trying to find the words to explain what she thought had happened in her dream. "It is all very confusing, you understand, but I wasn't thirteen when the dream began. I think I was dressed so because I wanted to . . . to seduce you."

"I see," Rhys said slowly, the glimmer of a smile quivered on his lips. "And did you?"

"I think I started to," she answered seriously. "You didn't like the wig. You said my hair was too dark." Self-consciously she touched her burnished curls. "This color must bother me more than I thought."

Rhys was fascinated by the blend of reality and unreality in her dream though he didn't have any clue as to what it meant or why it existed. "What happened then?"

"We kissed."

"Aaah," he said wisely. "Then the wig did not concern me overmuch."

Kenna gave his hand a little shake in reproof. "I was holding onto you very tightly. It was as if you were carved from stone. And then, without warning, you *were* stone, and I found myself in the cave. I wanted the dream to end then, for something told me it was a dream this time. But knowing did not help. I could not back away from the antechamber entrance. It was as if some force compelled me to go through the sequence of events again."

Rhys heard a certain breathlessness enter her voice and she was beginning to rush her words. "Slowly, Kenna. Go through it with me now, but slowly. You can stop any time you wish. I won't force you."

Kenna felt her palms begin to sweat. "I was crouched against the wall, listening to the argument that was going on in the chamber. The two men from the boat . . ." She stopped. "You know about the boat, don't you?"

"Yes. Nick told me that you swore a ship signaled from the channel and a pair of men rowed up on the beach."

"That's right. Their backs were to me and they partially hid you. I mean the man I thought was you," she corrected quickly. "But I could see Victorine clearly enough. She was arguing, or perhaps pleading would explain it better, with the Frenchmen."

"Are you certain they were French?"

"As certain as I am about anything else, which is to say everything is open for interpretation."

"Go on."

"My father came then. Rhys, I never saw it happen this way before, but I swear my father walked through the chamber wall. I know it is too much to be believed but that's what seemed to happen." She laughed uneasily. "Why am I telling you this? It sounds more incredible when I hear it aloud."

"Never mind," he cut in. "Tell me what happened next."

Kenna was slightly taken aback by the tenor of seriousness in Rhys's voice. Even she did not credit her own memory on this count, yet Rhys was hanging on every word. "Well, he stepped into the chamber and the gap in the rock behind him simply disappeared. He ordered Victorine to come to his side and chastized her for putting any credence in the plans of her escort or those of the Frenchmen. I was frightened for my father then. The Frenchmen were agitated and Victorine was sobbing. I edged toward the entranceway, thinking that disguised as I was, I could help my father."

"But he recognized you, didn't he?"

"Yes." Her breath caught on a harsh sob. "I cannot forget how he looked at me. There was so much grief in his eyes that I was paralyzed by the enormity of what I was doing. I used to believe Victorine diverted his attention so the lantern light was knocked out, but I know it was me. Do you think this is what I don't want to remember? That I am the one who killed my father?"

"Kenna! No! You're wrong!" Rhys let go of her hand and cupped the side of her face, brushing away salty tears with the pad of his thumb. "You did not kill your father! Think back, Kenna. You told me much the same thing

292

the night I came to your bedchamber at Dunnelly. Remember? You mistook me for Nick on that occasion. There is something else you do not want to recall, something more painful perhaps than your father's grief at seeing you in the cave."

"I don't know what it is, Rhys! I don't!"

"Who is the man who stood at Victorine's side, Kenna?"

"I don't know!" She closed her eyes tightly and her head swayed from side to side in negation. "I cannot remember! The lantern goes out. It is so dark! So dark! I can't see anything. If only it would stay lighted longer. I would see his face clearly. But I can't see it now, Rhys! Don't make me try to see it now!"

"All right, Kenna. That's enough." He slid off his elbow and put his head next to hers. One arm embraced her shoulders and his even voice calmed her. "You don't have to remember anything. I told you, you are safe here and I meant it. It is all in the past."

"Then why must I go on reliving it?" she asked plaintively. "I want to be done with it."

The only answer Rhys had was one she didn't want to hear. He doubted she would ever be free of her nightmare until she knew with certainty who murdered her father. He wisely kept his counsel. A short time later her question was forgotten as she fell asleep in the security of his arms.

The pleasant, familiar aroma of coffee woke Kenna. She opened her eyes and saw Rhys sitting at the table, drinking from a steaming mug while he read the captain's log book. Some movement she made must have caught his eye because he looked up and smiled at her. He raised the cup slightly.

"Would you like some? There's plenty."

"Please. It smells delicious." She threw back the covers and went to the wardrobe to find her dressing

293

gown. "I thought you would be on deck," she said, tying her sash.

Rhys handed her a cup. "Careful, it's hot."

She sipped it gingerly and made a face. "I don't think I shall get used to this. I much prefer tea." She glanced out the window and saw that the sun had barely lifted above the horizon. The sky was as sharp as blue crystal and without a single cloud to bear evidence of last night's storm. "I had no idea it was so early."

Rhys laughed at Kenna's wistful sidelong look at the bed. "Put it out of your mind. If you truly want to begin learning at my side, it starts at daybreak. You had only a few minutes more sleep before I rolled you out of bed myself."

"Brute. You would have done it, too. And no doubt taken pleasure in it."

"I'm not about to deny it and have you call me a liar," he said pleasantly. "I admit there would have been a certain amount of satisfaction in it after last night."

Kenna paled as she lowered herself into a chair. "I'm sorry about the nightmare, Rhys, I couldn't help—"

Rhys's gray eyes widened in alarm. "Kenna! I wasn't referring to your dream! Have I given you cause to think I would not let it rest?"

"No," she said guiltily.

"Well then, what I was referring to was your presence on deck, or should I say, above deck?"

"Oh, that."

"Oh, that," he mocked. "*That* likely caused me to lose a score of years. What possessed you to do such a dangerous thing? And don't tell me again that you fell out of bed. One event does not necessarily lead to the other."

Her chin lifted a notch. "Of course one does not lead to the other," she said loftily. "I am not such a nuncheon that I would climb that rigging because I fell out of bed. I

294

was on deck because I fell out of bed. I was in the rigging because at the time there didn't seem to be any choice but that I help."

"I vow I am an old man, growing older by the second," he sighed, rolling his eyes above the rim of his coffee mug. "I may have understood that explanation ten or more years ago when a certain Miss Scrapegrace offered it so charmingly, but I believe time has addled my brain. More clearly, if you please. And more slowly."

Kenna took a quick gulp of her coffee to brace herself for a full explanation, then had to fan her open mouth with her hand.

"I warned you it was hot."

She wrinkled her nose at him. "Strive not to always be right. It could become frighteningly boring."

"Point taken. Now your explanation, please."

"Very well. I woke when I fell out of bed."

Rhys feigned dismay, shaking his head. "That effectively puts a period to my sleepwalking theory."

"Do you mind?" she asked frostily. "As I was trying to say, I was rather frightened when the ship's rolling tumbled me out of bed. You were not here and I surmised, quite correctly I might add, that you had gone above to help the others in the storm. I did not feel at all comfortable waiting in my cabin while the wind tossed this ship around like so much driftwood, so I decided to find you. Thinking I might begin my education immediately I borrowed a few of your things to wear and went on deck. Before I had even the opportunity to look for you, not that I could see much in that rain, someone who plainly did not recognize me, ordered me to help secure the mainsail. I said no, Rhys. Honestly, I did. But who could hear me in that gale? I was practically dragged to the rigging and there was nothing for it but to begin climbing."

Rhys's jaw was working from side to side and his eyes were flinty. "I'll have the man who forced you keel-hauled."

"I haven't vaguest notion who it was," she said. "And if I did, I wouldn't say. He didn't know who I was and he was only carrying out the captain's orders. Anyway, keel-hauling, whatever it is, sounds positively barbaric."

"It is," Rhys assured her with no remorse. "I may yet use it on you."

"Well, that would be different, because I probably deserve it," she pointed out calmly.

"Don't tempt me. Carry on." He added "please" as an afterthought.

"There is not much more to explain. I was fearful of disobeying because I didn't know what would happen. For all I knew I might have been tossed overboard. I started up the rigging. Oh! That's when I kicked off your shoes. Have they turned up?"

It occurred to Rhys that for his patience he should have been nominated for sainthood. "Someone found them and brought them here after I carried you to the cabin."

"Imagine that. I can't quite think how they weren't washed away."

"A bloody miracle," he gritted.

Kenna could not fail to miss the edge of frustration in his voice. She took a more cautious sip of her drink and continued quickly. "I think you know the rest. I climbed the rigging and helped the others secure the sail. I don't mind telling you I was frightened and there is no need for you to forbid me to do it again because I've already made up my own mind. Nothing could induce me to go up there a second time. I kept telling myself that I would prove I was no hothouse flower, that I was up to the task, but it was silly, really. And useless. My feet touched the ground and poof!" She spread her hands and fingers. "I wilted like a plucked daisy."

Rhys doubted this was the moment to point out that a daisy hardly qualified as a hothouse flower. He fought down a smile. If she suspected how effectively she had disarmed him, he would forever be at her mercy. "Then this is the end of it," he said tersely.

"The end."

"And I will never have to look overhead to find you."

"Never."

"And if I should find you in the rigging . . ."

"I know," she said sagely. "Keel-hauling would be too good for me."

"Exactly." Rhys hesitated, thinking over his words carefully. "All things considered, it was a good piece of work, Kenna."

Her cheeks reddened a bit beneath his praise, knowing what it cost him to voice it. "Thank you."

A genuine smile touched Rhys's mouth and he eased back in his chair and relaxed. "Now, why don't you finish your coffee, eat some of your breakfast, and dress? There are some papers and things in Johnson's cabin that I want to share with you."

During the weeks that followed Kenna proved herself to be more than an eager pupil. She was a bright and learned one as well. Rhys marveled at her quick grasp of figures and her ability to plot a course with unfailing accuracy. They shared every idea, every scheme, that would bring Canning Shipping back from financial disaster. With Captain Johnson's knowledge of the type of ships remaining with the line, Kenna and Rhys planned the actions they needed to take. The problem loomed clear before them. They needed to raise capital by taking command of the quickest routes with the best profits.

A scant two weeks before the *Carasea* would dock in Boston Harbor Kenna was still mulling over their chief concern. The task was made difficult because Rhys was nibbling her neck and showed every sign that he was not going to content himself with only one portion of her anatomy.

Kenna was languishing in the copper tub, up to her shoulders in water scented with a few drops of perfume. The cabin was lighted by more than a dozen candles Rhys had set out on the table and Kenna was not insensitive to the romantic possibilities. Some evenings they were so exhausted from their labors they simply fell into bed and were asleep before their heads touched the pillow they shared. Tonight was definitely not one of those evenings; not after nearly a week of abstinence when Rhys was considerate of the embarrassment she felt because of her monthly courses. "I thought you were going to wash my back," she said. Dipping her fingers in the warm water, she flicked a few drops backward and hoped they met her target.

"I thought that's what I was doing," he whispered against her ear. The light from the candles flickered across the strands of red-gold hair. Rhys never admitted how happy he was to see the last of the mahogany dye wash away.

"Then you should have paid more attention when I was scrubbing yours. I don't think you've mastered the way of it."

"Pity. I think I've lost the cloth."

Before his hand could dive beneath the water, Kenna stopped him. "I'll find it. Don't trouble yourself."

"No trouble," he assured her, grinning wickedly behind her.

She slapped his hand again for good measure. "I can always count on you to state the obvious." Kenna groped beneath the surface and came up with the cloth. "Here it is." She handed it over her shoulder and leaned forward, hugging her knees and sighing with pleasure as Rhys trickled water over her back. He applied the cloth gently in an ever-widening circle. "I've been thinking," she said dreamily, then qualified quickly. "About the routes and cargoes."

"Pity." Rhys echoed his earlier sentiment.

"If we were unscrupulous we would have the problem of capital solved."

Rhys knew precisely to what she was referring. "Could you live with yourself if we involved our ships in the slave trade or opium smuggling?"

"You know I couldn't. And neither could you."

"Are you certain about me?"

She knew Rhys was teasing. If she had felt more confident of his feelings for her she would have told him then that she loved him, and loving him made it quite impossible for her to believe he could engage in any illegal or immoral trade. "I'm certain," she said simply, but with complete conviction.

"Good." He lifted a handful of hair at her neck and kissed the damp, baby soft skin.

"I've been thinking of alternatives," she said, unable to hide the frisson of pleasure that ran down her spine.

Sighing, Rhys sat back on his heels and began scrubbing again. This time the cloth covered her slender back in long even strokes, dipping below the water to touch the curve of her buttocks. "So? What weighty thoughts have occupied your mind?"

"Fresh fruit and coffee."

"Again, please?"

"Fresh fruit. I miss it dreadfully. So must New Englanders in winter time. Oranges. Lemons and limes. Bananas from South America. All manner of fruit from the West Indies. And coffee. Judging by the Americans I've met, they cannot seem to get enough of the bitter stuff. Who are we to change their tastes? Canning ships will bring it to ports in the north in record time."

Rhys stopped scrubbing a moment. "May I be skeptical?"

"Of course."

"Well then, aside from the fact that a taste for coffee is not peculiar to Americans and that Lloyds of London had its beginnings in an establishment that served the bitter stuff by the gallon—"

"I concede your point."

"How do you propose we transport our cargo? According to Johnson we have but one ship with a hold of any credible size, and we're sailing on it. The others were lost in the war when they attempted to carry on trade in the face of English guns."

"But we have the privateers. The light, swift schooners that could elude British frigates and capture prize ships."

"Would that they had captured more. We wouldn't be in this predicament."

"It's unimportant," Kenna said airily. "These ships could be our beginning. The captain says they are like quicksilver gliding over the water. And from the plans he showed us, their holds are more than adequate to carry a goodly supply of coffee and fruit. More importantly they can carry it quickly, over an established route, and bring it north before the cargo spoils. With the profits we will build ships equal to this one, for the longer routes, say to China and India."

"China? India? You have no small dreams, Kenna." He began washing her arms though his movements were haphazard, thoughtful. "Not that I expected less. It would be possible, I think."

"I *know* it would be." She took the cloth from his hand, lathered it, and began soaping her neck, shoulders

300

and breasts.

Rhys moved to the side of the tub and watched her. He wondered how guileless her gentle motions really were. There was nothing innocent about the sideways glance she gave him beneath her thick lashes. His heart began to hammer. He cleared his throat. "It's an excellent idea."

"I'm glad you think so."

"You do realize that when we arrive in Boston, winter will be more than seven months away? Fresh fruit from the Indies may not be in great demand."

"I think there is always a demand for fruit. Granted, the winter months would be more profitable, but we can earn enough for a good beginning. I think coffee will not present the same problem." Kenna leaned back in the tub, raised one leg, and began to wash it with languid strokes.

"There may be other lines with the same idea."

She nodded. "I already thought of that. Canning will simply be the best."

"I believe you." He reached over the tub and placed his hand on hers, stopping her movement. He took the cloth away from her. "Let me finish."

Kenna closed her eyes in acquiescence as Rhys began washing her leg. At his hands bathing became a highly erotic experience and Kenna cheerfully gave herself up to the delicious sensations he created. He lifted her calf higher to wash the back of her knee and paid particular attention to her toes. Once he tugged on them with his teeth and she shivered in spite of the warm water that lapped at her skin. In turn he washed the other leg, though Kenna found his actions more of a caress and less of a good scrubbing. At some point he abandoned the cloth and continued with only the soap in his palm, dipping his hand below the water and lathering her thighs and belly until her lips parted on a near purring sound

301

born of excitement and contentment.

Her tongue peeped out to moisten her lips then retreated when she felt the warmth of his face very close to hers. She waited, anticipating the moment when his mouth would seek hers. When seconds went by and he did not fulfill the promise of his nearness, Kenna cautiously opened her eyes.

Rhys's face was indeed very near hers. His eyes were dark with desire, only a sliver of silver ringed the black centers. He was searching her face as if making a memory. The tenderness, the heat, of his gaze as it slipped over her brows, her cheeks, and settled on her mouth, touched Kenna's soul. This beautiful man wanted her. And she wanted him no less.

"Rinse."

Kenna blinked at the command, tersely and huskily given. She hesitated a second too long as she realized his order was all in aid of teasing her.

"If you don't rinse I'm coming in after you."

Kenna slid lower in the tub and calmly brushed away the remains of soap on her shoulders. She had no idea that the smile that crossed her face beckoned him to join her anyway. Nor had she any conception of the willpower it required on his part to ignore her invitation. Her eyes followed his movements as he stood and skirted the tub to get the bucket of fresh water warming on the stove. Kenna stood, not only comfortable with her nakedness, but proud of it also. Some imp made her ask, "Do you remember the first time you saw me in a tub?"

Rhys began pouring the fresh water over her shoulders to wash away the last of the soap. Kenna tipped back her head, arching her neck and breasts to feel the water cascade over her tingling flesh. Rhys felt a hard knot of desire form in his loins and had difficulty understanding her question, let alone answering it. It was not until

302

Kenna had casually relieved him of the wooden pail that he realized where it would have lead. He backed away from the tub, but not quickly enough to get out of the line of fire.

"You practically drowned me on that occasion!" she announced, heaving the contents of the bucket in his direction.

Rhys sputtered and coughed and wondered why he had bothered lifting his hands to protect himself. That had certainly been a useless gesture, unless, of course, she had followed through by pitching the bucket. He came out from behind his dripping hands and grinned wickedly. "If you thought to cool my ardor, madam, your plan has failed."

Kenna's eyes dropped to the bulge wetly outlined in his trousers. "Oh, my!" She quickly jumped out of the tub and grabbed the towel that hung over the back of a chair, holding it up in front of her like a shield. She backed away from Rhys's slow advance around the tub and bumped into the table. The candles swayed alarmingly, their yellow light flickering wildly. She would have liked to rub her bruised hip but it was clear Rhys was giving no quarter. Hastily she moved away from the table and looked for something to put between them.

Rhys laughed as he saw Kenna's eyes dart about the cabin. "I suggest you see to your comfort, Mrs. Canning, for I swear I'll take you anywhere I find you." He pointed to the massive desk that Kenna was nearing. "Anywhere."

Kenna's cheeks pinkened at his announcement, knowing he meant every word. One afternoon he had surprised her while she was reading at the windowseat, blithely unaware of the seductive picture she made curled in the corner, head tipped to one side as she studied a dusty old manual. On that occasion they never made it as far as the bed.

Kenna remembered the floor hadn't become uncomfortable until after they finished making love, but then, it was horribly unyielding. The bed offered the most sensible alternative and Kenna nearly leaped for it as Rhys made a grab for her. Her towel tangled in her legs, offering no protection whatsoever. Kenna reached for the pillow and flung it at him as he approached the bed. Rhys brushed it aside with his arm, letting it fall to the floor, and began stripping off his wet clothes. Kenna observed him unabashedly, her attention riveted to the play of his muscles, the tautness of his belly, and the undeniable evidence of his need. Rhys watched her watching him and was caught unaware by the pleasure her desire gave him.

"The bed was a wise choice, Kenna. We can save the desk for another time."

She took the towel by its opposite ends, spun it so it wrapped along its length, and snapped him on the thigh with it.

Rhys was too quick for her and before she could bring it in he grabbed it. "That was too close," he said pulling it out of her hands and tossing it beside the pillow. He knelt on the bed and took her by the shoulders. "If you have such strong objections to the desk, I wish you would voice them rather than attempt to do me grievous injury."

Kenna's hands slid along his waist then over his hips. "You appear none the worse for it." Then she began to fondle him, smiling shyly up into his eyes.

Rhys growled deep in his throat as his mouth came down on Kenna's. She savored the urgency of his kiss, the flavor of this special communion. She knew that she loved him and wished for the confidence to say the words. In the end she said it with her body, with the mounting tension in her flesh, hoping he would understand that her giving was the expression of all that she felt.

She caressed him with her hands and mouth, whispering words that she never could have uttered in any other circumstance. She grew brave, taking the initiative and becoming the aggressor, stunning Rhys with the force of her passion. He let her explore his body until she knew the sensitivity of his flesh, knew precisely where to touch him to trip his heartbeat or cause his breath to catch. In turn she surrendered her body to the same exploration and offered herself up to the skillful hands of her lover. Nothing he did to her was shameful or ugly. Kenna could find only beauty and pleasure in the touch of his mouth on her breasts, at her hip, and between her thighs.

Rhys gently urged Kenna to lie on her stomach then knelt behind her and raised her hips. His palms stroked her back, came under her to caress her breasts, and then he thrust deeply into her. The unfamiliarity of her position gave Kenna a moment of alarm, then her senses took over and she welcomed the sensations that flooded her.

Her fingers dug into the feather tick as Rhys carried her with him on a sharp crest of pleasure. For long minutes after he had given her his seed her flesh still tingled.

Rhys waited for his own breathing to still before he slipped out of bed, giving Kenna a kiss on her mouth as he did so. Eyes closed, Kenna heard Rhys washing at the commode then rummaging through the wardrobe. Curious, she opened her eyes and saw him pull out his dressing gown. But instead of putting it on he carried it over to the bed, searching its pockets all the while.

305

She lifted the covers as he slipped back into bed and turned on her side. "What are you looking for?" Rhys palmed something, then threw his robe on a chair. "I amend my question. What have you got in your hand?"

Rhys did not answer her right away. He made a fist around the gold band in his palm. "I don't know if this is the proper time. Hell, I don't know if there even is a proper time. I thought I would wait until we were in Boston and I could have it fitted, but I realize I want you to have this now. I'll understand if you don't want it, it was rather forced on you the first time, though if you recall, you did agree to the ceremony."

"Rhys, what *are* you talking about?"

"This." He held up her wedding ring between his thumb and forefinger and waited for Kenna's reaction.

She stared at the ring in mute astonishment.

It was not quite the reaction Rhys was hoping for. He could read neither pleasure or dismay in her expression. "Translation, please. I haven't any idea what you're thinking."

Tears welled in her eyes. "You dear, dear man," she said as they overflowed. She cupped his face and covered it with kisses and tears.

Rhys was overwhelmed. He knew what the ring meant to him. Dare he hope it meant the same to her? He took her trembling hand and slid the band on her finger, then he lifted her hand to his lips and kissed it. Kenna very nearly hugged the breath out of him, admiring the ring from over his shoulder.

"You always meant for it to be a real marriage, didn't you?" she asked wonderingly.

"I think that's what I meant when I said there would be no divorce," he said dryly.

"No divorce," she echoed, drawing him down on the mattress and snuggling close. "You said something about

306

this being forced on me the first time. What did you mean?"

"I gave you that ring when we were married. I gather you don't remember."

"No," she said sadly. "But I wish I did. So much of that time is vague."

"It's just as well. It was not exactly filled with pleasantness."

Kenna refused to dwell on that unhappiness. "Tell me about our wedding. I recall what I was wearing and I remember a ride to the church. Someone was with me, holding me."

"That was Polly. I wish you had been able to know her, really know her. There is not another like her."

Even with a ring on her finger Kenna was not so secure that she cared to hear the virtues of another woman, especially one she thought held a great deal of her husband's affection. She wondered why she was plagued by the vision of the women Rhys had held in his arms when there were so many things she had forgotten.

Rhys was blithely unaware of the turn of Kenna's thoughts. "It was Polly who arranged the marriage. She knew a priest, you see, who regularly tried to save those souls living at the Flower House. She convinced him it was his duty to marry us."

Kenna frowned, thinking hard. "Rhys, who *is* Polly? And *what* is the Flower House?"

"You have forgotten rather a lot, haven't you? The Flower House is an establishment much like Mrs. Miller's and Polly Dawn Rose is the proprietress."

Kenna couldn't credit it. "Do you mean that I was rescued from one brothel and hidden in another?"

"Does sound rather unlikely, but that's the gist of it. Of course no one at Polly's was preparing you for—" he groped for a delicate word—"for service. The girls there simply wanted you to get well. When they took you from Mrs. Miller's they hadn't the slightest notion who you were."

"This is a Banbury Tale if ever there was one."

"Quite. Now do you want to hear about our wedding?"

"Later," she said, intrigued in spite of herself. "If they didn't know me, why did they bother taking me from Mrs. Miller's? Was that your doing?"

"No," Rhys sighed, realizing he was going to have to explain the whole of it. He told her everything, beginning with the search for her that covered all of London and finally how he found her at Polly's and his connection to the Flower House.

"I can scarcely take it all in," she said when he finished. "It's as if it happened to someone else. I am going to compose a letter on the morrow, thanking Miss Rose and the others, and send it on the first packet back to London."

Rhys grabbed Kenna's wrist, unaware he was hurting her. "No! No letters! P.D. is the only person in all of England who knows you are alive. Even her girls think you dead. If one of them came across the letter and spoke without thinking, you would not be safe."

Kenna stretched her fingers when Rhys let go of her wrist. "No letter," she agreed slowly.

"I'm sorry. Did I hurt you?"

"No," she lied.

Rhys massaged her slender wrist anyway. "Why are you smiling?"

She shrugged a trifle self-consciously. "I was thinking how fierce you can be at times, then so tender. I like you both ways."

"You can be fierce yourself."

She had no illusions about what he was referring to. There was no denying she had bitten his shoulder earlier.

She kissed him where she thought the mark should be. "And tender, too." She laughed when he made a playful grab for her. "I think you'd better finish telling me about our wedding." Kenna held her hand a few inches from her face as he spoke, letting the candlelight catch the burnished gold. When he was done she turned her face to him. "I'm glad you didn't wait until Boston to give this to me, Rhys. I didn't know how much importance I had placed on a ring until tonight. It's silly but it's as if there is more permanence now. I'm not so afraid."

"It's not silly," he said softly. "I didn't know you were afraid."

She nodded. "Sometimes, when I wake and you're gone, I think you've left me. Then I'm frightened."

Rhys understood that emotion. He had thought Kenna was lost to him for so many years that when she wasn't in his sight it had the power to chill him. "I'm not going to leave you, Kenna."

"I think I know that now."

For a long time after Rhys fell asleep, Kenna stayed awake, watching him. She would always remember it as one of the most uniquely peaceful nights she spent in his his arms.

That memory helped sustain her until the following afternoon when, in the course of three hours, Rhys called her sprite more than two dozen times. He was sitting at the desk, studying some papers, and Kenna was sitting on the desk top, leaning over the very same charts. They were trying to determine the extent of the cargo their schooners could carry as well as a realistic timetable for the run from the Indies to New York and Boston. She had gritted her teeth the first time he had casually dropped the hated nickname but when it tripped off his tongue again and again she could no longer let it pass. Did he want a wife, a lover, a partner, or a child?"

"Approximately once every seven minutes," she said, scribbling down a few numbers on a scratch paper. She pushed the paper in front of him.

"That can't be correct, sprite," Rhys said good-naturedly. It was not often she made a mistake like that.

Kenna took back the paper, scratched down a few more figures and gave it to him again. "You're right. Make that closer to every six and one half minutes."

Rhys leaned back in his chair. "Kenna," he said patiently. "How can we send off a ship every six and one half minutes? We'd need a fleet of vessels larger than . . . well, beyond my imagination anyway."

Kenna was tapping her fingers on the desk. "I was not referring to our shipping timetable," she said sweetly. "Those calculations are based on 180 minutes, which is the length of time we've been working here, and 27, which is the number of times you've called me by that ridiculous nickname. Have done, Rhys!" She jumped to her feet and walked away from the desk, spun around, arms akimbo. "Do I look like a sprite?" she demanded. "Sprites are small, airy things, impossibly delicate and equally mischievous. Forget I said the last," she added when she saw a smile tug at his lips. "I am not small, nor am I airy, and above all I am not delicate!" To prove it she thudded her foot against the deck so hard the papers on the desk shuddered.

"Come here, Kenna," Rhys said in a voice that brooked no argument.

Kenna hesitated until one of his dark brows raised, issuing a challenge she could not ignore. She walked toward him. The sunlight at her back filtered through her yellow muslin day dress, outlining the length of her long legs and the slenderness of her waist.

"Closer." Rhys pointed to a spot directly in front of

him, directly between his splayed legs. "Right here."
Kenna took the final two steps a shade defiantly and
Rhys closed his legs, trapping her. "All right. Let's
address these issues. First, your height. Even on tiptoe
you are still shorter than I am. Therefore, to me, you're
small. And airy? Kenna, if you saw the way you looked
coming toward me, light and ethereal, you would not
doubt me on this point." He reached for her wrists and
raised them in front of him. "That brings us to delicate.
These are delicate." He dropped them and spanned her
waist with his hands. "This is delicate." He drew her
down on one knee and brushed her lips with the tips of
his fingers. "Not delicate. Exquisite."

"Rhys," Kenna sighed. "You present a lovely
argument. But I don't think you understand the
problem."

"I'm listening."

"It's this: when you call me sprite I feel like your
sister, or worse, the wretched little girl who dogged your
every step at Dunnelly. More importantly, I wonder if
that is how you see me. Is it, Rhys? I want to be your wife,
your lover, your friend. Am I still a child in your eyes?"

"Child? No." He shook his head for emphasis. "I
haven't thought of you as a child since your seventeenth
birthday."

Kenna could not hide her surprise. "You were on the
Peninsula then. You hadn't seen me for nearly three
years."

"I was on the Peninsula, yes, but Nick sent me a
miniature of you. He commissioned a portrait of you for
your birthday and asked the artist to duplicate the
painting in miniature."

"I never knew."

"Nick knew better than to tell you. You wouldn't have
sat for the portrait."

"God, I could be cruel!"

"You thought you had reason enough to hate me," he reminded her. "When I saw the painting I saw a woman, Kenna, not a child. Your face was so solemn, so grave, that I wept for the loss of your childhood and wondered if you had even noted its passing. There was a frailty in your expression, a certain vulnerability in your eyes, and I mourned the absence of your spirit. It was not the wistful face of a child the artist had captured on canvas; it was the haunting face of a young woman who was completely unaware of her own beauty.

"I had a locket made for the miniature and I carried it everywhere. It was my good luck piece. To this day I don't know what happened to it. I was preparing for a battle and reached in my pocket to get it, just to hold it for a moment, and it wasn't there. I shall never forget how scared I was to face the enemy that day."

"You didn't need it." A lump in her throat made it difficult to get out the words.

"You'll never convince me of that," he said in self-mockery. "That was the day two of my finest animals were shot out from under me and a pistol ball creased my hairline." He caught her horror. "I was unconscious for a while, that's all. It was not much more than a scratch."

"Oh, Rhys," she said miserably.

"Don't think on it, Kenna. I don't. Think on this: when I call you sprite it is because you've triggered a chord that responds to your spirit. Don't ask me to ignore it. I don't think I can. I loved you as a brother when you were a child. Not any longer. I thought you understood. I love you as a man can only love a woman. There has been nothing less in my heart for years."

"You never said . . . I thought everything you did for me was protecting me. I thought you were sacrificing your life for mine."

"I am not a sacrificing man," he denied. "I'm a selfish

one. Very, very selfish. You are as necessary to me as air itself. I would guard you as jealously as a thirsty man would guard his last few drops of water. That is the sort of protection I've always offered you."

"I love you," she said. Kenna leaned her head against his shoulder. "Dear God, how I love you!"

Chapter Eight

"Do you feel as if you're coming home?" Kenna asked curiously. She was standing in front of Rhys at the taffrail. His arms were resting lightly on her shoulders and over the top of her head his eyes were watchful. Boston was becoming more than a point on a map as the *Carasea* sailed closer to the harbor.

"Yes. Frankly, it surprises me. I hadn't thought I'd feel this way."

Kenna reached back and put her hand on one of his. "Is any of it familiar to you?"

He nodded. "See the building there, the one at the end of Long Wharf? That's the State House. The Declaration of Independence was announced to Bostonians from its balcony."

"Eloquent, but treasonous, literature," chided Kenna.

"Indeed it was."

"What is that building there?" She pointed to the second cupola rising to the left of the State House.

"That's Faneuil Hall. At least I think it is. I was nine when I left Boston. I'm afraid my memory may not serve me. It has market stalls and in one of the upper meeting rooms Sam Adams planned the tea party."

"Why would one have a tea social above a market place?"

Rhys laughed outright at her question. "What did your tutor teach you in the schoolroom? I was talking about the famous, or infamous, Boston Tea Party."

"Hmmpf. I never heard of it," she said tartly. "Pardon me for pricking this newfound American pride of yours, but I had *hundreds* of years of *English* history to study. Your little rebellion was a mere blink in time."

Rhys laughed again, giving her a tiny shake. "I hope you don't intend to make your view common knowledge. Americans like to think the English still smart a bit at losing their colonies."

"I doubt the subject will come up, and if it does, well, I shall try not to embarrass you."

"You couldn't embarrass me." He kissed the top of her head. "Have you ever heard of Paul Revere?"

"No. Is he someone you shall be doing business with?"

Behind her Rhys rolled his eyes heavenward and found himself giving Kenna an impromptu *American* history lesson as he pointed out the Old North Church. He told her what he remembered of the early colonists, the transplanted city dwellers who had aspirations of becoming gentleman farmers but had little knowledge of the soil. He explained how the natural resources of the untamed land led the colonists to seek sustenance from the sea. It began with codfish, the lifesaving food of the settlers, then ship building followed, to export the fish to other settlements. As New England learned to sail, Boston became the center of the coastal trade.

Kenna hung on every word, eager to learn all she could about her new home. By the time the *Carasea* docked at the wharf she admitted to some newly found American pride herself.

Captain Johnson came to stand beside them as their trunks were loaded on a carriage. "I'd be happy to escort you to your home personally," he offered.

"No," said Rhys. "I know you have matters here that

require your attention. It was kind of you to arrange for our transport and give us two men to help with our things."

Johnson had to smile at that. "Hardly gave them to you. After all, you employ them."

Rhys grinned then. "That will take some getting used to."

"Thank you for all your patient assistance, Captain," Kenna said sincerely. "You made the voyage a delight. As soon as we are settled I want you to be our first guest at dinner."

"Happily, ma'am. Most happily." The easy smile faded from his face. He looked beyond Kenna and Rhys and tugged at his chin thoughtfully.

Kenna and Rhys turned simultaneously to see what had captured Johnson's attention. A three-masted schooner was swiftly approaching the harbor. It was an elegant vessel, flawless in design, bearing red and white markings of another line.

"She's yare!" breathed Kenna. "How I wish she were one of ours! Look how she flies!"

"That's your competition, Mrs. Canning," Johnson said gruffly, though he could not quite keep the admiration for the sleek vessel out of his voice. "She's a Garnet schooner and they don't come any finer. If you'll pardon me for saying so, Mr. Canning, your father didn't have much good to say about the Garnet Line. Says they're no better than pirates. There's no love lost between the families."

"My husband is not his father," Kenna said, unknowingly echoing Rhys's earlier sentiments. "The Garnets will have ample opportunity to discover that for themselves."

Johnson coughed to cover his astonishment at Kenna's spirited defense of her husband. "There are no Garnets any longer, ma'am. The family name's been gone

317

more than eighty years though it's still a family enterprise. Tanner Cloud runs the business now. Has since the end of the war. His wife, his sister and her husband all have an interest in it. In fact his wife comes from a Caribbean shipping family. Ever heard of Quinton Lines?"

"I have," said Rhys. "It was mentioned in my father's notes."

"Quinton Shipping *is* Mrs. Cloud. Tanner did all right by himself. That marriage to Alexis Quinton is what kept Garnet afloat when things turned bad during the war."

Later, as they were passing Boston Common, Kenna asked Rhys something that had been in her thoughts long before Captain Johnson spoke of Alexis Quinton Cloud. "Do you mind that I didn't bring anything to our marriage?"

"So that's why you've been so quiet," he said. "You were working yourself up to ask that ridiculous question."

It was true that she had hardly heard Rhys as he pointed out the various Boston sites. She hadn't been able to appreciate the fragrant spring air or the greening of the common. Still, that didn't make her thoughts ridiculous and she told him so. "If things had been different I could have brought my inheritance into this marriage. As it stands I can't even offer you a rowboat."

"I don't want a rowboat, or even a schooner that can chase the wind. I thought I was quite clear. I want you."

That mollified her a little. She stared out the carriage window. "Still," she said softly, looking at a row of yellow daffodils that brightened the side of the road, "you should have held out for my little pond trawler."

Rhys smiled and leaned back in his seat, shading his eyes with the brim of his hat as Kenna moved back and forth across the opposite seat, trying to see Boston from

318

both sides of the carriage.

The carriage stopped in front of a large wooden-framed house which sat on several acres of woodland property outside of Boston proper. Black shutters on every window of the three story home relieved the pristine whiteness of the building and gave it a stately air. Twin chimneys rose above the mansard roof and an iron railing, also painted white, formed a boundary around the roof's less steep first slope. The entire third floor of the house was formed by the slate roof's second slope and a series of white dormers that were built three to a side. Four white columns rose in front of the main entrance and supported a balcony on the second floor.

Rhys liked the house, had always had a fondness for it, but he said nothing as he waited for Kenna's reaction. She, after all, had grown up in a veritable castle.

"Oh, Rhys! It's lovely. Why didn't you tell me?" She tugged at the sleeve of his greatcoat, urging him up the cobbled walk.

"It's not Dunnelly."

Kenna stopped in her tracks and looked at him suspiciously. "I can *see* that. For all that I loved it, Dunnelly was still a tomb! This is fresh and alive. I'll wager there's not a single musty corridor to be found. When was it build?"

"About sixty years ago. I know it's only a blink in time compared to Dun—"

"I had no idea I would have cause to regret that statement so soon. I hope you aren't going to hold it over my head forever. Did you think I might not like your home?"

"It had occurred to me," he admitted sheepishly. "Your family owned a minor property in Brighton that was larger than this."

"What has size to do with anything? I'm certain this

319

house will accommodate us, the servants, and a half dozen children without any of us living in one another's pockets."

Rhys opened his mouth to say something, then shut it abruptly. The mention of children effectively silenced him.

Kenna laughed at his confusion. "Come along. We can talk about the exact number some other time."

The door was opened for them by the butler and Kenna immediately noted a certain chill in the air. Rhys had sent a messenger on ahead to give the servants notice of their arrival, but from their expressions it appeared they were much put out by the disruption to their routine.

They had crowded in the hallway in their best dress and the first thing Kenna noted was that they were all wearing black armbands. Neither she nor Rhys observed any sort of mourning for his brother and father, a fact which could hardly go unnoticed since she was wearing the peach gown beneath her redingote. Kenna looked at Rhys for direction but he seemed unperturbed by the situation, handing the butler his greatcoat and helping Kenna out of her coat.

Behind them two sailors from the *Carasea* stood patiently, waiting to be told where to deliver the trunks. Rhys told them to leave everything in the foyer while the butler was motioning them to use the house's rear entrance. They obeyed Rhys and the trunks thudded to the parquet floor.

The butler, a portly gentleman with red cheeks which gave him a perpetually flustered look, swallowed hard. His adam's apple did not even break the surface of his thick neck. "Welcome home, sir," he said stiffly. He nodded at Kenna. "Madam. I'm Alcott, head of the household staff. We would like to offer our sympathies on the passing of your father and Mr. Richard."

"Thank you," said Rhys with no show of emotion.

Alcott cleared his throat. "May I introduce you to everyone?"

"Please."

It was then Kenna realized that Rhys did not know any of the people working for him and her heart went out to him. What must it be like to be welcomed home by strangers who obviously resented his presence and wished for the return of the old guard?

"Nicholas would not have tolerated it," she told him later when they were eating dinner. The supper room was pleasant enough, she thought. The wallpaper was pale blue, patterned with tiny white flowers. Above the round walnut table hung a crystal chandelier whose candles gave off a warming light. Gold drapes with sweeping valances hung at the tall windows and there was a door leading to the gardens which could be opened in warmer weather to let the fragrance of the outdoors sweep the room.

"What wouldn't have Nicholas tolerated?" Rhys asked patiently as he cut his meat.

"Their insolence," she whispered, looking around quickly to make certain one of the servants hadn't suddenly walked into the room. "He would have dismissed them at once."

"Then he would have been without any staff. Circumstances are different here, Kenna. Domestic help is harder to find. If I let these people go they would be snapped up before their bags were packed."

"How do you know these things? If I didn't know better I would think you never left the United States."

"I know because I anticipated the reception I would get and I asked questions of other Americans before I left London."

"Do you mean we must keep them no matter how

321

much they dislike us?"

"For the time being I think it would be best," he said. "And I doubt if they actually dislike us."

"The cook does," Kenna said with conviction, pushing away her plate. "The meat is without texture, the potatoes are watery, and the vegetables have had the color cooked out of them. I think I would gladly put up with Monsieur Raillier's temper if I could have his food now."

"At least you don't have to worry about arsenic here," Rhys pointed out.

Kenna stared at her plate. "Pardon me if I doubt your word," she said dryly.

Rhys started laughing and Kenna soon joined him, tears gathering in her eyes from his infectious amusement. They sobered long enough for their half eaten repast to be exchanged for dessert by a grim-faced serving girl. As soon as they were alone they glanced at the pudding in front of them which had the consistency and color appeal of mud and simultaneously burst into laughter.

Kenna wiped her glistening eyes with a corner of her napkin and dared Rhys to try it.

He shook his head and backed away, scraping a leg of his chair on the polished hardwood floor. "You try it."

"We both will. We have to," she insisted. "If we don't touch it the cook will think we just weren't hungry and she's likely to serve this again. But if we eat a few spoonfuls—all right, just one spoonful—she'll know we tried it and found it wanting."

Rhys was skeptical of her logic. "You first."

"Together," she told him sternly.

They put their spoons in the pudding at the same time, and watching each other carefully lest one of them falter, they brought the spoons to their mouths. The spoons hovered for a moment, then Kenna and Rhys cast caution aside and took a bite, swallowing quickly. Their eyes widened in mutual amazement.

"I'll take yours if you can't eat it all," Rhys said, trying to draw her crystal cup in front of him.

Kenna grabbed it back. "There are some things I won't do for you, Rhys. And giving up this—this—whatever it is—is one of them."

After dinner they went to the music room where Kenna played the spinet while Rhys relaxed in a chair with his feet propped up on an ottoman. He winced, looking over the top of the Boston paper, when Kenna hit some sour notes.

She made a face at him. "It's badly out of tune," she defended herself.

"I didn't say anything," he said innocently and lifted the paper again to hide his grin.

"Beast!" Kenna dramatically pounded out a minor chord. She rose from the bench and sat on the ottoman, pushing his feet to one side. "Rhys, the servants are all observing mourning."

"I didn't fail to notice that."

"Won't it seem odd if we don't?"

Rhys dropped the paper. His eyes were cold. "I have already given my father and brother more attention in death than they ever gave me in life. I did not wish them dead, Kenna, but just because they are does not mean I must forgive or forget the past. If there had been some sort of reconciliation, or an overture on their part when they were in London, I might feel differently now. There wasn't and I don't. I will not observe mourning for the sake of appearances. I have too much respect for my father and myself to mock us both."

Kenna was stricken by Rhys's response. "I did not know you felt so strongly about it," she said quietly.

He folded the paper on his lap. "I hope you are not going to try to change my mind."

"No. It never occurred to me!"

"Good. Now I wish you would rest your concerns about the servants. This is a trial period for all of us. If you have any problems dealing with them, if their resentment causes you the slightest difficulty, or if you are not satisfied with their work, speak with me about it. We will decide what is to be done then. Does that meet with your approval?"

"Yes." She lifted her chin a notch. "They haven't intimidated me, you know."

Rhys's lips twitched. "I never thought they would. I didn't marry an insipid English miss. Besides, there are only eight of them. You had more servants than that taking care of the grounds."

"True," she admitted. She gave his knee a squeeze then absentmindedly rubbed his taut thigh. "Are you going to the shipping office tomorrow?"

"Yes, and the lawyer's. Do you want to come with me?"

"I don't think so. Not tomorrow. It's certain to be hectic and there will be enough here to occupy me. Will you mind if I have your father's and Richard's clothes packed and their rooms aired? I peeked in them earlier. Nothing's been touched."

"Do whatever you want. There must be some charitable organization which would welcome the clothes."

"Is there anything I should think about keeping?"

"No. Nothing I can think of. What made you go in their rooms?"

Kenna shrugged. "Mrs. Alcott pointed them out when she showed me around the house. I suppose I was curious. I never met either of them."

Rhys held back a retort rooted in bitterness and placed his hand over hers.

"There was a painting in your father's room. A portrait of a very lovely woman. There was a resemblance . . . is she your mother?"

Rhys nodded. "Her name was Elizabeth."

"You have her eyes, her coloring."

"I know. It's why I was sent away. My father couldn't bear to look at me. Do you know I once tried to destroy that portrait? I thought if I could change it, color the hair differently or alter the eyes, my father would not think of her when he looked at me. Even as a child I knew why he resented me. I had lived and she had not."

Kenna knew the painting had not been damaged. She had to ask. "What happened?"

"Father caught me as I was ready to glob the canvas with my brushes. He didn't say a word. Simply carried me out of the room. Four days later I was on a ship to England."

When Rhys made love to her that night there was a certain halting sweetness in his touch that made Kenna want to weep. She felt a sadness for the father who had died loving a canvas and never known the warmth and kindness of his younger son.

"Put the portrait in the library," said Rhys.

"Yes," she said. "I will."

After Rhys left in the morning Kenna met individually with each of the servants to discover their particular area of expertise. She was tactful, but firm, and by lunch time she was finished walking on eggshells and was confidently in command of the running of the house. She even managed to glimpse a look of grudging admiration on the faces of the butler and his housekeeper wife. While the two bedchambers were being aired and clothes packed, Kenna consulted with the cook about the evening meal. Years of dealing with Monsieur Raillier served Kenna well. She managed to convey her displeasure without stinging Mrs. O'Hare's pride. During the course of the conversation Kenna learned that the cook was more capable than the meal she served would lead one to believe. Kenna crossed her fingers hopefully and told the cook she could be as creative as she wished.

After Kenna saw to it that Elizabeth's portrait was given a place of honor above the library mantel she toured the gardens and the stable. Neither Roland nor Richard had been any great judge of horseflesh and she wistfully thought of Pyramid and Higgins. The groom informed her apologetically that there was no lady's saddle to be had and Kenna was not prepared to shock him by offering to ride astride.

Because she couldn't ride Kenna decided there was nothing for it but to work on her gowns. She had two bolts of rose and cornflower blue muslin that she spread out on the supper table and began cutting. The grim-faced girl who had served dinner the evening before made no attempt to hide her interest when she brought Kenna tea.

"I could sew that up beautifully for you, Mrs. Canning," she offered a shade defiantly.

"Are you a seamstress then?" Kenna asked, though the words were tangled around a mouthful of pins. She removed the pins and directed Alice to put the tea tray on a chair since the table was covered with fabric.

"I'm saving for my own shop some day," Alice said proudly, her sharp face softening a bit. "I have a talent for stitching and design."

"And not much opportunity to use it here."

"No, ma'am." Her glance strayed to the material again. "It's excellent fabric."

"Yes, it is. And I'm afraid I will not do justice to it," she sighed. "My skills are merely adequate. Would you really like to work on the gowns?"

Alice nodded and the ruffle on her cap fluttered a little.

"Very well. I'll inform Mrs. Alcott that you're to have

326

lightened duties so you'll have time for this."

"If you don't mind, ma'am, I'd rather sew in my spare time and earn something extra if you like my work."

"Of course," agreed Kenna. "I should have thought of it myself since you are saving for a shop. That will be quite satisfactory."

Once Alice had removed the material Kenna knew herself to be monumentally bored. Just to pass the time until Rhys came home she went to the library and began searching through his papers, collecting anything of interest on Canning Shipping. In the middle of the pile there was one paper that caught her attention sharply. It was a guest list for the night of the masquerade written in Victorine's hand.

Rhys could not fail to notice Kenna's unusual quietness at dinner that evening. He had expected her to be full of questions about his visit to the lawyer's and the office, yet she asked very little. He probed gently to discover what was bothering her.

"This dinner is excellent," he said. The meal began with a cold soup and later came thin, tender slices of beef cooked in its own juices. The potatoes were roasted and the carrots and baby peas retained all their color and flavor. "You must have had an eventful conversation with the cook."

Kenna smiled faintly. "Did you know your father had poor teeth and a stomach condition?"

"I didn't know. But what has that to do with anything?"

"That's why our meal was so bland and soft last night. Poor Mrs. O'Hare has been cooking like that for years to please Roland's palate. And since Richard never complained she thought perhaps all the Cannings suffered from the same ailment. She was actually trying to please you with the dinner."

"Amazing," Rhys said, shaking his head. "This meal is

evidence you were successful convincing her otherwise. You must have had a busy day."

"Not so busy," she disagreed. "I'm afraid I had some time for snooping."

"Oh? And what horrible Canning secrets did you uncover?"

Kenna put down her fork, unable to do justice to her meal. "I found a guest list, Rhys. I know it was the one for the masque given by Victorine and my father. I recognized some of the names and several of the people are no longer alive. That's how I knew it wasn't a recently planned list. Why is it in your possession?"

Rhys did not answer her question directly. There was something almost accusing in her tone that weighed heavily upon him. "Why do *you* think it is in my possession?"

"I don't know," she said honestly. "At first I thought you must have helped Victorine plan the list, then I realized how impossible that was. You were on the Continent then."

"Why in the world would it even cross your mind that I would help Victorine plan her gala?"

Kenna bit her lip then blurted out, "You were her lover."

"What!"

Rhys's astonishment was genuine but Kenna didn't know if he was denying the charge or only surprised that she had discovered it. Still, her poise faltered under his glaring expression. "You and Victorine were lovers then."

"No, we were not. I met Victorine briefly before she and your father were married and I went to the Continent. We were not lovers then nor when I returned."

"But I saw you kissing her in the gallery," she insisted.

"The way you saw me at her side in the cave?"

Kenna ignored his question. "And you and she had been in the summerhouse!"

"Did you see us there also?"

"No, but I could smell her perfume and the bed was mussed. I know she took her lover there."

"She may have taken a lover there, but I was not that man! Have you seriously thought all these years that Victorine and I cuckolded your father?"

"Not all these years," she said, choking on the words. "Victorine only began to appear in the dream recently."

"About the same time the attempts on your life began?"

"Yes . . . no! I don't know! Victorine can't be responsible! She would never harm me!"

Rhys gave her his handkerchief to wipe her glistening eyes. "Where is the guest list?"

"In the library. I put it back with your papers."

He stood. "Stay right here. I am going to get it." He returned in a few minutes and saw Kenna had taken him literally and had not moved so much as a fraction.

She looked up when he came in the room. "Rhys, I'm sorry. I don't know why finding it upset me so. I suppose I thought I had put it all in the past. It was a shock seeing that list among your things."

Rhys sat down beside her and smoothed out the paper between them. "That's why we are going to settle this now, Kenna. This list is not the original and if you had looked more carefully you would have noted it. I asked Nick to supply me with these names the last time I was at Dunnelly before my father died. Victorine composed the list for him. Your brother did not have the time to look over it. You disappeared then and his mind was naturally on that. This is the first time I've seen it since he handed it to me. Quite frankly, I forgot its existence."

"Why did you ask for it in the first place?" She tucked the handkerchief in her sleeve and stared at the names scrawled on the paper.

"I had hoped it would give me some clue as to your father's murderer and eventually lead me to the person responsible for the attempts on your life."

"But surely these people were questioned at the time of the murder?"

"Many of them were. But there was a lot of confusion that night. I was going to seek the guests out and speak with them again. You would have been safe with Yvonne. It seemed the perfect time."

Kenna nodded, her eyes misting again at the thought of all he had tried to do for her. She pointed to the third name on the list. "Squire Bitterpenney," she recalled fondly. "He made the most ridiculous Roman senator that evening." Her finger dropped to the next pair of names. "And here is Lord and Lady Dimmy. I don't remember what he was wearing but she was one of the shepherdesses. Oh, and Lady Barthel! She was another. Here is a name that is not familiar. Michael Deveraux. Probably an emigré friend of Victorine's. She kept in close contact with others who had fled the Bonapartists. See, here is Paul Françon and the Comte and Comtesse Lescaut. My father was instrumental in helping the Lescauts leave Paris. They stayed at Dunnelly for several weeks while the Comte recovered from the ill-treatment he received in the French prisons. They live in New Orleans now so you wouldn't have been able to talk to them."

"What other names do you recognize?"

Kenna continued to go through the list and point out people she knew and their connection with either her father or Victorine. "It's not been very helpful, has it?" she said when she was finished.

Rhys folded the paper and slipped it in his pocket. "At least I know a few names of those it couldn't be. The Lescauts, for instance, since they've been in the United

States for several years. And Lord Rilling. He left for India about the same time I went to the Peninsula. Seven of the guests have passed away which I didn't know before this evening. It narrows the list a little." He put Kenna's fork in her hand. "I insist we both eat something before Mrs. O'Hare decides we don't care for this either."

Their dinner was cold by now but Kenna ate dutifully under Rhys's watchful eye. "You're not angry, are you, about what I said?"

"You mean about me being Victorine's lover? No. I'm not angry. I wish that you had mentioned it before. I suppose I should have realized you believed some such nonsense. You've connected her name and mine on several occasions. I never understood why until now."

"I couldn't confront you with my suspicions," she said softly. "Or Victorine. I think I was afraid of what you would tell me."

"And now?"

"I believe you, Rhys, and feel foolish for all the times I did not."

They shared a glass of wine later, sitting on the floor in front of the hearth in their bedchamber. The spring nights were still cool and Kenna welcomed Rhys's suggestion of a fire in the grate. She was wearing one of the gauzy nightgowns that Rhys had bought her and didn't suspect that his offer to build the fire was prompted in part by his desire to keep her out of her less revealing robe. She sat with her legs curled to one side and Rhys's head rested in her lap. Her fingers threaded through his hair absently as she stared at the ephemeral shapes made by the flames.

"I was not very good company at dinner," she said. "Will you tell me about your day?"

"The lawyer had better news than we suspected. There is a large reserve of funds he had been urging my father to put back into the line. Enough to build several ships the equal of the one we saw yesterday in the harbor. My father wanted to move ahead more cautiously, waiting for the economy to strengthen. Mr. Britt was too polite to say it outright but I gather my father had lost interest in the line. His political aspirations had taken precedence in recent years and he was grooming Richard for a position of greater responsibility in the government. The day-to-day decisions concerning the business were left to Joshua Grant, a capable man by all acounts, but without any real authority to bring about change."

"Did you meet Mr. Grant?"

"In the afternoon. He impressed me as knowledgeable and reliable but also as the sort of man more comfortable receiving directives rather than issuing them. His relief was almost palpable when I said I would be taking responsibility for the operation. I discussed plans with him to build two ships, both with large cargo holds, as well as your idea about the schooner runs to the Indies and South America. He believed both were excellent ideas."

"Was he merely saying that because he thought it was expected of him?"

"No." Rhys chuckled. "He must have seen that I wondered that also. He summoned all his stiff Boston pride and informed me rather coldly that he had been offered a position with Garnet Lines on several occasions. If he didn't like what I was doing he could say so without fear of being unemployed for long."

Kenna smiled, imagining Rhys's response. "You increased his salary, didn't you?"

"Of course. I was not going to let him be lured away. How did you know?"

"It's what I would have done," she said simply.

"I had no idea I had married such a shrewd businesswoman. Your ancestors must be appalled. Imagine, one of the Dunnes in trade."

"My father would be proud," said Kenna wistfully.

Rhys took her hand and held it to his lips. "Yes," he said gently. "Yes, he would."

In the morning Kenna went with Rhys to the harbor. The offices of Canning Shipping occupied several rooms on the second floor of a warehouse along the wharf. The odor from hundreds of barrels of cured cod being transported from the warehouse to a waiting ship permeated the office. Kenna had a scented handkerchief in her reticule but she refused to take it out and hold it to her nose.

"It takes some getting used to," Rhys told her when he caught the pained expression on her face.

"I wasn't complaining," she said tartly.

"I wouldn't expect you to." He picked up some heavy ledgers that were lying on top of an oak filing cabinet and placed them on the desk. "Are you certain you want to go over these by yourself? I could help you with them later."

"No, let me sort out the accounts. I like working with figures and you know you don't. More to the point, I would probably be a hindrance to you if I attended your meeting with the merchants. Not everyone will appreceate my interest in the line's operation."

"All right," Rhys gave in graciously. In truth he did not care what others thought but he knew she was right. "Let us plan on having luncheon together. We'll find a respectable tavern."

"I'll look forward to it."

Rhys grinned at her absent reply. She had already opened the first ledger and was scanning the accounts thoughtfully. He picked up her redingote which she had thrown over a chair and hung it up on a hook by the door. He doubted she even heard him bid her good day.

Immersed as she was in her figures, Kenna did not glance up whe she heard the door open several hours later. "I'll be with you in a moment, Rhys. I have only this column to do."

Alexis Cloud shut the door softly behind her and sat down in one of the pair of chairs in front of the desk. Her striking amber eyes studied Kenna's intent posture thoughtfully. If Alexis had relied on the rumors already circulating Boston concerning the Cannings, the last place she would have expected to find Mrs. Canning was in her husband's offices. It was thought she would be making a triumphant entrance into society based on her late father-in-law's power and position. It was expected that she and Rhys Canning would attend the splendid affairs given by their wealthy peers, thus filling the void left by Roland and Richard. The fate of all that Canning money weighed on everyone's mind. Or nearly everyones's mind. The Canning wealth had been used generously to hold a number of people in the Canning pockets. Alexis Cloud was not one of that number.

When Kenna finally looked up from her work she found herself staring into a pair of the most intriguing eyes she had ever seen. Amber, with flecks of gold, they seemed to reflect the light in the room. The woman seated across from her was naturally poised, confident, and clearly beautiful. Kenna estimated her age was very near Kenna's own. From beneath her attractive bonnet wisps of bright gold hair framed an oval face that was more lovely than the sum of its features. Kenna found herself admiring the character she saw and it was only after smiling in welcome that Kenna realized she had been under similar scrutiny and had not been found wanting.

"I'm Mrs. Canning," she introduced herself. "Pardon me for keeping you waiting. I thought you were my husband come to take me to luncheon." As a smile dimpled the corners of the woman's mouth Kenna realized the woman must think her remarkably unconcerned about her husband's feelings. "You were infinitely more patient than he would have been."

"I confess I have kept my husband cooling his heels while I attended to some matters also," she said in the manner of a fellow conspirator. "Now that we share that much in common, permit me to welcome you to Boston. I am Alexis Cloud."

Kenna could not suppress her shock. "But you can't be."

Alexis's laugh was genuinely pleased. "I do enjoy that reaction. Tell me, what have you heard?"

Kenna was embarrassed at her lack of manners. "It doesn't bear repeating. It was plainly untrue." She was not the sort of woman who would permit her wealth to be bartered into marriage. "Would you like a cup of tea? I was going to have one myself."

"Yes. I'd like that."

Kenna poured hot water from a kettle on the stove into a pot and measured out the tea. While it steeped she found a second cup in one of the drawers of the desk and set it out. "Your accent surprises me," she said. "I did not realize you were English."

"I'm not."

The reply was so terse that Kenna felt as if she had somehow given offense where none was intended. "Have I said something wrong?"

"Forgive me," said Alexis. "Cloud always says I am too quick to take issue with comments like that. I was born in England and lived there until I was thirteen. Breecham Lane. Have you ever heard of it?"

"Oh, but that's—" She stopped before she offended Mrs. Cloud again.

"It's all right. I know very well what it was. If there was a poorer, dirtier section of London, I've yet to learn about it. After I left England I lived on Tortula with George and Francine Quinton for six years. I assume you

335

heard my name in connection with Quinton Shipping."
Kenna nodded. "I thought so. When they were killed by
a British naval officer, I severed the last ties with
England. I'm American now." She said the last with
unmistakable passion.

Kenna poured their tea. She was filled with curiosity
but held her questions. She felt certain this woman could
be her friend and in time they would share their pasts.
"I've rather had the country thrust upon me, but I admit
there is much to admire about it." She handed a cup to
Alexis then sat down, but instead of putting the desk
between them, she took the chair beside her guest. "It
was kind of you to come here today. Do you know you're
the first person to welcome me to the city?"

"Quite honestly I had come to welcome your husband
and extend an invitation to you both for dinner in my
home some evening this week. It was an unexpected
pleasure to find you here. At this very minute there are at
least four of Boston's bloody blue matrons on their way
to your home to look you over."

"Are there really?" asked Kenna, plainly astonished.

"Oh, yes." Alexis sipped her tea. "I saw them
gathering on Beacon Hill this morning when I left the
house. They will be quite put out that I found you first."

"It amuses you," Kenna observed. "Why is that?"

"I'll let you discover that for yourself," she replied
enigmatically. "I'm of no mind to spoil it for you."

Kenna realized she was going to have to be satisfied
with the explanation. "When Rhys and I arrived the
other day we saw one of your schooners coming into the
harbor. It was truly a beautiful ship. Rhys said she could
chase the wind. Have you many like her?"

"She's one of a kind," Alexis said, pleasure in her
voice. "Responsive to the slightest touch. Yes, I believe
she can chase the wind. I will have to tell Cloud that. He
designed her. You saw her coming in on her maiden

voyage. I took her out to get the feel of her."

"*You* took her out?" Kenna's awe was transparent.

"Not alone, you understand. I have an excellent crew," Alexis added without a trace of conceit. She finished her tea and placed her cup on the desk. "I have to be going. I've taken up enough of your time and your husband will no doubt be here shortly. Will you think about my invitation? Say for Friday around seven? Cloud and I would both enjoy your company."

Kenna rose to her feet when Alexis stood. She found one more thing to like about Alexis Cloud. The woman was every bit as tall as she was. Kenna opened the door for her. "I don't have to think about it. Rhys and I would be delighted to come."

"Good," said Alexis, meaning it. "Enjoy your luncheon."

Kenna stood in the doorway with a rather bemused expression on her features as Alexis Cloud walked confidently through the outer office and disappeared in the corridor. Rhys appeared a moment later, looking somewhat preoccupied himself. He crossed the outer office and gave Kenna a light kiss on the cheek she offered.

"Who was that striking woman I saw leave her?" he asked.

"That," Kenna said a trifle smugly, "was Quinton Shipping."

"Mrs. Cloud?"

"One and the same, according to Captain Johnson," Kenna reminded him.

Rhys looked at the two cups on the desk. "And you had tea with her? They've not spared a second becoming acquainted with their competitors, have they?"

"They?"

"I was talking with Tanner Cloud only an hour ago. That's why I'm late. He took me on a tour of some of the

337

Garnet ships."

Kenna did not know what to make of that, but she voiced her first impression. "Rhys, I quite like Mrs. Cloud. I hope you are not saying we cannot be friends simply because our lines are rivals."

Rhys laughed openly. "Damned if I didn't like Tanner, too. I accepted an invitation for dinner in their home on Saturday evening. Does that meet with your approval?"

Kenna paused as she reached for her coat. "That at least proves they were not rushing their fences together," she chuckled. "Mrs. Cloud asked us to dinner Friday night."

When Kenna dressed for the dinner Friday evening with the Clouds she chose the rose gown Alice had just finished that morning. Kenna discovered when she tried the gown on that Alice had not lied about her talent. The fit was excellent and the fine detail surpassed Kenna's exptectations. The gown bared her shoulders and the delicate line of her collarbones while the empire cut hugged her breasts. Tiny rose beads dotted the puffed sleeves, a touch that Alice had taken upon herself to add, and one that Kenna thought added greatly to the gown's simple elegance. She wore long white gloves, rose slippers, and carried a white shawl. When she turned away from the mirror after giving a wayward curl a stern admonition to lie quietly she feared from the dark speculative look in Rhys's eyes that they might not arrive on time.

"I hope you were dressing for me when you chose that gown," he said, his sharp silver gaze glancing off her bare shoulders and taking note of her barely concealed bosom.

"I was dressing to please myself," she said tartly, then lost the effect because she smiled flirtatiously. "But I'm glad you approve."

One of Rhys's brows kicked up. "Approve, madam? I don't know that I approve at all. Haven't you got one of those things, you know, to cover your . . . .your . . ." He pointed to his own chest.

"Bosom," she said sweetly, grinning at his stammering. "And the thing is called a fichu and it simply would not work with this gown. Now put your eyes back in your head." She made an assessing sweep of his appearance. He was wearing a dove gray tail coat and trousers a shade darker. His cravat was a snowy fall of white linen impeccably arranged and in the crook of his elbow he carried a top hat. "You are looking more handsome than you have a right to. Don't cast stones in my direction."

Rhys wasn't mollified in the least by her backhanded compliment. He arranged the white shawl over her shoulders to his own satisfaction while trying valiantly to ignore Kenna's blatant amusement. In the end he surrendered to it. "I sounded rather priggish, didn't I?"

"Endearingly so." She patted his cheek as if he were a naughty boy.

Rhys took exception to that and kissed her hard on the lips until she gave a little moan against his mouth. Pleased with himself, he drew back and mocked her gesture by patting her flushed cheek. "Shall we go, sprite?"

Kenna took the arm he offered. "Rogue," she said, not unkindly.

By the time their driver stopped the carriage in front of the Clouds' Beacon Hill home, Kenna's cheeks matched the rose of her gown and her lips had a decidedly well-kissed look. When she tried to scold Rhys he swept aside her concern by reminding her they were still newlyweds and it was expected. Kenna was skeptical but his kisses wreaked havoc with her common sense.

Kenna's first glimpse of Tanner Cloud, scion of the Garnet wealth, gave her a clue to Rhys's earlier protectiveness. He was a vital man, tanned from long hours out-of-doors with a broad-shouldered frame that

339

bespoke of his labors. He might design ships, she thought, but he helped build them as well. He probably acted as his own foreman, working beside his men. His hair was the color of copper and his eyes were as deeply green as emeralds. He greeted them warmly as the butler took Rhys's hat.

"I'm delighted you could come," he said with genuine pleasure. "Alex tells me that she is hosting this affair and tomorrow night is my turn. God knows, life would become too simple if we consulted one another at every turn."

Kenna laughed. "About Saturday's invitation. We would like you to come to our home."

"That's very kind of you, but I've already made reservations for the four of us at Forrest's. The owner used to be the cook on a ship I commanded, but don't let that frighten you away. He doesn't actually do the cooking and therefore has promised me an excellent meal."

Rhys chuckled appreciatively while absently straightening the shawl on Kenna's shoulders. "I've heard Forrest's is an excellent establishment. And quite a popular place."

Tanner nodded, his eyes amused as he watched Rhys's hands on his wife's shoulders. "That's because no one knows he once headed a galley. I'm going to ask you to keep the secret." He motioned them toward the drawing room. "Come. We'll have a drink before dinner," he said. "Alex is waiting. She'll be wondering what I've done with you." In an aside to Rhys as they were entering the room Tanner said, "In your place I'd want to wrap her in that shawl, too."

Kenna glanced over her shoulder and saw a touch of red creep over Rhys's face though at the same time he looked absurdly pleased by the compliment to her appearance. She sighed, wondering if she would ever understand the vagaries of a man's mind, and loosened the shawl, draping it over her arm as it was meant to be worn.

When Kenna saw Alexis she was once again struck by the woman's cool beauty though not at all intimidated by it. She realized in that moment how much of her confidence she had regained since being away from Dunnelly. In part it was due to Rhys because of his unflagging belief in her, but Kenna also knew she had a well of strength that existed with or without Rhys Canning. She had proven that when she had pitched Mason Deverell's vile drugs overboard.

Alexis was pouring them drinks in long stemmed crystal glasses. "This is a very light, dry wine," she said. "I hope you like it." She gave a glass to Kenna and Rhys. "Mr. Canning, I'm Alexis Cloud. It's a pleasure to meet you at last."

Kenna noted Alexis's stare was not bold but she was studying Rhys's face thoughtfully, clearly making up her own mind about the man her husband had told her about.

"I can say the same," Rhys said gravely, not flinching from the steady gaze of his hostess's striking amber eyes. Whatever she was searching for she must have found it in his serenely confident features because she smiled then, looking very nearly radiant as she did so. Rhys returned the smile and understood what Kenna admired about this woman. "Kenna has scarcely stopped talking about you. She tells me it was you commanding the schooner."

"And you came to dinner anyway," Alexis said in self-mockery. When she saw their puzzled faces, she explained. "My penchant for sailing the ships Cloud builds has kept more people than I can name from coming here. It is something of a scandal here on Beacon Hill."

Tanner chuckled deeply and raised his glass of wine toward his wife. "To my notorious wife," he said, a secret

341

smile lifting the corners of his lips.

Rhys and Kenna were a little bewildered but they drank dutifully. "This is very good," said Kenna. "Is it a domestic wine?"

"It's French," said Tanner.

Kenna looked quickly at Rhys. The smile around his mouth had become a little strained.

"What is it?" asked Alexis quickly, alert to the sudden tension that existed in the room.

"It will take some time getting used to," Rhys said, twirling the stem of his glass in his long fingers. "In England it is tantamount to treason to drink French wines. Some do, of course, lifting their glasses and cursing Napoleon at the same time, but I—" He stopped, shrugging his shoulders as if what it were no longer of any importance.

Tanner stepped forward and drew the glass from Rhys's hand. "But you never could. It's understandable. You fought that bloody Peninsula War, didn't you?"

"How did you know?" Realization dawned in his eyes. "No, never mind, I know where you heard it."

"Roland could not accept that Rhys would not come here three years ago to fight on the side of the United States," Kenna said quietly. "It was a difficult decision for my husband but he wanted to remain in England."

"As I would have in his place," said Tanner. "What is the latest word on Napoleon?"

"You probably know as much as I do," Rhys said. "When we left England he was rallying his armies. He has likely taken over the reins of power in France. If he is not checked by the English he will have the entire Continent again."

Alexis placed her hand on Rhys's forearm. "It cannot be easy for you to know he is free after so many years of fighting."

"It's not. But my part in it is over. I've had my fill of

342

war." His eyes were soft as he looked at Kenna fondly. "This is where I want to be now." He touched the slender hand Alexis had placed upon his arm. "But I seem to have left my manners in London. Forgive me for becoming so tiresome about something as trifling as a glass of wine."

"There is nothing to forgive," Alexis said simply. "I am happy you spoke your mind."

Tanner offered his arm to Kenna. "A moment ago I saw Widdoes motioning from the hallway that our dinner is ready. Shall we go?"

Kenna went happily on his arm while Rhys escorted Alexis. The Clouds entertained in their small intimate supper room. Fresh, beautifully arranged flowers filled several vases on the sideboard and the room's light came from the candelabras which had been set on the mantel, sideboard, and the dining table. The room had a mellow warmth about it that made Kenna very comfortable. She touched Rhys's hand beneath the table and saw by his gentle smile that he was also quite content.

The meal was served with unobtrusive flair by Widdoes and the conversation flowed easily while they dined on fresh lobster served with hot melted butter, mushrooms stuffed with crabmeat and herbs, and a colorful rice and vegetable dish. Kenna laughed at her clumsy efforts to separate her lobster from its meat. She had difficulty peeling back the softened and cut shell and pushing out the meat.

"It requires a little perseverence," Alexis assured her.

Kenna tried again, pressing the back of the shell, and the white succulent meat flowered to the top. She poked at it with her fork to separate the juicy flakes of meat.

"I always think this food is meant to be enjoyed with one's fingers. Go ahead. It's quite acceptable here." Alexis graciously demonstrated, then Kenna and Rhys followed suit. Tanner grinned, shrugged, and not to be

343

left out, joined them.

"You were correct about the four Boston blue bloods, Mrs. Cloud," Kenna said.

"Please call me Alex."

Kenna nodded and offered the same informality of address. "They arrived just as you said they would and, according to the housekeeper, were plainly shocked that I was not at home to greet them. Imagine, expecting me to be there just because they had come calling!"

"It would be considered something of an honor that they deigned to visit you at all. The usual thing would be for them to simply command your presence. They left invitations though, didn't they?" Alexis said wisely.

"Yes. How did you know?"

"It is the expected thing. They are all curious about the Cannings. You must know Roland wielded a great deal of power in this state as well as nationally. Richard was considered by many to the likely winner of a senate seat in November. Their deaths shocked Boston. Naturally there is a lot of speculation about Roland's estranged son."

"I was prepared for that," said Rhys. "I am fated to disappoint them. I have no political aspirations whatsoever. Canning Shipping is enough to keep me occupied for quite some time." He hesitated slightly. "The captain of the *Carasea* led me to believe my father did not have much respect for the Garnet Line. Frankly, I'm curious as to why that was. Kenna and I have been impressed by what we've heard and seen."

"If I may speak plainly," Tanner said, raising his eyebrows in question.

"Please."

"Roland was an astute business man. There was much about his management of the line that I admired. But Canning Shipping became the means to an end in his hands. His end was power; for himself and for Richard.

344

He used political leverage to win special concessions for his line and he used money from the line to further his political ambitions. I spoke out against sending him to London to work out the terms of peace treaty and I was opposing Richard's bid for the senate seat. Roland took exception to my right to free speech."

"What did he do?" He waved away Tanner's look of surprise. "I knew my father well enough to know he would not take exception quietly. He must have acted against you in some way."

It was Alexis who spoke. "It's unimportant. We did not ask you here tonight to speak of these matters or to insist you do anything differently than your father has done. I will tell you this, your father's displeasure with us existed before Cloud spoke out against him."

"Alex," Tanner said warningly.

She touched his hand lightly. "It's all right. I want to tell them." Her gold flecked eyes traveled from Rhys to Kenna. "Roland believed I was responsible for the death of one of his dearest friends."

"Were you?" asked Rhys directly without the slightest fear of offending her.

Alexis's admiration grew. Not many people would have asked, preferring to reach their own conclusions based on the slim body of evidence available to them. "Two years ago I was responsible for the arrest of Senator Howe on charges of treason. He was a popular man here in Massachusetts and, as I mentioned, a good friend of your father's. He was found guilty after a short trial and later he hanged himself in prison."

Rhys grimaced in disgust. "That is hardly your fault."

"Roland didn't think so. When the war was officially declared at an end in December of last year, Cloud and I came to Boston to help his sister and brother-in-law with the Garnet Line. Roland made it quite clear that not only were we not welcome, but that we were to blame for

Howe's death. Reasoning with him was out of the question. He remained adamant."

"Yes, he would. He did not stray easily from a course once it was set."

"Not an entirely unadmirable quality," said Tanner. "I admit to a stubborn streak myself."

Alexis feigned surprise, laughing lightly, easing the strain in the room. "You do?" She spoke to Rhys and Kenna. "This is the first I've heard of it."

The conversation continued in a bantering manner throughout the remainder of the dinner. A plate of cheese and fresh fruit was served for dessert. They took the tray and their cups of hot spiced coffee to the music room where Kenna was coerced into playing something on the spinet.

"Alex doesn't play," Tanner told her as he put out the sheet music. "She keeps threatening to learn."

"She has other accomplishments," Kenna said a trifle wistfully. "I should love to learn to sail." She ignored Rhys's affected groan. "I lived along the Channel my entire life and never once was allowed to put out in a boat."

"The Channel waters can be treacherous," said Alexis.

Rhys added quickly and significantly, "And so can these waters."

"I take your meaning, Rhys," she laughed and began playing.

Shortly after Kenna's impromptu concert was at an end she and Rhys bid the Clouds goodnight. Kenna sat in the carriage beside Rhys, her head on his shoulder.

"It was an enjoyable evening, wasn't it?" she yawned sleepily as the carriage rocked them gently over cobbled Boston streets.

"Yes."

His quiet, single-word response gave Kenna pause. "What are you thinking?"

"That my father was a true bastard." The cords of his neck were knotted with tension. "I know he found a way to retaliate against the Clouds. I only wish they could have told me what he did. I could set it to rights. They don't deserve my father's revenge for speaking their minds."

"I think I know what he did," Kenna said quietly after a long silence had separated them. "There were things . . . .they didn't make sense then, but now, after tonight's conversation, well, I think I know what they mean."

She had his complete attention. "Kenna, what are you saying?"

"I found some items in the accounts that I was going to discuss with you because they made no sense to me. Were you aware your father was making regular payments to the lumber mills and iron forges and getting nothing in return? He was also making payments to certain individuals like foremen, carpenters, and laborers who were not employed directly by Canning Shipping. Not only that, but I found contracts with some merchants, no doubt good friends of your father's, that set ridiculously low prices for importing or exporting their goods. Rhys, Roland was paying people *not* to supply materials or work for the Garnet Line!"

"Dear God! That he could be so vindictive! It is nearly beyond belief!"

"I want you to look over everything, so you can be certain in your own mind, but I believe you will find that the evidence is there. The payments date back years, probably beginning at the time of Howe's suicide. That Tanner and his family have been able to keep Garnet in operation must have sorely taxed their resources, even with Quinton Shipping becoming part of the entire business."

Rhys could not take in the depth of Roland's

treachery. His flinty eyes narrowed as he stared out the carriage window. "They would have had to import the materials to build that schooner and cut their own prices to compete with Canning. And do you know what makes no sense?" he said bitterly. "My father was slashing his own throat to achieve his ends. He was so bent on destroying Garnet that he was sacrificing his own business."

Kenna folded her arms around Rhys's. "I suspect that he believed when Garnet was finished there would be time enough to recover what he paid out and more. Roland was in the stronger financial position. The Clouds would have had to declare bankruptcy eventually."

"I think my father seriously underestimated Tanner Cloud. Garnet Shipping would have held on for years."

"I don't know that Roland cared how long it would take, Rhys. I think he believed, however erroneously, that he was avenging a friend."

"A treasonous friend," Rhys said tightly. "I shouldn't wonder that my father had something to do with that."

"Oh, Rhys! Don't even think it!"

He said nothing in reply, remaining deep in his own thoughts during the rest of the drive home.

Rhys's withdrawn mood had not changed when they went to bed but when he reached for Kenna in the darkness of their room, she went to him gladly, laying her arm across his chest and her head in the crook of his shoulder.

Her soft breath caressed him. "I love you, Rhys Canning," she said. "Nothing your father ever did can change the way I feel about you. I hope it hasn't the power to change the way you feel about yourself."

Rhys stared unblinkingly at the ceiling. "I could not love my father, Kenna. But until this evening I was never ashamed of him. I feel it so deeply within me now that I ache with it."

"Don't do this to yourself," she pleaded softly.

"We're going to be very alone, you and I," he told her, his voice rasping. "I will not let his injustices stand, Kenna. In the morning I will begin putting a stop to wages given for no work and bribes that were used to keep Garnet without lumber and iron. I am going to tear up the contracts that kept fares unreasonably low. In fact I'm going to tear them up in front of the merchants who signed them. You know what will happen once the word is spread, don't you? When the reserve of Canning money is no longer in circulation, we are going to be shunned. Have no doubt, my father's business friends are going to revile us for laying open their immoral conduct."

"You're hardly going to put a notice in the *Gazette*, Rhys."

He smiled as if the thought appealed to him and knew a moment's pleasure. "No, I'm not going to do that," he sighed. "This affair does not have to reach the public. It will be enough that those men who entered into agreements with my father learn from me that it is finished. We won't be welcome in many homes after that."

"I can think of one place where we would be welcome, even if you had not discovered Roland's dealings a year from now. Alexis and Tanner don't bear any ill-will, Rhys. Why, they wouldn't even speak of what Roland had done this evening, which is why I remained silent about my suspicions. They certainly did not invite us into their home to win our support. If you had not asked about Roland, I sincerely doubt the topic would have been broached."

"You're right, of course. And I value their friendship, too. But aren't you in the least curious why they never fought my father publicly on this count? They could have stopped him by acknowledging openly how he was trying to ruin them. He would have been afraid of the scandal."

"Perhaps they had no tangible proof," she suggested. "Or it simply may be that they thought they could overcome the pressure Roland was placing upon their business. Does it really matter?"

"No, I suppose not." But still he was curious. Something that Tanner had said about his notorious wife refused to be silenced. Was it more than a lover's tease between them? A truth, perhaps, that his father had known? His thoughts strayed from Tanner and Alexis to his wife, who was rubbing the sole of her foot along the length of his calf. "I never asked what you think, Kenna. Do I have your support in this? It will not be easy on you either, you know."

"What do I care for being sought after for every social affair?" she said, mocking his question. "Of course you have my support, darling. We are hardly going to be pariahs. Alex and Tanner will see to that. There are hundreds of people in Boston who had no dealings at all with Roland Canning." Her hand slipped across his abdomen and pressed against his thigh. "Can we speak of this on the morrow, please. I would dearly love . . ." She whispered her desire in his ear.

"Kenna!" Rhys pretended shock. "Where did you learn those words?"

Her teeth tugged on his ear lobe. "From you, dearest. Where I learned everything." She slid down his body and her tongue flicked across his flat male nipples, arousing them as he did hers.

"Not everything," he denied huskily, brushing his fingers through her hair. "You're very . . ." She pinched the back of his thigh. "Creative! I swear I was intending to say creative!"

She lifted her head and looked into his dear face which was graced at the moment by an impish smile. "I love

350

you." She kissed the faint dimple in his chin. "You can't imagine . . ." Her mouth brushed his and the kiss deepened as desire swelled between them.

Kenna was an impatient lover that night, rousing them both to a fiery passion that left them breathless in its aftermath. Their skin misted with love's labors, their bodies tensing and arching, then curving into one another as pleasure's demands were surrendered to. They curled spoon fashion, Rhys's arms beneath the tender curves of Kenna's breasts, and slept that way most of the night.

In the morning Rhys went to the warehouse alone, but promised Kenna he would review the ledgers before he did anything. He admitted to himself that he had harbored a niggling hope that Kenna was wrong in her assessment of the irregularities in the accounts. That hope was extinguished by early afternoon. There was simply no other explanation that made sense. Rhys had a lengthy conversation with Joshua Grant but was finally satisfied that the man was guilty only of not questioning some of Roland's practices. Grant had never concerned himself with finances, his position demanded only that he make decisions about the cargo and sailing schedule and report back to Roland's lawyer, Mr. Britt. Britt, in turn, notified the bank to release funds for wages or made the deposits for Roland. Entries were made in the ledgers on a weekly basis by Britt's clerks.

Rhys's meeting with Britt lasted less than twenty minutes, long enough for him to terminate their business relationship. Though Britt protested he was only directing payments according to Roland's wishes, Rhys knew the man had understood all along what Roland was really asking him to do.

"I told you I advised your father to turn the profits back into his own line," Britt argued heatedly, pushing back his wire spectacles until the lenses seemed to press

351

against his eyes.

"The fact remains that you did as he wanted," Rhys said coldly.

"He employed me, for God's sake! He was my most important client!"

Rhys opened the door, tipping his hat with mocking politeness. "Then I hope you can find other clients, but I will not be among them."

Rhys managed to pay a visit to three merchants on his list before the closing of the business day. After informing them their contracts with Canning Shipping were void, he told them the new rates and left it up to them to decide if they wanted to continue using the line. He did not wait around to hear their protests or their decisions.

Before returning home Rhys visited the two ironworks that supplied anchors and chains, nails, hooks, and tools, to Canning Shipping. And none to Garnet. Neither of the owners were at the works and Rhys decided against explaining the problem to the foremen, preferring to deal directly with the owners.

When he arrived home Kenna was already dressed for their evening out. She was wearing her peach gown with the garland of flowers embroidered on the hem and looked achingly lovely to his weary eyes.

Kenna turned from the mirror where she was adjusting the pearl choker around her neck and stood, walking quickly toward Rhys to greet him. She brushed a lock of hair away from his brow, noting the lines of strain, and kissed him on the mouth.

"Would you rather not go this evening?" she asked, concern making her eyes the color of sweet dark chocolate. "We could send the groom with our excuses. Alex and Tanner will understand."

Rhys shook his head, shrugging out of his coat. "Thank you for asking, but there's no need to change our plans." He brushed her cheek with his mouth. "Mmmm, I like your perfume. Help me out of this shirt. I'd like to wash. I shouldn't wonder that I feel dirty after this day's work."

Kenna loosened the studs on Rhys's cuffs and shirt front. "Was it difficult for you?"

"I don't know that I thought about it," he said as she drew the shirt off his shoulders. "I went through the motions, but I didn't let myself think."

Kenna set out his evening clothes while Rhys poured water from the pitcher on the nightstand into a white porcelain bowl. "Do you want to tell me about it?"

Rhys began washing. "I confirmed your suspicions after a few hours. My father and Richard, and later Britt's clerks, kept excellent records. I spoke with Grant and he cleared himself to my satisfaction. My conversation with Britt was briefer. We will not be doing business with him any longer. I spoke with Franklin Anders, Thomas Hamilton, and Harris Feilding and let them know our rates would be increasing. Neither Brown nor Sampson were at their ironworks so that will have to wait until Monday."

"What was the response from the men you did speak to?"

"To a man it was the same. Incredulity, sputtering protests, and then resignation." He threw down his washcloth and turned to Kenna. "On Monday, after word has traveled, I expect the denials of wrongdoing to flow smoothly from glib tongues. I doubt I shall be amused."

"Can I help in any manner?" she asked.

"Knowing that you are willing to is help enough. Just keep loving me, Kenna."

Her heart went out to him as he stood there, vulnerable with his open hands at his sides and a pained look in his glistening eyes. She had not suspected that he needed the same reassurances that she did. Lifting his hand to her breast, she held it there a moment, then raised it higher, touching her lips to the center of his palm. "That I should ever stop loving you is the last thing you should worry about."

Rhys's eyes closed and he pulled Kenna into his embrace. "I don't want Tanner to know about what I've done today. Let us put business aside this evening."

"They're going to find out."

"But not tonight, please."

"Of course, Rhys. Whatever you wish."

Alexis and Tanner were waiting for them at Forrest's, though they swore they had only arrived minutes before. They were shown to a private booth at the back of the tavern by Forrest himself, a gruff man with an impatient air about him who kept calling Tanner Captain Cloud in spite of Tanner's objections.

When Forrest left them Alexis patted Tanner's hand consolingly. "You'll always be the captain to him, so you may as well save your breath. Besides, you know he was doing it in part to needle you." She turned to Rhys and Kenna. The delicate silver necklace at her throat sparkled in the candlelight. "We have been promising to come here for over a month and never found the time. Forrest is not about to let it go lightly."

Kenna looked around her, admiring the tavern's warmth and nautical decor. "This setting is very attractive," she said, gazing up at the fisherman's nets that hung from the ceiling. "Rather like being at sea."

Tanner rolled his eyes. "Don't let Forrest hear you say that. He envisioned his tavern becoming a place for rowdy sailors to swap outrageous stories. He hasn't accustomed himself to the fact that most of his patrons pay for their passage when they sail, and know nothing about trimming canvas or mending split taffrails."

Their meal arrived from the kitchen a short time later, scarcely interrupting their laughter at the tales Tanner

354

shared with them about his former galley cook. They dined on stuffed flounder, small potatoes dripping with butter and garnished with flakes of parsley, artichoke halves, and sliced tomatoes sprinkled with cheese.

Kenna glanced at Rhys secretly several times throughout the meal, her eyes soft with concern, and each time she was relieved to see him genuinely enjoying himself. His rich laughter made her heart lighter and she was glad she had not talked him out of coming. Even when the conversation accidently took a more serious turn as Napoleon's name was mentioned, Rhys appeared unperturbed by the discussion.

"It's hard to credit," he said, "but Napoleon's return to power could have been avoided. That is what makes it so difficult for me to comprehend what is happening in Europe now."

"Avoided?" asked Alexis. "But how? Who could suspect he would escape Elba?"

Rhys chuckled mirthlessly. "Exactly the skepticism I encountered when I tried to tell the Foreign Office that a plot to release him was beyond the planning stages."

"Rhys!" Kenna murmured, shocked. "Is this true? You knew of a plot to free Napoleon?"

"I did," he said succinctly. "Don't you believe me?"

"What I don't believe is that no one else did!"

His features softened at the unwavering trust for him in her voice. "You should have been working in the Foreign Office." He touched her hand beneath the table, squeezing her fingers, and explained to the others. "I overheard the plans for the escape some seven weeks before the event. Oh, the Foreign Office had every right to be suspicious. I couldn't even present the case myself and I had none of the names of the perpetrators. They dragged their feet too long making a decision, and then, well, you know what happened." He shrugged. "It scarcely can be changed now. Wellington will have to defeat him in battle."

Tanner and Alexis sympathized with his frustration at being unable to have made a difference but Rhys could not fail to notice that Kenna had become withdrawn. During the remainder of the evening her laughter alternated between being brittle and too bright and she drank rather more wine than she was used to. The carriage ride home was taut with silence and Kenna held herself so stiffly that Rhys finally withdrew the arm he had around her shoulders.

Immediately upon returning home she went upstairs. Rhys would have followed her but Alcott drew him to one side.

"There are four gentlemen waiting for you in the drawing room, Mr. Canning," he said, looking more flustered than usual."

"I don't want to see anyone. Tell them to leave."

"They refused, sir, when I asked them before. I doubt they will go now, especially since you're here."

"Very well," Rhys sighed. He would handle them rather than risk causing a disruption which was certain to bring Kenna. "I'll see them. But don't bother bringing refreshments. They won't be staying long."

Rhys was as good as his word. Britt had brought three of his friends, men Rhys had not yet met but who were due to make his acquaintance on Monday. Rhys showed them that at least in one way he was very much his father's son: he refused to be moved from his position. He listened politely to their arguments and protests and then repeated his dissolution with Britt and the increase in his shipping rates. Then he showed them the door.

When they were gone he went to his bedchamber, having forgotten Kenna's strange mood until she failed to respond to his presence.

"I know you're not sleeping," he said as he stripped of his clothes, taking note of her stiff form beneath the

356

bedcovers. He sighed heavily as she turned on her side and gave him her back. Rhys put on a nightshirt and walked around the four-poster, slipping between the cold sheets. He lay on his back, staring at the play of shadows on the ceiling made by the fire in the grate. "I'm of no mind to tease you from this mood, Kenna. I wish you would tell me what has upset you and be done with it." She was silent so long that Rhys thought she had no intention of answering him, then he heard her muffled sob and realized she could not speak.

His impatience faded and when he spoke it was with gentleness. "Why are you weeping, Kenna?"

"Why did you n-never tell m-me?" she choked out, lifting a corner of the sheet to wipe her eyes.

A thread of impatience returned to his tone. "Tell you what? I don't know what you're talking about."

Tears spilled through her lashes again. "N-Napoleon. You n-never said a w-word."

"It never came up before tonight. I put it all behind me once we sailed for America. Why should it bother you?"

Kenna's fist hit her pillow in frustration and she sat up, drawing a deep breath. "B-because the conversation you heard happened at Dunnelly!" Even through her tears she could see Rhys's surprise as his mind worked furiously to discover how she knew.

"I never said it did," he said slowly.

"Seven weeks! You said you heard it seven weeks before the event. You were at Dunnelly then!"

"Kenna! Calm yourself!"

She came very close to raising her hand against him then. Instead her fingers curled into bloodless fists. "Ooooh! I will *not* calm myself! Who spoke of the plans for escape, Rhys? Was it one of the servants? Mayhap you think it was Nicholas! Is that why you came to Dunnelly? To spy on my family, listen at keyholes, and poke your nose into my brother's private papers?" She gave him no time to respond as anger fired her senses. "You lied to me, Rhys! Not once, but twice! You first said you came to Dunnelly to get away from your father in London! Then you told me, oh, so sweetly, that you were there because of Yvonne's letters. To protect me, you said!"

"Those were not lies, Kenna," Rhys denied, sitting up himself. "They were but two parts of the truth."

Kenna's eyes darkened and widened. Her brows lifted disdainfully and her laughter was mocking. "Two parts of the truth? Since when is the truth divided like a recipe ingredient? What do I add? One part confidence? Equal portions of faith? A dash of deceit?" She knuckled a tear that dripped from her eye. "Tell me, Rhys. How many parts make up the whole? Three? Four? How many, damn you?"

Rhys got up from the bed and poured himself a measure of brandy from the cabinet beside the window. He gulped it back quickly, poured another, and stood at the window, watching the moon scatter its white light on the edge of the clouds.

"Do you think what I had to do at Dunnelly is the sort of thing I could talk about?" he asked quietly, turning slowly in her direction. "The Foreign Office frowns on that kind of sharing."

"So you *were* sent to Dunnelly."

His expression was bleak and pale in the moonlight. "I thought you didn't have any doubts."

"I didn't . . . I don't." Her eyes pleaded with him. "Please, Rhys, tell me what your purpose there was! I cannot bear these half-truths and you knowing things about Dunnelly that affect me too. Don't let there be any more secrets between us!"

"The secrets had to be there, Kenna," he said slowly, putting down his drink. "I could only tell you what you could bear to hear."

"That's no excuse."

"No, it's not." He sat on the edge of the bed beside her. "Do you remember the first morning of my visit? You asked me there in the wood what my purpose was for being there. Could I have told you then that I was there to protect you? Would you have believed that someone was trying to end your life? More to the point, could I say that I loved you when you only felt hatred toward me? Those were things you could not listen to, Kenna, so I compromised and told you what you could hear. And it was no lie. My father's presence in London was enough to send me packing for Dunnelly even had there been no other reasons."

Rhys lifted his legs on the bed and sat cross-legged in front of Kenna, leaning a little forward with an earnestness about his posture. "And on the ship, when you were finally able to hear another truth, that I had gone to Dunnelly to see that you were safe, could you have listened to me tell you that protecting you was irrevocably intertwined with finding a traitor, perhaps a member of your own family? Could you have listened and believed me then, when you didn't even realize I loved you and would never do anything to harm you?"

Kenna closed her eyes, wishing she could answer him differently. "You know I wouldn't have believed you," she said, defeated. She raised her eyes to him. They hinted at her pain. "I can bear it now. I promise I can listen to you." She reached out impulsively, touching his arm. "I must know, Rhys. Why did the Foreign Office send you to Dunnelly?"

Chapter Nine

Rhys admitted to himself it was time to tell Kenna everything, yet he wished this moment had not come. Almost immediately he wondered if that were entirely true. Perhaps he had wanted to share this with her, else why had he spoken of the overheard conversation at dinner? He sighed, thinking reflection in this instance was not productive, and Kenna was still pleading her question with her beautifully eloquent eyes.

"In order to answer you I must go back more than a decade," he said finally, his voice heavy.

"To my father's death?"

He shook his head. "Before that. To the fall of 1804, when I went to the Continent."

Kenna nodded wisely and spoke, thinking to save him a painful explanation. "I know why you went to France, Rhys."

"You do?" he asked, brows lifting.

"Nick told me."

That clearly shocked Rhys. "He did?"

"Yes. He told me all about his love for poor, mad Lara and how you fought the duel in his place while he acted as your second."

"I see," Rhys said thoughtfully.

Kenna frowned at his tone. "It's true, isn't it?"

"It's true. Or rather it is the truth as Nick knows it. There are other things which I could never speak to him about, things that I must tell you now if you are to understand." His eyes did not waver from hers. "When I finished at Oxford your father approached me, asking if I would be interested in working for the Foreign Office. The position as he outlined it entailed going to France and acting as a conduit for highly sensitive information between Napoleon's government and the crown. More simply, I was being asked to spy for England. There was nothing I would not have done for your father, Kenna, but I cannot lay my acceptance of the request solely at his door. In truth, I found the idea intriguing and I felt, as your father did, that I was highly suited for the task.

"My American citizenship would make me more acceptable to the French and my command of the language was excellent. But my relationship to the Duchess of Pelham was bound to be remarked upon should it be discovered. Neither Robert nor I thought it would be wise to dismiss the possibility. It therefore remained for me to find a reason for going to France that would not be questioned."

"The duel," she breathed softly.

"Yes. You must believe I did not plan it to happen the way it did. When Lara's brother asked Nick for satisfaction I took responsibility for the affair and offered to meet him. I honestly don't know if I would have acted in the same manner if it were not for the other problem. I like to think I still would have stood in Nick's stead, for we both know he is a poor shot and Lara's brother was intent upon murder. But it is hardly debatable because the other problem did exist and I responded accordingly."

Kenna did not agree. She touched his knee lightly. "You would have helped Nick. I know it."

"Thank you for that." Rhys's bleak smile faded slightly as he basked in Kenna's confidence. "The wound to Lara's brother was more severe than I intended. I did not anticipate he would flinch at the last moment and I was thankful I had not killed him. Dueling was all that was necessary, not murder. I believe you know what happened next. I fled to France with my great-grandmother's blessing. She expressed an interest in never seeing me again and formally broke all ties with me. Your father as well made it publicly known I was not welcome in his home. My grandmother was sincere, Robert only appeared so."

"Nick said father was gravely disappointed in you both."

"He was disappointed in Nick, for he knew the reason I had taken your brother's place. He thought I was reckless and gave me a stern dressing down. Afterwards he shook my hand and wished me luck."

"What did you do while you were in France?" Kenna asked with ill-concealed curiosity.

"I attached myself to a circle of people which included some of Napoleon's confidantes as well as Josephine's. I listened to every small bit of information that came my way, whether or not it seemed to have any significance at the time. All that was expected of me was that I report what I heard, not analyze it. Interpretation was left to agents more skilled than I or the Foreign Office. As I proved myself I was given more responsibility and eventually I was chosen to lead an important operation. There were still a number of men and women of noble birth in France who had offended Napoleon in some way. Some were in prisons, others were closely watched on their estates by Napoleon's spies. For obvious reasons they were not able to leave the country. My assignment was to provide the means for them to do so.

"From the time of the Terror on, your father was

involved in helping people flee France. His political influence and financial support was crucial in making the operation a popular one. Your sister, as I discovered much later, was one of the first children brought out of Paris with his help and years later Victorine was able to follow. When we were reviewing the guest list the other day you pointed out the Comte and Comtesse Lescaut. They left France under my direction, as did Michael Deveraux and Paul Françon."

Kenna shook her head wonderingly. "You never said a word. It did not seem then as if you even knew them. Why didn't you tell me how you had helped my father?"

"It was not relevant at the time," he said simply. "I was more interested in what you knew about the guests."

Kenna had to accept that explanation. "You do tend to be bloody single-minded," she said, sighing. "Tell me how it came to pass that you returned to England. I should have thought your work on the Continent would have lasted longer than one year."

"It should have," Rhys agreed. "But I received a communiqué from your father, asking me to return to Dunnelly. He did not relate much information in the missive but I understood its urgency. He mentioned the plans for the masquerade and said I should make every effort to arrive before that night."

"And you did."

"Just. I reached Dunnelly only an hour before the ball was to begin. It did not give Robert much time to speak with me privately. It was agreed between us that I should pretend to be there at Nick's invitation, for your brother had also written to me of the masque and asked me to come. Nick, knowing nothing of my work in France, was of the opinion I had been away long enough."

"Why the subterfuge? Why not simply say it was my father who invited you?"

"Robert thought it was necessary in the event I would

return to France. He did not want anyone to know he approved of my presence in his home."

"I see," she said slowly, trying to take in the depth of caution intrinsic to Rhys's work. "And why did my father want to see you?"

"He suspected that Dunnelly's coast was being used as a location for Napoleon's spies in England to pass information. It was a dangerous place for the spies to use, given Lord Dunne's influence, but it was in the same respect a very safe place, because who would think anyone would have the backbone to use it?"

"Obviously my father did."

"Yes, Robert was suspicious, though he never had time to tell me what was responsible for his concern. He related only that he anticipated contact would be made during the masque, in Dunnelly's coastal caves, and that all his guests were suspect."

"Only his guests?" Kenna asked shrewdly.

After a moment's hesitation Rhys surrendered to her sharply discerning gaze. "His words as I recall were that everyone at Dunnelly was suspect."

"And you took that to mean the servants and his family?"

"Yes. If Robert meant to exclude anyone I believe he would have said so."

"Perhaps," she said, though it was clear she was unconvinced.

Rhys did not comment upon her skepticism, recalling his own at the time. "As I said, my time alone with your father was limited. He asked me to be his second pair of eyes that evening, looking for anything beyond the ordinary. Of course I agreed, though I hadn't the slightest idea what to expect. I dressed for the masque, talked very briefly with Nick, and started downstairs, only to be waylaid by a young miss with a scheme in her eyes."

"You went along with my plans," she reminded him.

"Yes, I admit to a soft spot in my brain as well as my heart where you were concerned. The guests had not all arrived by that time and I could see that little would be lost if I delayed my arrival downstairs by a few more minutes. I also had hoped Nicholas would take more responsibility for looking after Yvonne. He was helpful in the beginning, but when I saw him desert her and disappear from the ballroom I took her to one side and asked her to return to her room. Thinking that she would do as I requested I went in search of Nicholas."

"That must be when I came downstairs. I could find neither of you in the ballroom. There were no other highwaymen anywhere."

"That would account for me, but Nick's costume was that of a devil."

"He told me that, but I have found it hard to credit. In my dream he is always a highwayman," she said.

"I think we both agree now that there are serious distortions of reality in your dreams," he said gently. "But perhaps you were there then because I found Nick in the study, brooding over a half-finished tumbler of whiskey. I did not need to be his closest friend for twelve years to know something was troubling him."

"Did he tell you what it was?" Kenna asked anxiously, fearing the worst.

"His brooding had nothing to do with why your father sent for me," Rhys told her. "With Nicholas it was women. It was always women with your brother."

"Poor Nick," Kenna said sadly.

"Poor Nick, indeed," Rhys said dryly. "This time he had foolishly allowed himself to be involved with a married woman."

Kenna gasped. "Who?"

"He would not say. He told me her identity did not matter in the least because he was calling an end to their affair that very evening."

"Then she was at the masque!"

"It would appear so. And you can keep your next question, for I haven't any idea who the woman was. Much later that night, hours after we had found you in the cave, Nick told me that he had put a period to their relationship."

"He told me there had been other mistakes with women of good birth and breeding," said Kenna. "It's how he justifies his penchant for actresses and opera singers."

"I know. Nick has not been so fortunate as I."

"Nor I," she said serenely. "What happened after you left Nick in the study?"

"I mingled with the guests. It was deuced difficult to keep a watch. They were flitting here and there, leaving the ballroom for trysts in other parts of the house. Your father needed more assistance than just me. I stationed myself near the entrance to the ballroom at one point and my vigilance reaped results almost immediately. I saw a man dressed in rogue's garb leave the gallery, brush past Henderson, and go outside."

"That was me!"

"I didn't know that at the time. If I had I would have stopped you and sent you to your room. I thought I was witnessing the guest whom your father suspected would meet with the French. You must admit your movements bore me out."

"You followed me!"

"Naturally. First you went toward Dunnelly's gate but when you got there you paused, looking around as if you thought you might be followed. When you thought yourself alone you circled around the south wing of the manor and went toward the summerhouse. I knew of the steps leading from the summerhouse to the beach and I assumed that is how you were going to arrive at your meeting place."

Kenna's eyes widened as she listened to the meaning Rhys had attached to her innocent movements of that night. In his place she would have been equally suspicious.

Rhys continued quitely. "I went back into the manor to tell Robert what I had seen but he was no longer in the ballroom. Yvonne was still there though, so I took her firmly in hand and led her straight to her room. After I left her I caught a glimpse of your father turning the corner to the south wing and I followed. When I arrived in the south corridor your father had disappeared and I had to open a number of doors before I discovered where he had gone. Did you never know about the passage?"

It seemed impossible that Kenna's eyes could grow even rounder, but they did. "Passage?" she choked on her surprise. "What passage?"

"I can see that you didn't," said Rhys. "Amazing, considering the number of hours you used to spend exploring Dunnelly. The third bedchamber on the left has a wall with a false panel. It can be removed without much difficulty if one knows the trick of it. I didn't then, of course, but Robert had been in too much of a hurry to secure the panel behind him so I was able to follow. There is a narrow spiral staircase which winds between Dunnelly's walls and far below me I could see the light Robert carried. You cannot know how many times I wish I had had the foresight to have brought such a light myself. Once Robert's lantern vanished and I could not see my hand in front of my face. I found my way by keeping one arm in front of me and one on the wall."

"Why didn't you call to him to wait for you?"

"I did. Several times. If he heard he gave no sign of it. I kept to my path but my progress was slow and it was only when I reached the bottom of the stairs that I realized where the passage was leading me."

"To the caves," breathed Kenna. "I had always imagined there was a way, but . . ." her voice trailed off. "What then?"

"I kept walking until I reached a dead end, or so it appeared to be to me. It was a small chamber with no way out except by the way I came in. I thought I had taken a wrong turn and was about to retrace my steps when I heard voices on the other side of the chamber. If I had had a lantern of my own or had had the luck to stumble upon the one your father had snuffed and left behind mayhap I would have found the way out of the chamber. I had never experienced such helplessness as I knew then. All I could do was listen to the raised voices and nothing I heard was clear." His voice deepened as the ache in his throat conveyed his pain at the memory. "Nothing. Until the shots echoed in the chamber."

"Oh, Rhys." She felt his pain as keenly as she felt her own. Without hesitation she went into his arms, offering and receiving comfort in the healing circle of his arms.

Rhys's chin rested against her soft red-gold hair. "I broke two knuckles beating uselessly on the face of that damn rock before a measure of sanity returned. By that time there were no more sounds coming from the chamber but I would not let myself believe anything had happened to Robert. I forced myself to calm and waited interminable minutes for your father to return by the same method he exited. I did not know then that it would have been impossible, even if he were alive. After the stone has been rolled back the only exit from the chamber is by the beach. When Robert did not reappear and I could still find no way to reach the outer chamber I returned to the south wing. I was on my way to search for him when Yvonne stopped me in the corridor, asking if I had seen you. I confess I hadn't much patience for her and would not have paid her any heed if she hadn't finally blurted out that she thought you had gone to the masque

369

after all—dressed as a highwayman."

"And you knew—"

Rhys nodded. "I knew then it was you I had seen and wondered why I hadn't guessed it before. Your stride, your profile, it was somehow familiar, yet I ignored the signs. I remember running for the caves, praying all the while you had only gone as far as the summerhouse, that you had not accidentally stumbled into the dangerous situation below. I caught sight of Victorine in the garden, in earnest conversation with your brother, the devil. I yelled to Nick to bring several servants, a lantern, and meet me at the cave entrance, then I went on. A quick search of the summerhouse revealed you were not there and, fearing the worst, I headed down to the beach. It was deserted. No ship was in sight, no boat, no sign of the men your father had argued with. Even the footprints had been obliterated. The tide was coming in and I waited for Nick as long as I dared, calling for you and Robert all the while. When Nick did not appear soon enough to suit me I entered the cave. You know what I found."

She shuddered in his embrace, chilled by the memory. Her escape was more narrow than she had imagined.

Rhys's hand slid soothingly along Kenna's spine, warming her. "Your screams led me to you else I would have taken the wrong passage. When I finally reached you, you were unconscious. There was nothing I could do for your father, Kenna."

"I know," she said sadly. "He was already dead when I found him."

"I carried you out and met Nicholas in the passage. The servants brought your father out. Nick wanted to take you from me, but —"

"You wouldn't let him," she finished. "He told me that. That, and other things. Like how you stayed by my bedside nearly the entire two weeks I was unconscious." Kenna pulled back a little so she could see his face. "I was

370

so miserable and hateful toward you then." She would have apologized for her actions; it was there in her eyes. Rhys put a finger to her lips, stopping her.

"You were a child, Kenna. What you saw, or rather what you thought you saw, was more than anyone should see, child or no. I don't blame you or think less of you. I cannot deny I was hurt by your accusations, but we are past that now, aren't we?"

Her gaze was steady. "Yes, we are."

"Then I hope you can understand that I accepted the Foreign Office's most recent assignment because I knew I was going to Dunnelly anyway. I was there for you, Kenna. I agreed to keep a watch on Dunnelly's coast, but frankly I did not expect any activity. Napoleon was safely away on Elba; peace between England and France seemed as if it would continue without disruption. But something must have roused the suspicions of my superiors because they were adamant that I go to Dunnelly."

"Their suspicions were founded. You heard of plans for the escape."

"I did. But I think that news was rather more than the Foreign Office anticipated, else they would have acted with more haste. The first night I was at Dunnelly I saw someone walking toward the summerhouse. In my mind there was only one reason that a person would go there in the middle of winter. I was with you that evening. Remember?"

"That was the night you practically threw me from your bedchamber."

"Precisely. After you were gone I used the passage in the south wing to go to the caves. By now I knew all its secrets. I had explored the passages and chambers many times since I first used it. I knew exactly where to stand to hear the conversation being conducted in the outer chamber. Unfortunately, the stone wall distorts the voices so I still did not know the identities of the people in the cave. At this moment I know no more than I did then. I sent Powell directly to London to tell of what I had overheard and I was determined to establish the identity of the traitor once you were safely at Cherry Hill with Yvonne. But my plans came to nothing. My father and Richard died, you were abducted, the guest list was forgotten, and Napoleon escaped. It now rests with Powell. He is employed at Dunnelly and I can only hope he has more success than I."

Kenna was not certain she wished Powell the same. She would not let herself dwell on the possibility that someone she knew, even loved, was a traitor. "Have you any suspicions?" she asked, dreading Rhys's response.

"It would be folly for me to speak of them. I have no evidence. I did not even share my thoughts with Powell, preferring that he begin his work uninfluenced by my judgment."

"That is no sort of answer at all. If you suspect some member of my family you should tell me."

"It is the only answer I will give you, Kenna," Rhys said sternly. "Please do not ask me again."

"Now I shall think the worst."

"I cannot be responsible for that. Think whatever you wish." His expression softened as did his hold on her. "I'm sorry. I did not mean to be so brusque. This is a matter on which I do not care to dwell either. But, Kenna, while I have only suspicions, I would swear on my life that you know the truth."

"I know nothing of traitors!" she denied hotly.

"Don't you? What of your dreams? Isn't the truth there somewhere?"

"You mean—" She was too astonished to finish her thought.

Rhys nodded, reading the expression on her face with perfect clarity. "I believe the person responsible for your father's death is the same person I overheard receiving information of Napoleon's escape. There has always been much more at stake than you merely discovering who murdered your father. That you could identify a traitor who is still working for Napoleon ten years later threatened everything he is doing. It mandated the attempts on your life."

It made an awful kind of sense to her but Kenna did not want to believe it. "No, Rhys. You are wrong."

Rhys would not argue over this matter. "Mayhap I am," he agreed quietly.

It occurred to Kenna that Rhys was patronizing her but it was not in her at the moment to take offense. "I need time to think on it," she said, admitting to herself there might be more than a grain of truth in his suspicions.

"Of course."

"You must admit it is difficult for me."

"I admit it."

She went on as if he had not spoken. "I mean, it is a fantastic idea."

"Fantastic."

"That the traitor of ten years ago could be the same traitor you overheard. It is hard to credit."

Rhys simply drew her closer. "I know."

Kenna's lashes fanned her cheeks, blending into the shadows beneath her eyes. "Just hold me, Rhys. Hold me forever."

"I will." And he did. Long after Kenna had fallen asleep Rhys held her in his loving embrace and stared at the play of shadows on the ceiling.

Something soft touched the bridge of Kenna's nose. She wrinkled it. There was another touch, light and airy. She passed her hand in front of her face, brushing aside the teasing caress. When it came again she buried her face in her pillow.

Rhys chuckled, ruffling the red-gold curls at the nape

373

of her neck. "Slug-a-bed," he said affectionately.

Kenna nodded happily in agreement.

The knuckle of his index finger traced the length of her spine, eliciting a sleepy, but satisfied sound of pleasure. "It's a beautiful day, Kenna," he said, looking past her to the window. The sun was shining in a cloudless azure sky, coaxing pink and white blossoms on the cherry tree beyond the window to lay open their petals.

"That's nice," she said, yawning hugely.

Rhys was uncertain if she was commenting on the day or the pressure of his hand in the small of her back. He bent his head, blowing softly in her ear. "I was thinking of a picnic. We could ride to the brook that Alcott says skirts the edge of our property, lay out a rug, and breakfast on muffins, honey, and tea."

She turned her head a little and snuggled closer to Rhys. "That sounds lovely."

"I cannot help but notice you are making no effort to rise."

Kenna's hand slipped beneath the covers and tugged at Rhys's nightshirt. She ran her fingers lightly over his inner thigh, then her touch grew bolder, fondling him. She giggled when she felt his immediate response. "No, but you are."

Without conscious thought their bodies made the necessary adjustments, melding with a complete naturalness that took Kenna's breath away. Her gown was pushed up around her waist and like the blossoms outside their bedroom window she unfolded to receive Rhys. She had not realized how ready she was for him until he thrust into her. It faintly embarrassed her that she could accept him so easily, so quickly, that her body had prepared for his entry as if it were inevitable.

And perhaps it was.

She felt the heat of his gaze upon her and she lifted her eyes to his, caught at once by the desire darkening his smoke gray eyes.

The swiftness of their passion had surprised Rhys also but he reveled in the hunger they shared. His mouth sought Kenna's, tasting, teasing, exploring the full curve of her sensitive lower lip. He pressed kisses along her jaw, at the tip of her sometimes impossibly determined chin, traced the delicate sweep of her cheekbones and touched his lips to the corners of her eyes. He felt her need in the throaty way she murmured his name and in the arching of her body against him. Her breasts swelled in his palms, the nipples becoming erect under the insistent pressure of his thumbs. The tips of her tapered nails made small crescents in the flesh of his shoulders as she held him to her. Her legs wrapped around him, smooth and white against the darker texture of his skin. His hand slipped from her breast to her thigh, stroking the taut curve of her leg.

"I love touching you," he said, his own voice husky and edged with desire.

Kenna's hands caressed the length of Rhys's broad back then cradled his buttocks, keeping him deep inside her. There was an infinitesimal pause in the rhythm of their love. "You cannot imagine . . . how good you feel."

His response was a growl from deep in his chest as his loins gave an involuntary jerk and he felt himself lose control. Kenna met his quickened thrusts and knew her own pleasure was but moments away. Her neck arched, exposing the slender column of her throat and the little pulse there, beating wildly as she finally gave in to the mounting sensations. She opened her eyes because she wanted to see his face and found Rhys watching her expectantly as if he had commanded her attention. Her lips parted but her thoughts remained unspoken. Their mouths touched, then clung, as if sharing the same breath in the moment their bodies shuddered with the force of pleasure's release.

"It's a lovely day," Kenna said some minutes later. She rubbed her cheek against the smooth linen fabric that covered his chest.

Rhys gave her backside an affectionate pinch. "You have yet to look out the window," he observed.

"I don't have to," she answered tartly. "One knows these things."

A dark eyebrow lifted. "Does one really?"

Kenna sat up and pulled her nightgown over her head, giving Rhys an uninhibited view of the beautiful thrust of her breasts. She laughed when she saw her actions had the effect of raising his other brow. She leaned down and droped a kiss on his forehead, bounding off the bed and neatly eluding Rhys's play to grab her. "I thought you wanted to go on a picnic," she said, glancing over her bare shoulder as she retreated into the dressing room.

Rhys rose somewhat reluctantly from the bed and followed her. The smooth routine of dressing was interrupted periodically as they found excuses to touch and tease one another. By the time Kenna smoothed Rhys's jacket over his back her cheeks were warm and her eyes were suspiciously bright. As Rhys followed her downstairs, watching the graceful sway of her hips, he admitted to being warm all over.

In the days that followed Kenna clung to the memory of Rhys's roguish glances as he threw himself into his work. Though she often accompanied him to the warehouse she returned hours before he did and was not nearly as tired when he finally joined her in bed. He slept restlessly as the day's events would turn over in his mind and she held him, troubled by the shadows beneath his eyes and tension in his body. He spoke to her of the difficulty of righting his father's wrongs against the Clouds but Kenna knew he did not share his innermost feelings. It was in the darkness of their chamber when he would reach out to her and love her with a desperation that made her ache, that she knew how troubled he was by the course he had set for himself.

There was increased resistance from the merchants he dealt with as they balked at the rates he had set. Monitoring the accounts as she did, Kenna could not fail to notice the sharp decline in the number of businesses that used the Canning Line. Even some of the merchants who had no personal dealings with the late Roland Canning shied away from dealing with Rhys, giving in to pressure exerted by Roland's friends.

Kenna honored her invitation to Captain Johnson the evening before he set sail for the Indies. She almost regretted that she had asked him to dine with them when he insisted upon mentioning the state of affairs of Canning Shipping.

"You've made some powerful enemies," Johnson said, pulling on his chin thoughtfully before he helped himself to a second portion of halibut steak. "I don't pretend to know why it's so, I simply know what I hear. A lot of people, important people, are upset with you, Mr. Canning. Can't remember the last time I heard Boston Wharf so noisy with rumor."

"More coffee, Captain?" asked Kenna politely, trying to divert the conversation. Johnson was insensitive to her mood, but Rhys was not.

"It's quite all right, Kenna. I'm interested in what the captain has to say."

Johnson held out his cup. "Have I gone and put my foot in it?"

"No," denied Rhys. "My wife is simply concerned for me. There have been a number of threats recently."

Now Johnson was alarmed. "Threats? I hadn't heard any talk of threats. Pardon me, Mrs. Canning. I didn't know it had gone so far. Of course you don't want me talking about it now."

"I think it's a little late for that, Captain," said Kenna.

"Please tell us what you've heard."

With additional encouragement from Rhys, Johnson related what he had learned at the docks. There were complaints from men who had been employed with Canning that Rhys has fired them unfairly.

"They were being paid by my father *not* to work for Garnet," Rhys pointed out.

"Doesn't matter to them. They're talking now like you owe them a wage. Employment is harder to come by these days. None of the other lines have a place for them. Then there's this matter of your rate increase. Folks are saying you're profiteering."

Kenna laughed at that. "Hardly. They could glance at our books and know otherwise."

Johnson shrugged. "Truth is, Canning Shipping is setting the precedent. The other lines will be raising their rates in turn. No one is happy about that."

"It will balance in the end," Rhys said with a shade more confidence than he felt. "Our prices are fair. Far more than they were under my father's leadership. The rates he proposed could not keep this line afloat."

"That's because he was trying to sink Garnet."

Rhys could not hide his surprise. "You knew that?"

"Course. I'm not saying it was common knowledge, you understand, but I worked for your father long enough to know the bent of his mind. I told you he didn't have much good to say about Garnet. I hated to see Canning floundering as he tried to run Garnet aground, but it wasn't my place to say anything. If it means anything to you, Mr. Canning, I think you're doing the right thing."

It did mean something to Rhys, Kenna realized, as she saw some of the tension seep out of him. He respected Johnson's opinion and though he would not have changed what he was doing even if the captain had thought him foolhardy, it gave him a measure of strength to know someone else believed in him. She was happy that Johnson had come to dinner after all.

The following morning Kenna and Rhys stood in a bank of fog and bid farewell to the *Carasea*. They waited until the ship was no longer in sight before they turned away, Kenna to the office and Rhys to supervise the work being started on their new vessel.

Kenna had been working on the books less than an hour when her attention was drawn to the window by the rough and raised voices outside on the wharf. Pushing aside the ledger she ran to the window, wiping a pane clean with the heel of her hand so she could have a clear view of the commotion.

At the building site, less than fifty yards from where she stood, she saw a gang of men surround Rhys and his employees. The dozen or so men were armed with clubs and appeared to have every intention of using them if their demands were not met. Rhys seemed to be calm in the face of the danger but Kenna saw his hands were clenched at his side, giving lie to the unconcerned expression on his face. The shouting became two-sided as one of the Canning men took exception to something that was said. Kenna never saw who threw the first punch but suddenly there was chaos as fists and clubs swung wildly.

Her thoughts were all for Rhys as she fled from the window and raced down the steps to the front of the warehouse. Uncaring of her own safety she ran directly into the melee, picked up an unattached two by four, and began swinging with the rest of them.

Rhys saw her out of the corner of his eye and his misdirected attention allowed his opponent to knock him backward into a stack of barrels with a well-aimed blow to the chin. In turn the man who laid him low never knew what hit him. He felt as if he had been kicked in the head by a mule as Kenna brought down her plank on his bald spot. Groaning, he fell on all fours and Kenna walloped him again from behind, sending him sprawling.

"My God, Kenna!" Rhys shouted, extricating himself from the barrels. "Would you get out of here!"

"Thankless wretch!" she yelled back. She spun on her heels and directed her plank between the brawny shoulders of yet another ruffian.

Rhys pushed her out of the way as the man turned and lifted his own club to lay his assailant out. Rolling with the blow to his shoulder, Rhys grunted as he fell to the deck. Kenna's scream alerted him and he was able to scramble to his feet as the club whistled past his ear. He caught the plank she tossed him and used it to defend himself, warding off the man's wild swings.

"Kenna! Over here!"

Kenna recognized the familiar voice of Tanner Cloud and responded to the thundering command a moment before Alexis raised one of the pistols she carried and fired a warning shot into the air. Even before she reached their side the fighting had stopped. The pistol spoke nearly as eloquently as the veritable army of men standing behind the Clouds.

One by one the gang of ruffians dropped their clubs.

"That's better," Tanner said, his hard green eyes surveying the gathering, committing every unwanted face to his memory. "Now get out of here."

The self-appointed gang leader got to his feet and drew himself up to his full height. He had a formidable presence that would have intimidated Kenna if it weren't for the lump already developing on his head. She reminded herself that she had put it there. The man glared at Rhys, who not only did not flinch, but gave as good as he got. It was the leader who finally looked away, jerking his chin in the direction of the wharf and indicating to his followers it was time to leave. Everything in his demeanor said it was not over yet.

Rhys ordered his own men back to work, then joined

Kenna and the Clouds. The Garnet crew was already dispersing as he held out his hand to Tanner. "A timely arrival. Thank you."

Tanner took Rhys's hand in a firm grip. "I was glad to help, though I think Alex is disappointed she couldn't fire at something more substantial than the air overhead."

Rhys grinned at Alex, who did indeed look a trifle disappointed as she gave the pistols to Tanner, then leveled his flinty eyes on his own wife, who shrank a little behind Tanner. "I noticed Kenna did not experience the same sort of problem," he said dryly. There was a promise in his tone that told her they would speak of her part in the fight later.

"If my opinion matters," said Alexis.

"It doesn't," Tanner warned her, knowing full well he had wasted his breath.

"I thought she was wonderful."

Kenna began to feel as if she wasn't even present; they were talking about her as if she had ceased to exist. She stepped out from behind Tanner and cleared her throat to remind everyone she was still around. "I thought I responded adequately to the situation," she said with a show of defiance. "At least I am not the one sporting a purpling chin."

Tanner's lips twitched as he looked at Rhys's bruised chin and Rhys was hard pressed to temper his own smile. He touched his chin gingerly, wincing at the swollen tenderness.

Kenna took his arm. "Come back to the office. I'll put something on that to keep it from getting worse, though it does have a certain rough appeal."

Tanner and Alexis followed Rhys and Kenna back to the Canning warehouse. While Kenna applied a wet pack of tea leaves to Rhys's chin Tanner outlined some of the precautions they would find it necessary to take to prevent another incident.

"I appreciate your offer, the additional protection of your men, but this is not your concern," said Rhys.

"I disagree," Tanner said. "There would have been no interruption at the construction site today if you hadn't taken steps to put an end to Roland's scheming. Alex and I are united on this. We want to help."

Kenna bit her lip and remained quiet, hoping Rhys was neither too proud nor too foolish to accept the Cloud's assistance. She needn't have worried.

"Then I am not going to turn you away," said Rhys. "We'll use patrols of men from Garnet and Canning to watch the wharf. Do you think fire is our biggest worry?"

Tanner nodded. "It is now. Wilson—that was the leader—tried his own method of reasoning with you first. There's no way to be certain what manner of persuasion he'll use next, but destroying your fleet by fire is as good a way as any."

"Can't we go to the authorities?" asked Kenna, "You know it was Wilson who started the trouble. Can't we have him arrested?"

"He won't be easy to locate," Alexis told her. "And I do not believe for a moment that he is acting on his own. Even if he is arrested there will be someone else to take his place."

Kenna frowned. "Then who is responsible?"

"Britt, perhaps," Rhys said.

"Our lawyer?"

"Our former lawyer," he reminded her. "Or any of his friends. We haven't enough hours in the day to list all the people I've offended of late. Any of them might think I've given them just cause for retaliation."

"It is not so bleak as all that," said Alexis. "You have your share of supporters also. News of what happened today will spread quickly. The other lines will not stand idly by and wait for Wilson to torch your ships. Self-preservation, if nothing else, will make them want to help you. A fire on the wharf is likely to rage out of control. No one will want to risk that."

"Alex is right," Tanner agreed. "You've gained more friends than you've lost by your actions. Others will offer their assistance."

Over the course of the next hour the four of them set down the plans that would keep Canning Shipping safe from another attack. Kenna offered suggestions periodically but she acknowledged early in the conversation that she had few strategic skills. This was not the case with the other three. Alexis was as quick as either of the men to point out the particular follies of one plan or the benefits of another. Kenna marveled at Alexis's command of the situation, her knowledge of the harbor area, and the sharp clarity of her thinking. She could not help but wonder what had prepared this other woman to approach this problem as if she were readying for battle.

A collective sigh of satisfaction was drawn from all of them when the business was at an end.

Alexis laughed at herself, her amber eyes bright with the knowledge that she had met a challenge. "You must believe me, Rhys, when I say I wish it were unnecessary to do all this plotting, but I confess I enjoyed it."

"I rather enjoyed it, too," he replied easily, not taking offense.

Tanner glanced at Kenna. "You probably think us quite mad."

Kenna smiled. "Quite," she said, but there was no sting in her ready agreement. "It sounds as if it will work."

"It will," Rhys said confidently. "You know, Tanner, it was a good piece of luck that you showed up this morning."

"Not luck. We heard rumors. Alex and I became concerned the moment you began making changes at

Canning. We've been dealing with Roland's allies too long not to suspect they wouldn't do something like this."

Alexis nodded, securing a tendril of gold hair behind her ear. "We were somewhat surprised by how quickly you discovered what your father was doing."

"I hope you weren't surprised that I decided to do something about it," said Rhys.

Alexis was visibly shocked. "No! I like to think I am a good judge of character. Neither Tanner nor I thought you would do anything but what you did. Still, we did not think you would uncover your father's dealings so quickly. You had barely taken command of the line."

"As it happens I was not the one who learned how my father was trying to bankrupt you. Kenna made the discovery. If she had not taken the time to unravel the accounts I would still be without that knowledge."

Kenna's cheeks pinkened a bit under the thoughtful regard of Tanner and Alexis. She smoothed the folds of her dress in her lap to give her fingers something to do while her eyes appealed to Rhys.

"You're too modest by half, Kenna," Rhys said, taking one of her hands in his.

"Not so modest," she argued, looking at him askance. "I thought I was splended earlier, swinging that piece of lumber."

Tanner and Alexis laughed as Rhys cleared his throat and tried to look stern. "*That* piece of work is going to be discussed at another time."

"Before you two take up cudgels," Alexis said, "there is a small matter I want to bring to your attention. Tanner and I will be entertaining some dear friends who will be visiting in two weeks. It's been in the planning stages, off and on, for months, but I just recieved word that their arrival is definite. We'd like you to come to the ball we're giving on Saturday of that week. It will give you an opportunity to meet some of the friends you didn't know you had."

Tanner smiled. "You can be certain Britt, or any of his cronies, is not on the guest list."

"Not that you would recognize him anyway," said Alexis. "It's a masked affair. I wanted . . . what's wrong?" Her face softened with concern as she saw Kenna pale.

"Nothing," Kenna said quickly, too quickly to reassure any of the others. "A masque sounds wonderful. I know exactly the sort of costume I want to wear. I've had it in my mind for ages but the occasion never presented itself." She laughed, hoping it did not sound as stilted to them as it did to her own ears. "Or rather, I could not present myself at the occasion."

There was an awkward little silence following Kenna's speech and she looked down at Rhys's hand, squeezing hers with gentle strength. She knew what he was going to say before he said it. "Kenna's father was murdered at a masque ball," he said quietly. "It was nearly a decade ago, but the memory is still painful. I hope you'll understand why we regretfully decline your invitation."

"Of course I understand," said Alexis, her voice soft with sympathy for Kenna's loss and pain. "But my plans are not set in stone. I can easily send word around that I've changed my mind and costumes will not be necessary."

Kenna was more than a little touched that Alexis would change her plans simply to accommodate her. "Nonsense," she said firmly. "Rhys and I will be there and we'll feel terribly embarrassed if we're the only ones in costume." She turned to Rhys. "Really, it's all right. I want to go."

Rhys was skeptical but he did not show it. He looked at Alexis. "It appears we will accept the invitation—in costume—so don't make any changes. I admit I fancy seeing my wife as Queen of the Nile."

"Cleopatra!" exclaimed Alexis.

"You'll be stunning," Tanner said. "No shawls this time, Rhys."

Kenna giggled as Rhys shifted uncomfortably. "May I ask what you'll wear, Alex?"

"It only seems fair that I tell you, now that Rhys has given away your surprise. I've been giving some thought to a pirate's garb."

Kenna's brows rose nearly to her hairline. "A pirate? Surely there are no women pirates."

Rhys choked back his laughter. "And what of highwaymen?" he asked his wife.

Alexis did not understand the byplay between Rhys and Kenna but she saw that it had effectively banished the sad look from Kenna's large eyes. "I know nothing of highwaymen," she told Kenna, "but have you never heard of Anne Bonney? She sailed with Ned Teach."

"More familiarly known as Blackbeard," Tanner put it. "But, if I am not mistaken, I think Alex wishes to dress as another pirate of more recent fame. Am I right, Captain Danty?"

"You know you are," she said with pleasure.

Rhys was thoughtful, rolling the name on his tongue to place it. "Danty. Isn't he the man who was sinking British frigates even before 1812?"

"The same," said Tanner.

"I remember now," Kenna said, snapping her fingers. "The London papers were full of his exploits. Most of it happened while you were in Portugal, Rhys. Danty's dealing with the British Navy did not set well with the Admiralty. As I recall he boarded ships and took off sailors who claimed they were impressed into service."

"It was no idle claim they made," Alexis said. "They *were* impressed."

"The *London Gazette* would beg to differ the point.

Pirate was one of the kinder names they used for Danty. No one understood his motives. I think that is what troubled the Admiralty most. After taking the impressed men with him he allowed the other sailors to set out for shore before he sank the ships. No one was quite certain of his purpose. From the accounts of the surviving men it appeared Danty was seeking a particular man. Is that what you heard?"

Tanner answered her question. "Yes, Danty was pursuing one man. A British commander. A murderer."

"I never knew that. I never even knew if Danty was an American. No one was certain. Shortly after the war began there was no more news of Danty. I thought he was killed, but perhaps he finally found his man." Kenna's expression was thoughtful as she recalled something else. "I seem to remember speculation that Danty was horribly disfigured. The papers said he always wore a mask. Is that why you chose him, Alex, because of the mask?"

"Yes," she said. "Because of the mask."

As Rhys had listened to Kenna speak his features became progressively clouded. Now the shutter over his thoughts lifted and his focus shifted from Kenna to Alexis. "But the mask never hid any disfigurement, did it, Alexis?" he asked, studying her through narrowed eyes.

Alexis shrugged, unmoved by the steady gaze. "How would I know?"

"Yes, Rhys," Kenna said. "How would Alex know?"

Rhys leaned back in his chair, folding his arms across his chest, and smiling for all the world like a cat who had got the cream. "I may not be as good with figures as you, Kenna, but even I can add two and two and arrive at the appropriate sum. Do you recall Captain Danty's Christian name?"

"Why, I think it was Alex."

"Not a diminutive of Alexander though, I'll wager.

Would I win my bet, Mrs. Cloud?"

A half-smile touched Alexis's lips. "I believe you would, Mr. Canning."

Kenna's eyes went perfectly round with shock. "You are Alex Danty?"

"I was." Alexis's smile became full blown as she looked at her husband. "Danty was a name I chose for myself before the Quintons adopted me. But I'm Alexis Cloud now, and I've a fondness for the name, so I'll ask you not to repeat the other. There aren't many people who know the truth."

"How did you know, Rhys?" asked Tanner.

"Something you said when we first dined in your home. You toasted your notorious wife."

"Aaah. Then I shall have to guard my tongue more carefully in the future."

"It wasn't merely that," Rhys said to Alexis. "As I listened to Kenna several things began to make sense in my mind. For instance, the fact that you were the one commanding the schooner the day we arrived in Boston. And the way you held those pistols this morning. If that weren't enough to make me suspicious, you had already told me that you were responsible for the charges of treason brought against Senator Howe. At the time I did not ask myself how it was possible that you could be in a position to make those charges, but now I see it was not Alexis Cloud who made the claim, but Alex Danty. Is that correct?"

"Yes."

Rhys leaned forward. "And my father knew who you were. That is why you never fought him, never publicly acknowledged what he was doing to Garnet Shipping."

"Yes. Roland knew. He visited Howe in prison several times and Howe must have told him. Do not mistake our reasons for silence. Neither Cloud nor I are ashamed of who I was or anything I have done. But I have no wish to have it known that I was Alex Danty. There are still those in England who would pay dearly for that knowledge."

"If they believed it," Kenna said. "I am finding it quite difficult."

Tanner laughed. "You would not be the first. It is for precisely that reason that Roland never spoke publicly of his knowledge. He would not open himself to ridicule any more than we would open ourselves to the possibility that he would be believed. Even though Danty is something of a folk hero on these shores, Alex would be ostracized by most of society if the truth were known."

"I don't care so much for myself," Alexis said softly, "but it would be a burden for the children we may have some day. It is better that everyone think Alex Danty is dead."

"You didn't have to admit the truth to us," said Rhys. "Why did you?"

"Because I trust you, both of you, and I think you had a right to know what Roland was holding over our heads."

"I thank you for that."

Tanner stood and Alexis followed suit. "We have to be going. I'll speak with my foreman about our plans to keep the wharf safe. You'll have some additional men by this afternoon."

Rhys escorted the Clouds to the street then returned to the office. Kenna had moved behind the desk but her attention was directed absently on the window rather than on the ledgers in front of her. Rhys shut the door behind him and leaned against it, studying Kenna. There was a serenity to her expression that captivated him. The corners of her beautiful mouth were turned up in the merest suggestion of a smile; her eyes caught the light filtering in the window and glistened with a far-away look.

"What are you thinking?"

Kenna started guiltily at having been caught daydreaming. "Just things," she said, shrugging off her thoughts as if they could be of no importance to him. In truth she was a little embarrassed by the direction her mind had taken after Alexis and Tanner had left. Rhys had come upon her while she was thinking of children. One of Alexis's last remarks had started her thinking about a family again.

Rhys pushed away from the door and rounded the desk, sitting on the edge with one foot propped on Kenna's chair. "Just things," he echoed softly. "They were lovely thoughts, whatever they were. You looked beautiful thinking them."

"How kind of you to say so," she said, tilting her head to one side and looking at him with a coy sideways glance.

"I'm no idle flatterer, Mrs. Canning. And if you keep looking at me that way I'll not prove reluctant to show you what's on my mind."

"Rhys!"

"Kenna!" he mocked, grinning wickedly.

"I forbid you to make advances in this office!"

"Forbid, madam?"

She relented, knowing he would take up the challenge and she would inevitably surrender. "All right. I don't forbid it, but if you ever want me to work in here again you won't do it. I won't be able to concentrate for thinking of other things."

Rhys tossed his head back and laughed. "When you put it that way, I have no choice. I cannot afford to lose my best unpaid employee."

Kenna pushed his foot off her chair and struggled to temper her own mirth. "Go on," she said severely. "That ship is not going to build itself."

At the door he smartly saluted her, winking for good measure, then ducked outside before he made himself a target for the book she was preparing to throw.

Rhys arrived home quite late that night. Kenna was reading in bed when he entered the room and she could smell spirits on him before he crossed the floor to kiss her.

She wrinkled her nose and gave his shoulders a shove. "Before you went to the tavern were your plans to drink your liquor or wear it?"

Rhys pulled the lapel of his jacket close to his nose and sniffed. "I swear I meant to drink," he laughed. "I'm not foxed, but I'll forgive you if you don't believe me. One of Tanner's men upended a tray of rum and most of it landed on me."

Kenna got out of bed and helped Rhys get out of his sodden jacket and trousers. "I had one of the maids draw you a bath. Here, I'll take these clothes and you deposit yourself in the tub. There's a kettle of water heating in the fireplace. You'll need it, the water's no better than tepid by now."

Rhys stripped off the remainder of his clothes and handed them to Kenna. He slipped into the tub while she deposited the reeking material in the dressing room and instantly regretted he had forgotten to add the hot water. He looked at Kenna plaintively when she reentered the room, making his teeth chatter to call attention to his plight.

"I've a good mind to let Alcott chip you out of there in the morning," she said. She used a mitt to remove the hot kettle from the hearth. "Move your feet if you don't want them scalded." Carefully she poured the water into the tub. When she had emptied the kettle Rhys slid lower, resting his head on the edge and closed his eyes.

"You're a kind woman, Kenna Canning," he sighed.

She knelt beside the tub and took the sponge and soap in hand. "Simple-minded would be a more accurate description," she said, mocking herself as she began to lather Rhys's smooth chest.

"Mmmm."

The gentle massage stopped. "Are you agreeing with me or simply enjoying my attentions?"

"The latter, dearest." He smiled complacently as the sponge was drawn across his chest again.

"How did it happen that you went to the tavern?"

"Tanner came by the construction site an hour or so after you left. He offered a few suggestions on the design and I offered to discuss it over a few pints. I didn't think you'd mind."

"Oh, dear. Have I sounded like the veriest fishwife?" She brushed his mouth with hers. "Honestly, I don't mind. But, given the unsavory events of this morning, perhaps you would send someone out to the house with word that you are going to be delayed."

His eyes flew open. "You were worried!"

"Did you think you had an exclusive right to that state of mind? I love you, Rhys Canning. Of course I was worried." She touched the bruise on his chin. "I don't like to think of someone marring this perfectly beautiful face."

"I could remind you that this handsome visage you affect to admire would have been unscathed if I had not been distracted by a sprite wielding a veritable battering ram. I *could* remind you of that. But I won't."

"Your reticence to dwell on past events is one of your most admirable qualities."

"I'm glad you think so." He closed his eyes as she tenderly bathed his face. "If I plan to work late in the future I'll send someone round with a message." His concession was rewarded by a very warm kiss.

"Thank you." She brushed a bubble of soap away from the corner of his mouth. "Lift your foot."

He curled his toes over the edge of the tub so she could wash his leg. "Do you really want to attend the Clouds' masque, Kenna?"

"Yes. I really do. It's absurd to let the past interfere with present."

"If you're certain then."

"I am. Other leg please." She paused, waiting for him to comply. "What will you wear?"

"I've already decided against a highwayman. And pirate garb is out of the question. Alexis has priority there."

"Most definitely. She's quite something, isn't she? I'd love to know her story. Did I tell you she grew up on Breecham Lane? Can you imagine? One would never think it to hear her speak."

"I'm certain, given time, she'll tell you how she became Captain Danty. And if you don't share it with me I doubt I shall ever speak to you again."

"As long as you don't deny me the pleasure of bathing you," she said, dipping the sponge beneath the water and running it along his thigh. "So what are you going to wear?"

"I thought you had lost interest."

"Hardly, though I admit my interest is beginning to take another turn." She leaned over the tub to reach his other thigh. Rhys's eyes fluttered open and he knew himself to be quite taken with the view of Kenna's breasts thrusting against the bodice of her low cut nightgown.

"So is mine," he warned her as she leaned back and he saw her bodice had become damp, outlining her every curve.

Kenna tossed the sponge at him so that he caught it reflexively, thus foiling his attempt to grab her. Laughing, she went to the vanity and gave her hair a few hard strokes, watching Rhys in the mirror as he finished bathing. "I believe we were discussing your costume," she reminded him.

Rhys climbed out of the tub and hitched a towel about

his waist. "I am not going as Marc Antony or Caesar so you can put that from your mind, Cleo."

Kenna affected disappointment. "Oh, and you look so dashing in a sheet."

Rhys grunted as he dried himself off. "I was thinking of a musketeer. When I was in France I saw a number of paintings featuring them. Do you think Alice could copy their uniform if I sketched it for her?"

"It will cost you dearly. She is already working on Cleopatra's gown."

"Why do I feel as if I am the sole contributor to that dress shop of hers?"

Kenna put her brush aside and turned to him. "Perhaps because you are." She rose from the vanity and skirted past Rhys while he had his head buried in a towel, briskly drying his hair. "Are you ever coming to bed?" she asked, slipping between the sheets. She reached over to the nightstand and put out the lamp, then lay on her side, warming a spot for Rhys with the palm of her hand.

Rhys slid into bed a few moments later and reached for Kenna. She went into his embrace willingly. His fingers threaded through her hair as her fragrance teased his senses. "Care to share a pillow?"

"I'd like that very much," she said, responding to the phrase that had come to mean he wanted to love her.

Rhys teased her face with kisses until Kenna was forced to take him in hand, directing his mouth to the one place he had neglected—her soft, moist lips. They made love slowly, savoring the tension building between them. He adored her with his mouth and hands, knowing precisely where to touch her to elicit her small cries of pleasure. She caressed him with her slender fingers, cherishing the husky sounds he could not hold back.

Afterward they lay curled against one another, listening to the cadence of their breathing as it slowed in unison. Kenna reached for Rhys's hand which rested lightly on her hip and brought it around to the flatness of her abdomen.

"I was thinking about children today," she said. "Our children."

Rhys's caressing hand stilled. "So those were your beautiful thoughts."

"Hmmm."

"Then, my very dear Mrs. Canning, I shall try my best to accommodate you."

"I thought you might," she murmured sleepily.

Chapter Ten

Kenna adjusted the coal black, shoulder-length wig on her head and secured it with the finely crafted gold leaf band Rhys had presented her at breakfast. The front of the head piece was adorned by the slender coil of a snake with fiery ruby eyes. She darkened her brows and lashes and enhanced her eyelids with kohl. Kenna lifted her chin a regal notch and stared at her reflection, pronouncing herself quite mysterious and every inch a queen. Then she wrinkled her nose and made a face just to remind herself who she really was.

Rhys's shout of laughter came from the other side of the room. "I saw that!"

"Quiet, slave! Or I swear I shall have you entombed in a pyramid," she announced dramatically. "Alive!" She rose gracefully from her seat and crossed the room to Rhys. Her gown shimmered as she walked, caressing her body in a film of golden threads. The broad onyx necklace that she wore lay flat against her chest, accenting not only the slim column of her throat but the delicate curves of her breasts. Each of her bare arms was adorned by a coiled golden bracelet and the hem of the dress swayed softly about her ankles, allowing an occasional glimpse of the thin leather straps of the sandals that wound around her calves.

Rhys made a deep bow as she approached, flourishing his broad hat in a grand manner that made the white plume dip and sway.

"You may rise," she said grandly. "Let me look at you." Rhys straightened. "Oh, my. Alice has outdone herself." She walked around him, surveying him critically from every angle. The sleeves of his white linen shirt billowed on his arms and tapered at his wrists in tiers of lacy ruffles which lay over the backs of his hands. His long, lean fingers appeared more masculine for the contrast. The loose fitting vest he wore was royal blue, emblazoned with the gold insignia of the old guard of France. His dark velvet breeches disappeared into black leather boots that were softer and allowed more room than the current fashion. The lethal looking rapier Tanner had lent him for the occasion was fastened to his side.

"*Magnifique!*" Kenna pronounced when she came to stand in front of him again.

"I'm so very pleased you approve," Rhys said dryly. "I cannot remember a time when I felt so . . . so . . . You see!" he accused. "The proper description is foreign to me."

Kenna gave him an affectionate kiss on the cheek. "Remind yourself that you could be wearing a sheet, dearest. That should help you put this in perspective." She offered him a saucy smile before she swept out of the room.

When they arrived at the Clouds there were already more than a dozen couples dancing to the lilting waltz melody the stringed orchestra was playing.

"Do you know that I've never waltzed before?" Kenna whispered to Rhys.

"Regretting not having that London Season after all? You could have waltzed until the wee hours of the morning at Almacks."

"I'll make up for it this evening," she promised, casting a glance at his feet. "I hope your boots are comfortable."

"The only part of this costume that is," he whispered back. He started to say something else but Tanner approached them then and Rhys grinned when he saw him. Tanner was wearing a swirling desert robe, much like those worn by the Infidels the English had fought during the Crusades.

"Alex said I looked quite fierce," Tanner gritted, almost daring his friend to laugh out loud.

"Oh, you do," said Kenna quickly, reminding Rhys of his manners by giving him a poke in the ribs. "Doesn't he, Rhys?"

The plume in Rhys's hat wavered as he nodded and bit back his smile. "Quite fierce."

There was laughter in the emerald depths of Tanner's eyes as he turned his attention to Kenna. "And you, my lovely queen, are radiant." He lifted her hand to his lips and kissed it.

Kenna fluttered her darkened lashes at Rhys over Tanner's bent head. "So gallant, my lord." She laughed gaily as Rhys pretended to prepare to draw his sword.

Tanner caught Rhys's feint out of the corner of his eyes and straightened quickly. "As lovely as you are, Kenna, I am not prepared to fight a duel for you."

"Very wise of you," said Rhys. "And where is your wife? I have a mind to ask her to dance."

Tanner laughed and pointed to the pirate dancing with a lovely, dark-haired woman dressed as the Greek goddess Hera. "Don't spoil her fun by asking her to dance, Rhys. Only a few people realize it's Alex under all that black and they've sworn secrecy. That's my sister Emma she's dancing with now."

Rhys and Kenna could not help staring at Alexis. She

was wearing a loose fitting black silk shirt and dark breeches which concealed her feminine curves. Her golden hair was covered by a black bandana and her face, with the exception of her striking amber eyes, was hidden beneath a cloth mask the color of midnight. She threw back her head and laughed huskily at something her partner said.

"Now *she* looks fierce," Rhys said admiringly.

"Oh, the dark lady is," agreed Tanner. "And please don't tempt her into a mock duel. She knows how to use the rapier at her side."

"I believe you," he said feelingly.

Tanner chuckled deeply. "Come with me. I want you to meet our guests from New Orleans. We met them several years ago when Alex and I were running blockade at the port. We were married in their home. Their presence is the reason we're hosting this masque." He led them across the floor, skirting the dancers, and brought them to a couple watching the dancing from the sidelines with obvious enjoyment.

Tanner's guests had at least a score of years on him but their welcoming smiles were young. The woman's silver hair was attractively arranged high on her head and adorned with tiny powder blue bows. The bodice of her dainty flowered gown was laced with ribbon of the same color and a white apron slanted across her hips. In one hand she held a staff, decorated at its crook by a large blue ribbon.

Kenna held back a smile, thinking that there would always be shepherdesses at masqued balls, and looked from the woman to her companion. The gentleman was dressed in 17th century courtier and he made a handsome leg as Kenna approached.

Tanner took a step toward the couple, taking the shepherdess's hand. "Mr. and Mrs. Canning, I would like you to meet—" He never finished his sentence. Much to

400

his surprise the Comtesse Lescaut tore free of his hand and launched herself at Rhys.

"My dear, dear boy!" She hugged him, pushed at his shoulders to look at him, then hugged him again. "I never, never thought to see you again. Oh, this is delightful! Wonderful!" She turned to her husband. "Do you see who it is, Etienne? It is Rhys. Rhys Canning!"

"I see very well, my dear," said the Comte. As his wife stepped aside he took Rhys firmly by the shoulders and kissed first one cheek, then the other. "This is indeed a pleasure!" There was a faint sheen of tears in his eyes as he stepped back, studying Rhys from head to toe. "A pleasure!"

Tanner was feeling a trifle superfluous. "You know each other?" he asked finally.

"Of course we do," the Comtesse answered. "This is our dear Rhys Canning!"

"*I* know who he is, Madeline, but how is it that you know him?"

Madeline looked at Tanner as if she could not understand his confusion. "We told you about him, I'm certain of it. This is the young man who helped us flee France!"

"You never mentioned his name," said Tanner. His eyes were faintly accusing as he looked at Rhys as if to say, "Why didn't you tell me you knew the Lescauts?" then he remembered he had failed to tell Rhys the name of his guests.

"Didn't I? How careless of me." She gave a beautiful Gallic shrug. "Well, this is he! And a friend of yours, too! *C'est incroyable!* Rhys, you must meet Michael. Michael Devereaux. Do you remember him?"

"I do," Rhys smiled. "I thought he was still in London."

"He came to New Orleans not long ago. He's been staying with us and Tanner was kind enough to include him in the invitation to visit Boston. Oh, he will be delighted to see you!"

The comte's attention shifted from Rhys to Kenna who had been watching the proceedings with stunned pleasure. "You must introduce me to your lovely companion, Rhys. Dare I hope she is your wife?"

"She is."

Kenna found her voice at last, sweeping into an elegant curtsy for the comte, and the comtesse. "Do you not remember me, Uncle Etienne? Aunt Madeline?"

"Uncle?" sputtered Etienne, his brows knitting together. "I have no niece."

Kenna smiled. "You said I might address you as such when you came to stay in my father's home."

The Comte's eyes widened further. "Could it be? *Non! C'est impossible.*"

"Kenna Dunne!" Madeline announced breathlessly. "Why you were just a child when we stayed at Dunnelly Manor. And look at you now!" She pulled Kenna to her ample bosom, greeting her in the same manner she had Rhys. "What has become of your fiery hair? Please tell me you are wearing a wig!"

"It's a wig," Kenna said quickly. "But I'm afraid the hair beneath is not the veritable torch it used to be."

"My dear Kenna," Etienne said fondly. "Forgive me for not recognizing you."

"It has been a long time. And I think I've changed a little."

"You always were a diamond, darling," said Madeline enthusiastically. "But I think you've acquired a polish. Isn't she stunning, Etienne?"

"Stunning," he agreed dutifully, but meant it with all his heart. "Will you honor me with this dance?"

Kenna agreed happily as the orchestra struck up another waltz and glided onto the floor with her handsome partner.

"If you'll excuse me, Madeline. Rhys. I must be greeting my other guests." Tanner shook his head ruefully as he saw Alexis circle the dance floor with another feminine partner. "I fear Captain Danty is going to break some hearts this night."

Madeline laughed lightly as she watched Tanner stride away. "Now there is a man hopelessly in love with his wife." She looked at Rhys slyly, tapping his shoulder with her staff. "But I think you have some knowledge of that state of affairs, yes? These old eyes observed how you looked at Kenna."

Rhys held up his hands in mock surrender. "You have found me out."

"I cannot believe you are standing in front of me! And married to Kenna Dunne! You must tell me everything! How is it that you've come to Boston? How long have you been married?"

Laughing, Rhys drew Madeline onto the dance floor and proceeded to answer her barrage of questions, albeit with a fair amount of prevarication. There were some secrets he would not share even with the Comtesse Lescaut.

Kenna was enjoying herself immensely. Etienne was an excellent dancer and she had no difficulty following his lead. He spoke fondly of the weeks he had spent at Dunnelly recovering from his illness and when he mentioned Robert Dunne it was with great respect. Kenna was pleased she could listen to Etienne's recollections without experiencing a familiar tightening in her stomach. She was able to respond to his inquiries about Nicholas and Victorine and never indicated the circumstances in which she left England were the least unusual.

Etienne partnered her through two numbers before he reluctantly released her to her husband and joined his own wife.

403

"Etienne did not hold me so closely, Rhys," Kenna said as the large hand at her waist drew her nearer.

One of his eyebrows arched in question. "It's Etienne now? What happened to Uncle Etienne?"

"He said it made him feel uncommonly old now that I was no longer a *jeune fille*."

"I see." He executed several quick turns, lifting Kenna off her feet to keep her in step. She was beautifully flushed when he set her down and clung to him. The pressure of his hand was incidental. He kissed her temple. "One would never suspect you are but a novice at this dance."

"Etienne said I learn very quickly," she said, fluttering her lashes again.

He chuckled at her attempt to make him jealous. There was no point in telling her he already was. She would not believe he had been envious of the comte for having the pleasure of leading her in her first waltz. "What else did Etienne say to you?" he asked teasingly.

"He said you are very fortunate to have married me."

"I know that. Did you tell him how I came to be so fortunate?"

"Yes, but don't alarm yourself. I said nothing awkward."

"He has no contact with anyone in England then? No one to whom he might mention he saw you?"

"I cannot be certain, but I think not. Many of his friends have emigrated to the French quarter in New Orleans."

Rhys breathed a little easier. "Madeline says much the same. It does not appear she has any close friends in England. I was stunned to see them here this evening."

"Rhys? Mayhap we should tell them the truth. Then we would be sure they wouldn't say anything. Etienne says he owes you a debt he has never repaid. He would consider what we ask a very small price indeed."

Rhys spun her again. "Let me think on it. There is still the matter of Michael Deveraux. If he left England only a short time ago then it is possible he heard of your abduction and your death, and more than possible he still has friends in London. Please, until I can decide what is best, avoid him if you can."

"How am I to avoid someone I can't remember? Can you point him out to me?"

Rhys shook his head. "I haven't seen him in years and I cannot recognize him for all these costumes. I will have to wait until Madeline of Etienne introduces us—or Michael recognizes me."

"Doesn't Monsieur Deveraux owe you a debt also?"

Rhys did not want to worry Kenna unnecessarily, but his memories of Michael Deveraux did not point to a man who believed he owed anyone anything. "Perhaps he thinks he does," he said. "I'll know better once I've spoken to him." There was a lull in the music and Rhys was going to ask Kenna if she wanted some refreshment when he felt someone tapping him on the shoulder. He did not have to turn to know who it was. The amusement in Kenna's eyes told him everything. He gave Kenna over to the only person he could watch her dance with and not feel the smallest twinge of jealousy. "Do not tread on her toes, Captain Danty."

Kenna's laughter covered Alexis's deeper tones as the music began again. "You are a rogue, Captain Danty," Kenna said, falling in step.

Alexis's amber eyes sparkled. "The charade is soon at an end, I think. I find that I want to dance with my husband. Even Cloud draws the line at partnering me while most of the guests think I'm a man."

"I can see his point."

"Would you mind if I took off this mask and bandana while I'm dancing with you? If you can laugh at yourself for dancing with another woman, then I think the others will also."

"Of course you can take it off."

"Good," she sighed, then added quickly, "At the end of this waltz." The ballroom floor had become more crowded as guests continued to arrive. Laughter and music mingled pleasantly, as if giving sound to the bright array of colors the dancers wore. "I had a word in passing with Cloud. He told me you know the Lescauts."

Kenna nodded and briefly explained their relationship. "It was quite a shock to see them here tonight. A pleasant one though."

"It is odd to think that if Rhys had not helped the Lescauts leave France, Cloud and I would never have had the opportunity to know them. I would—Kenna? What is it? You're pale!" Alexis's steps faltered as her eyes darkened with concern. "Do you want to stop?"

"No!" she said hurriedly. "No. Please, keep dancing." Her gaze was fastened on a point beyond Alexis's shoulder. "Who is the man speaking to my husband?"

Alexis turned Kenna so she could see Rhys. "The devil?"

Kenna nodded. "Yes, the devil. Do you know him?"

"That is the Lescauts' friend, Michael Deveraux. Haven't you met him?"

"No. That is, I haven't met him tonight." She smiled weakly, fighting for composure. Her heart was pounding rapidly. "There is something vaguely familiar about him."

"He frightened you," Alexis observed shrewdly.

Kenna shook her head in denial. "The costume . . . it startled me." Deveraux wore a close fitting crimson leotard and carried a trident which he leaned on while talking to Rhys. A blood red satin cape covered his broad shoulders and fell in an elegant line to his knees. The upper part of his face and his entire head was hidden beneath a hood. Kenna could only make out the shape of

406

his mouth and chin but the familiarity of those features tugged at her memory in an unsettling fashion. "I've seen one like it before. Years ago," she added on a mere thread of sound. "Please, is there some place I could go to rest a moment? I'm not feeling quite the thing."

"Certainly." Alexis quickly escorted Kenna off the floor and took her upstairs to a guest bedchamber. She discarded her mask and bandana, tossing it on a chair, while Kenna lay back on the bed. "Is there something I can get you? Tea? Brandy?"

"No, nothing, thank you. I'll be fine in a moment."

Looking at Kenna's pale face and trembling hands, Alexis doubted it. "I'll send Rhys here."

"Please. Don't mention anything to him until he is alone."

Alexis's brows drew together. "Kenna, is it the costume that has made you uneasy or the man?"

"I don't know," she said truthfully. Now that she was away from Michael Deveraux she could not remember his features clearly. It must have been what he wore that troubled her. "See to your guests, Alexis, and please don't put on that mask again. I fear Captain Danty's ruined my reputation by accompanying me to a bedchamber."

Alexis laughed because she knew it was expected of her. When she shut the bedchamber door, however, her smile was bleak. She wished she had Kenna's confidence so that she might somehow set what was bothering her friend right again.

As minutes passed Kenna began to feel like the veriest fool for taking to the bedchamber. She was made of sterner stuff, she told herself staunchly. Hadn't she climbed a rigging in gale force winds? Hadn't she overcome an addiction? What was it about that devil that made him so difficult to face? What did she know that she did not want to remember?

She was sitting up, holding her fingers to her throbbing temples, when the door opened again and Rhys entered the room. He crossed the floor quickly and sat beside her.

"Alexis says you are not feeling well. What is it?"

"A headache, nothing more."

"An odd sort of headache that begins when you see a man looking like Satan himself."

"Oh, Alexis told you."

"A good thing she did, else you would have not. Why?"

"I feel so foolish, Rhys. Why should I react so violently to the man?"

"I was startled when he approached me also, Kenna," he admitted. "With his head and most of his face covered, Michael looked very much like Nick did at the masque at Dunnelly. For a moment I imagined myself back ten years."

Kenna's head lifted sharply and she looked at Rhys with troubled eyes. "Nicholas? That is how Nicholas looked?"

"Yes. You really don't remember, do you?" He wondered if he would ever get used to Kenna's distorted memory.

She shook her head. "No, I don't. But if he looks like Nick did, mayhap that explains why I reacted so. Or it could be he reminds me of the man I spoke to that evening while Victorine and my father were dancing. It could be the same person. Michael Deveraux's name was on Victorine's guest list. Maybe I am beginning to remember."

He put his arm around her shoulder. "Perhaps you are, but don't force yourself, Kenna. Would you like to go home?"

"Oh, no! I am fine, really. I'd like to stay. But what

408

about Monsieur Devereaux? Have you told him who I am?"

"I didn't have to. He already knew you were Robert Dunne's daughter."

"How odd," Kenna said slowly. "I'm certain I never met him formally before."

"Any one of Tanner's guests might have told him your name and he made the connection. Kenna is not of the common mode, you know."

"Could anyone have told him my maiden name as well? Only Etienne and Madeline know it."

"Then they must have said something to Michael before I had the chance to speak with them."

"I suppose." Kenna was not convinced. She hadn't seen the Lescauts speak with Deveraux, hadn't even noticed him in the room until she saw him with Rhys. But then, she reminded herself, there were any number of guests she had not really seen because her attention had been all for Rhys.

"If it concerns you overmuch then we'll leave," he offered. "I would not have you making yourself sick with worry."

Kenna looked at him appealingly. "I want to stay, Rhys."

Rhys relented to the persuasion in her dark eyes, but he stayed by her side the remainder of the evening. It turned out to be an unnecessary precaution as Deveraux never introduced himself to Kenna. In truth, it troubled Rhys that Michael seemed to be avoiding them, though he told himself he was making much of nothing. If Deveraux was with a group of people and Kenna and Rhys approached, the man made some excuse and quickly left. Though Kenna danced with many different partners, Deveraux was not one of them. Because Kenna appeared to notice nothing odd, Rhys kept his thoughts to himself and after a time he put his worries to one side.

It was an easy thing to do, given the number of new acquaintances Rhys and Kenna made that evening. The Clouds' guests were very friendly, very gracious, and many took it upon themselves to offer Rhys their support for what he was doing with Canning Shipping. Neither Rhys nor Kenna quite understood how the business dealings of the line had become common knowledge but they accepted the assistance gladly.

Rhys and Kenna were enjoying a precious moment alone, sipping chilled wine by the doors that opened onto the verandah, when Tanner interrupted them.

"Widdoes just brought me a message from two of my men who were patroling the wharf tonight. Wilson and three others were caught while trying to set a fire at your construction site. Garrison and Springer are waiting outside for instructions. Would you like to speak with them?"

Rhys found Kenna had plucked the glass of wine from his hand before he answered. "Most assuredly. I'll only be a few minutes, Kenna," He brushed her cheek quickly, making her smile with his distracted air, and left with Tanner.

Kenna looked down at the two glasses she held and smiled ruefully. She was wondering what to do with one when Alexis joined her.

"Here, let me relieve you of one of those." She gave a little toss of her head and the long golden braid that had fallen over her shoulder settled properly at her back. "Where have Rhys and Cloud gone in such a rush?"

Kenna related what she learned from Tanner.

"That's very good news." Alexis sipped her wine. "How predictable Wilson was," she mused, her smile flattening in disgust.

"What do you mean?"

"Cloud knew he would attempt something tonight,

410

thinking it would be safer because so many of us are here. Wilson fell into the trap very neatly, I would say."

"But you said even if he were caught there would be another to replace him."

"True, but not if he can be persuaded to talk. Who did Cloud say brought the message?"

"Two men, Springer and Garrick, I think he said."

"Garrison," Alexis corrected, smiling broadly now. "Mike has fists like brass bookends. If your husband wants Wilson to name his employers, then Mike Garrison is the man who can get those names."

Kenna took several large swallows of wine, her eyes widening. "And Springer?" she asked carefully. "What does he do?"

"Oh, dear. I've shocked you, haven't I?"

"No. Well, perhaps a little. It sounds rather cold-blooded. Tell me about Mr. Springer."

Alexis laughed as Kenna's curiosity won out over her disgust of violence. "Springer is there to prevent Mike from using his fists. He'll pretend to want to save Wilson from experiencing Mike's wrath and he'll reason, coax, and cajole. All the while Mike will be growing restless in the background. If you were Wilson in those circumstances, wouldn't you give Springer what he wanted?"

"Most certainly."

"It's a very effective technique. The threat of force is in many cases more persuasive than violence itself."

"I can understand how it would be." She hesitated a moment then asked a question that had long been on her mind. "Why do you always call your husband by his surname?"

The warm blush that touched Alexis's cheeks was at odds with her pirate costume and her eyes became so soft that one could be forgiven for forgetting she was skilled with the rapier resting against her thigh. "I thought Tanner Frederick Cloud too arrogant for my tastes when

I first met him. I should have properly addressed him as Captain Cloud then, but I wanted to irritate him."

"And did you?"

Alexis sighed. "No. He was more amused than annoyed. I think that is when I fell in love with him."

Hours later when Kenna had removed her wig and was cleansing her face of makeup she told Rhys what Alexis had said. "Don't you think that's just like Tanner? Can't you see him simply smiling to himself and letting Alexis go on and on? Poor Alex. She must have been furious."

"Did I miss something?" he asked. He flopped back on the bed and attempted to remove his boots, using the toe of one foot against the heel of the other. Given his slightly foxed state it was not the best of strategies. "Why would she have been furious?"

Kenna took off her necklace and armbands and put them in her jewelry case. "Because she wanted to make him angry. Why is that so difficult to understand?" No reply was forthcoming and in the mirror Kenna could see Rhys was losing the battle with his boots. Taking pity on him she went over to him and helped him out.

"I think you overdid the celebration," she observed as the first boot thudded to the floor.

"Wilson naming Britt, Anders, and Fielding was cause enough for a little indulgence."

"It was the first time I ever drank a toast because someone was going to go to prison." She grunted softly as the other boot gave way.

"I believe it was a first for me also." His legs collapsed and he was motionless, showing no indication that he intended to undress.

Kenna hiked up her gown and crawled onto the bed, straddling Rhys. "Lift your arms. Alex explained the procedure Garrison and Springer used on Wilson to encourage him to talk. Apparently it worked brilliantly." She sighed deeply, hands on her hips. "You can put your

412

arms down now, Rhys." Kenna leaned forward and unfastened the studs in his shirt, tossing them randomly until they glittered on the bed. She slid the shirt off his shoulders, down his arms, and pulled it out from under him with a magician's flair. Next she concentrated her energies on the waistband of his breeches. She loosened them, then yanked them rather roughly down his thighs, following their path by shimmying down his legs.

Rhys rolled over on his stomach and gave a sharp yelp as several of the studs poked him in the chest and arm. He brushed them away and closed his eyes.

"Serves you right," Kenna laughed. "Are you going to get under the covers or sleep on top?"

His speech was slurred. "Sleep right here."

"Now why doesn't that surprise me?" She picked up his clothes and laid them over a chair then undressed herself and slipped into one of her most revealing nightgowns. Kenna climbed in bed, pushing aside a few more studs and cuddled close to Rhys, pressing her body seductively against him. The few glasses of wine she had were making her feel decidedly amorous. She whispered in his ear. "I was thinking of something other than sleeping."

But apparently Rhys was not. His soft snore told her that.

Kenna smiled, drew the coverlet around them, and was asleep herself in a matter of minutes . . .

. . . She rubbed her eyes, waking to the sound of frantic, whispering voices. Cautiously she raised her head over the back of the settee and stared narrowly at the couple at the other end of the room. Victorine was engaged in pleading urgently with her red-caped companion. The devil's hood covered his head and half his face but Kenna thought she recognized the shape of his

413

mouth and the stubborn thrust of the Dunne chin. Nicholas! Nicholas and Victorine! Her hands slid beneath his cape and pulled him close, standing on tiptoe to reach his mouth. Nick's hands caressed Victorine's slender back as their kiss deepened.

Kenna left the gallery shortly after Victorine and Nick and stormed out of the house. She walked briskly toward the main gate, paused, then circled around to the summerhouse. There she uncovered more evidence of Victorine and Nick's perfidy and was promptly sick on the steps leading to the caves. A light flashing over the water caught her attention and when two men came ashore she scrambled down the steps to investigate. Her entire body trembled as she watched the proceedings through a narrow fault in the rock face.

She could clearly see Victorine, then, when the Frenchmen moved, she saw the devil, his leotard and cape more orange than red in the dim lantern light. Nick again! Then her father appeared, drew Victorine to his side, and began berating his son. "Would you have her betray us all so that you might venture into some new scheme?" he said bitterly. "I had not thought you could be capable of this—not betraying your country for some notion of world peace designed by Napoleon. I should kill you, you know. But I can't. At the very least I should bring you before the courts but I find my pride too great to allow you to shame my house. I will grant you the opportunity to leave Dunnelly and England. It is better than you deserve."

Kenna stepped into the entrance. She could not let father and son go against one another. She had to try and stop them. There must be an explanation for Nick's actions. Her movement startled the Frenchmen. The lantern was pushed from the ledge it rested on but as it fell Kenna looked up in time to see a hand come down hard on her father's wrist, making him lose his grip on

414

one of the pistols he held. Before the pistol reached the cave floor the lantern crashed, plunging the chamber into unrelieved darkness . . .

. . . "Nicky. Oh, no! Don't Nicky!"

"Kenna!" Rhys shook her shoulder. "Wake up! Kenna!" He grabbed her flailing arms and threw a leg over her calves to keep her from kicking him again. "You're dreaming."

Tears trickled down her cheeks. She sobbed brokenly, trying to catch her breath. "Rhys! It was Nick! It was Nick in the cave with Victorine!" She repeated it over and over, shaking her head from side to side, until she exhausted herself.

As soon as she was quiet Rhys leaped from the bed and poured a brandy for her. With hands that shook he held it out to her as she sat up. "Here. Drink this."

"I don't want any."

Rhys's arms remained extended. "Drink."

Kenna took the glass and sipped from it cautiously. It was like fire going through her veins but it cleared her head and calmed her nerves. "I had the dream again," she said unnecessarily.

Rhys said nothing. He pulled at the covers, arranging them as he should have when they had first gone to bed, then he took the brandy from Kenna's hand, set it on the nightstand, and got in beside her. He took her clammy hands in his, massaging them. "Whenever you want to talk about it, I'll listen. Whatever you want to tell me is enough."

If he had demanded to know her dream Kenna would have balked and told him nothing. His gentleness was her undoing and the words tumbled out so quickly she could barely make sense of what she was saying.

Rhys understood enough to realize Kenna was accusing Nick of killing their father. With the same fervor and assurance she had once leveled her accusations at him, she was now making the same claim about her own brother. Was it true, he wondered. Is this what she had fought so hard not to remember or were her dreams confusing her again? Was Nick the murderer as well as the traitor?

Rhys considered a number of things while Kenna spoke. Nicholas had never really investigated the tampering of Pyramid's girth that led to Kenna's near fatal fall. Nor had he pursued any of the other incidences. He either genuinely believed they were accidents or he was responsible for them. He could not take the middle ground. There was the pistol ball that had wounded Tom Allen. An accident? Nick was never much of a shot. The poisoning? If he were in league with the French then Monsieur Raillier was probably his accomplice. Rhys could not forget trying to carry out Kenna's broth to see if it was tainted, only to bump into Nick and lose it all. Nicholas could have easily arranged Kenna's abduction. Mason Deverell, Thompson, and Sweet were merely his hirelings. But Nick had searched all of London for Kenna. Was he only acting? If that were the case then Nicholas Dunne had missed his calling. He belonged on stage.

"I don't know, Kenna," he said when she finished. He could not point to what troubled him, only that something did. "I just don't know any more."

It was not the response she had expected. "How can you say that? Haven't you heard what I've said. You told me I knew something I did not want to remember and now that I've remembered it you doubt me! Do you think I want to accuse my own brother? Dear God, Rhys! What sort of person do you think I am? Do you realize what I am saying? Nick killed our father! He is a traitor! And he tried to murder me!" Kenna's features contorted with pain and she buried her face in her hands.

Gently Rhys pried her hands away and drew her into

his embrace. She sobbed on his shoulder. "Think, Kenna. What prompted your dream tonight? Why did you suddenly see Nick as the devil when you have never done so before?"

"The costume at the party tonight."

"Precisely. And I was the one who suggested he looked like Nick. It never occurred to you before."

"What are you saying? Don't you believe what I'm telling you?"

"I believe you believe it, Kenna. Beyond that, I don't know."

"Don't you see, Rhys? I always knew it was Nick. Always! But I could not admit it. You said so yourself. That is why Nick was dressed as a highwayman in my nightmare. It made it convenient for me to confuse him with you. When I was thirteen and was forced to choose between my brother and a dear friend, I protected my brother. I loved Nick, Rhys. God help me, I still love him. But I love you, too. It is no longer convenient to remember Nick as a highwayman. He was dressed as Satan that night and that is how I finally remember him. I saw him with Victorine in the gallery. Do you understand, yet? Victorine was the married woman my brother loved! You told me you saw them yourself in the garden, talking earnestly. He must have been trying to break off with her."

Rhys remembered how long it had taken Nick to join him in the caves on that occasion. Had he been slow to come because he wanted to make certain his father and the intruding highwayman were dead by the time he arrived with help? Rhys did not know the answer. He was silent for so long that when he finally spoke his voice was rough. "If I told you I was going to write to Powell, informing him of what you've said this evening, that Nick is the traitor we've been searching for, would you still swear that your dreams are true?"

417

Kenna gasped. "You wouldn't!"

"Answer my question, Kenna. Do you have that much confidence in your dream that I would not be accusing your brother unjustly?"

When Rhys put it like that, Kenna found herself wavering. Hadn't she already claimed Rhys was the murderer? Was she any more certain she had the truth now? "No," she admitted. "I do not have so much confidence."

"Neither do I," he said softly. "Perhaps I was wrong to rely so heavily on your dreams, for I find I cannot accept this explanation either."

"Why?"

"There are many things I could name that would seem to incriminate Nick, but I cannot forget how he looked when he told me you had been abducted. Have you ever thought Nick much of an actor, Kenna?"

"No. He is not adept at hiding what he feels or pretending to feel something he does not."

"That is what I think, too. He was shattered that day he came to see me. I cannot make myself believe he had a part in any of it. It's odd, you know, but before tonight I would have wagered Canning Shipping that Nick was the one. Now I wouldn't put a farthing in on it."

"What happened tonight to change your mind?"

"Actually it was Alexis Cloud that made me rethink the matter. Or rather her costume. I kept asking myself if I could have recognized her if Tanner hadn't pointed her out or if I hadn't known how she would be attired. And the answer was no, I could not. I wondered if the same thing was not also true the night of your father's ball. Who did I really see in the garden with Victorine? Nick, or somebody wearing a similar guise? You must come to your own conclusions about the gallery. I don't doubt you saw a devil. But was that devil Nicholas?"

Could she really accuse her brother on the basis of a

chin and the shape of his mouth? "I thought . . . no, I cannot be sure."

"It seems to me that we should talk to Madeline, Etienne, and Michael. The opportunity may never present itself again. If I show them the guest list they may remember what some of the people were wearing. Perhaps, like the four shepherdesses, there was more than one devil afoot that night."

"What of Victorine, Rhys? Have I mistaken her, too?"

"I don't know." He kissed her temple as she lay back. "But don't think about it now. Let's get some sleep." Though Kenna did so quickly it was a long time before Rhys took his own advice. Something still troubled him and it was made all the more agonizing because he could not name its source.

Rhys and Kenna went riding on Sunday, racing their new mounts over the fields with carefree abandon. Kenna pronounced her bay mare nearly the equal of Pyramid while Rhys continued to withhold judgment on his horse. By some mutual agreement which neither expressed aloud, they did not speak of Kenna's dream at any time.

On Monday several letters addressed to Rhys arrived at the office. It was the first mail Rhys had received from any of the packet ships leaving London. Kenna recognized the handwriting on two of them as Nick's and Victorine's. The third letter still carried a faint fragrance that Kenna immediately associated with the time she spent in the Flower House. The letter could only be from Polly Rose. She was tempted to open the letters, hungry as she was for news from home, but she controlled her excitement and took them to Rhys at the building site. He opened them immediately while Kenna read over his shoulder.

Polly's letter was amusing, full of anecdotes about the girls and the latest bit of mischief they had perpetrated on

419

Mrs. Miller's establishment. Kenna sniggered at Polly's wicked sense of humor but pretended shock when Rhys looked at her consideringly.

Victorine had news of Yvonne—she was expecting another child—and of Nick—he was spending a great deal of time in London of late—and she hinted delicately that he had acquired a mistress. She wished Rhys well and hoped he would write soon with news of how he was faring in Boston.

Nick's missive was the most sobering. He confirmed the reports they had heard that Napoleon was gathering troops and was expected to make his first strike in Belgium. He wrote poignantly of how much he still missed Kenna and how little time he spent at Dunnelly because she was no longer there. "I cannot help but think," he wrote, "That had I forced her to marry you her death could have been avoided. Victorine says I blame myself unnecessarily but I cannot change what I think. Perhaps in time . . . Victorine is herself in no position to cast stones. She has not been well since Kenna's death. Even when I am in residence she takes to her room most of the day. Doctor Tipping assures me there is nothing physically wrong with her but her melancholia saps her strength. I fear that time itself will not be enough to heal her." The remainder of the letter was brighter in tone, yet Kenna and Rhys shared a common guilt when it was put aside.

"Cannot we write to him, Rhys?" pleaded Kenna. "Listen to what he says of Victorine! She is ill because of me. If she dies it would be as if we had murdered her! What can the harm be? I am with you now, thousands of miles away from Dunnelly, and very safe. Please let them know I am safe!"

Rhys did not even hesitate in his answer. He gathered the letters and put them in his vest pocket. "No," he said and walked away before Kenna could realize she had the power to make him change his mind.

Kenna returned to the warehouse and wept bitter tears in the privacy of the office. When she was unable to cry any longer and the ache in her head became unbearable she left word with Mr. Grant that she was going home. On the way there she decided what she was going to do.

It did not take her long to find the guest list among Rhys's papers. Stuffing it in her reticule, she informed Alcott that she was going to the Cloud's home, then eschewed the offer of a driver and took the carriage out herself.

The accident happened while she was crossing the common. A horse and rider coming hellbent from the opposite direction veered too close to the carriage causing Kenna to pull the reins sharply to one side. Startled, her horse reared, tipping the carriage dangerously. Before the buggy could right itself it hit a rut in the rough path and twisted as the axle broke. Kenna hadn't the time to scream as she was hurtled from her seat. She gasped for air, weakly trying to raise her head as people who saw the accident came running. The last thing she saw before she lost consciousness was the distant, retreating figures of the horse and rider who had caused the mishap.

Someone in the crowd recognized her and set off to get Rhys at the wharf. By the time he arrived Kenna had already recovered her wits and was resting her head on a blanket someone had found in the carriage and put beneath her for her comfort. Her smile was meant to reassure Rhys as he knelt beside her. It fell a little short of the mark.

"Nothing's broken," she said. "Oh—except the carriage axle."

"I don't give a damn about the carriage. What about you?"

"I'm fine." She clutched her reticule to her stomach.

"Really. No one would let me move until you came, but I can get up now. I'm just a bit shaken, but otherwise fine."

Rhys ran his hands over her quickly but thoroughly, judging for himself that she was all right. He told her to lie still while he spoke to the people around them, gathering some information about the accident. It was an unsatisfactory inquiry. No one had clearly seen the rider whose recklessness had caused the accident; their attention had been diverted by Kenna's efforts to keep the carriage under control. Rhys thanked them for their assistance and asked them to let him know if they remembered anything that would help him identify the rider. To a man they apologized for the rider's inconsiderate, incautious behavior as if it reflected badly upon themselves in particular and Boston in general.

When the crowd had dispersed Rhys unhitched the horse from the wrecked carriage and tethered it to the reins of his own mount. "Can you ride, Kenna?"

"Yes." She sat up slightly, propping herself on her elbows.

Rhys grimaced. "I suppose I should have asked you that before I sent everybody away." He scooped her up into his arms. "I find I am not so level-headed when you are involved. Are you certain you're all right?"

"Yes."

He nodded and helped her onto his horse then took his place behind her. Immediately upon returning home he carried her to their bedchamber. In spite of her protests to the contrary Kenna was glad of his attention. She could not deny the trembling in her legs.

It was not until she was resting comfortably in bed that Rhys began questioning her. He learned nothing from Kenna that he had not learned from those who had offered their assistance.

"It could have happened to anyone," she said when he

continued to glower.

"It didn't. It happened to you. Why did you have to set off in such a rush for Alex's?"

Kenna did not bother to defend herself. What good would come of telling him that she was not rushing anywhere? "I was angry with you and I wanted to show the Lescauts and Deveraux the guest list. I want answers, Rhys. I cannot be happy here while my family is miserable because they think me dead. If the Lescauts can tell us something then I want to know!"

"Did you have to go alone? Couldn't you wait until I could go with you?"

"I didn't want to wait for you and I didn't want to argue about it in case you put me off. I have no patience about this, Rhys. Either we discover the truth or —"

"Or what?" His eyes were as cold and biting as winter wind.

"Or I will write to Nicholas myself and tell him I'm alive. You said yourself that Nick was no longer a suspect. What can be the harm?"

"I did not precisely say that your brother was no longer suspect," Rhys corrected. "I said I simply did not know any more. And the harm is clear. He will tell Victorine. She will mention it to Janet who will tell Raillier. In hours all of Dunnelly will know and before long, all of London. And six weeks later, long enough for a ship to cross the Atlantic from London to Boston, there will be more incidences like today. Only they won't be accidents!"

"Then we had better identify the real murderer, Rhys, because I may take it in my mind to present myself on Nicholas's doorstep!" She didn't mean it. As soon as the words were out she regretted them. She had no intention of leaving Rhys, but the look on his face told her he believed she could. By the time she started to deny it she was talking to an empty room.

Kenna was sleeping when Rhys returned to the bedchamber. There were tear stains on Kenna's flushed cheeks and a near empty glass of brandy on the nightstand. She would sleep quietly through the night, he thought, and proceeded to go through her reticule for the guest list. When he found it he left as quietly as he had come then saddled his horse and rode furiously to Beacon Hill.

Rhys brushed past Widdoes when he opened the door and called to Tanner as he was about to step into the music room.

"Rhys! Good to see you. We were just about—"

"I want to see the Lescauts," Rhys said brusquely. "And Devereaux."

If Tanner was surprised by Rhys's impatient manner he did not show it. "Of course. Madeline and Etienne are with Alexis. I was about to join them. You've missed Michael, I'm afraid. He left today."

That stopped Rhys in his tracks. "Left?"

Tanner nodded. "Yes. This morning. He booked passage back to London."

Rhys followed Tanner slowly into the music room. "Wasn't that rather sudden? I thought he was staying with you as long as the Lescauts."

"We thought so, too. But Madeline says Michael always intended leaving Boston for London. He simply neglected to mention it to us."

Etienne stood, holding out his hand to Rhys. "How good it is to see you again. I could not help but hear you were discussing Michael. It was a matter of finances, *comprenez-vous?* The passage to England was less money if he departed from Boston rather than New Orleans."

"We tried to lend him the money," Madeline said. "But he wouldn't hear of it. He accepted passage to Boston instead."

"Come, sit down," said Alexis, pouring Rhys a tumbler

of scotch. "Where is Kenna?"

Rhys accepted the drink but remained standing. "Kenna is sleeping. There was an accident this afternoon. Her carriage overturned." He raised his hand to stop the questions they all voiced at once. "She's fine." He gulped back two swallows of scotch. "God, I wish Michael were here. I needed his help."

Alexis's eyes were watchful, following Rhys's movements as he paced the floor. She knew a helplessness that was foreign to her and looked to Tanner for guidance.

"Rhys," Tanner said.

The single utterance had an immediate calming affect on Rhys. There was a strength in Tanner's voice that edged his concern and Rhys stopped pacing the floor. Although he knew there was nothing either Tanner or Alexis could do, they would listen, and for now that was enough. His hope for a chance at the truth still rested with the Lescauts. And so he told them everything, beginning with events leading up to the death of Robert Dunne, and, sparing himself nothing, Kenna's threat, only hours old, to leave him if he could not single out the one person responsible for all that had happened.

When he finished speaking there was a heavy silence in the room. Rhys reached in his pocket for the guest list and handed it to Madeline. Etienne edged closer to his wife to see the paper. "If you could remember anything—anything at all—that would help me, I would forever be in your debt."

Madeline waved Rhys's statement aside. "Nonsense," she said briskly. "Sit over there, Rhys." She pointed to the empty space on the sofa beside Alexis. "I cannot think with you hovering."

Rhys sat down but could not completely relax. He sat on the edge of a cushion, leaning forward and saying nothing when Alexis poured him another two fingers of scotch. Madeline and Etienne went through the list, commenting on names they recognized, people they knew, and whenever possible, the manner in which they were dressed one evening ten years earlier. When they encountered Michael's name they both registered surprise, then sighed, agreeing with Rhys that his presence would have been helpful, acknowledging his eye and his memory was superior to their own. In the end they could tell him nothing.

"I'm so sorry, Rhys," Madeline said. "I wanted very much to be able to help you. That night . . . oh, but it was *très horrible, n'est-ce pas?* So much confusion. Some things I recall so clearly, but others, not at all."

"It is much the same with me," Etienne said heavily. "In truth, Rhys, I had no knowledge of your presence at the masque until you caused such a stir carrying Kenna in the house. I did not recognize Nicholas before he pushed back his hood and announced his father's death. I could not imagine how Michael could be of help to you until I saw his name on the list. I do not even recall that he was there that night. He certainly never spoke to me."

"Nor me," said Madeline.

"You mean none of you spoke of the circumstances of Lord Dunne's death after seeing Kenna again?" That seemed odd to Rhys. He would have thought, human nature being what it was, that they would have talked among themselves.

"Etienne and I discussed it privately. But Michael said nothing about it." Her eyes traveled from Rhys to Alexis and Tanner. "Did he mention anything to you?"

"Nothing," said Alexis.

"No," Tanner replied. "I found Deveraux to be the sort of man who keeps his own counsel."

"Yes, I remember him that way also," Rhys said. "Damn! I wish I had spoken of this with him Saturday night. How many hours is he out of Boston now?"

Alexis looked at the mantel clock, an excitement growing in her. "Ten. At approximately eight knots an hour that would put his ship some eighty nautical miles from here. A little over ninety land miles," she translated for the Lescauts. "With a strong wind in the sails I would say he is already more than a hundred miles from Boston."

"Can the ship be caught?"

Alexis glanced at Tanner. He was with her. She could see in his dark emerald eyes that he had already accepted the challenge. "It can," they said simultaneously.

Rhys's heart lightened and for the first time since he entered the room he truly felt some hope. If he could speak with Deveraux, even if the man could tell him nothing, at least he would have the satisfaction of knowing he had done everything in his power to find the truth for Kenna. "I'll speak with one of my captains immediately." He stood, anxious to be on his way.

Tanner stepped in front of him and put a hand on his shoulder, pushing Rhys gently back into his seat. He was glad his friend did not require more persuasion than that. Not only would have he regretted using more force, he wasn't at all certain he would win. "I think you've misunderstood, Rhys. When Alex and I said Deveraux's ship could be caught we did not mean to imply that any ship in your fleet was up to the task. Not only that, but there is the matter of the *Harmony*'s course. There are several general routes the ship might take. Plotting the wrong one would make your pursuit as hopeless as catching a shooting star."

"Then there is no way," said Rhys. He wanted to hit something. Instead he squeezed the tumbler in his hands until his knuckles whitened.

Alexis eyed the tumbler. "Tanner is not saying that, Rhys. When we saw Michael off this morning I spoke with the *Harmony*'s captain. Just small talk while the

427

Lescauts were escorting Michael to his cabin. Rhys, I know what route the *Harmony* is taking."

Rhys laughed and though his tone was rough there was genuine enjoyment in the sound. He dropped the tumbler, took Alexis by the shoulders and kissed her cheek. "I should have known your small talk was like no other woman's."

"But, I will not tell you," she finished, immediately dampening Rhys's enthusiasm.

"What?" He could not believe what she was saying.

"I will not tell you because you still haven't a prayer of catching the *Harmony*."

"However," Tanner added quickly, "the *Artemis* can."

"The *Artemis?*"

"The Garnet schooner you saw your first day in Boston," Tanner explained. "The one that you said could chase the wind. She can. And Alex and I will prove it by going after the *Harmony*."

Rhys was stunned. "I couldn't ask you to do that."

"You haven't," Alexis pointed out. "We offered."

"But your guests."

"We don't mind," Madeline said. "Do we, Etienne?"

"Not at all. Do not be so foolish as to turn them down, Rhys. You are a master of campaigns on the land, but Tanner and Alex, well, they have few equals at sea."

Tanner anticipated Rhys's next question. "My sister and brother-in-law will see to everything here. Alex and I will not be gone long and they've shouldered the sole responsibility for the line before."

Rhys surrendered. "You've no need to waste more time convincing me. You'll bring Deveraux back so I can talk to him?"

"We will."

Rhys did not doubt it. Their confidence washed over him like a healing spring rain. An hour later he was bidding them farewell from the docks as the *Artemis'* sails caught the invisible force of the wind.

It was a few minutes before midnight when Rhys returned home. Kenna was sitting up in bed, a cold compress over her eyes. At the sound of the door closing she dropped the compress.

"I thought you would be sleeping," he said quietly, shrugging out of his jacket.

"Mrs. Alcott woke me when she brought me a late supper. She told me you had gone. I wasn't able to sleep after that." She hesitated, twirling a strand of hair between her thumb and forefinger. "I was hoping we could talk."

"And say what? I heard you clearly this afternoon, Kenna. You did not mince words about your intentions." He yanked off his boots, taking a perverse pleasure in seeing Kenna flinch as they dropped to the floor.

"I didn't mean it, Rhys. I spoke in anger. What I said about presenting myself on Nick's doorstep . . . it wasn't true. I wouldn't leave you."

Rhys did not respond to her statement. He finished undressing and put on his nightshirt. He did not join Kenna. Instead he took blankets and a pillow from the base of the wardrobe and walked into the dressing room.

"Where are you going?"

"I'm sleeping on the daybed in here."

"But why?" she asked anxiously.

He stepped into the doorway. "Because I am so angry with you, Kenna, that I may very well strangle you if I come within arm's reach." He disappeared into the room again and Kenna could hear him snapping out the sheets and thumping the pillow.

"Please don't do this, Rhys. Won't you say something? Don't you believe me?"

He stepped in the doorway again. "Did Mrs. Alcott mention where I went this evening?"

"No. I don't think she knew."

Rhys spoke in brief, hard sentences. "I went to talk to Madeline and Etienne. They couldn't remember anything that would help us. Michael Deveraux wasn't there. He's already left for London. But what does that matter? Tanner and Alex departed not above an hour ago to bring him back. They abandoned their guests, abandoned their business, just to make certain my wife doesn't leave me." It was an exaggeration but Rhys found he wanted to hurt her as much as she had hurt him. "And now she says she didn't mean any of it. Be certain to tell them that when they return. Oh, and make your apologies to Michael. I'm sure he'll be very happy about having his voyage home interrupted." He pulled the door to the dressing room shut, effectively ending conversation.

Kenna had no more tears to weep. She blew out the bedside lamp, then tossed and turned, alternately pressing the compress to her eyes then staring blankly at the ceiling. An hour passed, then another, and she was no closer to falling asleep than she had been when Mrs. Alcott first told her Rhys was gone. Finally she could stand it no longer. Throwing aside the covers she strode across the cool floor to the dressing room and flung open the door.

Rhys had not had any better luck going to sleep and he knew better than to blame it on the discomfort of the daybed. His entire body jumped when Kenna threw open the door. "Kenna! What's wrong?" He sat up. He had discarded his nightshirt and the sheet slid down his naked chest, folding around his waist.

Kenna threw up her arms. "My husband is sleeping in another bed, a full foot too short for him, and he asks me what's wrong!" She dropped her hands to her hips and peered through the dark, trying to make out Rhys's outline. She could see the muscular expanse of his chest where it rose above the white sheet and her heart did a

430

flip. "I want to know one thing, Rhys," she demanded. "Does this mean you don't love me any more?"

She held her breath in the terrible silence that followed. It seemed to her that Rhys had no intention of answering her question and every second that passed served only to confirm her worst fears.

"No, Kenna. It doesn't mean I don't love you any more."

She released her breath and her hands fell from her hips to lie uselessly at her sides. "Well . . ." One foot rested on top of the other and she swayed slightly, feeling all at sea of a sudden. "That's all I wanted to know. I'm glad. I mean . . . thank you. Good night." She backed out of the room, closing the door quietly behind her.

Kenna was within three steps of the bed when Rhys's hands gripped her waist, spun her, and lifted her the few inches necessary to bring her lips to his. His mouth ground against hers in a kiss that was not punishing, but desperate.

Rhys swallowed Kenna's soft moan as he lowered her to the floor. Stunned by the quickening of her own desire at Rhys's demanding caresses, Kenna guided him into her, unwilling to tolerate the sweet torment of his mouth and hands. Rhys's thrust was hard, claiming her powerfully and, in turn, finding himself claimed.

"Look at me, Kenna," he ground out as their bodies thrummed with sensuality.

She did. She wanted to. The darkness surrounding them was not so dark as Rhys's eyes and she lost herself in the black whirlpool that was his gaze. She did not know that her own features held Rhys spellbound. He stared at her mouth, her moist, slightly parted lips, waiting to hear the soft sounds of her pleasure then take them from her, feeling the vibration of her urgent little cries against his mouth.

His body excited her, incited her. Kenna was greedy

431

for his every touch. Her hands clasped his taut buttocks, pressing him inside her, loving the warm intimacy of his lean body.

Her body fired him, fevered him. Rhys was eager for her every touch. His hands cupped the underside of her breasts, feeling the quickening of her heart, loving the heated response of her supple body.

The tension in Kenna and Rhys exploded and shimmered through their bodies. Tiny bursts of tingling pleasure pulsed in their flesh, touching their very souls.

Their ragged breathing slowed in unison. Rhys started to lift himself from Kenna.

"No, stay."

"I'm too heavy."

"I like it. Just a little while longer."

He kissed her and rolled onto his back so that she covered him. "I like it, too."

Kenna pressed her face against his neck. "I love you."

"You make me happy, Kenna."

"I make you angry."

"That, too. But I've never stopped loving you. Not for a moment."

Kenna touched her mouth to his throat in the lightest of kisses, then drew back. "Where are we going to sleep?"

For an answer Rhys reached for a blanket hanging over the edge of the bed and dragged it to the floor. A pillow dropped beside it. "That damn bed is simply too far away."

Kenna murmured her agreement as she slipped to her side and Rhys covered them with the blanket. In minutes they were asleep, oblivious to the unyielding hardness of the floor.

Alexis gave a happy shout as she sighted the

Harmony's square rigging. She handed her eyeglass to Tanner and ordered the appropriate change of course. In under an hour the *Artemis* pulled alongside the ship she had been relentlessly pursuing for five days. Alexis and Tanner boarded the *Harmony* as Captain Botti extended a rather bewildered greeting.

"This is most unusual," he said in the next breath, returning his cap to his head. "Most irregular."

"We cannot argue with that," said Tanner.

Botti was somewhat mollified. "What can I do for you?"

"We're here about one of your passengers."

The captain paled. He could think of only two things that might induce the Clouds to chase him: one of his passengers was wanted by the authorities or worse, was suspected of carrying disease. The thought of his ship in quarantine did not set well with him. "Who are you looking for?"

"Michael Deveraux," Alexis explained.

Color returned to Botti's sea-toughened features. "The same young man you escorted to the ship?"

"Yes."

He shook his head. "Can't help you then. Deveraux never sailed with us. Left the ship before we weighed anchor, not long after you and your friends walked away from the docks. Claimed he had forgotten to tell you something. I told him I wouldn't hold the ship for him. Wind was right and I've got a schedule of sorts that I pride myself in keeping. Said he understood and took his things with him. Waited as long as I could. He never returned."

Alexis frowned, turning troubled eyes to Tanner. "Is it too late to say I never much cared for Michael Deveraux?"

Tanner's expression was just as grim as his wife's. "Yes, I rather think it is."

Chapter Eleven

"Alice? Where does Mrs. O'Hare keep the cinnamon?" Kenna pushed aside a lock of hair with the back of her hand, unwittingly leaving a streak of flour on her cheek. All of the servants had the day off and only Alice chose to remain at the house, doing some intricate needlework on the hem of one of Kenna's gowns. Kenna shot a glance in Alice's direction. The girl was sitting on a stool by the back door and her fingers hadn't moved in more than ten minutes. Sighing, Kenna expertly peeled and quartered the last apple for the pie she was preparing. When she was done she began opening cupboards in search of the cinnamon.

"The one on your left, ma'am," Alice said suddenly.

Kenna found it. "I thought you didn't hear me. It must have been a pleasant daydream."

Her voice was as wistful as her expression. "Very."

"Why, Alice! I believe you were thinking of your beau!" The house had been abuzz this past week with the rumor that Alice had a suitor. The tasty bit of gossip had not bypassed Kenna who was told smugly by Mrs. Alcott that it wouldn't last.

Two bright spots of color appeared in Alice's cheek but her lips flattened in a sullen line. "Are you making light of me, Mrs. Canning?" She raised her chin a notch, ignoring Kenna's obvious shock. "Just because I'm not beautiful like you doesn't mean I can't have a suitor." She sniffed her contempt. "Some folks round here like to think they're better than me."

"I'm not one of them, Alice. And I wasn't making light of your feelings. I think it's wonderful that some young man has noticed what a fine person you are." Kenna arranged sliced apples in the pie shell as she spoke. "What is he like?" she asked with sincere interest.

Alice was pacified. She returned to her embroidery. "He's very kind," she said. "And handsome."

"Two qualities that have much to recommend themselves."

She nodded thoughtfully. "He makes me laugh."

Kenna smiled to herself as she added sugar, cinnamon, and freshly churned butter to the apples. "Then I wish you all the best, Alice. He sounds wonderful."

"Hmmm. He is."

"Is he coming by today?" Kenna rolled out another circle of dough then placed it on top of the filling. She sliced away the overhanging edges of dough from the pie plate then pinched the rim of the crust between her thumb and forefinger. "Is that why you stayed here?"

"Yes. He said he would," Alice admitted, looking somewhat defiantly at Kenna as if she anticipated her disapproval. "Are you angry?"

"Not at all." Humming softly, Kenna placed the pie in the oven then wiped her palms on her apron.

"He said you wouldn't be," Alice said thoughtfully, then explained quickly. "I told him I wouldn't be alone here, as if I would invite him if I were. I said you never went to the warehouse on the day you give us off, that you liked to fix Mr. Canning's dinner yourself."

"I like to prepare my own dinner as well," she laughed. She looked around the kitchen, surveying the disorder with a certain amount of pride, then proceeded to begin cleaning up. Mrs. O'Hare had never made it a secret that Kenna was an intruder in *her* kitchen. The cook would not speak to her for a week if she misplaced so much as one spoon or left the kitchen in any condition but immaculate. "Would you like to meet with your suitor in the parlor?"

Alice shook her head. "I thought we would go for a walk."

"It's a lovely day for it." Kenna looked out the window above the sink as she wiped scraps of dough off the bread board. Sunlight touched her face, caressing her features with its pleasant warmth. "Can I prepare you something for lunch?" She wished it were not so many hours until Rhys came home. She wished they were sharing the day as Alice planned to do with—. "What is your young man's name, Alice? You never said."

The back door opened and Alice gave a little squeal of delight. "Here he is, Mrs. Canning. This is—."

"It's all right, Alice darling. Mrs. Canning and I have already met."

Kenna dropped the bread board as she spun away from the sink. "You!" It was the only thing she could think to say. How in God's name had he found her? Her hands clutched the counter for support as she faced the man she knew as Mason. She searched her memory for his last name. Rhys had mentioned it once. Devon. Devers. Deverell. That was it! Deverell.

Kenna glanced at the paring knife on the table and in the next second leaped for it. She held it up threateningly. "Get out of here, Mason!"

Mason leaned against the door frame, perfectly at ease. "So you do remember me. How flattering."

Alice's face registered equal parts horror and bewilderment. "Mrs. Canning! What are you doing?"

Kenna ignored her. "Alice," she said sharply. "I want

you to take the carriage and go directly to the warehouse. Tell my husband that Mason Deverell is here."

"But—"

"Now, Alice! Go now! Hurry!"

Alice was certain Kenna had taken leave of her senses but for all her defiant airs, Alice was used to taking orders. She put her sewing on the stool and took a step away from Mason, an apology in her eyes for her employer's strange behavior.

Mason grabbed Alice's wrist and pulled her to him. Neither of the women saw how he produced a knife, but suddenly it was there, its cutting edge against Alice's slender throat. "Put your knife down, Kenna, or I will not hesitate to use this on Alice."

Kenna did not doubt him. His crystalline blue eyes bored into her and her fingers unfolded. The knife clattered to the floor. "Let Alice go. You don't want her."

Mason chuckled. "Truer words have never been spoken."

Alice's face crumpled and she sobbed once. The knife nicked her throat and a drop of blood appeared on the wound.

"Careful, Alice," Mason warned her. "Come here, Kenna."

Kenna shook her head. The subtle hint of an accent in his speech grated on her nerves.

Mason pressed the knife against Alice's throat. Another drop of blood appeared, staining the edge of the blade. "Come here." Kenna stepped forward and Mason held out his free hand. "Give me your hand." Kenna put her hand into his. Mason gave Alice a hard shove and pulled Kenna against him, holding the knife to her throat now.

Alice bumped into the corner of the table, clutching her throat and weeping piteously.

438

"Leave here, Alice," Kenna said. "Leave while you can."

"Don't do it," Mason countermanded Kenna's order calmly. "You don't want to have Mrs. Canning's death on your conscience, do you?"

Alice shook her head, unable to lift her head and meet Kenna's eyes. She was sick with shame that she was somehow responsible for what was happening.

"Good. I want you to go upstairs and pack some clothes for Mrs. Canning. Put whatever you think necessary into a valise. Pack a few things for yourself as well. The three of us will be leaving shortly. Go on, Alice." When she hesitated he snapped. "Now!"

Alice fled the room, her sobs fading as she took the stairs two at a time.

Mason pushed Kenna toward the table where he picked up the paring knife and pocketed it. "I want you to clean up this mess and do it quickly." He could feel her resistance and gave her a little shake. "Do it, Kenna."

"Why should I? You're going to kill me. Why should I care if I leave a clean kitchen behind?" She despised the quaver in her voice.

"Because I am not going to kill you, unless you become completely uncooperative, that is. If I had wanted to kill you I had opportunity some time ago. Have you forgotten the carriage accident?"

"That was you?"

"It was. But it was also an accident. I saw you coming down the path and was afraid you would recognize me. I spurred my mount on but he veered too closely to your carriage. You handled it very well. As I said, I have no plans to kill you. I am going to hold you for ransom and a clean kitchen is necessary to my plans."

"Rhys will not give you a *sou*." She finally identified his faint accent as French. His command of English was

439

truly remarkable.

"Clean the kitchen, Kenna," Mason said tightly. He eased the knife from her throat.

Kenna took off her apron and used it to wipe off that table. She wrapped the apple peelings in newspaper and threw the bundle in a barrel standing in one corner of the pantry. Next she washed the few utensils she used, put them away, then threw out the dishwater. "Satisfied?" she asked scornfully.

"Put the apron away. Sweep the floor."

Kenna did as she was told. Alice returned to the room with two valises as she was putting the broom away.

"Sit down at the table, Kenna. Alice, get some paper, ink, and a pen for Mrs. Canning. She has a letter to compose."

Alice dropped the valise and fled the room. Kenna sat down, her shoulders slumping as she stared helplessly at her hands. Much too soon Alice returned with the writing implements and under Mason's direction she placed them on the table in front of Kenna.

"Come here, Alice." She cast one fearful glance in Kenna's direction before she stepped in front of Mason. He twisted her around and pulled her hands behind her back, putting his knife between his teeth while he bound her wrists with a length of rope he extracted from his pocket. He took the knife from his mouth, shoving Alice into a chair. "Now write, Mrs. Canning. I want you to compose a suitable missive to your husband, telling him you have reconsidered your position and have decided you cannot live here any longer. Explain that you cannot be satisfied with your husband's attempts to find your father's murderer and Dunnelly's traitor. You have decided to find these things for yourself, therefore, you are leaving him."

Kenna paled as Mason basically outlined the content of her last argument with Rhys. "How did you know these things?" Alice's sharp sob gave her the answer. The girl had been listening shamelessly at the door! "Alice! How could you!"

"I heard you scream one night," Alice defended herself. "I came to see if you were all right. I thought Mr. Canning was beating . . . but then I realized I was wrong and I listened to you, just to make it right in my own mind. I heard what you said about your father. Then the day of your carriage accident, I was bringing you tea, and I heard you arguing again. I didn't mean to eavesdrop. I couldn't help myself. I was worried for you. Honestly." Two tears slipped from her eyes. "I didn't want to tell him. I didn't! But he had a way of getting me to talk without my even knowing it."

Kenna quite believed it. Mason Deverell was as handsome as he was unscrupulous and Alice would have been totally vulnerable to his easy, practiced charm.

"Be quiet, Alice. Write the letter, Kenna. Oh, and make some mention that you are taking your personal maid with you."

A protest came automatically to Kenna's mind but she hurriedly bit it back. So Mason thought Alice was a lady's maid, did he? No doubt Alice had thought to elevate her position in the house and told Mason the lie to impress him. Kenna could have kissed the girl then for giving herself airs. It was precisely the thing she needed to write that would make Rhys suspicious. What a lovely irony that Mason had ordered her to do it!

Mason looked over Kenna's shoulder while she wrote the letter. It took three attempts before he announced he was satisfied. He folded the letter, put it in his pocket then tied Kenna's wrists as he had Alice's. Making a quick tour of the house with both women in front of him, Mason made certain Alice had left no incriminating message behind in her own room or Kenna's. He returned the ink, pen, and paper to the study and left

Kenna's letter on the desktop. Pushing the women toward the kitchen again, he forced them each to carry a valise then directed them out the back door.

Alice glanced at Kenna nervously as they were ordered to enter the closed carriage in the stable. Kenna realized that Alice was looking to her for guidance, expecting her to somehow put everything right again, and Kenna hadn't the vaguest notion of how that could be accomplished. Mason had planned this abduction with infinite care.

Kenna and Alice followed Mason's curt instructions and lay down on opposite seats with their backs to one another. Mason tied Kenna's ankles first then used a short length of rope to lash the ankle and wrist cords together, making it impossible for her to do anything but roll or perhaps move about on her knees. When he had done the same to Alice he gagged them both with rags he found in the stable. Just when Kenna thought he could not do anything more to either of them Mason proved her wrong. After tossing the two valises on the floor of the carriage he disappeared for a few minutes and returned with a bridle. Using his knife to cut away the reins, he tied one of the leather ribbons around Kenna's neck, one around Alice's, then attached the ends to the carriage's door handle.

"In the event either one of you decide to throw yourself from the carriage," he explained, throwing the damaged bridle on top of the valises. "This is fair warning that you'll likely break your neck." He closed the carriage door, slackening the tethers, then harnessed and hitched two mounts. His bound companions rocked helplessly as the carriage jerked once before it started on its journey.

With a great deal of difficulty Kenna managed to turn over so she could see Alice. The other girl struggled to turn also. When they finally faced each other they independently decided the effort was worth it. There was a certain amount of comfort in being able to see one another even though they remained powerless to do anything about their situation.

Kenna estimated an hour had passed when the carriage was brought to a halt. She glanced up at the door, trying not to show her fear as Mason appeared. He shook his head as he noted their rearranged positions. "I can see these tethers were necessary," he said with a trace of smugness. He loosened Alice's leash on the door handle and gave it a rough tug so that Alice was pulled to the floor. Her cry of pain was muffled by the gag. Kenna watched in horror as Mason grasped Alice's shoulders and hauled her out of the carriage. He did not bother to close the door and Kenna realized a moment later he had left it open on purpose. He wanted her to see what he was doing to Alice.

Kenna's view of the surrounding landscape was not wide enough for her to get her bearings but she supposed they were on some portion of the banks of the Charles River. She did not have to see more to know the area was deserted. Mason would not have stopped the carriage otherwise. He carried Alice to the edge of the bank, seemingly oblivious to her struggles, then with no sign of hesitation or the briefest of second thoughts, he dumped her unceremoniously into the churning water.

When Mason returned to the carriage a minute later he discovered Kenna had fainted. Shrugging indifferently, he closed the door.

Rhys tethered his horse outside the stable, thinking he could coerce Kenna into going for a ride before dinner. He walked in the back door, expecting to find her deliciously disheveled. He only had to look at her apron to know what manner of feast she had decided to prepare.

She wore a bit of everything on it by the time dinner was ready.

Rhys wrinkled his nose, wondering if he should suggest they dine with the Lescauts. Kenna had obviously burned something. There was still a hint of smoke in the air. He left the back door open and threw open the window above the sink. How could she have left everything closed? "Kenna!" he called out as he searched the kitchen for the source of the odor. He found the charred remains of a pie he supposed might have been apple in the hearth's oven. The oven itself was cold and there was no fire in the hearth. He set the pie on the table, calling for Kenna again.

There was no answer and Rhys felt the beginnings of fear clutch at his gut. His first thought was that she had managed to burn herself so he went to the bedchamber, expecting to find her lying abed. When he didn't find her there he forced himself to remain calm and searched every room on the second floor and the servants' quarters on the third. Had she injured herself so grievously that she had to go somewhere for help? That thought led him to the stables where he discovered the covered carriage and two mounts gone. He leaned against one of the stalls, breathing easier. She was not hurt. She would have never taken time to ready the carriage if she were.

Clearly she left the house on some errand and simply had forgotten the pie. Perhaps in ten years or so he would let her forget about this incident. Rhys sauntered back in the house, wondering when Kenna would return. She must have left hours ago, judging by the coldness of the oven. There was no evidence that she had started preparing their dinner.

Rhys vowed he was not giving all the servants the same day off in the future. Kenna liked having the entire house to herself on occasion but if just one person had remained behind he would know where his wife was. It occurred to Rhys then that Kenna may have left a note.

He found it on the desk in the study. In the few seconds it took him to read her missive Rhys's world shattered—but not because he believed a word of what Kenna had written. A note was not her way. She was infinitely more honest than to leave while his back was turned. Kenna would have faced him and boldly announced her plans.

Rhys reread the letter. His eyes kept returning to the line where she had written she was taking her personal maid so he needn't trouble himself about Alice. Alice? In other circumstances Rhys might have laughed. That young woman had her heart set on her own shop. She would hardly agree to become a lady's maid. And trouble himself about Alice when his wife had left him? It was an absurd notion.

If he had entertained any doubts that Kenna had willingly left him the pie would have put a period to them. No woman he knew, certainly not Kenna, would have baked a pie for her husband's dinner if she was preparing to leave him.

But knowing Kenna had not written the letter willingly was not enough. Rhys had no idea who could have forced her. He considered Britt. The lawyer and his friends were facing a possible prison sentence for their part in the fire at Canning Shipping. The trial date had already been set. Had Britt somehow arranged for Kenna's abduction, hoping that Rhys could be forced to drop the charges? Rhys dismissed Britt as a possibility. The contents of the letter did not make any sense if that was the case. The purpose of the missive as far as Rhys could tell was to make him believe Kenna had left of her own accord. The intention was clear: Rhys was not meant to follow.

Rhys's expression was grim. He was supposed to believe Kenna was going to London but it did not necessarily follow that it was her abductor's true destination. Forcing himself to think calmly and logically, Rhys pocketed the note and returned to the bedchamber, looking for anything that might help him understand what had happened. Everything appeared to be in perfect order. The same was true of Alice's room. Rhys went back to the kitchen.

Mrs. O'Hare had returned while he had been upstairs. She was muttering under her breath, pulling open drawers and slamming them again, working herself into a temper in keeping with her fading red hair.

Rhys was not amused. "Dammit, Mrs. O'Hare! Will you have done with it!"

Mrs. O'Hare gasped and spun on her heels. She was not used to be spoken to so roughly and she was more than ready to pitch a fit. "Mrs. Canning has made a complete shambles of my kitchen!" she announced, throwing her hands wide so that Rhys would take in the total picture of Kenna's irresponsibility.

Rhys glanced around the kitchen. Other than the burnt pie on the table, which he had put there himself, he failed to see anything out of order. "I don't have time—"

"Look at this!" She held up the bread board. "She put it away with my kettles. And this!" She brandished a wooden spoon. "Does this look as if it belongs with the knives?" Mrs. O'Hare reached in the sink and picked up something that looked like a damp crumpled newspaper to Rhys. She dropped it on the table and unfolded the paper, revealing Kenna's apple peelings. "Do you know where she put this? In my flour barrel! She knows we feed these scraps to the animals! And I can't find my paring knife. The spices have been misplaced. I don't like—"

"Sit down, Mrs. O'Hare!" Rhys roared. "Now!"

Mrs. O'Hare sat. Never in her life had she witnessed such fury as she saw on Rhys Canning's face now. His jaw

446

was clenched. A muscle jumped in his cheek. When he braced himself against the table and leaned forward, towering over her, Mrs. O'Hare recoiled in fear.

"Has my wife ever left the kitchen in this condition before?" he grated.

"No," she said quickly. "Never. Mr. Canning, I'm sorry—"

"Be quiet, Mrs. O'Hare. Please, just be quiet. I want to think."

Mrs. O'Hare's mouth snapped shut, wringing her hands in her lap. Rhys's eyes were closed, his brow furrowed. The tips of his fingers were bloodless where they pressed agaient the table top.

Rhys let out his breath slowly and willed himself to speak in clear, calming tone. "Mrs. Canning is not here, Mrs. O'Hare. I don't believe she has been here most of the day. Someone came to the house and forced my wife to leave. Do you understand me thus far?" Mrs. O'Hare's head bobbed in assent, her eyes widening in shock. "Given the state of your kitchen it would appear the intruder came while Kenna was working here. In order to give the impression that she did not suddenly take it in her head to leave in the middle of baking he cleaned the kitchen himself or—"

"Or made Mrs. Canning do it," Mrs. O'Hare finished. "And she made a muddle of it on purpose!"

"Very good, Mrs. O'Hare." He pushed the blackened pie in front of her. "I found this in the oven. Stone cold. Until you mentioned the misplaced items it was the only hard evidence I had the Kenna did not leave willingly. Now I need your help, Mrs. O'Hare."

She sat up a little straighter. "Anything, Mr. Canning."

"I want you to read this." He handed her the letter Kenna had written. "Carefully. Tell me if anything strikes you as odd."

447

Mrs. O'Hare squinted, holding the note at arm's length then bringing it closer as she attempted to make the spidery handwriting clear. She set down the note triumphantly. "Mrs. Canning always did for herself here. She doesn't have a lady's maid. Certainly not Alice."

"Exactly my thoughts. But I don't know what to make of it. Why did she write it?"

"For the same reason she made a mess of my kitchen."

"I don't think so. Whoever forced her to write this would not have let her mention Alice without reason. But why? Alice had the day off. She was gone with everyone else."

"No, she wasn't."

"What?"

"Alice stayed here today. Confidentially, I think she was expecting a visitor."

Rhys frowned. "A visitor? Who?"

"Someone she met in town. A man." Her voice lowered as she imparted her opinion. "I think it was too soon to be inviting him here. Sure, and didn't I tell her so myself. But she wouldn't listen. Hussy. And her only meeting him not much over a week ago."

"Do you know his name, Mrs. O'Hare?"

"Made it a point to know," she said proudly. "Alice said his name was Mike. Michael Downing."

Rhys's shoulders slumped. He had hoped for something more, something familiar. Why could he not understand what was happening? Was he overlooking something obvious and dwelling on the unimportant? "Did you ever meet him?"

"No. Mrs. Alcott saw him once though. She and Alice were in town on an errand and he spoke to Alice. Bold, Mrs. Alcott says. But a splendid looking man."

Rhys was about to ask her if Mrs. Alcott had perhaps described Mike Downing in a bit more detail when the back door was flung open and Mr. Alcott stumbled in. His face was mottled and he was breathing heavily. He leaned against the wall, clutching his crushed hat over his heart. "Mr. Canning! Thank God you're here!"

Rhys pushed away from the table and went to the butler's side. "What is it? Are you hurt?"

Alcott shook his head, struggling for breath. "Not me. Alice. Someone tried to . . . she's in a bad way . . . they found her near . . . she's asking for you, Mr. Canning. Not much time."

Rhys's insides roiled. "You'll take me to her?"

Alcott nodded. "Right away, sir."

Rhys held the door open and followed Alcott outside. Alcott's horse was lathered but he refused to take the time to harness another. "Have to return the animal anyway, " he told Rhys. "Borrowed it. Mrs. Alcott is waiting with the buggy and one of your horses is still hitched to it."

"Where are we going?"

"Out of town. Follow the Charles."

Rhys was unhappy with the pace Alcott set but he had no choice but to keep his horse in check. Alcott was exhausted and doing the best he could to ride and answer Rhys's questions.

"Mrs. Alcott and I were in Cambridge, visiting her sister," he explained. "We were just about to take our leave when a young man announces himself without even so much as a knock on the door. He tells us there's been a horrible thing happen along the river and the girl was asking for us. Poor Alice." He shook his head sadly. "She didn't have anyone except us to turn to. Knows we spend our days off in Cambridge though, so that was lucky. I don't think she knew quite where to find you. Mrs. Alcott and I went with the boy right away. He took us to his father's farm, not much above twelve miles from here. Said he found Alice when he went fishing, lying curved against a rock. Barely able to keep her head up.

Arms and legs bound, then bound together, bending her like a bow."

Rhys listened to the remainder of Alcott's recitation with a growing tightness in his chest. If Alice had suffered so at the hands of the abductor, then what of Kenna? He would not allow himself to consider the possibility that she was already dead.

When they arrived at the farmhouse Rhys was immediately shown inside and led to the back bedroom where Alice lay. She appeared to be sleeping but when he knelt beside the bed her eyes fluttered open. For a moment they were dull with pain, then she recognized him and they cleared. She opened her mouth but no sound came out.

Rhys thought he was prepared to see Alice after listening to Alcott's description of her condition but he realized nothing could have prepared him for this. Her face was lacking all color though a livid bruise circled her throat like a choker. Her thin arms, lying outside the blanket that covered her, were all that Rhys could see of her body. It was enough. They were marked with ugly scratches. Her left arm was held at an awkward angle and Rhys sucked in his breath as he saw that it was broken.

"Mr. Canning."

"Ssshh, Alice." He touched her head gently. "Don't talk." No matter that he had a hundred questions for this girl, there was nothing he would ask of her now.

Tears appeared in her eyes. "Must," she whispered. "Mrs. Cann . . ."

Rhys said nothing. He took out a handkerchief and wiped away the tears that slid over Alice's hollow cheeks.

"It was my Mike. Sorry. So sorry."

"I know you are."

"Don't hate me," she begged piteously.

"I don't, Alice."

"He didn't want me. Wanted . . . her." Her voice

faded and Rhys had to lean closer to catch her next words. "She knew him. Called him Mason. I just wanted you to know." She coughed and gasped for breath, looking to Rhys wildly for help, fear clear in her eyes. He reached for her hand and felt her squeeze his fingers in an amazingly strong grip.

A tiny bubble of blood and river water came to her lips and Rhys touched the linen to the corner of her mouth. Her fingers relaxed. With infinite gentleness Rhys closed Alice's sightless eyes and brushed his lips against her forehead. He adjusted the blanket so that it covered her arms then he left the room.

The *Artemis* was two days out of Boston when her lookout sighted a ship bearing down on them from the northwest. Tanner Cloud gestured to his wife. Alexis disengaged herself from the conversation she was having with two crewmen and went to stand beside Tanner at the starboard taffrail.

"What is it?"

"You know Harry sighted a ship?"

Alexis nodded. "I heard him. He said it was an American merchant. Is there a problem?"

Tanner gave her the eyeglass. "Tell me what you make of it."

Alex peered through the glass, silent for several minutes as the two ships sailed steadily closer. "It's a Canning ship."

"Yes. And the man at the bow?"

Alexis put down the glass, frowning. "It looks like Rhys, but that couldn't be."

"That's what I thought, which is why I called you over."

There was a shout from above. "Her captain's signaling! They want to board!"

Tanner gave orders which altered the course of the *Artemis* and cut her speed in half. Twenty minutes later he was extending his hand to Rhys.

Rhys exchanged brief greetings with Tanner and Alexis then grimly explained his purpose. "I need to talk to Deveraux. Kenna's been abducted."

Alexis gasped, putting her hand on Tanner's forearm. "When? How did it happen?"

At the same time Tanner spoke. "Deveraux's not here."

Rhys felt as if he had been kicked in the gut. He had barely slept in the last three days, making arrangements to leave Boston, plotting the course of the *Artemis* based on what Alexis had told him, and then taking most of the watches, afraid to trust anyone else lest they miss sighting the Garnet vessel. Now he was finally here, prepared to force Michael Deveraux's memory if he had to, and he was being told the man wasn't on board. "You never overtook his ship?" he asked.

"We caught the *Harmony* days ago. Michael wasn't there. He never sailed with the ship, Rhys. He's still in Boston."

"Not any longer." Rhys slammed his fist against the taffrail. "Dear God! That I could have been so thick-witted!" It was clear suddenly. So transparent that he could not forgive his own stupidity. "Michael Deveraux. Mason Deverell. Both the same person. Why didn't I know? Why didn't I see it before?"

Kenna had no concept of time. In the dark hold where Mason Deverell kept her like an animal she could not distinguish between day and night. Time flowed unhindered by the interruptions that would have oriented her. She was served two meals each day, always the same fare of broth, hard tack, fruit, and cold biscuits. No one spoke to her. No one answered her questions.

Her room had few amenities. There were several thin blankets which she laid out on a bed of straw, a chamber pot that was emptied when she complained about it, and an empty crate she used as a chair. She had her valise, filled with the clothing Alice had packed for her, but Kenna had no use for any of it. She was too dispirited to care about anything so inconsequential as her appearance.

Days and nights melded, becoming weeks. The steady motion of the ship rocked Kenna to sleep at odd hours. She never dreamed and she never saw Mason Deverell.

Nicholas Dunne frowned at the interruption. He had finally been dealt a hand worth playing and now a stone-faced waiter was hovering at his shoulder bearing a message for him on a silver salver. With thinly veiled impatience Nick put down his cards and took the note. He read it once, then, hands trembling, he read it again. Ignoring the questions and protests of his fellow players, Nick excused himself, a curious tightness in his voice. "I must return to Dunnelly," he said. With no more explanation than that he turned on his heel and strode briskly out of White's.

Rhys was not the sort of man who usually questioned his decisions, yet he found himself wondering time and again if he had done the right thing by telling Alexis and Tanner to return to Boston. They were more than willing to take him aboard their ship, change their route, and sail for Dunnelly, but Rhys refused their help. He had not done so out of hand. Rhys had carefully considered their offer, yet he felt bound not to involve them in this matter. He could not be certain that Mason was taking

453

Kenna to England. He hadn't even the assurance that Kenna was still alive. He was resting his entire hope on past evidence of Mason's greed, motivated, he was certain now, by Deverell's loyalty to Napoleon's cause. Mason was pursuing money to finance Napoleon's return to power and he saw Kenna as a means to his ends. Rhys was convinced that if Deverell had only been interested in protecting his identity, his links to Dunnelly, he would have killed Kenna at the house. The elaborate charade he had undertaken would have been unnecessary. Mason seemed to be after a larger prize and the only place where Rhys could imagine him going was back to England.

Rhys blamed himself for helping the man he had known as Michael Deveraux to excape from France. He and Robert Dunne had been used to place a traitor on English soil. The Lescauts, genuinely fleeing France for the sake of their lives, had been similarly used, acting as unwitting blinds to keep suspicion away from the traitor in their party.

Rhys shook his head, clearing the recriminations from his thoughts. He did not need to feel any more powerless than he already did. The captain of his ship had already informed him they were less than a day from the Channel. Rhys needed to direct his energies elsewhere. He picked up one of the pistols lying on the desk in front of him and began cleaning it.

"Allons!" Mason demanded impatiently. "Come out of there! *Vite!*"

Kenna shielded her eyes from the lantern light that blazed at Mason's side. How dare he order her to hurry! She raised her chin a notch and straightened her shoulders.

Mason's laugh mocked her. "A pathetic show of defiance, Kenna. Do you recognize this?" He held up a

454

vial, thrusting it into the light so that she might see it. Her absolute stillness told him that she clearly under-stood its contents and its purpose. "Good. It would be awkward if I had to use this, but I assure you I will if you do not cooperate of your own accord. Now, come here. Bring your valise."

Kenna stood and walked slowly toward him, picking up the valise. He stepped away from the door and ushered her into the empty passageway. Mason closed the door, put a hand at the small of Kenna's back and urged her along the corridor. Her legs were weak as she climbed the narrow stairs to the upper deck awkwardly and Mason finally took the valise from her. He stopped her in front of the door to his cabin, opened it, and motioned her inside. Kenna glanced at the cabin's single porthole as Mason set down the lantern on a trunklid. It was dark outside. She wondered what time it was, what day. "Why am I here?" she asked.

Mason pointed to a wooden tub sitting in one corner. "I want you to wash." He put the valise on the bed and opened it, rifling its contents until he found the clothing he wanted. He laid out clean undergarments, smoothed the wrinkles from Kenna's peach gown, and put her kid slippers on the floor. When he turned back to Kenna he saw she hadn't moved. She was watching him warily. "Undress. Wash yourself."

"Why?"

Mason ignored her question. He walked toward her, turned her around, and began undoing the fasteners at her back.

Kenna pulled away. "I'll do it."

"As you wish." Mason sat on the bunk.

"May I have some privacy?"

"No. There are some matters we must discuss."

Fingers trembling, Kenna began to undress, keeping her back to him. The water in the tub was cold but Kenna entered it quickly, hunching her shoulders to keep Mason's eyes from violating her anymore than they already had. She found a sliver of soap and a cloth and began washing.

"Do you know where we are?" he asked.

"No. Near Paris?"

"Near Dunnelly." He saw her grow still with shock, then resume washing again. "You and I are going ashore in a few hours. I have already arranged the meeting. There will be an exchange—you, for a great deal of money."

"I see," she said slowly. It explained the bath. Mason did not want her to look as if she had been mistreated. "If money was your objective all along then why not ask Rhys for it?"

"Your husband is a wealthy man, but not nearly so wealthy as your brother. It is Dunnelly funds I want. You and I will be met in the caves. You're familiar with the caves, I believe."

Kenna nodded.

"*Bien*. I will expect your cooperation. I regret that it will be necessary to bind your wrists. However, you will be able to walk on your own. The entire affair will be accomplished in a few minutes and I will leave. I hope, for your sake, that no one tries to stop me. You would do well to consider that before you take it upon yourself to play the heroine."

Kenna closed her eyes briefly to hold back the rush of tears. She willed herself not to cry in front of this man. Kenna dipped her head in the water to wet her hair then began to wash it, digging her fingers into her scalp painfully so that she could think of nothing else. When she finished rinsing she rose from the tub and clumsily wrapped herself in a towel. "Nicholas will not give you money."

Mason shrugged, getting to his feet. "I'll be back in an

hour. Make yourself comfortable."

"Bastard," she said under her breath. "Satan's spawn."

Mason opened the door to the cabin, laughing shortly. "You are not the first person to call me a devil, Mrs. Canning. But in your situation one should practice more discretion. It would not cause me the slightest inconvenience to break your nose a second time."

Kenna stared mutely at the door as it was locked from the other side. Too late she found her voice. "Wait!" she cried, running to the door and pounding on it with her fists. "Come back here! I want to know what you meant!" There was no reply, not that she had expected one. Kenna sagged against the door, sobbing raggedly.

Nicholas was pacing the floor in Victorine's room. Without fail he would glance at the mantel clock as he turned sharply on his heel to resume pacing in the opposite direction. "I cannot let you do it, Victorine. It is too dangerous."

Victorine's fingers plucked nervously at the folds of her dress. "There is no other way. The note is very specific. I must go to the caves myself with Kenna's ransom. If I do not—"

"I read the damn message," Nick snapped. "I know what it said. What I don't understand is why! Why you, Victorine? Why must you be the one to deliver the money?"

"I suppose because I am a woman. I do not present the same threat as you do." Victorine's hair had become markedly gray in the weeks that followed Kenna's funeral services. For years she had given the appearance of being much younger than her age. It was no longer true. There were deep lines about her mouth and eyes and her normally clear complexion was pasty white. "I wish I had not called you down from London," she said bitterly. "I knew you would argue. I would have done this thing myself if it were not for the fact that you control the money and there was no time for me to sell my jewels."

"Thank God you did send for me! I would not for the world wish you to do this thing yourself. But, Victorine, you may be risking yourself without cause. Can either one of us be certain that Kenna is truly alive and that this message you received is not some cruel joke? Let me go in your stead. If I have the money with me do you really think Kenna's abductor will turn me away? Of course he won't. And if Kenna is there I am better suited to protect her from further harm."

"I am afraid. You could be watched as you enter the caves. Kenna's abductor may not come if he sees you."

"That is a chance I'll have to take." Nick's fingers threaded through his hair. The smile that touched his lips and blue eyes was bleak. "Victorine, I have put the gold and silver in the valise as directed. In truth, I doubt you could carry it, certainly not the entire way to the caves. If I leave now I will reduce my chances of being seen entering the cave."

Victorine nodded. "Then go, Nicholas. Godspeed." She waited until she heard Nick's steps recede along the corridor, then Victorine went to her chiffonier and opened the bottom drawer. She sifted through dainty undergarments and hose until she found what she wanted. Cautiously she removed the pistol she had kept hidden there since Robert Dunne's murder.

Rhys was waiting impatiently for Powell at the edge of the woods. When the older man inadvertently crossed his path Rhys stepped out from behind a tree and called to him.

Powell jerked with surprise, twisting around quickly.

His eyes narrowed as he made out the figure of his friend. "God almighty! You've likely pushed me nearer my grave! I couldn't believe it when I received Polly's note that you wanted to meet with me. What are you doing in England, Rhys?"

Rhys offered Powell the briefest of explanations, telling him only the most necesary details. "I arrived in London less than forty-eight hours ago. I spent one night at Polly's and I had planned to talk to Nick yesterday. I found out he left a card game at White's to return to Dunnelly the day before. I can think of only two reasons he would walk out on a wager. How is Victorine?"

"Much the same. Not in good health, hasn't been since . . . well, you know. But she's no worse. It was she who sent for Nick. I know because I saw her give young Billy the note."

"That leaves something to do with Kenna. Which is why I think we haven't much time. Hours. Days. I don't know. But something will happen here before the week is out."

Powell nodded heavily. "That's a certainty. Deverell will have to move quickly if he wants to be any help to Napoleon. You've heard that Wellington will make his stand soon?"

"Yes. Everyone in London is talking of it. At Waterloo, I believe."

"If Deverell knows, then he will want to ransom Kenna soon and leave the country."

"I agree. Can you get me into the house? Hide me until we know something?"

"We can go now. The house is quiet. There are still a few hours left before the servants are up."

Rhys followed Powell across the yard, keeping low as a precaution. They had just rounded the rear corner of the manor when Powell came to an abrupt halt, holding out his arm to keep Rhys at his back. "Look there! Near

459

the summerhouse!"

Rhys eyes narrowed in the dark as he tried to identify the figure hurrying toward the summerhouse. "My God! Is that Deverell? Look! He's carrying something!"

Powell had to put a restraining hand on Rhys's shoulder to keep him from running out and stopping the man. "Not Deverell. That's Lord Dunne. Or at least that's Lord Dunne's cape."

"I cannot afford another case of mistaken identity. I'm following him."

"No. Let me. I'll go to the summerhouse and watch the beach. You take the passage to the caves. You can take the stairs quicker than I can. Are you armed?"

"Yes. Is the lantern still at the top of the stairs?"

"Aye. Everything's much as you left it. No one's used that passage but me. There's been no activity in the caves since you went to America."

"Small wonder," Rhys said dryly. "What with our traitor out of the country as well. Be careful, Powell."

"You also." He gave Rhys's shoulder an encouraging squeeze, then the two men parted company.

"It's time," Mason announced. "We're expected."

"You were there the night my father was killed," Kenna accused.

"How clever of you," he said sarcastically. "Come on."

Kenna refused to move. "You're Michael Deveraux, aren't you?"

"On occasion. I confess I am surprised that it took you so long to realize it."

"The only time I saw you as Michael Deveraux you were wearing a costume," she reminded him.

"Effective, wasn't it?"

"Very. You must have been relieved that the Clouds'

affair was a masque. I would have had no difficulty recognizing Mason Deverell."

"No difficulty at all," he agreed. "If you recall I did not press my good fortune that night. I made it a point to avoid you. Frankly, I did not know you even knew my surname."

"Rhys discovered it when he was tearing apart London to find me."

Mason appeared uninterested. "I would rather you save the whole boring story of how he managed to find you for another time. We must be going." He withdrew a length of rope from his pocket. "Turn around and place your hands behind your back."

Kenna hesitated, then did as he asked, remembering the vial he carried with him. He would drug her if she refused him and Kenna believed it was better to have her wits about her. Mason tied her hands with practiced efficiency then took her by the elbow and led her topside. Kenna looked around curiously when she reached the upper deck. There were only a few men in sight.

Mason caught her puzzled expression and explained. "It only takes a small crew for a ship this size. The others are sleeping now, waiting only for my orders that we leave for France."

"You're confident."

Mason shrugged. He helped Kenna into the boat that would take them ashore. After he stepped in, bringing an unlighted lantern with him, two men lowered it over the side. Mason took up the oars and rowed competently toward shore.

Kenna recognized the stretch of beach they were heading for. It was a little under a mile from the cave and with the additional cover of darkness Mason's ship could not be detected even from the vantage point of the summerhouse. Mason took the boat as close as he could to the beach, got out himself, and dragged it a few more

461

yards so Kenna would not have to walk in the water when she stepped out. His gallantry unnerved her. He extended his hand to her with the same cool indifference he had exhibited when he had dropped Alice into the Charles River. Kenna shuddered and shook off his touch. "I can walk myself."

"As you wish." He took the lantern from the boat and fell in step beside Kenna, forcing her to keep close to the base of the cliff so they could not be seen from above.

It took them a little more than fifteen minutes to reach the entrance to the cave. Mason told Kenna to step inside before he lighted the lantern. She started to walk toward the rear of the chamber but Mason caught her elbow and held her back. He lifted the lantern, pointing to the footprints he saw. "I believe we have a large problem," he said lowly, "judging by the size of those prints. You will walk ahead from now on." He drew a pistol from his waistband and pointed it at her. "Remember this will be at your back."

"I don't think I could forget." Kenna could barely hear herself over the pounding of her heart. When Mason nudged her with the barrel of the pistol she began slowly walking forward.

She had never returned to the caves after her father's death and with every step she took her mind was filled with returning visions of that night. Her nightmares were never as clear as the things she saw in her mind's eyes now. She stumbled a little, balking at going deeper into the cave.

"Go on," Mason whispered harshly.

"I can't. Please don't make me."

"Damn you! Move!"

Kenna forced herself to take one step, then another. She saw herself as she was ten years ago, clutching the damp cave walls, trembling as she listened to the argument in the chamber. She knew now what she did

462

not know then. It *had* been Nick she saw in the gallery. She could remember with startling clarity that Victorine had cried out his name. But just as she knew it had been Nick in the gallery, she knew with equal certainty that it *had not* been Nicholas with Victorine in the cave. At thirteen, her young eyes still filled with betrayal of Nick's affair with his own stepmother, she had confused Nick with Mason Deverell, an easy enough mistake given their costumes. Robert Dunne's words to Mason that night echoed in her head. She could hear her father's bitter pronouncement: "I had not thought you could be capable of this—not betraying your country to some notion of world peace designed by Napoleon." At the time Kenna thought the country he was referring to was England. She realized now her father was accusing Mason of betraying France by choosing to follow the Bonapartists. "At the very least," her father had said, "I should bring you before the courts but I find my pride too great to allow you to shame my house." Kenna could well imagine the humiliation her father must have felt, knowing that he had helped bring Mason to England.

Kenna could understand now what she could not imagine then. It only remained for her to discover why Victorine had been with Mason and why Robert had merely chastized his wife for not trusting him, absolving her of all guilt and protecting her until the end.

Rhys cursed softly as he searched the top of the passageway for the lantern. Damn, Powell had assured him it was here. He pulled back his hand sharply as he touched a jagged piece of glass. After a few seconds of cautious groping Rhys found the bent lantern frame. Useless! The damn thing was useless. Fearful of wasting more time acquiring a lantern, certain he could roll away the stone in the dark if he had to, Rhys started down the steps. He proceeded in exactly the same way he had when he had followed Robert, holding one hand in front of him and passing the other along the wall. He despised the slowness with which he was forced to move but resigned himself to it. He would be of no help to anyone if he broke his neck on the stairs.

"Nick!" Kenna cried his name as she entered the antechamber. He was standing near the far wall. A valise rested near his feet and the lantern he had brought sat with chilling familiarity on the natural stone shelf. Kenna started to go forward automatically and Nick even took a step toward her, but then she was pulled back sharply as Mason dropped his lantern and grabbed her bound wrists.

"Stay where you are, Dunne," Mason ordered. "Tell him, Kenna."

"He has a pistol, Nick. At my back."

Nick clenched his teeth, nodding shortly. He remained where he was. "Are you all right?"

"Yes. Oh, Nick, I'm so sorry for—"

Mason poked Kenna with the pistol. "Enough. Why are you here, Dunne? I specifically requested Vic—"

The wall behind Nick opened up suddenly, startling everyone in the chamber. Nick, closest to the gaping hole that appeared, leaped forward in alarm. Mason did not realize that Nicholas was acting on his instincts, therefore Mason acted on his own. Pushing Kenna to one side he leveled his pistol at Nick and fired. The lead ball caught Nick in the shoulder and he fell backward, hitting his head against the chamber wall. He was unconscious before he fell to the ground.

"Damn you!" Kenna shouted, running to Nick's side, unafraid of Mason's pistol any longer. Once fired, it was useless until he reloaded. Kenna dropped to her knees, her head snapping up when she saw Victorine step into the chamber. "Oh, why did you come here? Look what has—" She broke off abruptly as she noticed the pistol Victorine held in a tight double grip. Her weapon was pointed directly at Mason's chest.

Mason had seen the pistol before Kenna and he decided upon his action quickly. He kicked the lantern at his feet, sending it skidding wildly toward Victorine. At the same time he dove for Kenna, using her body to shield him. Startled, Victorine stumbled backward as she tried to avoid the lantern. She fell against the stone, releasing the spring, and it rolled easily into place, blocking the exit she had planned for Kenna and Nicholas.

Mason stood up, bringing Kenna to her feet in front of him. "Your calm surprises me, Victorine. I thought you would fire your weapon. But look at this situation carefully. You still have a primed pistol and I have Kenna. It would appear we have a stalemate. Do you agree?"

Tears sprang to Victorine's eyes but she did not lower the pistol. "You are a bastard, Mason."

"A popular opinion this evening," he said easily, getting to his feet and dragging Kenna with him. "Give me the valise and I'll bid you *au revoir*."

"If you want it, you will have to get it yourself."

Kenna was frightened for her stepmother. The pistol seemed impossibly heavy for her thin arms to support much longer "Let him have it, Victorine," Kenna said. "What can it matter now?"

"It matters, Kenna. Once he has it he will kill us."

"But his pistol—"

"Mason is never without a knife. Isn't that so, Mason?"

Mason grinned. "You know me so well, but then our association goes back many years, doesn't it. Mayhap you

465

wish me to explain it to Kenna?"

"I wish you to cut her bonds."

"I don't think so."

"Cut them, Mason."

He shrugged. Watching Victorine carefully, he slowly pulled his knife from where it was sheathed against his calf inside his right boot. He cut the ropes at Kenna's wrists but did not let her go. Placing one arm across her chest, he held her back while he pointed the tip of the blade beneath her chin. "I have done as you asked, Victorine, though I fail to see what you have gained."

What Victorine had gained was the possibility that Kenna could defend herself. Before her bonds were cut she hadn't the remotest chance of doing anything to save herself. "Now release Kenna and I will let you have the valise."

Mason shook his head. "And shoot me when I pick it up. I have not forgotten that you can use that thing, though perhaps Kenna has. You are not so successful at distances—witness how you missed Kenna in the wood and shot that old poacher instead—but you are more than competent at this range, aren't you, Victorine?"

Kenna gasped, her features contorting in a mixture of pain and horror at her stepmother's betrayal. The last veil over her memory was lifted. She closed her eyes briefly and in milliseconds she saw what she had never seen before: Victorine picking up the pistol that her father had dropped a moment before the lantern was extinguished. Kenna opened her eyes and stared hard and accusingly at Victorine. "You killed my father! You murdered your husband!"

Mason tightened his grip on Kenna. "You are half right," he said. "She shot Robert Dunne but she did not murder her husband." He jerked his chin in Victorine's direction. "Tell Kenna why we were here that night."

Victorine's thin shoulders sagged a little. The pistol

wavered as her arms slackened. "I came with Mason to discover word of my husband, the Comte Dussault."

"But—" Kenna's protest was cut short as Mason pressed his blade more firmly against her neck.

Victorine did not seem to notice Mason's action, nor that he was slowly, cautiously, moving himself and Kenna toward the valise. She continued to speak, her voice low and strained. "I know you thought I was a widow. Everyone did. But my husband was still alive in France . . . I would have done anything to see him released . . . and I did. I was told I could save him by coming to England and working for the Bonapartists as a spy. I accepted Robert's marriage proposal because I thought it would give me access to information. I never intended to care for him, Kenna, but I could not help myself."

"He loved you," Kenna said bitterly. "He tried to protect you that night."

"I know." Her head drooped and her eyes lowered sadly. "He knew more about me than I had ever suspected. He slowly realized my purpose in England and gave me bits of useless information."

Kenna looked away from Victorine to the unconscious form of her brother. The darkening flower of blood on his shoulder needed attending. "That is when you turned to Nick."

"Yes. But it was not what you think. Nick was simply infatuated with me and I used it against him, teasing him along. Until his own sense of guilt played upon him Nick was unknowingly helpful."

"Then who was with you in the summerhouse?"

A single tear trickled down Victorine's cheek. In the lantern light her complexion was sallow. "Mason," she said quietly. "Mason was my lover. Not that I wished him to be, but because I had no real choice. Even before I came to England Mason was using my body. I laid with him because he saw to it that my husband was not tortured." She glared at Mason. "He made no such promises about my parents. They were murdered by the Bonapartists. As was my husband, eventually." Victorine came out of her reverie suddenly, tightening her grip on the pistol. "Stay there, Mason!"

Mason halted but he began talking, lowering Victorine's guard as he filled in the gaps for Kenna. "Victorine arranged that I should wear the same costume as Nick at the masque. It was merely a precaution to throw suspicion toward Nick and away from myself. She said she had important information to give our contacts so she took me through the passage which Robert had shown to her and I responded to the signal from the ship. But she had lied to me. She only wanted news of her husband. Unknown to either of us your father followed."

"It was an accident, Kenna!" Victorine cried out. "You must believe me! It was an accident! I picked up one of the pistols Robert dropped when Mason chopped at his wrist. The lantern went out then and I could not see how I held it. I was so frightened! I did not know I had fired it until your father fell against me. I screamed and one of our contacts found me and pulled me away from Robert."

Kenna was unmoved. "You left me here," she said coldly. "My hands and feet were bound and you left me here to drown."

"I did not know it was you! None of us did! I wouldn't have left you if I had known!"

"You will understand if I find it difficult to credit. There is the matter of a fall on the stairs, a boating accident, a tampered girth, Tom Allen's death, poisoning, and finally, arranging my abduction."

Mason smiled malevolently at Victorine. "Kenna has a remarkable memory for certain facts, don't you think?"

"It was all Mason's idea, Kenna! He was forcing me! If I did not stop you from remembering the events at the masque his operation would be in jeopardy. I would go to prison! I couldn't go there! I couldn't! But I don't care any more."

Kenna wondered if she could believe Victorine. Some part of her doubt must have shown on her face for Victorine continued.

"It's true! I don't care what becomes of me now! But I cared what happened to you, Kenna! Yes, I tampered with Pyramid's girth, but in the end I went riding with you. I couldn't let you go alone. I saw your saddle begin to slip. Do you remember? I called to you then to slow down. I saved you from a fatal fall." Her expression appealed to Kenna for forgiveness. "And I set the trap in the woods for you but when you arrived safely back at Dunnelly I knew I couldn't go through with it. I went to retrieve it but you were already there with that poacher. I was afraid! I could have killed you then, Kenna, but I didn't!"

"Instead you protected yourself by murdering Tom Allen," Kenna said with bitterness.

"I had to!"

"You tried to poison me, Victorine!"

"I tried to frighten you," she corrected. "I knew you suspected Rhys. Who didn't? Mason said you could not be allowed to marry Rhys. You would be beyond our control then. If I had wanted to kill you I could have done so easily and the suspicion would have fallen upon Rhys or, thanks to your maid, Monsieur Raillier."

"Did you meet Mason in this chamber and discuss the plan for Napoleon's escape? Were you helping to finance that escape?"

Her question shocked both Mason and Victorine.

"How did you know?" asked Victorine.

"It is unimportant."

"I had to, don't you see? Mason was not giving me a choice. I had to provide financing for his plans. There

469

were others that offered support. I was but their link to Mason."

"What about my abduction?" Kenna asked coldly.

"That was Mason's idea. I inadvertently told him you were going away. He did the rest. He finally realized I could not hurt you. Didn't I beg you not to go to Cherry Hill?"

Victorine began to sob jerkily, giving Mason the opportunity he had been waiting for. He pushed Kenna hard toward Victorine. Victorine's hands lifted higher to remove the pistol from Kenna's path and as Kenna fell into her the weapon was fired harmlessly at the roof of the chamber.

Kenna rolled off Victorine and quickly scrambled to her feet. Mason's attention was distracted as he tried to lift the heavy valise. With no thought for the consequences, Kenna locked her hands together in a double fist and swung her outstretched arms as if she were swinging a plank. Her fists smashed against Mason's nose at the same time she felt a sharp pain in her thigh. Mason staggered backward, withdrawing his blade from Kenna's leg. Blood gushed from his nose and he howled once in pain before he advanced on Kenna, revenge sharply defining his features.

Kenna backed away, limping as she edged toward the lantern on the stone shelf. She could not think of any way to escape him save under the cover of darkness. Kenna leaped for the lantern, knocking it off the ledge at the same moment the wall of the chamber opened for the second time that evening.

Rhys had only a second to mark everyone's position in the chamber before the lantern crashed to the floor, but he marked them well. The shots from his pistols thundered in the chamber, then there was an even more thunderous silence.

"Kenna?" he ventured softly.

470

Kenna was so stunned by the sweet familiarity of Rhys's voice that she couldn't say anything. She clung to the sheer damp wall for support, not believing he was really here.

"Dammit, Kenna! Say something!"

"I'm here, Rhys."

Rhys started forward but Victorine's warning scream came in time to halt his steps. Mason's knife caught the sleeve of Rhys's jacket before Rhys jerked away. There was a heavy groan from Mason, a pained sob from Victorine. Their bodies crumbled to the floor, then thick silence pervaded the chamber once more.

"Rhys!" Kenna cried out. "What happened? Victorine!"

Rhys did not answer immediately. Cautiously he bent over, groping in the dark for proof of what his mind was already telling him. He found Mason's body first. There was no pulse. He pushed at Mason's lifeless form and his hands brushed Victorine's shoulders. A moment later he found Mason's knife, embedded to the hilt in Victorine's breast.

Rhys's voice was heavy. "She's dead, Kenna."

Kenna's harsh sobs led Rhys to her side. She felt his arms circle her and she clung to him tightly, weeping with shock, bitterness, and finally thankfulness for the security of his embrace.

Epilogue

"Goodnight, Nick." Kenna touched his uninjured shoulder, giving it a gentle squeeze, and kissed his cheek. His tender smile warmed her heart. In the six days since Victorine's funeral she had despaired of seeing her brother smile again. He seemed haunted by the discovery of Victorine's betrayal, as if he believed it had been in his power to make things different. He blamed himself for not providing protection for Kenna and for not recognizing Victorine's perfidy. He despised himself for the youthful passion he had once felt for Victorine. Kenna felt helpless in the face of Nick's decision to accept responsibility for all that had happened. That neither she nor Rhys blamed him for anything did not seem to matter.

Nick laid his hand over Kenna's. "I dearly love you, sprite," he said. "I'm going to miss you and Rhys."

"We could stay longer," she offered quickly. They were due to leave in the morning but she knew Rhys would not object.

He shook his head and released her hand. "No. You both need to return to Boston. The only reason you would stay here is for me and I am going to be fine."

"You'll visit us?"

"I promise," he assured her. He pointed to the clock. "Your husband is no doubt pacing the floor, wondering what's kept you. You'd better go, Kenna."

Realizing he was politely saying he wanted to be alone, she shut the study door quietly behind her, leaving Nick to his own thoughts. When Kenna reached the bedchamber the first thing she noticed was that Rhys was not pacing the floor. He looked very comfortable in bed, his back propped against several plump pillows, reading the London paper. He was hungry for all the available news on Wellington's defeat of Napoleon at Waterloo but he put aside the paper when Kenna came over to the bed.

He patted a spot beside him, gesturing her to sit down. "You were a long time with Nick this evening. How is he?"

"Better, I think. Do you know what he said tonight?"

"What?"

"He said he envied us. He wants a wife, a family. I think that's good, don't you?"

"Very."

Kenna nodded happily. "Will you unfasten this dress?"

"Certainly." His fingers nimbly undid the tiny hooks.

Kenna slid off the bed and began to undress. "Do you know," she asked, her voice muffled as she pulled her gown over her head, "I've been wondering about something Nick said a long time ago. He said that he was with Victorine when Father was murdered. But he wasn't. Why did he tell everyone he was?"

"Why didn't you ask him?"

"I couldn't. I was afraid he might think I was accusing him of something." Kenna laid her gown aside and stripped off her undergarments, completely unaware of the attractive picture she made as she danced about on the cool floor, looking for her nightgown.

"Forget your nightgown," Rhys said huskily.

Kenna needed no further encouragement. She slipped between the covers that Rhys held open for her and snuggled beside him. He wasn't wearing anything either. "So why do you think he said it?" she asked.

"Oh, we're still speaking of Nick, I take it."

"Yes."

"Pity." He put an arm around her shoulder. "I believe Nick thought he was telling the truth about that night. Everything was so confusing. There were only a few of us who knew the exact time of Robert's death. If you recall, I thought I saw Nick and Victorine in the garden. He really was with Victorine a short time later when she left Mason and ran to get him and told him I wanted him at the cave. He was simply mistaken about the time everything happened."

That explanation more than satisfied Kenna. "Poor Victorine," she said after a moment. "Mason used her vilely for his own ends, baiting her with news about her husband when all the time the comte was dead. I cannot hate her; I feel so sorry for her."

"Then you believe it was an accident that she killed your father."

"Yes, don't you?"

Rhys was not so certain. Victorine had shot Tom Allen, then found the resolve to brutally strangle the injured man. She had arranged accident after accident to protect herself against the power of Kenna's returning memory. Simple luck had prevented Victorine from suspicion on a number of occasions. Nick's confusion and innocence had protected her the night of the masque. Nick again, accidentally bumping into Rhys when he carried the broth, and Janet's own suspicion that Monsieur Raillier was responsible for the poisoning, carried Victorine safely through another dilemma. But it was truly Robert Dunne's own trust in Victorine that kept her safe, because Kenna could not believe her father would seek to protect his wife if he did not truly think her innocent. Lord Dunne's judgment became his daughter's until Kenna learned of the betrayal from Victorine's own mouth.

Rhys thought this all, but he said, "Yes, it was probably an accident. She said she had come to care for Robert. And you know, in the end, she proved her love for you. She went to the cave with no other thought in mind than to kill Mason and bring you and Nick out safely. Nick even said that Victorine begged him not to take the ransom himself."

"And she saved your life," she said softly. Even now it was hard to imagine how Victorine had sensed Mason moving in the pitch-black cave and gave her life to stop him.

Rhys pressed a kiss to Kenna's soft temple. Beneath the sheet his hand touched her thigh where Mason had stabbed her. He ran his finger lightly over the tender scar. "I'm very happy that you chose not to tell Yvonne everything."

"I just couldn't," she said, her voice breaking. "What purpose would it have served? Better that Yvonne thinks only that her mother gave her life to protect us. There is truth in that, too."

"I love you, Kenna."

"And that makes me very, very happy." She turned into him, curving her body against his own. The lean, wiry strength of his body never failed to thrill her. "Very happy," she repeated softly.

"Hmmm. What say you to a physical display of affection?"

"Does that mean—"

"Yes. I want you to share my pillow."

Kenna answered him with sweet kisses on his brow, his cheeks, his chin. Her mouth brushed his. Her fingers traced the line of his chin, his throat, and teased his nipples into hard arousal. Their legs twined, rubbing sinuously together, pale and dark, rough and smooth, in perfect contrast. They loved one another, giving, taking, eager in their desire and greedy for the pleasure that lifted their hearts and bound their souls.

"I think you've given me a baby," she said later, turning sleepily in his arms.

Rhys smiled, not at all adverse to the idea. "How can you be certain?"

"One knows these things," she said wisely.

"Does one really?" he asked, tongue in cheek.

Kenna said nothing then. She was patient. She waited nine months, then presented Rhys with an eloquent, if somewhat squalling example of "I told you so."